Advanc

"What an extraordinary world Christine Estima has created for her readers! She has breathed exquisite life into the world of Austria and Czechoslovakia in the interwar period, where intellectuals and artists live on the brink of horror, while pinching pennies, creating immortal works, and falling madly in love. Her portrait of the Czech writer (and thief!) Milena Jesenská, and her love affair with Franz Kafka, brings to life an extraordinary, whimsical, subversive young woman, roaring with talent and courage. I adored every word of this novel and could not put it down."

—Heather O'Neill, author of *The Capital of Dreams*

"*Letters to Kafka* by Christine Estima is a startling debut novel about a brilliant woman refusing to give in to her period of history. Estima has an astonishing command of setting, invoking a dark and dynamic prewar Europe—abuzz with a large cast of literary figures, artists, and hangers-on—with the facility of someone playing with a bauble between their fingers. In that milieu, Estima's Milena stands out as a memorable tour de force, full of ravenous intellect, cutting humour, and gusto. Through her heroine's unabashed insistence on recognizing and satisfying her emotions, Estima's novel explores the chasm between writing about life and actually living it. Estima's vivacious, ultra-sharp prose only accentuates that fascinating journey. This is a stunning achievement in historical fiction."

—Saeed Teebi, author of *Her First Palestinian*

"*Letters to Kafka* is an enthralling debut novel that is both ambitious in scope and rich in character. Christine Estima skillfully takes us back to one of the most explosive moments in world history and makes precise space for an important woman—Milena Jesenská—often overlooked both in literature and the historical record. Estima's keen eye for detail yields a truly picturesque and enchanting setting, and her superb and compassionate storytelling bears a love story for the ages."
—Waubgeshig Rice, author of *Moon of the Turning Leaves*

"Deftly imagined and passionately felt, *Letters to Kafka* is a tribute to the beauty of words and their power to forge an unbreakable bond between two brilliant minds. As the love story between Milena and Kafka unfolds through their letters, the streets of Vienna and Prague in the roaring twenties come to vivid life, crystalline in detail and rich with wonder. This is a luminous debut novel by a gifted writer."
—Corinna Chong, author of *Bad Land*

Letters to Kafka

Also by Christine Estima

The Syrian Ladies Benevolent Society

Letters to Kafka

A NOVEL

CHRISTINE ESTIMA

ANANSI

Published in Canada and the USA in 2025 by House of Anansi Press Inc.
houseofanansi.com

House of Anansi Press is committed to protecting our natural environment. This book is made of material from well-managed FSC®-certified forests, recycled materials, and other controlled sources.

House of Anansi Press is a Global Certified Accessible™ (GCA by Benetech) publisher. The ebook version of this book meets stringent accessibility standards and is available to readers with print disabilities.

29 28 27 26 25   1 2 3 4 5

Library and Archives Canada Cataloguing in Publication

Title: Letters to Kafka : a novel / Christine Estima.
Names: Estima, Christine, author.
Description: Includes bibliographical references.
Identifiers: Canadiana (print) 20250172356 | Canadiana (ebook) 20250172372 | ISBN 9781487013318 (softcover) | ISBN 9781487013325 (EPUB)
Subjects: LCSH: Jesenská, Milena, 1896-1944—Fiction. | LCGFT: Historical fiction. | LCGFT: Novels.
Classification: LCC PS8609.S865 L48 2025 | DDC C813/.6—dc23

Cover and text design: Alysia Shewchuk
Cover photograph: Nancy Landin / Millennium Images, UK

House of Anansi Press is grateful for the privilege to work on and create from the Traditional Territory of many Nations, including the Anishinabeg, the Wendat, and the Haudenosaunee, as well as the Treaty Lands of the Mississaugas of the Credit.

Canada Council for the Arts | Conseil des Arts du Canada

ONTARIO ARTS COUNCIL
CONSEIL DES ARTS DE L'ONTARIO
an Ontario government agency
un organisme du gouvernement de l'Ontario

With the participation of the Government of Canada
Avec la participation du gouvernement du Canada | Canada

We acknowledge for their financial support of our publishing program the Canada Council for the Arts, the Ontario Arts Council, and the Government of Canada.

Printed and bound in Canada

This book is dedicated to every woman throughout history whose baptism by fire gave a lovely light.

And to one in particular: my mother, Joan Zarbatany

"Only to the rude ear of one who is quite indifferent does the song of a bird seem always the same."

—Rosa Luxemburg, 1917

10 November 1939
Attn: The German Legation in Prague

In a conversation held in Prague on the 10th of November 1939, between the undersigned and Obergruppenführer Reinhard Heydrich, the latter stated that he endorsed the former's order of the arrest of Frau Milena Jesenská, suspected of Rassenschande—a disgrace to the race by having carnal and marital relations with Jews. The arrest is to occur forthwith. It has been requested that, because of her prominent position within Czech society, Frau Jesenská not be sent with a mass transport to the eastern territories but rather be held in a special camp in the Reich in order to be available for eventual political use.

Heil Hitler
Konstantin von Neurath
Reichsprotektor of Bohemia and Moravia

1

The Obergruppenführer

PRAGUE

1939

Milena was locked in a cell with a bare wooden floor, a latrine in the corner, and a small high window. She shared it with a dozen women. Pankrác Prison—Prague's main jail—was built only a few years before she was born. Formerly a banking institution, it was now used for Gestapo interrogations. Women were dragged from their cells to "sessions"; some returned with a split lip or a black eye. Some of their screams echoed throughout the lower levels. Some were never heard from again.

Milena was dragged to her session and forced into a chair. The lower-level chambers stank of septic damp, the ripped moulding along the walls showing this was surely where the bank safes had once been. The brick walls were cold, but the flooring was warm, like bodies had been lying on it all night. There was no window. Gales whistled through the cracks around the door and all along the exterior corridor. She could have sworn she heard his voice—the voice she had missed for fifteen years—saying her name.

Two men entered the room then turned the key in the lock before turning to her. One was tall and fair. His quotation-mark eyes were the colour of French chartreuse, his cheeks were flushed with salmon-toned blotches, and he had a long aquiline nose. His hair was slicked to the right in a deep left part, and he sported fat lips, big ears like two open car doors, wide forehead, strong jaw and chin, a bulbous head. He looked like a goose-stepping chump.

He wore a suit. The other wore a tweed cap and suspenders. He was short, with a flat nose and a flabby jawline. Milena was sure she had seen him in Wenceslas Square on occasion, buying roasted chestnuts from one of the hot carts and talking about the latest picture showing at the movie house. Yet, he also looked like a milkman she once employed when she lived in Malá Strana with Jaromír. He would deliver milk bottles with either brass or chrome caps, depending on how much cream she wanted. Whoever he was, if he also recognized Milena, his expression, perfectly controlled, revealed nothing. He spoke first.

"What were you burning when you were taken into custody?"

When the SS detectives had burst into Milena's home, she had been waiting for them. The pan in the fireplace was smoking. The letters were burning too slowly; she tossed them in by the bundle, her eyes seething red, like she was swimming through sand.

The telephone call to her Resistance contact had raised

her suspicions. The voice at the other end was not one she recognized. It sounded like the thick, viscous drip of honey, rather than the abrasive coffee grinder she had grown used to. She needed to pick up the latest copies of *V boj*. Into the Fight. The Resistance paper she was editing and distributing clandestinely to all Czech patriots. Sending her eleven-year-old daughter, Honza, to do the distribution might have seemed like a shrewd idea at the time, but when Honza didn't return an hour later, Milena estimated she had an hour, maybe two, before the men in suits came for her.

She could have fled, but she was stubborn, always stubborn; Kafka had accused her of this several times. It was her worst fault.

Stubborn when she watched her newspaper *Přítomnost*—for which she was the first female editor-in-chief in its history—abolished. Stubborn when she watched her neighbours fling themselves from their balconies as the Brownshirts paraded up Wenceslas Square. Stubborn when she sent Honza to distribute *V boj*—what a thing to make a child do! Honza would be all right, of that she was certain. Why, that girl could sell rotten eggs to hens. Milena knew her father, Dr. Jesenský, would take charge of his granddaughter.

Milena had grabbed the *V boj* carbon copies and thrown them into the blaze. Letters from Jochi; from Schaffgotsch; from her first husband, Ernst; from her second husband, Jaromír. "Forgive me, my dears." She winced as their words turned to ash.

The letters from Kafka. They must burn. She had turned her head in the direction of the hollowed-out spinet piano. The false backing held every letter, telegram, and handwritten note Franz had ever sent her. She was reaching for the piano when a pair of hands grasped her arms. They began to lead her out, but she knew what fate awaited a woman imprisoned by the fascists. "Halt!" one of them shouted as she wrenched off his hands. She ran toward the open window. A long way down. They lunged at her feet. She screamed like a thornbird that had pierced its own heart as it fell in a death spiral. Legs grabbed, body lifted before she could start her own death spiral. The defenestration was stopped before it could begin. Instead, she was dragged down the stairwell.

Now, Milena looked at the interpreter, and then at the fair man in the suit walking the length of the room and back again without meeting her gaze.

"Badly written drafts."

The interpreter immediately translated her words from Czech to German for the fair man, who looked at her for the first time and said in German, "She writes for the underground subversive paper *V boj*. Ask her about that." But what the interpreter relayed in Czech was, "You managed to slip some coded language into your newspaper past the censors. Why?"

As the editor of the *Přítomnost* newspaper, Milena had cued her readers to how they could operate in this newly occupied state. But her passport had been confiscated and her paper banned entirely by the Nazi censor when she wrote, "Czech soldiers pass by under a window and the pavement rings a little. Only one German soldier has to pass by a café for the glasses to shake and the plaster to fall from the ceiling."

Milena looked from one to the other narrowing her eyes. "I have never heard of this underground paper."

The Czech translated that she said the accusation was a lie. The German officer looked closely at Milena's face. Hands folded behind his back, he bent at the waist so his eyes were level with hers. She jutted out her chin defiantly. No man had ever made her blush or look away. The German let out a snort and shook his head in amusement.

He turned to the interpreter and said, "Sie versteht Deutsch." *She understands German.*

The interpreter straightened his back, and then began to fumble out some kind of explanation—that direct translations between Czech and German were impossible. Milena snorted loudly at that, which caught the two men off guard. The German paced the length of the room again, hands neatly clasped behind his waistcoat, and then back once more for what seemed to Milena the duration of a Bible.

Then he came face to face with the Czech and said, with the same honey-dripping voice Milena had heard over the telephone before her arrest, "Raus." *Out.*

The interpreter bowed his head, tipped his tweed cap, and disappeared on the other side of the locked door.

Milena and the German looked at each other; she with eyes of bone.

"Shall I speak to you in Czech or in German?" he asked in German.

Milena, mindful of being tricked, remained silent. German had been made the official language of Czechoslovakia since the Munich Agreement, which annexed the Sudetenland. White socks were once again seen in Sudeten villages, and black paper covered every window. Czech street signs were changed to German, Czech social clubs were forced to close, and the Germans even insisted on everyone driving on the right side of the road. The First Czechoslovak Republic had, like Britain, driven on the left. The streets became dangerous with traffic collisions. Then, in late summer the following year, troops had marched into Poland. Britain and France declared war. Occupied Czechoslovakia was now a Reich protectorate.

"No answer is wrong, I promise you," he added.

Milena shook her head. "In Czech, I'm sentimental, sad, and truthful. In German, I'm sober, brief, and good-humoured. Which person would you like best?"

The fair man cracked a momentary smile before catching himself. He smoothed his suit and tugged at his vest. He pulled out a folded document from his breast pocket. It was a carbon copy, so Milena could see through the limp paper and noticed it was probably typed on a Rheinmetall, a Kolibri, or an Olivetti. He read through the document, taking his time, before finally breaking the silence.

"It says here you fancy yourself a descendant of the seventeenth-century Catholic dissident Jan Jesenius."

Milena pursed her lips.

"You might be the equivalent of Prague royalty, as it were." He smirked, and then barely took a breath before asking, "You like to sing?"

"Pardon me, Herr Hauptmann, I—"

"—Obergruppenführer."

"—am not a songstress."

"No, but our guards have reported hearing you singing in your cell at night."

"I know I'm no cabaret singer, but—"

"Singing is forbidden."

"But it's Lotte Lenya."

He paused. He knew that name. How could he not? "As in, Lotte Lenya and Kurt Weill?"

"I have always thought the tunes from *The Threepenny Opera* were the prettiest German songs, wouldn't you agree?"

"They are classed by the Reich as degenerates."

"Oh, come now." Milena cleared her throat. "'Gentlemen, the smiles will leave your faces when the walls come tumbling in! The towwwwwwn will be razed to the grouuuuuund.'"

The Obergruppenführer folded his arms.

"'Oh, show us! The way! To the next! Whisky bar! Ohhhh don't ask why. Ohhhh don't ask why ...'"

He drew back and slapped her across the face, splitting her lip open. She blinked in shock for a moment, before sucking in her lip. If she bled on him, he might deal her another blow. He leaned forward at the waist again, drawing her gaze into his. "Forbidden. Degenerate. Music. Understood?"

She blinked again and nodded.

He tilted his head and surveyed her features from ear to ear. "Most women become hysterical right about now."

"I've been hit before."

He narrowed his eyes. "You're not afraid of me."

Her lip pulsed like the tap of Morse code. She tasted her blood to prevent him from taking pleasure in his handiwork. "You're not very frightening. Violence is a lack of self-control. You should be pitied, not feared."

He snorted once again. "God will be my judge. And I will be yours."

She gritted her teeth. "If you're asking to be crucified, Herr Obergruppenführer, I know where to procure two planks and some nails."

He grabbed her by her Peter Pan collar and yanked her face toward his. "Don't forget, Frau Jesenská, you are a prisoner here."

"And when I get out, I will write about the conditions of this prison and my treatment."

"*If*. Not *when*."

Milena straightened her back. "Herr Obergruppenführer, I am forty-three years old. My brother died in infancy and my mother died not long after. I survived the lash of my father, an unjust confinement in an asylum, the Great War, the Great Depression, two unfaithful husbands, and a criminal conviction for theft. To earn my keep, I ported suitcases for rich people and taught their bratty children languages, all while thanklessly writing articles for the *Národní listy*, the *Tribuna,* and the *Přítomnost,* working my way up to editor-in-chief only to see the paper banned by your fragile censors. Almost everyone I know has fled the country, been deported, or died before my eyes, yet I'm still here. Do not for one minute assume you can break me. I wouldn't even blink if my hair was on fire."

His eyes flashed brilliant for a moment, and he released his grip from her collar. He straightened and walked the length of the room again. She wiped her lip with the back of her hand and lightly touched her cheek, hot and raw from his hand.

He read from the document as though it were an indictment: "Frau Jesenská has smuggled Jews out of Czechoslovakia and into Poland." He looked up at her and she quickly folded her hands. "Much good that did, as Poland is now our territory." Back to the indictment: "She has a history of writing articles in support of Jewry. Is a Bolshevik and a Communist." He slapped the papers in his palm. "My, my, haven't you been busy."

"I am no Bolshevik," she replied.

"Is that so?"

"The movement at its core is pure and true, but there are no true believers to be found in Prague anymore."

He read aloud, "Has a slight limp." He looked at her feet turned inward. "Another lame Czech whore."

"Do you know of any little girl who dreams of being a whore when she grows up?"

"Frau Jesenská, you answer the questions, you do not ask them—"

"You're so beholden to these rules. Why is that?"

"—And you certainly cannot do both at the same time!"

"My knee was injured when I was pregnant with my daughter, and because of the strain on my body during childbirth, it never healed properly."

"A daughter out of wedlock, no doubt."

"I was married."

"Ah, yes, your marriages. Let's read more about those blessed unions. It says here your first husband, Ernst Pollak, was a Jew, was he not?"

"Pollak is no longer in Czechoslovakia."

"I'm not interested in locating him, not as much as you were in defiling yourself with him." He shook his head and tsked.

"At the time of my first marriage, there were no Rassenschande laws in Czecho—"

"Ah, yes, well, you're in luck then! Speaking of your first marriage, you were also a known consort of Franz Kafka at that time, were you not?"

Milena's lip throbbed and swelled.

He shook his head. "One Jew wasn't enough, you had to find another." Milena noticed one small strand of hair release itself from his carefully styled fop of pomade and flip down his forehead. He ran his fingers through his hair and settled it back in line like a truant child. "You wrote in *Cesta,* the weekly cultural paper that we mercifully killed, that Kafka was 'tall and emaciated, his face angular, pointed, beautiful, fierce, and good.' Is that so?"

Milena said nothing. She looked down at her lap, where she was folding and unfolding her fingers as if they were caught in a Chinese finger trap. A woman's muffled scream was carried on the gales that whistled through the lower levels. But then her voice was stolen as though suffocated by a handful of golden-throated dandelions.

He bent at the waist, his fair and freckled nose inches from hers. She could smell his pomade mingling with his eau de cologne, his breath like black tea from Café Union. "You just couldn't help yourself, could you?" He smiled for the first time, and she took stock of his gold-capped incisor. "Couldn't show a modicum of gentile restraint, could you, Milena?"

Her name on his lips felt like a swift kick to her torso,

one that could break her clavicle. It was his voice that had been calling her name on the wind, not Kafka's. She felt like she was falling to the concrete floor, certain she would end up as one of the bodies that kept it warm and stinking.

Meeting his eyes, she replied, "Maybe I'll show some restraint at your funeral."

He tightened his jaw. Without another word, he exited the session room and closed the door behind him.

THE THOUGHT OF ETERNAL rest seemed decisively attractive to Milena as she lightly touched her swollen cheek and raw lip. Before she was arrested, she had been walking in the New Jewish Cemetery to exercise her weak knee. Her flat on Kouřimskà Street was less than a five-minute walk from the cemetery, and she often went there for quiet reflection, for air, for a stroll through the tree-lined promenades or a rest on the benches curiously tucked against the outer red brick wall that kept the bustling, toxic traffic at bay. But if anyone was paying attention—and they never were—they would know that she came here to say hello to Kafka. He was buried about 250 metres from the main entrance, his grey obelisk standing like a solitary sentry over the cemetery gates. On days when her mind was a terrible place, she would sit with him and tell him about her day. He had always been a great listener. And she had always appreciated a captive audience. Since his death in 1924, his grave had become more crowded, with his father joining him in '31, and then his mother in '34. Milena remembered them fondly, how they welcomed her into their Oppelt apartment in the Old Town Square with ginger mint tea and rock candy. His epitaph was in Hebrew; she once had a friend translate it for her, yet she only remembered bits and pieces: *the magnificent, unmarried man ... of blessed memory ... may his light shine ... may his soul be bound in the union of life.*

Looking down upon his stone-peppered plot, she saw fountain pens, lead pencils, quills of varying size and plumage. The tradition of leaving behind a pen in deference to and reverence for the great Czech author continued. She smiled to see other acolytes had paid homage. It was a tradition she had started the day they buried him. The Jewish tradition was to leave a stone upon the grave, but she was not Jewish. Leaving her fountain pen seemed the best way to mark it. To mark him as a writer worthy of tribute.

Now Milena sucked up the blood from her lip the moment she heard the Obergruppenführer enter behind her. She straightened her back.

"Let us begin again," he said, as he stood before her, "and from the beginning. What is your full name and date of birth, for the record?"

Milena rolled her eyes. "What are the charges against me?"

"This habit you have of answering a question with another question—how long do you think I will tolerate it?"

"I have a right to know with what I have been charged so I may mount a defence."

"How proactive of you."

"When I get out of here—"

"Frau Jesenská, I am not one of your husbands who you can leave."

"Why am I here? Why did your men turn my home upside down? What were you hoping to find?"

The Obergruppenführer shook his head.

"Full name. Date of birth. If you please."

Milena met his gaze and didn't give him the pleasure of looking away this time. "Milena Jesenská. Daughter of Jan Jesenský and Milena Hejzlarová. Born on the tenth day of August 1896, in the Austro-Hungarian Empire, which no longer exists as per the Treaty of Versailles, which you no doubt will remember."

"Watch yourself, Frau Jesenská."

"My apologies, I was simply unsure whether Your Excellency remembers the 1918 Armistice that put an end to the war your men started, and signed freely, admitting culpability for the deaths of ten million people and the unlawful annexation of the western and eastern territories. I'm glad to hear I'm wrong. Surely the Treaty of Versailles has nothing to do with your presence in Czechoslovakia today. That would just be ludicrous."

"Hold your tongue, Frau Jesenská. I have half a mind to—" he stopped himself, tilting his head to analyze the theatre of expressions gracing her face. "Ah, I see." He sighed with a shake of his head. "What a clever girl you are."

"Don't you want to strike me?"

"I will not play this game, Frau Jesenská."

"You were willing to play it not a moment ago."

"I won't allow you to take the topic at hand three times around the dance floor until we've lost all sense of it."

"I'm sure I don't know what you mean."

"You and Kafka."

"What about him?"

"We have arrested Kafka's three sisters already."

"On what grounds?!"

"You will tell me everything."

"There's nothing to tell."

"You are forgetting yourself, Frau Jesenská. And Honza."

Milena's soft eyes grew to the size of harvest moons.

"You should think about Honza," he repeated, as he neared her face.

Milena's hands began to fold and unfold again and again in her lap. The tear in her lip seemed to widen, as if she were now vivisectioned from stem to stern. "What do you want with my daughter? She has nothing to do with Kafka."

"Then you have nothing to lose by telling me what I want to know."

Milena shrugged and looked about the cold room as if the answers lay in the cracks and creases of the concrete. "What can I tell you? I don't know where to begin."

The Obergruppenführer grabbed a second wooden chair from where it leaned against the back brick wall and dragged it, screeching, across the floor until it was directly in front of Milena. He jerked it into place, unbuttoned his waistcoat, lifted his trouser legs, and sat, heaving one leg over the other as if he were taking his front-row seat at the Paris Opera for Stravinsky's *Firebird* suite.

"You know exactly what I want to know."

There was no point in feigning ignorance or playing coy. Not anymore. Hesitantly, Milena nodded.

He folded his arms over his lap. "Begin."

2

Café Central

VIENNA

1918

By the light of oil lamps, I drink tea and wash my hair. I dip each tress in sugar water and roll it up in tissue paper to curl it overnight, but in the morning, my hair stands on end like unruly sprigs of mint. Ernst will notice, and so will Werfel. They will, as always, laugh about it among themselves at the café. I would never let them see it, but the pain they cause me has no equivalent. It is a spider with infinite legs, spinning a web around every waking moment.

My husband, Ernst, and I live in a four-room flat on Lerchenfelderstraße in Josefstadt, which borders the seventh and eighth districts. My sitting room overlooks the number 46 tram that rumbles across the avenue and shakes our walls. I wish it reminded me of the spacious trams in Prague, highlighted with mahogany accents, that ascend like the North Star to the St Nicholas Church's Staroměstská stop. But Vienna has neither the charm nor the beauty of my Bohemian days. Vienna is a broken city that stinks of rotting sauerkraut.

Everywhere I look, from the seventh district to the fourth, men are returning home without their legs. Beggars line the Ringstraße, especially at night outside the Burgtheater or the Rathaus, hoping that the rich and powerful—the very people who shipped them off to war—will take pity on their infirmities now. They have ghost limbs, faces hastily patched together with parts missing, and all are suffering from shell shock. Food shortages have crippled the city, and even the black market is too expensive. Ernst spent my dowry within weeks of our marriage, a fact my father will no doubt hold over my head until his last breath. So now we only get one loaf of bread per person per week from the state. It is the yellow, hard, mouldy body of Christ.

When I arrived in Vienna eight months ago, I spoke not a word of German. To my surprise, Ernst, who was fluent in both German and Czech, did not help me. Instead he left me standing there, porting my own luggage at the Westbahnhof, and went straight to his lover. Shock gave way to acute misery, and I stood there sobbing until he finally sent our housekeeper, Paní Kohler, to fetch me. One can get used to almost anything in time. But at that precise moment, I seemed so far from happiness, it was almost as foreign as the British.

Ernst doesn't share his wages from the bank with me, beyond covering the basic necessities, so every day I go to the communal kitchen and eat a poor man's meal made with cheap grease for 6.50 crowns. The soup, comprised of boiled barley, beans, and of course, sauerkraut, is made with unclean water. The meat is fermented salami coated in breadcrumbs. The cheese pastry is made with black flour and a lot of yeast so it rises quickly. How embarrassing it is to be forced to eat here among the laundry and factory workers while my taciturn husband dines on credit at the best establishments. He did not fight in the war. He doesn't know what war is and, therefore, what hell is. Everyone and everything—my clothes, my humidity-curled hair, the communal kitchen, every rooftop, and every cellar—stinks of nauseating sauerkraut. It's in all of our bellies and there is no escape.

We are just thankful that we have a coal-burning stove. We previously lived on Florianigasse in the eighth district, and then Nußdorferstraße in the ungodly ninth, where the city had cut off electricity for domestic use and we had to use candles, which were impossible to buy. No fuel, no coal, not even wood—nothing to heat with, nothing to cook with. Every day I had to go into the woods near the Meidling district to collect damp bits of wood and bark that would bake in the stove but give off no heat. Beyond the canopy of trees, I could see quite clearly the ornate Schönbrunn Palace, which was blessed by protections and fortifications during the war. If only the proletariat had been afforded such dignities.

All around us in the eighth district, people are dying every day of the Spanish influenza that has killed a good half of Europe—those who managed to survive the bombings and the gas attacks. I wish I were one of them. Twenty thousand Austrians, the papers say, have been lost to the pandemic. Hospitals are overcrowded, schools, theatres, and cinemas are closed, and train and tram services are limited.

The door clicks behind me and it is Paní Kohler, who pushes me to get dressed. As a young girl in an affluent household, I was weaned and raised by the housekeeper, who would dress me in the morning. Now, due to Ernst's tight purse strings, Paní Kohler only stays for a half-day and I have to dress myself. I am twenty-two years old and I have no idea how to lace and knot all these layers.

Paní Kohler has the kindness to at least lay out my clothes on the bed for me. I have no new clothes. The fashions of the day are changing, new styles and modern fabrics are in the shop windows of the Graben and the Kartnerstraße, but I wear my old dresses with the dated empire waists. How is a woman supposed to stay in her husband's good graces like this?

Paní Kohler watches me as I scan today's outfit with a disapproving eye. I meet her gaze. "Did he come home last night?"

She shakes her head.

I push past her down the hall and burst into Ernst's private bedchamber. The Egyptian cotton sheets and bed linen are undisturbed. The room is stale and stuffy, as the curtains haven't been drawn for some time. I jiggle the handle to his large burnt oak wardrobe, but I find it locked. Of course it is. It's where he keeps his coffers. I would grab one of his brass-studded highbacked chairs and smash the wardrobe to smithereens, but Paní Kohler's eyes bore into my back, searing my skin like a hot brand.

Apologizing to Paní Kohler for my shameful display,

I return to my room to dress quickly as the bells of the Alt Lerchenfelder parish next door ring out quarter-to. Paní Kohler sits me down for my morning tea and sticky bun and hands me today's *Neue Freie Presse*. The garish front-page headline says Mayor Richard Weiskirchner, a follower of intolerant former Mayor Karl Lueger, disapproves of the "press Jews," the "ink Jews," and the "money and stock market Jews." He promises to liberate the Viennese from the "shameful shackles of servitude to the Jews."

"Have you seen this, Paní Kohler?" I hold up the paper as she pours the tea through the strainer.

"Aye, ma'am. It's quite disgraceful, is it not?"

"That's an understatement. It is manufactured nonsense." I chomp down on my sticky bun. "Everyone in Vienna knows the Jews fought and died alongside gentiles in the war."

"Will you be staying in to teach today, ma'am?" she asks. I have taken gainful employment as a teacher of Czech. Viennese entrepreneurs are my biggest clientele, as the imminent dissolution of the empire means that most businesses will soon find themselves situated in Prague. I also teach their children on occasion. However, lately, the dire state of my finances has meant procuring a second source of income.

"Not today." I look up at her and she nods. "We all have to become charlatans in this new dog-eat-dog world, don't we, Paní Kohler?"

"Aye, ma'am." She wipes her hands on her apron and makes a move to return to the larder, but I grab her by the arm. "Please," I tug, "why don't you sit and join me?"

She holds my gaze tentatively, unsure if this is a test.

"Don't look so surprised," I say. "I would enjoy your company on this terrible morning."

She slowly lowers herself down into the chair opposite me and pours herself a cup of tea, plopping two lumps of rock sugar into her brew. Paní Kohler is a heavyset woman of indeterminate age. I realize now I've never taken it upon myself to ask. I know she has a family, and that they, like Ernst and me, came from Bohemia for work, but the war has made a mockery of their plans.

"Tell me," I say between munches, "how are things with Pane Kohler?" I ask of her husband.

She tilts her head and purses her lips. "It's difficult" is all she says.

"Has he found work?"

She shakes her head. "Machinery in the industrial factories remains quiet." The thought of her family suffering nicks at my composure. She appears to me as defeated as Austria. "You live in the tenth district, isn't that right?"

She nods. A pause hangs in the air. The reports coming out of the tenth have been abysmal. Greengrocers remain closed, their shelves bare. Consumption spreads pathogenically. Fathers send their starving children out into the streets to beg while the mothers queue for hours in the daily bread and soup lines.

"Well," I place one hand atop hers, "I hope things change for you soon."

"As do I, ma'am." She gives my fingers a pat before humbly removing hers. "Millinery shops and apothekes are still shuttered from the troubles last week."

"What happened?"

"There were protests against rising prices, but the march was stopped by the military police." She takes a sip of her tea, and droplets pepper her neckline. I don't dare tell her, to stave off embarrassment. "They bashed in the shop window at the Del-Ka shoe store and looted it. In a flash, all the security shutters slammed closed. I was nearly hit on the head with a stone! It was a very ugly scene."

"That's dreadful. Is there any bread for you and your family?"

"In the tenth one can only get a half-loaf. It is always the same miserable thing and tastes horribly of corn. One cannot get eggs anywhere either. The Consum will only sell you nine instead of a dozen, if it has any at all."

"Yes, I've seen the long queues growing outside of the Julius Meinl shop on Taborstrasse," I say, lifting up the newspaper again. "It says here Vienna is trying to procure food and fuel, but negotiations with Budapest, Prague, and Galicia advance too slowly."

"And people are starving!" she suddenly exclaims, then quickly composes herself.

Paní Kohler is a good housekeeper and often adds a calming, motherly presence to my life. Her jovial demeanour on mornings like this are a comfort, and when she is pained, she does her best to not let it affect the house. If I had never had a mother, I would wish her to be mine.

"Paní Kohler, feel free to take what you need from our pantry."

"Ma'am?"

"For your children."

"But—"

"Not another word." I rise from my chair and head for the hall wardrobe. "I have to go to work."

I set out into the morning in this boring city. As I move down Kaiserstraße and across Mariahilferstraße, I hum Czech folk songs to drown out the noise of the soot-lined streets. On Sundays, when I was a child in Prague, the Czechs and the Austrians would mill about Wenceslas Square, but each kept to their own side, like boys and girls at a mixed dance. The Austrians would mingle, gossip, and smoke cigars, but the Czechs, and even the Slovaks, would sing folk songs to taunt them. I hum one of those songs as I walk through this defeated city still yammering on about the Habsburgs and their loss of royal title.

When I arrive at the Westbahnhof, I notice a well-to-do couple emerging from their train cabin freshly arrived from Budapest. I spring into action. "Carry your valises for you, sir?"

He nods without looking me in the eye and motions behind him. I collect a small steam trunk and a Louis Vuitton hat carrier from his wife. I waddle in front of them down the arcade, through the portal with the large arches supported by ornate columns, and down the stairwell to the main taxi rank. The cumbersome cases slam into my legs, and the leather handles are much too small for anyone to get a good grip. I huff and heave. Luckily, today I am not requested to haul valises to the very doorstep of the hotel.

I may not be the strongest or sprightliest of women, but those are minor inconveniences. I was raised by a man of means and now I am a porter; there is no greater blow to one's pride. My pride is the only true inconvenience.

I open the cab door for them. The man gracefully holds his wife's gloved fingertips as she steps lightly into the cab and then follows her. I close the door behind them, and then hand their luggage to the driver, who hauls it atop the automobile and ropes it down. I swing back to the man's window and open my palm. He gives me half a crown and some remaindered hellers.

"I am obliged to your kindness, sir."

He does not once acknowledge me.

The cab jumps to a start and hurtles away toward the Ringstrasse. I watch it go, gripping the coins in my palm so tightly that they could disappear into my skin. What privilege must come with obliviousness. How enticing life must be as a man of means. Some of us will never know what that feels like. I work so hard, and my man-about-town husband gives me no money. My misery is like luggage: every day I carry something heavier than the last.

AS THE SUN GOES down, I leave the Westbahnhof and make my way to Café Central, which is around the corner from the Burgtheater. Ernst and his bosom buddy Franz Werfel will no doubt be there enjoying slices of Sachertorte or chocolate blancmange with cream. Café Central—with its unusual, vaulted dome ceiling, pentagram chandeliers, red cushioned booths, and pilastered columns with gilt maple leaves—is always full of journalists, writers, actors, artists, and philosophers. They celebrate newly published books and curse the bad reviews while musing about Bohr and Schopenhauer. In the quiet corners sit chatting ladies, silent lovers, and elegant waifs. Then there are the ladies who frequent the café on the arm of a new man each week. Everyone knows who first brought them, if they've been unfaithful to their lovers, and even the date for their decree nisi that will legally divorce them from their husbands. The ladies move from table to table to see their former lovers and husbands, who, in turn, are also here with new women each week. Everyone drinks hot chocolate topped with mounds of whipped cream delivered on silver trays, accompanied by glasses of mineral water.

After a day of heavy valises and poor tips, this is a most welcome highlight. Finally, an opportunity to sit among my intellectual peers on plush blood-red cushions and discuss truth, beauty, and art. Within an hour, the gaiety, the vivacity, and the radiance of the café will wash away all that troubled me today. I cannot wait for the night to begin.

The doorman ushers me over the threshold. My shawl is graciously hung, and a rack of daily papers on offer is next to the dessert tray, which today displays Damson plum strudel, Fleckerl semolina pudding, custard cream cakes, slices of sugared sponge gateau ... Oh, I could eat a dozen in one sitting!

I walk toward Ernst and Werfel sitting at their usual table in the back by the massive painted tapestry along with Gina and Otta Kaus, both writers and dramatists. I hope if I stay long enough, Ernst will come home with me tonight rather than head to his mistress, Mitzi.

Ernst spots me from afar, and his eyes scan my drab clothes with disdain. I stop in my stockings. I know that look. If I have any sense of self-preservation, I will turn on my heel and walk right out. But, like a buck caught in the crosshairs, I'm cornered.

"Oh, look!" Werfel announces loudly upon noticing me. "Here comes old Milena, looking like six volumes of Dostoevsky."

Everyone at the surrounding tables laughs, including the waiter, Anton, who lets Ernst dine on credit. I look to Ernst to come to my defence. He looks me dead in the eye and joins in the laughter. I have never felt more like a flag, half-mast in wind.

WERFEL HAS BEEN MONOPOLIZING Ernst's attention all evening, but when he rises for a trip to the gents, I lean in and whisper to Ernst, "Is Werfel still chatting your ear off about Klimt?" Everyone is talking about Gustav Klimt's death from a stroke earlier this year, but most suspect he was another victim of the Spanish flu. The architect Otto Wagner just died in April.

He snorts. "I wager I'll be stuck here listening to his diatribes until our waiter quietly shuffles us to the door at closing."

"Is Werfel still having an affair with Alma Mahler while she's married to Walter Gropius?" I whisper.

He nods vehemently. Alma had fallen under Klimt's spell in Italy when he joined her family for a Venetian holiday. "Well, I'm surprised Werfel hasn't written about this in one of his substandard poems."

"Milena ..."

"I'm sorry, but I find his writing to be boorish and overbearing, the typical indulgent musings of a man only concerned with men's business."

"I suppose some impressive books just aren't as thick as their authors," he says, reaching for his copita of port. Werfel returns to the table and leans in to Ernst to continue his pedantic gossip.

Rarely do I encounter Alma; she is too concerned with the fashions and follies of her social salons to mingle with the likes of me. But as I nurse my hot chocolate while Ernst and Werfel debate whether Klimt's contributions to painting were frivolous or scandalous, I see one of Alma's friends. A familiar face alone at a table in the back, drinking coffee and staring off into space. I put my glass down and place my hand atop Ernst's. That mere touch stops his words cold, and he looks at me to see what the fuss is before following my gaze.

"Come now, you two, what is it?" Werfel snaps, but then he also follows our gaze. His eyebrows drop and his voice cuts out like a skipping victrola.

"It's the woman from Klimt's portraits," Ernst breathes. "The woman from his *Judith*."

"The woman he painted in gold," I add.

Adele Bloch-Bauer.

Gina Kaus pipes up, "Didn't she have an affair with Klimt?"

"Shhhhh!" Werfel hisses.

I nod to her but keep my voice low. "They say she is the woman—not Emilie Flöge—in his shining masterpiece *The Kiss*."

"You don't say?" Otto exclaims.

I nod. "Her lame finger, which she tries to hide in her gilt portrait, is also visible in *The Kiss*, wrapped around Klimt's leaning neck."

All eyes are now on Adele's oddly curled finger. She has lost her secret lover to illness, and her husband doesn't seem to understand her passion. I can read it all so easily on her world-weary face. I have worn that look so many times myself. Except, Adele lives in the lap of luxury on Elisabethstraße, across the gardens from the Art Academy. And I live where the street sweepers rise at dawn to push away last night's cigarettes, ticket stubs, and confectionery wrappers.

Adele looks up from her drink, her dark eyebrows rise, and her pale skin is peach-blotched. Her gaze bounces aimlessly through the bustling café until it meets that of Werfel. It is customary for two people in this situation to look away quickly and pretend they haven't seen one another, but Werfel refuses to allow this. He gets up from our table and walks over. He does not sit, but he puts his hand atop hers and whispers something comforting. I assume so, because she looks down again and nods. Perhaps it wasn't a comfort. Perhaps it was a platitude. A reminder of her place. Of how improper her presence is. I look at Ernst and he nods, because Adele quickly gathers her shawl and coin purse and shuffles toward the exit. I am livid—Werfel has been such a pompous ass all evening and now he shames a woman in mourning. The gall is colossal. Someone really should put him in his place.

Adele leaves in such a hurry that she passes right by Klimt's protégé without noticing.

"Is that ...?" Ernst asks as Werfel retakes his seat in a huff.

"Why, it's Egon Schiele," Werfel gasps.

We all crane our necks.

"Don't all look at once!" Werfel hisses and we hunker our heads back down. He looks like he might die of embarrassment.

Egon Schiele is a regular at Café Herrenhof, just around the corner, where we often see him furiously scribbling with his charcoals, his wiry frame wrapped in darkness. I like his angry, erotic paintings. When I first saw his work at the exhibition in the Secession earlier this spring, I thought it was obscene: prostitutes in black stockings lifting their skirts to reveal engorged genitalia. The women looked almost contaminated. *Is that what he thinks of women? That we are monstrous mounds of diseased flesh?* But then I came across a large painting: *Liegende Frau*. The reclining woman—a woman unmasked in a manner beyond nudity—and I felt something for his work that I never had before.

Whereas Klimt depicted female nudes from his own perspective—a male perspective—where women are absent-minded objects, Schiele's portraits of female sexuality do not take on the feelings of the viewer. The subjects exude their own feelings, and they look at you from the canvas directly in the eye, taunting, almost accusatory.

Sigmund Freud, the local psychoanalyst from the Rossau part of town, often comes into Café Central and chit-chats about how the creative urge that consumes artists arises from a deep-seated need to resolve psychological conflict. Whatever that means.

Schiele was at that exhibition at the Secession, I remember, sitting in a corner, eschewing both conversation and glad-handing the benefactors. He was absorbed in his charcoals, labouring over each sketch like an invested lover. Ernst called the art show obscene and led me out swiftly by the arm. Lord knows Ernst would never acknowledge that I am a woman of flesh and blood, of longing and engorged desires.

"Who is that he's talking to?" Ernst stretches his neck to see above the canopy of heads, hats, and elaborate hairstyles.

"It's his sister-in-law, Adele Harms," I say, taking a sip of my hot chocolate, and we all exchange a look. Everyone knows Schiele still carries on with her, even though he married her sister Edith for money. It must be nice to live in a civilization that caters to your every whim and allows for such bad behaviour. I'd be pilloried on the spot.

The lovers whisper in their booth and exchange long, pregnant gazes. Her hair is a shock of ginger that brightens up the gauzed light of this wretched café.

"God in heaven, she looks just like Wally, doesn't she?" Werfel's belly rises with a chortle as he refers to the model, muse, and mistress that Egon bedded for years until his marriage.

Gina leans in and says in a hushed voice, "Do you know, after Christmas last year, word spread that Wally died in Sinj, the poor thing. She was a volunteer military nurse, after all. And ever since, Egon has borne all the hallmarks of an ill man."

As our eyes devour him from across the room, perhaps now I see the psychological conflict Freud is referring to. It is eating Egon alive—his body is wasting away, his cheeks sunken, his eyes enflamed.

What is it about artists and their ability to create flourishing tapestries or gilt portraits in an age when death and ruin abound on the streets? I think the world of an artist may differ from that of an ordinary man, as the world of the ordinary man differs from that of a dog. Lord bless all of them—the artist, the man, and the dog—for they cannot even manage their own feelings; that job lies squarely on women's shoulders every time.

As I sit sipping my drink while the gossipmongers spin their tales about the causes célèbres around us, I can't help but wish for a little autonomy from this role. What a different world I might live in if I could just free myself from these domestic shackles. Maybe in that world, possibilities would befall me. Maybe in that world, I never took up with Ernst. Maybe I stayed in my beloved Bohemia. Maybe we'd still have an empire. Maybe I would be happy.

AS BLOODY AUTUMN RAGES on, we sit in the coffee houses, all aflutter about the breakaways from the empire. The Slavs, the Poles, the Czechs, even the Galicians and the Silesians have declared their intention to secede. Every day at Café Herrenhof, men put their names on lists to be the next to devour the news in the papers slung on the wooden racks. Things are changing too fast for even the papers to print.

On the 28th of October, the Herrenhof is mad with whispers and gossip. I kindly ask a gentleman sitting alone in the corner if I might join his table just to read over his shoulder, but he prevaricates like a bratty schoolboy. So I simply reach out and swipe the *Neues Wiener Tagblatt* from his hands. He is outraged as I run back to my table to read the headlines aloud to Ernst, Werfel, Franz Blei, Gina and

Otto Kaus, and our new acquaintance, Hermann Broch, the writer.

"An independent Czechoslovak Republic has been declared!" I holler as I wave the front page for all to see. We clap our hands and stomp our feet in jubilation; finally, a place where the concerns of Czechs and Slovaks take precedence! A country of our own, if only we could go back!

On the 3rd of November, Austria surrenders. On Armistice Day, the 11th of November, the Kaiser leaves Vienna, never to be seen in this city again. The next day, the German Austrian Republic is declared. The news is on the lips of every man, woman, and child. Lamplighters converse with insurance brokers. Smithies clink beer glasses with civil engineers. Fishmongers toast with black marketeers. The war to end all wars finally has an end. We have survived, and now there is freedom and prosperity on the horizon!

As we sit at the Herrenhof, jolly and jovial, we see the hordes gathering in the streets, marching in one determined direction. We cram together at the windows of the café to catch a glimpse. There is revolution in the air.

Someone shouts, "Follow them!" and we smash through the front doors, running down to Michaelerplatz, under the arches of the Hofburg, and then across the Volksgarten to see a massive demonstration gathering opposite the parliament building. The Social Democratic Workers Party has the most support of late, well ahead of the Christian Social Party or the German Nationalists, and one of their own, Karl Leuthner, is speaking from the balcony of parliament. The crowd is yelling and shouting so much, I don't think any of us can hear a word.

People climb up on the parliament parapet and raise a banner that reads *Hoch die Sozialistische Republik!* It's raining, but nevertheless, people climb the lampposts, umbrellas waving in jubilation. Everyone is cheering. Thousands of tired labourers—nothing but skin and bone, yet with a new vigour—begin to holler. Even Werfel tears off his hat, waving it feverishly as he shouts, "Down with the Habsburgs! Long live the Republic!" Groups of workers wave red flags and sing "The Internationale." German Nationalists wearing black, red, and gold emblems sing "Die Wacht am Rhein." I grab Ernst by the arm, digging my fingers into his tweed jacket with the leather patches so as not to lose him. "It's like the premiere of Stravinsky's *Rite of Spring*!" I shout in his ear, but he can't hear me over the rhythmic beating of canes against the iron fencing of the Ringstrasse.

Farewell La Belle Époque, welcome the New Age.

"This is upsetting my digestion," Ernst whines, as the crowds begin to surge and wave in the direction of the city centre.

"Ernst, I want to march!" I cry.

"We're going home!" He steers me by the arm back and away from the throngs of the Ringstrasse, back to the eighth district of Josefstadt.

"You can't—"

"You're making a scene."

"You can't move me—"

"You won't embarrass me."

"You can't move me around like—"

"This isn't safe for women."

"Dammit, I will get to the end of this sentence even if it kills *you*!" I fight against him. "You can't move me around like a piece on a chessboard."

"This is an uncivilized gathering," he growls. "What do you even know of politics?"

"I know you traffic in mockery!" I yell at him as the joy bleeds from my cheeks.

He pushes us forward. "I won't have my wife hurt by charlatans, Bolsheviks, and anarchists."

"Oh, please," I wrench his hand off my arm, "you don't need a wife, you need a Greek chorus." I run back to the crowd. We, the new Viennese, march arm in arm, and we are going to chant and cheer all the way to the Prater.

But things devolve into puerile barbarity. The Bolshevik Red Guard tries to storm parliament. Windows are smashed and the sound of machine-gun fire suddenly rings out. Around one hundred shots are fired, some into the air, some at the building. Mass panic breaks out on the Ringstrasse. A man and a child are trampled to death, and many are injured. But the Communist coup fails.

By the time I make it through the blockades and burst through our front door long after supper, Ernst has left for his mistress. The lingering, nagging numbness inside my chest rushes through me like a tidal wave. My heart is a place that once was full, but now that I seem to be entirely unlovable to the man for whom I risked everything, it is a ship capsized at sea.

3

The Affable Thief

VIENNA

1919

If there's one thing I've learned, it's that rich people never notice when they've been burgled. You would think they'd be very prudent with their wealth and strive to keep note of everything. But no, they are careless. Tailored clothes. Gold jewellery. Antique bookplates. Coin collections. Terrycloth towels. Cotton bed linen. They never notice a thing.

In the beginning, I was scared of the consequences. I had to tell myself these people deserved it. Every sideways glance, every churlish comment, every knowing look at the state of my dress or unruly coiffure, I would visit back on them. This person I was becoming—the woman with the sticky fingers—was so far removed from what everyone knew of me. Not even Ernst knew. So many times I wanted to tell him, but I knew once the full extent of my deception was revealed, he could never again be prevailed upon to love me like he once did—and that has always been my hope for our union. So, I gave this person a name—the Affable Thief. So cheerful and pleasant I was, no one ever suspected me. The Affable Thief, or my "alter ego," as Freud might say, is the rightful heir to the Artful Dodger.

The first time I brought out the Affable Thief was as I ported valises at the Westbahnhof. The Affable Thief would slip a few fingers inside the luggage for loose coins or a stray silver pendant. Sometimes, as I extended a helping hand to a portly woman heaving herself into her waiting car, the Affable Thief would slip the platinum ring right off her chubby finger. "Much obliged to you, meine Dame!" I would call as her taxi pulled away, kissing my loot, leaving her to wonder why I was so joyful when she offered no tip. I would listen to the asphyxiating drivel of a Hungarian count, assaulting the very character of the Czechs and Slovaks ("who would be nothing were it not for the charity of Budapest!") as we awaited his taxi in the long rank, all the while relieving him of his silk scarf and platinum cufflinks tucked carelessly in his overcoat pocket. The bloviating numbskull couldn't shut his mouth long enough to realize he'd been had. It was such a gas! Running up and down the lower levels of the station, sliding a finger in a pocket here, lifting a money clip or a coin purse there. It was hilariously strange how no one noticed! I kept waiting to be caught, to be called out, to be sent away in chains, but no one ever took note of my face, let alone what my sticky fingers might be doing. So even if they ever suspected me of thievery, these "highly cultured" buggers couldn't pick me out of a lineup. No wonder we couldn't win a war. The police were so inept they couldn't even catch the Spanish flu.

One night soon after that first appearance of the Affable Thief, after Ernst had gorged himself at Café Central on grilled mutton chops, jacket potatoes, and custard pudding, he slammed our entryway door behind him as he went straight to his bedchamber, and I slipped out into the darkness and sold everything I had lifted to the back-door traders and black-market vendors on Pohlgasse. The men on Pohlgasse near St Vincent de Paul's shelter for wayward tramps and homeless vagrants were always eager to do business with me. To my surprise, the metal tins sold for greater value than the jewellery or the cocaine. In these hard times, when every prewar luxury like a bar of soap or an inkwell is impossible to come by, the Viennese will glue fragments of automobile tires to the bottom of their shoes instead of buying galoshes, or they will extract their own gold teeth and melt them down into counterfeit coins to avoid the long bread lines.

Even before I named the Affable Thief, during the Great War, so many of our friends and brothers were shipped off to the front, so on occasion, I would lift drugs from my father's oral surgery—opiates, morphine, cocaine, amphetamines—and sneak them to the boys on the train platforms, along with bags of talc and bars of soap from the pantry. I started to get careless when I lifted items from the fine shops that line the Na Příkopě. A bill of sale would appear at my father's door for the total amount, and we would have a calamitous row. My father would scold me, saying I craved attention. But it was so much more than that.

Everything was turned upside down when the Empire declared war on Serbia. The light patina of polite society was stripped clean to reveal nothing but chaos, rage, and distress. How can anyone punish a thief by the normal means when all morality is discarded with the declaration of war, when there is not a single normal day, not a single normal thing in our lives anymore?

Men were filling up the rail cars singing Czech folk anthems to the harmonica and the beat of the train wheels. They were coming back in coffins. Or not at all. My mother was gone, and my father was whoring and distant. Life seemed precarious and without a guarantee. So why not gamble? Why not strike out for deep water, daring yourself to drown? You almost never aspirate, but it's the gasp that offers the thrill of life.

I RUMINATE ON MY sticky fingers as I sit at Café Prückel on the Stubenring across from the School of Arts and Crafts, watching young pupils with easels and water-colours tucked under their arms run up through the entrance or bound down the steps. As I lick the mound of whipped cream off my coffee, men around me read the daily newspapers and waiters in black aprons whisper with their regulars. Then a voice over my shoulder asks, "Is that milchkaffee pulling its weight?"

I turn to find Max Brod, whom I once met at the Café Arco during my Prague days. "Herr Brod! You startled me!" I stand and extend my hand, but he kisses instead of shaking it.

"Please, call me Max."

"Do sit down."

"I knew you were in Vienna, Frau Pollak, but I did not expect to see you, as I am on such a short sojourn here."

"Please call me Milena."

"As you wish."

"What brings you to Vienna then? Last I saw you, you were deep in conversation among all the posturing peacocks of Herr Pollak's literary circle."

"My dear!" He gasps in delight. "I do remember you being rather opinionated, but it always comes as a shock, does it not? Egad."

"I am famous for my short fuse."

"God bless it." He runs his fingers through his hair. "I am in Vienna on business, but I am also conferring with a good friend of mine at Café Herrenhof."

"Ah, yes, I know the café well," I say. "Might you be meeting with anyone I know?"

"I'd wager you might, as he hails from the hallowed streets of Prague as well. Doktor Kafka?"

A dryness sets in my mouth like my cheeks are stuffed with sawdust. "Doktor Franz Kafka? Yes, I've read his work."

"Oh?"

"A few years ago. *The Metamorphosis*. It was ... something else."

"Did you not enjoy it, my dear?"

"Forgive me if I am too blunt. I am unaccustomed to social graces."

"Not at all, I would appreciate your thoughts."

"It was, in a word, disturbing."

"I do believe that was inten—"

"—and obscene."

"Obscene? That is quite the verdict."

"Tell me, Herr Brod—"

"Max."

"Max. Is Doktor Kafka as sullen and taciturn as his protagonist Gregor Samsa?"

"Why don't you accompany me to the café, Milena? You can determine that for yourself. It's been quite some time since I've had the pleasure of escorting a young, rosy thing on my arm."

I feel the crimson rising in my cheeks and along my neck. "Oh no, I couldn't. I'm not properly attired." I motion to my thick pleated skirt and un-ironed collar.

He rises, dropping a few coins on the table to pay for my hot drink. "I thought young ladies were consumed by shopping."

"Not this young lady. In fact, when I was a little girl I thought I would very much like to be a storyteller of some kind."

"You?" He raises a brow.

"Don't look so surprised, Max."

"I will try my best to hide it. What kind of storyteller?"

"I fancied becoming a novella writer like Doktor Kafka, or maybe writing feuilletons for the periodicals like my aunt Růžena."

"All the more reason for you to join us." He comes round to my side of the table and kisses the top of my hand. "We will be at Herrenhof well into the night. Do feel free to come by whenever you'd like. I'm sure your husband will be there as well."

"All the more reason to stay away."

Max winks at me and says, "Indeed," before tipping his bowler hat and pushing his way through the mahogany doors.

Shopping is not something I am accustomed to, despite my love of fashion and modern designs. It has always thrilled me the way the cut of a blouse or the length of a sleeve can make a body appear leaner in some areas while plumper in others. How colours, textures, and fabrics can reflect a personality. A black woollen shawl says to the world that I am sensible and modest, while a black lace shawl says that everyone at the speakeasy knows me by name and what I like to drink.

Perhaps, now that the Affable Thief has been turning a profit for some time, I can visit some of the shops on the Graben and Kartnerstraße. Perhaps I could go to Café Herrenhof tonight, meet the mysterious Franz Kafka, appease Max Brod, but above all, impress my husband. Impress him enough to come home to me this week, and every week thereafter.

I ARRIVE AT CAFÉ Herrenhof after the shops on the Kohlmarkt have graciously let me stay past closing. Money talks, as they say. The shopgirls dazzled me with garb in all colours of the season. Their hair swung as they showed me dresses of velvet and silk and ribbon and feather. Hats were everywhere in pastel shades, even sophisticated turbans for an evening out. I was shown new handbags and flashy brooches and ropes of pearls. The shopgirls were slender and well-coifed, with ivory-tooth complexions, each with a camellia in a buttonhole.

For the money I spent in their establishment, I could have bought box seats at the premiere of Strauss's *Die Frau ohne Schatten*, or procured five kilos of pork fat and maybe even a goose for Sunday dinner. Yet I do not feel an ounce of remorse.

The Herrenhof is one of the most fashionable cafés in Vienna, filled with red velvet armchairs, mirrored walls, and thick violet carpets. Flower arrangements as tall as trees adorn every surface—the marble-topped commode, the server's lectern, even the stairs to the lavatory. For once, my airs and attire fit this place.

I spot Max and Ernst, along with Werfel and Franz Blei, sitting in a corner booth. No one will dare say a word about my Dostoevsky-esque demeanour now.

"Gentlemen," I announce myself, and they all stand and drink me in.

My gingham dress is trimmed with cream rickrack, with a large diamanté clip at my shoulder, and I wear a ruby shellac silk shawl with a fringe and black sheath. A large black velour beret with fine mesh veiling sits atop my head. A pink chiffon scarf is tied at my neck, above my heart, and I'm wearing one-strap heels with alligator-finished leather. I look like one of those actresses from the moving pictures, here to dazzle everyone with my presence.

Werfel's mouth hangs like a dewdrop. Max and Blei grin with far-off looks in their eyes. Blei rubs his beard.

Satisfaction overwhelms me as I take my seat. Ernst, placing his hand atop mine, finally says something. "Milena, my dear, how chic and fashionable you look. I am in shock."

I take his copita of port right from his fingers and reply, "You'll be even more shocked when you find out where it all came from." I take a sip and watch the men laugh heartily.

"Pollak! How lucky you are!" Max says as he raises his schooner of sherry in my husband's direction.

"It would seem so." Ernst's face still has not recovered and I cannot hide my sheer delight.

"Are we missing someone?" I ask coolly, pretending I couldn't care less whether I am still the topic of conversation. "Isn't Doktor Kafka supposed to be joining us?"

"Ah, Kafka left hours ago," Max says, finishing his drink. "He was never one for prolonged social gatherings. More's the pity."

I have already stopped listening to Max as Ernst's hand has moved from atop mine, down to my lap, and across my thigh.

* * *

11 August, 1919

Appearance of Milena Jesenská before the General Court of Vienna

Presiding: Richter Georg Kaltenbrunner, Police Commissary Gustl Waud, Court Clerk Jochen Holz.

Prosecutor: Herr Helmut Gladigau

Defence Solicitor: Herr Janos Poellinger

PROSECUTOR GLADIGAU: State your name.

JESENSKÁ: Milena Jesenská

GLADIGAU: Date of birth.

JESENSKÁ: 10th of August 1896. Yesterday was my 23rd birthday.

GLADIGAU: Old enough to know better.

SOLICITOR POELLINGER: My Lord...

RICHTER KALTENBRUNNER: Herr Gladigau...

GLADIGAU: Withdrawn. What is your current address and occupation?

JESENSKÁ: Lerchenfelderstrasse 113. I am dually employed as an instructor of languages and a porter at the Westbahnhof.

GLADIGAU: Two occupations in such a time of dire need for so many in the former Empire, and yet you resort to wanton thievery?

JESENSKÁ: Yes.

GLADIGAU: Why?

JESENSKÁ: I was suffering from a crisis of love.

GLADIGAU: A crisis of love?

JESENSKÁ: An erotic crisis, if you will. It was a personal matter and it spiralled out of control.

GLADIGAU: Your personal matters are worth wasting the time of the state?

POELLINGER: My Lord, may I interject?

KALTENBRUNNER: Your witness.

POELLINGER: If it please the court, Frau Jesenská surrendered herself to the Commissariat, to which Police Commissary Gustl Waud, who is in attendance today, can attest. None of the victims of Frau Jesenská's petty thievery were even aware of any wrongdoing until she confessed to all her sins at the Commissariat. In fact, Herr Waud even turned her away, insisting she had imbibed beyond her limit and that she should return home. It is because of Frau Jesenská's deep state of remorse and regret that we are even here today. Frau Jesenská is a married woman, and deeply pious. I suggest that she be allowed to offer the state her deepest apologies and that she be released on her own recognizance.

GLADIGAU: My Lord...

KALTENBRUNNER: A mere moment, Herr Gladigau. Frau Jesenská, might you clarify for the court what exactly you mean by an erotic, or love, crisis?

JESENSKÁ: I am the devoted wife of Herr Ernst Pollak, whom you no doubt will have met in all the usual places. He is a man of many tastes and fashions, and I seem to have been disappointing him on both accounts. I wanted to purchase clothes to appeal to his appetite, so that perhaps the very thing which we have recently forgotten might be found in the dark recesses of our marriage. My two means of employment were insufficient, and in addition, my husband has some debts, which I was required to pay. My dowry has been exhausted and I was forlorn for weeks on end. There was another woman in our marriage, you see, and it was getting rather crowded.

GLADIGAU: Frau Jesenská, if you are unable to satisfy your husband, that is a failing that rests squarely on your shoulders. Theft is an unreasonable answer to an easily solvable quandary.

JESENSKÁ: Yes, I have often heard such remarks from men like yourself. However, considering it is callous, cold men like yourself who insisted upon marching toward war, and ultimately costing us an empire, I would think you would be rather eager for a change in perspective and to listen to the thoughts of the fairer sex.

GLADIGAU: My Lord, she is hysterical. Such comments surely should warrant a long custodial sentence.

JESENSKÁ: I've been confined to an asylum before. I am not afraid of your threats.

KALTENBRUNNER: Did your efforts satisfy your husband in the anticipated manner?

JESENSKÁ: Only in the interim. He was back with his mistress by the end of the work week. I did it all for nothing, and my errant ways caught up with my conscience. I am here because I am truly sorry for my actions.

KALTENBRUNNER: I've heard enough. Herr Poellinger, Herr Gladigau, please confer with me in my chambers.

[RECESS OF TWENTY MINUTES]

KALTENBRUNNER: Frau Milena Jesenská, it is upon consideration of your own testimony that we can agree you have been corrupted by your caste level and that you pose a threat to the very fabric that holds matrimonial unions together. The family unit is to be cherished and upheld beyond all other ideals, and should your husband seek other arrangements, it should be viewed as a rational response to an irrational spouse. I see no reason why, at twenty-three years of age, you shouldn't already have children to rear, but I suspect your obstinate independence might be to the detriment of your biological obligations. However, I have carefully considered the very manner with which you surrendered yourself and the fortitude of your honesty. Despite your testimony, it displays strength of character so rarely seen within these hallowed walls. Thus, it is the opinion of this court that you shall indeed be convicted of the criminal charge of minor theft. You are hereby ordered to pay the court a sum of 1,300 crowns and are sentenced to time already served. Next matter!

4

Café Arco

PRAGUE

1919

Apple blossoms fall into my hair. My lap. My hands. I am sitting in the gardens next to the Prater Ferris wheel, staring up at a sky the colour of a robin's egg. How did it all come to this? What kind of woman am I?

I look at my hands. They are strong, like my mother's. She was ill most of my childhood, but her strong hands used to hold me with a fortitude I will not soon forget. I may never really know what ailed her. One doctor called it "pernicious anemia," but I am certain I heard my father tell his colleagues it was cancer of the blood. I was sixteen years old when, at her bedside, it was obvious to me she would not make it any further out of 1912 than the *Titanic*. Her strong hands held mine as she said, "My little Milenka, there are two possibilities in life: to accept one's fate, or to seek one's fate." When she began to drift away from this world and into the next, the doctor turned to his tray of narcotics to attempt resuscitation. I grabbed the syringe right out of his hand and smashed it on the floor. The glass shards embedded in my knees when I fell upon them to pray by her side.

I can hear hoots and hollers from the children inside the wooden Ferris wheel pods. The view of Vienna is unparalleled and not for the faint of heart. All around me are families, young bankers, train engineers, high-society women with ever-rising hemlines, and roasted chestnut vendors. None of them has just emerged from the courthouse with both their freedom and their prison intact. I may not be incarcerated, but I am definitely imprisoned. My mother accepted her fate and what befell her. I will not allow that to happen to me.

Nothing could be better for me at this moment than a trip back to my homeland, my sanctuary, the hallowed streets of Prague.

RAIN SWOOPED THROUGH THE fields during the night ride as the train zoomed through Břeclav, Brno, Česká Třebová, and Pardubice. Bohemia and Moravia are now cut into islands. The Vltava River flows from a small stream into a tawny, opaque torrent that roars for miles, and as it reaches the heart of Prague, it is unfordable.

I left my valise with the hat check girl at the station and made my way straight into the pulsating arteries of town that intersect like starbursts. It is market day in Prague. There are heaps of peaches, plums, and apples at the Ovocny market, and snowdrops, violets, primroses, and Pasque flowers at the Uhelny market.

I stand on the Charles Bridge and survey the gilt streets, the intimidating arches, and the rattling trams that take their turns rather dangerously. My heart is in these stones. What was once to me a shining little rural community has overnight become a metropolis, full of variety. An empire collapsed, threatening to bury us, but we were seeds. Full of surprises, the city is growing, stretching, and reaching out. One day, she will be immeasurable.

I remember that day in 1914 when war was announced via the screaming black ink of the newspaper headlines. They reported that the regiments of the Cossacks and Uhlans were mustering in the firing lines, that Serbs, Austrians, Frenchmen, Germans, Britishers, Canadians, and Antipodeans were clashing in the clouds and dropping bombs onto capital cities and village hamlets alike. Wireless messages from as far away as India and Japan were hastily sputtering of conquests and extreme losses. Soon after, the first mutilated soldiers appeared over the horizon, slowly walking home in traumatized single file.

The war may be over, but it comes for us all in one way or another. Perhaps soon, we will find ourselves once again roasting in its ovens.

Prague sidewalks are made of small black and white stones that change pattern every block; diamonds give way to roses, then to pentagrams, and then to checkerboards. I walk past the Topič art nouveau building, up Na Příkopě, and past the apartment block at the lower end of Wenceslas Square that was once a credit union. When I was a little girl, we lived on the top floor, with my father's oral surgery on the first floor; my mother was still alive, and my father showed me more affection than he ever has in his later years. A statue of Mercy, the Roman God of commerce, with two angels at his side, peers over the balustrade of our attic apartment. This tableau used to give me nightmares of the acutest kind. I have many memories of growing up in this building in the heart of the city, where from our balcony we witnessed all sorts of festivities and massacres. I try not to think of them now. So, I keep walking.

Past Wenceslas Square. Past the Koruna palace with the corner cupola with stained-glass fittings, past the old casino and the Byvalem house, where Božena Němcová once lived and perfected her famous novel *The Grandmother.* Past the gothic Powder Tower and the Smetana concert hall, where Ernst and I used to buy nosebleed seats with obstructed views so that we could fondle each other in the dark during the last act of *Camille.*

Suddenly, the street merges into Hybernská street. And I find my old haunt: Café Arco.

Ernst first introduced me to this coffee house when we were young lovers defying convention. I was sixteen. I have never been here without Ernst, I realize now. To this day, it is the meeting place for young German-speaking Bohemian writers, intellectuals, and philosophers to talk about the zeitgeist, read the daily newspapers, and debate the merits of their rivals' latest publications. Ernst likes to call them the Arconauts. This was the one spot where the Czech and German cultural scenes would come together. Jews, the trading class, and the dominant political class all speak German. Czech has always been seen as the language of serfs and the unrefined folks of the countryside. These two Pragues could only seem to find common ground here inside the coffee house.

But as I enter through the glass doors, I hear nothing but German voices. The dialect is not so distant from what I use in Vienna, but it is notably its own. Copies of the *Národní politika*, *Le Figaro*, the *Prager Tagblatt*, and *Le Devoir*, among other foreign journals and newspapers, hang on the racks. The main hall is dominated by a large round table, and in the rear is a billiard room plus a reading room. Against the far wall are cubicles and private corners for the quiet and anti-social. There are tables earmarked for the *distinct* groups that patronize the café—the gentlemen poets, the gentlemen constructivists, the gentlemen pragmatists, and the old Christian gentlemen. Franz Werfel, Otto Pick, Willy Haas, Paul Kornfeld, Max Brod—I met them all for the first time here.

As I step inside now, I see writers Karel Poláček and Vladislav Vančura playing billiards in the rear. Johannes Urzidil is at a table with Alfred Fuchs, Ferdinand Peroutka, and Antonin Macek—the same table they occupied before the world was plunged into bloody conflict. I am surprised to see them. Many who once frequented the café had to enlist, and after the war, many never returned. All these men met me through Ernst, and as they notice me, they nod their heads in acknowledgement. Ernst might be my husband, but I will not allow him to claim Prague from my heart.

The head waiter, Mr. Počta, greets me by name—bless him—and pulls out my chair. "The usual?" he asks and then pushes the pastry cart past my table.

The owner, Josef Suchánek, is famous for posting

humorous notices on the walls of the café, including offering a reward of 100 korunas for reporting those who tear out the pages of the newspapers. A dirty theft, he calls this. He offers "severance pay for incorrigible guests in exchange for a written undertaking that they would never come back to Arco again." Another sign, tongue firmly in cheek, says, "Children not allowed in the café. If they are already in the café, they must behave well. If they do not behave well, they won't be fed. Unmarried parents are also not welcome." I let out a hearty snort.

My hot coffee arrives in a tall glass with a saucer upon a pewter serving tray where there is also a bowl with rock sugar in irregular lumps, a small brass creamer, and silver tongs with pearl handles decorated in the Dutch style. Dear, oh dear, these are exactly the kinds of accoutrements that the Affable Thief would love to add to her conquests. As I add my lumps, I can feel eyes on me from across the café: brooding, quiet, but ever present.

I look around to see the usual faces, until I spot a small figure in the corner, seated at a table for one. The light doesn't reach his face, but I can make out his lean shape, his eyes hooded under thick brows, and his angular face fashioned from years of jaw-clenching and handwringing. His drink cleared away long ago, there is nothing but strewn daily papers and a cloth serviette heaped upon the marble tabletop.

I look away to the scene outside the café windows, where children are shining a magnifying glass on a beetle as a tram rattles by. Its legs dance as it struggles on its back, and smoke wafts in concentric curls from the waltz of its six frantic feet.

The shadowy figure in the corner is Franz Kafka. Having just missed his company a few months ago in Vienna, I cannot abide another lost opportunity.

Eyeing the burning beetle, I very quickly and deftly elbow my glass of coffee. It makes a satisfactory smash at my ankles and I feign a gasp. The point of impact looks like a small meteorite crater, with brown liquid and opaque glass bursting forth like solar flares.

The legs of a distant chair push against the tiles, feet scurry. I lift the hem of my dress to just above my knees as the footfalls arrive to my left. He is kneeling next to me; I don't dare look down.

"Shall I get you another, Frau Pollak?" The voice is deep and rich.

I do look down. The eyes are a bit darker, the suit improperly tailored, and the hair peppered with wisps of grey, but it is him, collecting pieces of glass. He is extravagantly tall, lanky, and clumsy, as though unsure what to do with all that extra bone and muscle. He's as lean and slim as the day is long.

"Doktor Kafka? Thank you so much, I am entirely too clumsy for my own good."

Taking a good look at my scandalously inappropriate hemline, and my legs encased in silk stockings, he grasps my hand and brings it to his lips. I am not used to such pleasantries, and my skin thunders like a tempest at the touch of his hand, the brief brush of his lips against the back of my fingers.

"Please, Doktor Kafka, do not trouble yourself. Have a seat."

Grabbing the back of the other chair, he motions to

the head waiter for another coffee, and I do my best to calm down. I haven't employed such a shameless trick since I was a schoolgirl; I wasn't sure it would still work. His eyebrows are so thick, I am certain they are fluent in Hebrew. Nose like an arrowhead, ears perked to attention, he dons a slight smirk, which suits his fine, plush lips.

The waiter brings us two new drinks, but they sit on the table untouched. He is not drinking coffee or tea but rather a glass of steamed milk.

"What a pleasure, Frau Pollak, to see you back in Prague. We haven't seen you around here in many years."

"Please, call me Milena."

His lips curl like a hairpin. "Milena ..." He purposefully extends the pronunciation of my name. I am no longer Milena, I am Meeeeeee-lena. "What a rich, heavy name. Almost too full to be lifted."

I hold his gaze longer than one reasonably should before replying, "My mother gave me the sobriquet Milenka."

"Now that is a Czech name, to be certain. Milena feels too Greek or Roman, out of place in Bohemia." His eyes travel down to my legs again, and I feel a surge of power.

"Maybe that's why I don't live in Bohemia anymore."

"And correct me if I'm wrong," he has barely heard me, "but Milenka means 'sweetheart,' does it not?"

I bite my bottom lip.

"No matter the origin, Milena is most certainly the name of a woman." His eyes travel slowly from my knees, past my thighs and lap, up the lunar crescents of my hips, around the curve of my breasts, and linger on my clavicle before meeting my eyes again. "It is marvellously 'woman.' A woman whom one carries in one's arms out of the world and into the fire."

"Is that so?" I can feel the fire that he speaks of; it's in his voice and in my stomach.

"What else is a man to deduce when staring down the barrel of your elevated hemline?"

"I must say, the service is much better this way." I smooth my hair with my fingertips. "And I never have a problem stopping a taxicab or getting box seats at the opera house."

"Then I shall have to get the name of your seamstress so I might tip her handsomely."

I raise my eyebrow. He does the same.

"You flatter me, Doktor Kafka."

"My friends call me Franz. Or even Frank."

"Frank." I roll the name around my molars. "It's not very German."

"Indeed, I was about to comment on your impressive command of the language. I see living in Vienna has done you well."

"Thank you, though I was rather looking forward to speaking Czech while I was home."

"German is my mother tongue and, as such, more natural to me, but I consider Czech much more affectionate."

We both take a long, hard sip of our drinks, never taking our eyes off each other.

"Speaking of Vienna," I cut through the pause, "I heard you were there a few months ago. I had the good fortune of bumping into Max Brod, who invited me to evening drinks with the promise of your appearance."

"Ah, I must have just missed you."

"That must be it, yes."

"If I'm being honest," he lifts his warm glass again, takes a deep sip, and licks the foam from his lip, "I'm glad we didn't encounter each other then."

"Why's that?"

"The last time I saw you, it was many years ago, and it was here." He gestures across the airy, light café. "We were introduced, but you took no notice of me. I recall in detail your purple frock and your energetic, full mouth as you hunkered down with Pollak and read the musical score of a local concert."

"I vaguely remember that evening. I must have been eighteen years old."

"And hopelessly besotted."

"I really was." I thumb my glass and fiddle with my sugar spoon, but I do not drink. "But I was young and there was a war. Everything seemed so romantic."

We are interrupted by the pastry cart, and Kafka asks for a bowl of stewed peaches.

"Speaking of your husband," he says in between mouthfuls of the dripping, syrupy fruit, "it was not long ago that I encountered him most unexpectedly on the Franzensquai promenade."

"Oh, really?" The repeated mention of Ernst makes me take a long hard swig of my drink, as though it were spirits rather than a brew. "He does return to Prague often for work, but he made no mention of you."

"Well, our meeting was quite unmentionable. In fact, I can't remember exactly what happened. Either we walked along together chatting for a bit, or we passed each other with a brief nod. Both are entirely possible."

"And what was your impression of my husband?"

Kafka puts his spoon down and heaves one leg over the other. His legs are so long his tailor must work extra hours just to keep him in trousers. He folds his arms and takes his time. "He is a pious and humble Jew," he says, as he holds my eyes in his. "But then again, aren't we all."

I chortle and Kafka smiles.

"I am not a Jewess, if you haven't heard."

"Yes, you're what we might call a shiksa."

"Pollak has used that term on occasion, yes."

"Well, Rilke doesn't practise either."

"Rainer Maria?" I ask.

"I know him as Réné," he nods, "but yes. He's also from Prague, with a Jewess for a mother."

I lean in. "My father was none too pleased with me for carrying on with Pollak." Kafka's eyes are steady and true, but I can tell my words have given him pause. "I don't talk often about this shame I fear I've brought to my father," I continue. "I'm not sure why I'm even speaking of it now."

Kafka thumbs his cup. "Your father must have taken his cues from mine."

I can hardly breathe as we lock eyes again. There is nothing so corrosive as the parents you have, especially when contrasted with the parents you don't have. Most days, it is a struggle to even articulate it, but Kafka, with his narrow aquiline nose and eyes the velvet black of midnight, understands.

He raises a finger and, in one swoop, undoes the top button of his collared shirt. I can see his Adam's apple bobbing as he swallows hard, and I can also see the concave hollow at the base of his long neck. A bead of sweat jewels the hollow, and suddenly the scent of peach blossoms ebbs and flows around me.

I'm not sure what has passed between us in this moment. But something has happened.

"I'm terribly sorry, but I must be going." I smooth out the pleats of my dress and drop my hem as I stand.

Kafka rises and bows his head. "Of course, don't let me keep you. Allow me to cover this charge."

"Thank you kindly." I shake his hand and then pause for a heartbeat. "I hope you don't mind me saying so, but you are not at all like I thought you might be."

He does not let go of my hand. Rather, he thumbs my palm. "Oh?"

"I read *Metamorphosis* many years ago, and I thought—"

"—that I might be an insect?"

I giggle. "Not at all. No, I guess I thought you might be a horrible misanthrope. I'm delighted to see I was wrong."

His eyes follow the lines of my face. "Well, my dear Milenka, get to know me before you decide. I might be a misanthrope yet."

I reclaim my hand and gather my coin purse. "I look forward to it, sir."

Turning on my heel, I push my way through the glass doors. I will not look back over my shoulder. I will not glance behind me. I will not say goodbye. When trying to leave an impression, a woman must use all the charm at her disposal, and something tells me Doktor Kafka is just the man to impress.

When I am around the corner, I hear Mr. Počta bellowing my name down the street. I guess he noticed rather quickly that some of the Arco silverware was unaccounted for.

I've been lost at sea. And, for the first time, I've glimpsed the lighthouse on the shore.

5

The Master Key

PRAGUE

1939

Tell me about Minerva." The Obergruppenführer leered, looking up from his dossier.

Milena blinked. The cellar was cold with bitter drafts, but her body was steaming with sweat. "It was a gymnasium school for girls," she said flatly. "Where I learned Latin and Greek and benefitted as one of the first girls to receive an education comparable to the boys. Where I was afforded the opportunity to write the university entrance exams."

"Just one of the lads," he replied.

"I wouldn't say that."

"It seems to me that you are quite interested in behaving like a man."

She narrowed her eyes. "I'm afraid I don't know what you mean."

"The femininity of our women is under threat, and their masculinization is rather worrisome."

"Receiving a proper education is hardly a threat to womanhood, Herr Obergruppenführer."

"Quite right." He folded the dossier shut. "It's what you did during your schooling that troubles me."

Milena shifted in her seat, scanning her memories for indiscretions. The laughter of the little girls of Minerva rang in her mind. She thought of the green gates and the lunette carved with maiden faces that greeted the students as they passed under the stained-glass window depicting an art nouveau rose wreath with the erection date of 1906 in the centre. Founded in 1890 by local rabble-rouser and friend to all women, Eliška Krásnohorská, the school featured an old malachite pulley fountain on the front sidewalk. The water wasn't safe to drink, but the children on occasion filled their canteens and pails with it. The neighbourhood grandmothers used the water for their boilers, baths, and coppers. That section of the river was cleaner than in the Vyšehrad district.

"I never cheated on an exam, if that's what—"

"It's not."

"Then wh—"

"Who are ..." he opened the dossier once more and read the names like the ingredients for a recipe, "... Jarmila Ambrožova and Stanislava Jilovská?"

"Staša and Jarmila? They're my girlfriends."

"Whom you met at Minerva, isn't that right?"

"Is it an offence to the Third Reich that I have friends?"

The Obergruppenführer leapt from his chair and wrapped his fingers around her throat. "Would you like to die today, Frau Jesenská?" Her nostrils flared and her heart quickened, but she looked him square in his chartreuse eyes. He tightened his grip. "What was the nature of your friendship with Staša and Jarmila?"

"Do you think—" she gurgled.

"Yes, I do."

She fought against his fingers but couldn't win. "It's ludicrous."

"You seem to have no problem bedding Jews, so why not disgrace your sex by fornicating among yourselves?"

"Get your hands off me."

"Do you know what we do with homosexuals, Frau Jesenská?"

A piercing shriek penetrated the eerie stillness between them. It made her crane her neck to the side. A prisoner was being defiled somewhere in these dank cellars.

"If it's in any way similar to what you've done to the women here, then, yes, I can imagine."

He released his grip, but not without knocking her face backward with a smack. "Don't flatter yourself." Retaking his seat, he pulled a small flask from his inner breast pocket and, smoothing out that annoying lock of hair that kept flopping down upon his brow, took a big swig of strong, clear liquid. From the scent, Milena deduced it was Polish whisky. He resealed the flask and tucked it away. "When we spoke with Jarmila and Staša—"

"You arrested them?"

"We interrogated them."

"What for?"

"How much of your sexual proclivities and exploits did you share with Jarmila Ambrožova?"

"Why are you men so hysterical about sexual congress?"

"In your mind, did that qualify as an answer to my question?"

"She hasn't done anything wrong."

"Were you aware that Jarmila caused her first husband's suicide?"

"That's a scandalous falsehood!"

"He defenestrated when he learned she was spreading her legs for editor Willy Haas."

Milena's heartbeat was spilled ink, staining her chest cavity until its thump was all she felt. She'd had this conversation once before. The sun had beat down on her shoulders as the man she loved had questioned her about this very incident. To be questioned again about it by a man she hated was the ultimate act of fated retribution. Suddenly, she felt a tingle on her wrists. The scars. They were faded to light peach, fine as a razor, but she could feel them resurfacing. He mustn't see them. She pulled her sleeves down to her palms.

She sighed. "What does any of this have to do with me, Herr Obergruppenführer?"

He smirked, tapping the dossier on his knee like a winning lottery ticket. "You said you're not a Czech whore."

Milena gritted her teeth and clenched her jaw. "I am a respected author and columnist. My body is too sacred to be shared with any common Fritz like you."

"Yes, your body is so sacred." He guffawed, his breath stinking of alcohol. "It's like a temple, in fact, because sometimes your rabbi is in it."

"You know, Herr Obergruppenführer, I used to envy snake charmers for their ability to talk to vipers. But as it turns out, I've been doing it this entire interrogation."

When his backhand connected with her cheek, no blood spewed forth, but it felt as though her eye might jostle loose from its socket. His hand seemed to her like a shotgun or a cannon, the stability of her skin his target.

"You will answer my questions or I will lock you up in the stockade with the pedophiles and sodomites. They will make excellent work of you."

A choking wail tugged at her esophagus, but she refused to release it. She shuddered, but she managed to tamp the cries down until she was standing on them.

"Now," he stood and, clasping his hands behind his back, walked the length of the room as though on an evening stroll, "Staša told a very surprising anecdote: how the three of you stole the master key to the city of Prague."

Milena did not speak.

"Nothing to say, Milena?"

She pursed her lips like they were sewn together with wool thread. Before the Great War, Milena, Staša, and Jarmila had paid a black marketeer a couple hundred korunas for a copy of the postman's master key. Any apartment block, tenement building, or palais was suddenly accessible to them. There was no possession more valuable.

"Come now, Milena," he strolled back, his face remaining in the shadows, just shy of the light of the bare bulb above her head, "You've already admitted that you were a wanton, thieving slut in Vienna, convicted of theft by an Austrian court."

"So?"

"So what did you use this master key for?"

"It was..." she fumbled with her words as though fumbling with keys on a ring. "It was just..."

"Speak up!" he barked from the shadows, his voice bouncing off the walls like a ricocheting bullet.

"It was just a way to see Ernst."

The Obergruppenführer suddenly appeared under the glare of the bare bulb and thrust his face into her space. "You would sneak into his flat."

"Yes."

"And fornicate."

"Yes."

"Knowing full well he was a Jew."

"Yes."

"Were you carrying his Jew bastard?"

Milena closed her eyes.

"I can't hear youuu!" he bellowed, his voice scaring the roaches from the walls. "Answer me, Frau Jesenská. Yes or no. Were you pregnant with a Jew's baby?"

She gasped at the word. "Yes."

"And what did you do with the child?"

She couldn't stand on her suppressed wail anymore. She choked on it as it thundered out of her like a bat shooting from a cave. Collapsing into her hands, she sobbed while cursing her weakness.

The Obergruppenführer straightened, tugged on his suit, the row of medals across his heart clanging into one another, and headed for the latched door.

"I'll give you a moment to think about it," he said, before slamming the door behind him.

Milena clutched at her chest, the pain ripping at her organs as though they were impaled on a fishhook.

6

The Stoker

VIENNA

1919

As my train from Prague begins to slow, passing over the Danube, approaching Vienna's Westbahnhof, I cannot stop thinking of my encounter with Kafka. Every time I picture the shameless way his eyes lingered on my legs, or the unabashedly clumsy way he ate his stewed peaches, my back jolts with electricity.

Last night, as I reclined on my father's chesterfield after dinner, the housekeeper brought in a telegram addressed to me. It was from Kafka. The message was blank, but the return address was a health spa in Merano, Italy. Tucking it quickly into my blouse, I went to my father in his study, kissed the top of his head, and wished him a good night. He eyed me suspiciously for a moment but then returned to his newspaper without delay. Repairing to my bed chamber, I slept soundly with the telegram clutched in my fist.

I was always taught to bite my tongue. Spinning stories in my head—fanciful tales of great heroes fighting for the honour of flaxen maidens—I always knew I wanted to be a storyteller, but I was never allowed to consider this as a meaningful pursuit. Did I want to be on the stage? Or on the wireless? My focus eluded me, but no matter, since daughters of doctors weren't allowed to do such things. I was expected to immerse myself in my studies, but instead, I drifted from one infatuation to another, and this included men. Might I be satisfied with being a muse to a great man? Ernst moved among the great writers, philosophers, and thinkers of Prague, and I felt as though his desire for me shook the very foundations of his sensible life. I took great pleasure in thinking of myself as a Delilah, or a Helen of Troy. Marrying Ernst was the closest I've ever gotten to being a respectable woman. Yet that urge to use my voice, to tell all the stories waging war in my head, remains. Now, after meeting Kafka, I feel that urge rising up from my belly again, like an undigested bit of sauerkraut.

From the elevated tracks that wind through the city, I see street urchins burning nuts and playing tricks on the neighbours. During the war, matches all but disappeared, as did cigars, and we all learned to live without them, but now it is quite easy to procure automatic lighters, which inevitably find their way into the sticky hands of children. Women with generous bellies and hair piled high atop their heads are queuing for the public bathhouses—not to bathe, as that daily luxury has been reduced to once a week for the poor, but to wash their clothes and linens. Water is in such short supply that most have taken to dunking their unmentionables in the Danube, but the soap and bleach aggravate the fine layer of algae that sits atop the water like an oil slick. Their once pearl-coloured crinolines and bustiers come out permanently blotched with malachite. These same women take the slow-moving regional trains, two or three trains a day, out of the city to exchange soap and kerosene for food from the villagers in secluded huts. I don't have the hard lines around my mouth like some of them do. Although there are those in Prague who are destitute after the Great War as well, at least the Bohemians believe in banding together and sharing what they can with their neighbours. In fact, while home, I witnessed my own father, whose purse strings are tighter than a snare drum, donating the expired oils, unguents, and salves from his surgery to the orphanages in Malá Strana.

The train whistle blows as we lurch to a halt in the Bahnhof. My return to Vienna heralds a return to reality. I wish I had the resolve of Anna Karenina to throw myself upon the tracks, but I suppose I'm too old for that nonsense now.

I take the Stadtbahn a couple stops north to the Josefstädterstraße station. Day in, day out, I hear the roar of these tracks from our flat as the metropolitan trains pull in and out. Then the 46 tram chimes as passengers get on and off underneath the iron overpass. I walk two blocks to our building; the wrought-iron bars covering the double doors of 113 are decorated with twenty-four geranium Elke effigies buttressing the bars. Seven of the blooms create an arched proscenium over the main entrance. As I ascend the grand spiral staircase, I pass a sink on every other floor suitable for drinking and filling copper tea kettles in the morning. There is only one flat per floor, a luxury these days, as most of the buildings on Lerchenfelderstraße have two and sometimes three per floor! Overcrowding is everywhere. Our flat has been equipped with electricity and push-button light fixtures, but there is a porthole window in the stairwell as I climb from floor to floor, giving a little light so I can see where I step.

When I enter our flat on the fourth floor, I am surprised to find Ernst there during daylight hours. Paní Kohler is serving him two sticky buns and the tea has just been boiled.

"My dear, what a surprise." I take off my gloves and place them on the credenza.

Ernst smiles at me as he folds up the daily paper. He strides over and places a kiss on my cheek. "Welcome back. I'm afraid I will be out most of the night."

"Oh?" I remove my hat and hand it to Paní Kohler. "I've been gone for a week. I thought we might dine together tonight. I'm sure you're dying to hear the gossip from Prague."

He sits and takes a large bite out of a bun. Icing sugar sticks to his upper lip and whiskers. "It will have to wait for another time. I've been invited to a snooker challenge... mustn't disappoint."

I sit down next to him. "Yes, but I paid a visit to Café Arco."

"Ah, did you see any of the Arconauts we once knew?"

Running my hands along the ribs of my corseted dress, I say, "Yes," but I don't see the need to elaborate further. "And, well, I wanted to speak to you about that, my dear.

Being there among so many great minds made me think."

Ernst snorts as he pours milk into his black tea. "God help us."

Nervously, I let out a giggle. He lifts the cup to his lips as I say, "Yes, well, I think I'd like to try my hand at writing."

The cup rattles and hot tea sloshes onto his hand. He brays like an ass, and Paní Kohler runs to his side with a handkerchief. He rips it from her hands and dabs at his skin. "Milena … You? A writer?!"

"Yes, I think I'd be rather good at it. Don't forget, my aunt Růžena is a writer."

"Oh, she's just one scandal after the other. Didn't she have an affair with that artist, Mucha?"

"She's the editor of *The Calendar of Bohemian Ladies and Girls*. It's a high-quality literary review!"

"Last I heard she was in hot water for writing about Sapphic affairs."

"Oh, that's balderdash."

"Do you expect your narcissistic aunt—whom you never speak to, by the way—to offer you a position?"

"Not at all. I have a friend. She writes about manners and fashion for the *Národní politika*, and I think I might submit a story or two about life in Vienna."

He wipes away the last of the spilled tea and drops the handkerchief with exasperation onto the dining room table. "To what end, Milena?"

"Meaning?"

"What could you possibly want from this?"

"Well, it would mean extra wages coming into our household, for one."

"And you think someone would pay for your musings on Viennese polite society and high fashion?"

My blood begins to rise. His obtuse disdain is moving from challenging into the realm of insulting. "Yes, I damn well do."

"Milena!" He looks around to see if Paní Kohler in the larder has heard my profanity, and then he leans in with hushed concern. "We still have not erased the stain of your kleptomania, don't forget. I won't have you embarrassing me further with writing—of all things."

I lower my eyes at the mention of the thefts but quickly realize he is not allowed to see me like that. I won't give him the satisfaction. "I won't embarrass you." I meet his eyes and refuse to let him look away. "Ernst, I tell you, I can do this."

Paní Kohler enters the room. "Sir? The men are at the door for you, sir." She holds his trench coat in her hands. Ernst stands and she slips it onto him. "I have to go now."

"Not before I get your final word on this, Ernst."

"Do what you like, Milena." He pulls down his sleeves and smooths out the wrinkles in the cheval mirror in the hall. "I won't stop you, but don't be surprised if you cannot publish a word. Journalism is a man's domain, and only the greatest minds have any success at it."

"Then I imagine I will show the men how it's done."

Ernst snorts.

"You forget," I continue, following after him, "one of our greatest writers was a woman—Božena Němcová—and she lived one hundred years ago! I would have thought men's attitudes toward an authoress would have changed by now." I straighten his collar, and he juts out his chin.

"Božena Němcová died alone and without a kreuzer to her name, Milena."

"Well, how about this, then—if this endeavour lands us in destitution," I raise my brows, "I owe you a beer."

He rolls his eyes. "Oh, for pity's sake."

I place a big, sloppy kiss on his cheek. "Thank you, my darling. You won't regret this, I promise!"

He walks toward the door, but his hand pauses on the latch. "You know, Milena, when I first met you, I found you to be quite the social profiteer."

I tilt my head. "And now?"

"Now I find I was wrong. You're a goddamned racketeer."

He leaves and I clap my hands together with a joyful cheer. I run to the larder, grab Paní Kohler by the shoulders, and plant a kiss atop her head.

"Oof, my dear, what's the matter?"

"I have a fire in my fingers, Paní Kohler!"

I WRITE ALL NIGHT. Sitting in Ernst's study, at his Rheinmetall typewriter that he barely uses anymore, I type and I type until my forearms swell with pain and my fingers cramp. I use both sides of the foolscap so as not to run out of paper, and when the ribbon begins to fade, I re-ink it by unspooling it and running it, section by section, along his black rubber stamp pad.

Fingers darker than a smithy's, I write about Viennese café society. Bathing costumes. The types of people I encounter embarking and disembarking at the Westbahnhof. Roles for women on the eve of equal suffrage. The power of shop windows in the centre of

Prague. The age of opulence and refinement when so many on the streets of Vienna suffer. Those who are fond of the high life who turn away with disdain from the simplicity of a country fireside. Those who mistake ribaldry for humour. With so many opinions on the state of affairs, I never struggle to find my words. Words flow from me like life flows out of a skewered pig. The Alt Lerchenfelder church next door does not ring its bells past nine o'clock at night, so my only indication of the time is the amount of noise coming off the street, the echoing of voices from across the Josef-Strauss Park, the sound of footfalls and chair legs scraping the floors below.

I only pause a few times to stare at my surroundings. Ernst's study is decorated with odd portraits and drawings from a Viennese painter named Richard Gerstl. All we know of him is that he killed himself after an affair with the wife of composer Arnold Schoenberg. Ernst bought the paintings cheaply; he simply wanted something to cover the walls. They say art is an investment, and I doubt he will ever turn a profit on this unknown misfit. The one indulgence of his that I do admire is his customized Ex Libris bookplate stamp. He had Koloman Moser of the Wiener Werkstätte design it just for him: a woman in a black cloak carries an asp wound round her arm. Moser died a few weeks before Egon Schiele last year—the last of the Secessionists gone.

Unsure how to sign my finished essays, I try every variation on my name. Milena Pollak perhaps? MP? I could retain my anonymity this way. MJ. Even better. Maybe simply Milena? In the end, Milena Jesenská wins out. How could it not? I take great pride in my name, especially when it is on the lips of everyone in town. The praise, the power. Why, people still speak of that English authoress Jane Austen. Why shouldn't my name ring out through the decades? It's true that writers dearly want to be read. But secretly, we really just want to be remembered.

I set out at first light to the telegraphist and send a short but pleasant telegram to my old school friend who had told me about her mother's work at the *Národní politika*, offering my essays, banking on this connection to get my foot in the door. The response later that day is an offer to read what I wrote on spec, no guarantee. I race home, gather my papers, careful to set the carbon copies aside for my files, and hire a messenger to hand-deliver them to Prague at once.

When word comes back a few days later, I have already paced so fiercely about the flat that I've left permanent footprints in the hall runner. Paní Kohler has been lamenting that she can't keep the home in booze or butter with my anxiety.

And the word is not good.

Late at night, the murmur of the wireless waves hums through the apartment. I rest my head on the arm of the davenport and listen to the news service, the radio plays, the banter, the music, anything to fill my head. Idly roaming the stations, from Zurich to Munich to Berlin to Prague to Salzburg, I eventually pick up the wireless in languages I don't speak. Italian. Portuguese. The Slavic languages of the Croats and the Bosniaks.

Ernst will no doubt revel in this; I will never hear the end of his mockery. "What did I tell you, Milena?" and "Teaching languages is a much more respectable career,

Milena," and "Did you really think you had the fortitude and finesse?" So I listen to the wireless from abroad and daydream about a world where our men didn't come home to a falling empire in wooden boxes stacked neatly in sombre train compartments.

It is late, well past the black of midnight, when Ernst comes in and tells me to go to sleep. I turn away and ignore him. He exhales sharply and shakes his head. He leaves the parlour, and I hear the door to his private bedchamber click shut. I lean into the hum of the radio woofer, but the broadcast shut down hours ago. All I hear is the static hiss of dead air.

THE LAST DAY OF 1919 is upon us—I cannot wait to say goodbye to this year. The best thing to do is crawl into bed, cover myself up to my ears, and not come out until after the holidays. That's how I proposed to celebrate Christmas—but didn't—and how I have vowed to celebrate the new year—but alas, I have already broken that resolution.

I step out under the fading sky. The revelries are already beginning before night has had a chance to fall at our feet, and the town is like a fairground. The townhouses and businesses on Bäckerstraße are bathed in garish light. I shouldn't have bought that drink at the Alt-Wien Café, New Year's be damned. I can't afford it. These days, it costs forty hellers just to take the tram, when it used to cost nineteen. Why, I cannot even buy a copy of the daily *Kronenzeitung* anymore, because the price has gone up a whopping two hellers in just six months! Ernst believes the Austro-Hungarian Bank might soon move into liquidation and administration. None of the former Empire states are even allowing their circulating crowns to leave their borders. Each new country over-stamps them, making them worthless once they travel. Since the war, everything has been topsy turvy; the inflation makes beggars of us all. The only reprieve seems to be a dose of the playful New Year's spirit in the streets of a broken city that smells all day of sauerkraut and barley soup.

As I walk around the curved nave of the Stephansdom, and then up the Graben, a school of children races past, waving sparklers, bunting, and streamers in the air. A blast of rockets fires over the Habsburg Imperial Palace like a fusillade of bullets, and fireworks illuminate the night sky. *Kaboom!* A baptism by fire, a singed, fleshy smell. "What cracker is this same that deafs our ears?" And I am forced to agree with Shakespeare, as all the cooks, bakers, jugglers, and judges pile onto the Graben from St Peter's Cathedral to holler at the heavens. There are a thousand miseries in one explosion. *Kaboom!* My eyes burn. *Kaboom!* The world spins. *Kaboom!* Atoms collide. A new decade is upon us.

"Happy New Year 1920!" the harlots yell and the gypsies hoot. They exchange hugs and kisses and best wishes. Another chance to try again. Fireworks dot the horizon from the Prater Riesenrad to the Rathaus. Drunkards light their own fireworks on the streets. One cannot step too carefully, as firecrackers shoot in all directions. On Lerchenfelderstraße someone has lit an entire box of firecrackers behind the Alt Lerchenfelder parish. They echo off the quiet rear corridors and turn the rubbish bins into powder kegs.

The minute I walk through the front door, Paní Kohler takes my overcoat and muff and states ardently that she is certain the twenties will be the decade of peace, tolerance, and modernity. I smile at her and agree. But the promises of the night are made of butter and melt when the first sunrays appear.

Early in the morning of New Year's Day, before the infant year can even cry out, open its eyes, or suckle, I am awakened. I haven't opened my eyes, but there is a rustling in my bedchamber. The stench of brandy wine infects the air. Ernst stumbles in the darkness and plows through the room.

"Ernst, my darling, don't you think you should go back to your bed?" I mumble, unamused by his escapades. Had this been 1916, my twentieth year, I would have found this utterly amusing, even enticing, but now it strikes me as nothing more than intolerable weakness. There is an unmistakable burn that comes with being a woman among the fallout of men.

It all happens very quickly. He is on top of me, my bed linen ripped aside. He grabs my ankles and yanks me forward; my nightgown whips above my belly. My eyes open; the full force of what is happening shocks me into consciousness. I push against him, but I can hear him fumbling with his trousers with one hand while holding down my wrists with the other. His elbow comes down on my clavicle, knocking the wind out of me. "Get off me!" I scream, but he wraps his belt around my throat. Eyes bulging, nostrils stinging, lungs exploding like a cannon against my ribcage. In the name of Judas, I would shove my living body into a baking oven before I let my own husband defile me.

In one swift motion, I deliver a crushing knee between his legs. Immediately curling into a ball, he lets out a shriek so high-pitched that it would give the famous posturing soprano at the opera house a run for her money. Bringing my knee to my chest, I kick him off me and he flies off the mattress. Groaning and writhing on the parquet floor, he rocks in the fetal position while I throw his belt across the room, gather my nightgown, and stand over him with my fists clenched.

"Don't you ever do that to me again!" I scream down at him with all the white rage of a liquid hot Vesuvius.

"Milena, you're my wife!" he squeals like a pig.

"And you," I spit back, "are a mangled, bloviating hell-beast!"

"I didn't mean any—"

"How dare you treat your wife like this? You should be ashamed of yourself!"

"I thought that you—"

"Get out!" I grab him by his white collar, hoist him to his feet, and haul him to the door. He stumbles in the darkness, finds his footing, and gasps as he finally exits into the corridor.

Before I slam the door shut and collapse in a hysterical sob, I yell after him, "And don't come back until your cock has doubled in size!"

IN THE MORNING, I stand at the window overlooking Lerchenfelderstrasse. Heavy eyelids still raw, my neck turning a deep shade of mottled purple, and my skin still seething, I refused to even move a muscle in my bed until

I heard Ernst leave the flat, the door clicking shut behind him. When Paní Kohler locked it, I ran to the window.

The tram rattles by as men in hats run after it, and women with long skirts cross the thoroughfare arm in arm. One of them wears a cape the colour of lapis lazuli with gold-leaf flecks. It is long, like a kaftan, and she wears her hair in a clumsy hive piled high. Gold glimmers at her wrists and neck. I dare say it's Emilie Flöge, the longtime consort of Gustav Klimt. Her luminous, elaborate dress stands in stark contrast to the taciturn greys and ugly browns adorning the lower castes all around her. Klimt may be gone, but she is thriving. She goes unnoticed by Ernst, however, as I watch him emerge from our apartment block and head off in the direction of the bank. She no doubt is headed to her fashion house on Mariahilferstraße, near the Ringstraße. The two of them travel side by side—the coffers and life after death. Which one would I rather be?

Are those my only options?

Across the street at number 124, a mother-of-pearl edifice boasts a re-enactment of the Knights Templar slaying dragons and beasts with their spears, their steel jousting helmets marking each window.

As I stand here, bare feet cold on the floor and skin still throbbing, the thought of death makes me think about my future. I have always known, though not always admitted to myself, that I would never be happy in teaching or labouring servitude; in fact, I would be miserable. Journalism is the key to the realization of my hopes and ambitions. I would withstand any amount of hunger to be able to live the life I want. All the people I've met in the literary salons are doing the same, so I won't be alone. My multiple languages will be a tremendous help, so I must make hay! One cannot watch the play and act in it at the same time.

I turn on my heel, yank open my dresser drawer, and pull out Kafka's clandestine telegram. I sit down at the typewriter and slam the carriage into place.

My dear friend,
No doubt you will be surprised to receive word from me. I see you are at the bath and health spa in Merano, so I do hope this letter finds you well and in good spirits.

Our encounter at Café Arco has been fervently on my mind. I think about your expressive face as you listened—truly listened—to me speak, one leg crossed over the other. Your manner of walking with strides longer than the day. And the way you held my hand longer than one might expect.

All these seemingly unrelated events have culminated in a new passion, and it is with this in mind that I thought I might approach you with a request. As you know, I have read your works most ardently, but it is a shame that they are inaccessible to your countrymen. Those who live in the rolling landscape of the Sudetenland and the northern meadows all speak Czech, and they no doubt would surely love to read the words of our most famous son. I propose translating your stories from German into Czech, an exhaustive but important task, and I am just the right authoress to do it. Would you be so kind as to grant me permission to undertake such work on "The Stoker"? I read it many years ago in Wolff's volumes and its adequate length, intriguing landscape, and use of allusion and allegory would most definitely be of interest to Czech readers. Even, dare I say, to Slovak readers!

Please do let me know, and please remember me to our dear friend Max Brod. Vienna has been beset by incredible tempests of late. All is gloomy and grey in this new country without an empire.

With affection,

Milena

P.S. Please address your reply to the Poste Restante address included.

I visit the post office every day for a week, not wanting Ernst to find any telegrams or letters at our address. I don't want him to know about this encounter with Kafka, though Ernst probably wouldn't give a flying fig. Between his Herrenhof cronies, his work, and his mistress, I doubt he has much time to mind with whom his silly little wife is corresponding. It would take him longer to finish an aperitif with three onions and hum along to an Al Jolson song than to care about my written words. I shake my head. One day, he'll see. He'll turn his head and realize I'm so far above him, he's unable to reach me.

Finally, a letter arrives via my Poste Restante, but it's not from Kafka. Rather it's from Kurt Wolff, the man who originally published "The Stoker." I grab the courtesy letter opener on the clerk's plinth, rip open the envelope, and devour each line. Wolff has only written four. The first is a greeting. The second is the acknowledgement that Kafka has passed on my translation request.

The third grants my request. The fourth is his signature, which resembles the scratches of a crowing rooster.

Never have four little lines changed the course of a day or my outlook upon it more quickly. If those four lines were a kerosene lamp, they would burst open and singe every postman's sack in this small post office. If those four lines were a prayer, the Pope in Rome would bow before them. I could lose a stone in weight while eating a feast, just reading those four lines.

Hiking up my skirts, I race through the streets, dodging the workers who are replacing the cobblestones that were ripped out during the 1918 January Strike. Past the Theatre an der Wien where Beethoven's violin concerto was first performed while he lived in the building. Past the studio on Westbahnhofstrasse where Klimt suffered his fatal stroke. Past the tenement buildings abutting Seitenstettengasse where the Jews pickle everything in brine in the spring and dump the runoff into the sewers. Past the Kronenzeitung kiosks that clandestinely sell tobacco smuggled from Yugoslavia. Past all this, and then I dodge the rattling 46 tram as it hurtles toward the Volkstheater.

I turn the corner of my apartment block, Paní Kohler buzzes me through the gate, and I peel up the spiral staircase. I swing open the doors of Ernst's study. It is the only room in our apartment that looks as if it were furnished before the sinking of the *Titanic*. Everything is either cerulean or burnt copper. His cigarette caddy is even shaped like a Model A race car. Plunking down at his rolltop desk, I wind foolscap through his typewriter and fashion a series of letters. Sometimes, in this rough existence, being alive is a joy. Happiness is not a thing one can find; it simply assails a person when they least expect it.

Paní Kohler enters with a silver tray of tea, sugar, cream, and lemon biscuits. As she places it next to my fingers, which are flying across the keyboard, she remarks, "My word, what a lovely letter opener." She picks it up off the table, where it must have slipped out of my coin purse. The letter opener is sleek, brass, and sharp, with a snowy owl adorning the handle. "My dear, wherever did you find such a beautiful piece?"

Grabbing it from her hands and slipping it back into my purse, I say, "It was … a gift."

THE NEXT DAY, A reply from Kafka finally arrives.

> Dear Frau Milena,
>
> You may have already received a letter from Wolff. You're slaving over the translation in the midst of gloomy Vienna; it is somehow moving and embarrassing for me. Please send me the translation. I can't hold enough of you in my hands.
>
> Why don't you get out of Vienna for a while? After all, you're not homeless like other people. Wouldn't a trip to Bohemia give you renewed strength? And if for some reason you may not want to go to Bohemia, then why not somewhere else? Perhaps even Merano might do.
>
> It occurs to me that I can't remember your face in precise detail. Only how you finally walked away between the tables of the coffee house—your figure, your dress, these I can still see.
>
> Kindest regards,
>
> Kafka

I hold the letter to my chest as the post office clerk attempts to read over my shoulder. Joy rises from deep inside, as though I am standing on it; it sprouts roots that envelop my calves, my thighs, and wrap around my waist until I am gasping with sunshine. An invitation to join him in Merano! I am dually excited and afraid. Excited because it is no secret I have always been the type of person to run alongside the bullets, rather than dodge them, just to see where they lead. Afraid because I often forget to test for wood rot before stepping out onto the plank.

Carefully folding the letter along its lines and placing it in my blouse, I turn back to the clerk. "I require postage for a letter to Arnošt Lustig, the editor of the *Tribuna* in Prague," I say, as I bring forward a manila envelope containing the carbons of my essays. "In addition, I'd like to send a telegram to the literary weekly magazine *Kmen*."

As I'm plopping down my coins on the counter, counting them, and recounting them, the clerk asks, "Might you say that again, meine Dame?"

"Oh, for heaven's sake." I roll my eyes. "Tree trunk. *Kmen* means tree trunk. What did the empire teach us if not the importance of languages and cultural relations? Please tell me you have at least heard of Prague!"

The clerk counts the coins in her hand before depositing them in her till. "Prague? Yes, I know it. The Kaiser never did anything so clever as to fill it with Saxons."

Narrowing my eyes and pursing my lips at her, I am about to give her a piece of my mind when I notice a sleek new platinum letter opener on the desk. It is attached to a cord that is locked to the tabletop. She notices my look and folds her arms. I slide her the script for the telegram.

She counts the letters. "That will be one crown and three hellers."

"For a telegram!" I blurt out. "Does it also come with a slice of Sachertorte from Demel's bakery?"

The clerk shrugs.

"On second thought, send that telegram collect."

She blinks. "Collect?"

I lean in. "Coll-ect."

I gather my belongings and stomp out of the post office. Above the entrance, I notice a Latin inscription in the stone frame that I had never heeded before. It's from the 39th Psalm of David: *"My heart was hot within me; while I was musing, the fire burned."*

I RECEIVE WORD FROM Neumann at *Kmen* rather quickly. Although he indicated that his secretary would be sacked if she accepted another collect telegram from an expatriate, he was swayed by the idea of a translation. He agreed that the story of the oppression of a ship's stoker by the high ranks, henceforth known as *Topič*, would make a fine read for Czechs and Slovaks. Upon publication, he would wire me fifteen hundred crowns.

Fifteen hundred crowns! Who ever heard of such money? Not only could I finally pay my debt to the courts in full, but I would have enough left over for flour, for rice, for butter, for eggs, for coal, for oil lamps, for candles, for the trams, for Paní Kohler's wages. And maybe even, without anyone blinking or looking twice at my purse strings, to indulge in sweet Portuguese butter tarts decorated with honey-roasted pecans or rich Einspänners piled high with extra heavy Schlagobers from Café Prückel.

Ernst has been absent for days after the New Year's Day fiasco, so I make good use of his rolltop desk and typewriter. I sit all day and all night in my nightgown, surrounded by Kafka's original version in Wolff's volume, a German-Czech dictionary for the larger words, a grammatical instructional book in the style of Louis-Nicholas Bescherelle that shows how to squeeze Czech's seven cases into German's four, lots and lots of foolscap, and verbena tea. My fingers blur across the keyboard like the forest seen from a moving locomotive. The sun moves across the sky like a hare dodging the hounds.

The typeface of this typewriter is especially appealing and inexplicably satisfying as I churn out page after page. I love the operatic ding when I reach the end of a line; I love slamming the carriage back in place. I love the gorgeous *thack-thack-thack* the keys make. The workhorse shift, tab, and backspace keys make a *chunga-chunga-chunga* that tickles me. The keys strike the page with such torque, I half-expect blood to drip from the paper. If only it would.

The black ribbon is old and weathered, and I haven't the funds to visit Die Schreibmaschine Werkstatt on Siebensterngasse, so I roll the ribbon bit by bit over my husband's inkpad. I debate dropping dollops of ink from my fountain pen inkwell onto the ribbon, but the ink from stamp pads is designed to last longer and resist dryness. My fingertips and fingernails are blackened like the local colliers who fill our coal hole every fortnight. I leave my fingerprints all over Ernst's desk to soak into the English oak. Let him forever stare down at my marks and wonder how something so beautiful could come from someone so underappreciated.

One evening he finally comes home—merely for a change of attire and to collect some dossiers—and finds me: hair dishevelled about my shoulders, ink smudges across my cheek, tea and rock sugar spilled across the serving tray, and a wastepaper basket filled with crumpled attempts at Czech storytelling.

"Milena?" He enters the room as though he's barefoot on a frozen pond. "What are you—"

"Ernst! Quick, what is the difference between Kapitän and Hauptmann?" I slam the dictionary to the parquet floor next to my bare toes. I don't even remember where I last saw my slippers. "This wretched book is no help at all!"

"What in heaven..." He hovers over my shoulder and reads the foolscap wound around the platen. "Milena, this is by Kafka."

"Nothing gets by you, my darling." I pull the foolscap closer to my face to inspect my last line.

"Whatever you're doing with his manuscript, you better run it by—"

"Oh, for pity's sake, Pollak." I yank out Kurt Wolff's four-lines-from-heaven from underneath the heap of books and papers and shove it at him. "Here. And—" I find Neumann's telegram buried atop the desk "—here."

Ernst scrutinizes Wolff's letter with the intensity of a murder of crows, but when he comes to the end of Neumann's telegram, his pupils dilate as if they might give birth. "Milena, my dear," he looks at me, his head quivering like an arrow in flight, "this is wonderful."

I meet his gaze. He's wearing an expression I have not seen on his face in many years. A blooming admiration, on the verge of blossoming.

"Do you reckon?" I ask.

He nods, looking between the notes in his hands and me. "Yes, of course my dear. It is—" he pauses for the length of a Rudolph Valentino picture "—truly remarkable."

He hands the papers back to me, and as I take them, he extends a finger, caresses my thumb ever so slightly before I withdraw.

"Thank you." I smile.

"You're welcome." Something in my chest expands.

He retreats from the study, and I don't see him for an entire week. But on the seventh day, I receive a package delivered by bicycle messenger. The brown paper says it comes from Die Schreibmaschine Werkstatt. Unknotting the twine and ripping off the brown paper wrapping, I find two new octopus-ink black ribbons, a thousand pages of foolscap with attached carbons, a tin of paper clips, bull clips, a stapler with a full cartridge, three fountain pens, a bottle of fountain pen ink, a hole-punch, and a selection of brass fasteners.

Coming up behind me from the pantry, Paní Kohler sees me standing, very quiet and very still, by the front door in my bare feet and dressing gown.

"My dear," she wipes her hands on her apron, "is anything the matter?"

"No." I close the lid on the package and look up. "Nothing at all." For the briefest of moments, my heart is an island and I'm lost at sea. I retreat to the study, closing the door behind me.

7

The Letters of Eminent People

VIENNA
1920

As my drafts of *Topič* criss-cross the border during *Kmen*'s lengthy editing process, I mercifully receive a response from Lustig at the *Tribuna* after much waiting. Impressed with my writing, he had relayed the recent departure of the paper's fashion correspondent, Zdenka Wattersonová, whose immigration papers for the United States had finally been granted. And that is how, in late January 1920, my essay on what people eat in Vienna is published in the Sunday edition. Bursting with pride, I telegram my father to pay close attention to the paper that morning. There is no reply—not that I was expecting one. I am off to the races, and there is no time to be wasted on those who keep their praise locked away.

My melancholy melts like the winter snow, as, suddenly, spring is upon us. My world, once jostled by the war like a sack of pears, is now growing stronger, thicker flesh for the harvest. Ernst spends more days at home. He sits with me at teatime, while I rattle on like a macaw in a birdcage about my progress on the translation, and he even appears to be listening. He has adopted the routine of leaving me ten crowns a week to cover the postage and telegram fees arising from my burgeoning career, and he completely covers Paní Kohler's wages now. Oh, wings of spring, here you come. You saw me from afar and hastened your arrival.

As weeks pass and my musings on everything from war profiteers and barflies to Dostoevsky and American housewives are published, I think more and more about the words my mother spoke before darkness fell over her eyes, "My little Milenka, there are two possibilities in life: to accept one's fate, or to seek one's fate."

So, when Neumann suggests I send the final draft of my translation to Kafka for approval before it goes to print in April, I decide there is no harm in including a personal note. I eschew the typewriter this time. A letter written by hand reveals either haste or care, betrays lies, hints at truths, brings laughter, and commands reflection. If I get a letter from a friend written on a typewriter, it irritates me immensely. And I cannot deny this feeling that has been lingering all these months—that Kafka might be a meaningful friend in my life. All that, and more.

The notepaper is only the size of a gift tag, but I make good use of the space.

My dear friend,
Please accept the final draft of the translation with all my best wishes and affections. Do me the honour of replying at once. As Nietzsche once wrote, you have no idea what a charming memory you are to me.
Milena

The next day, the fire under my feet gets me to the post office on Bennogasse precisely at midday, when the mail sacks from Italy are being unloaded fresh from the train. There is a letter from Merano. I hike up my new cotton pongette dress, which falls scandalously just below my knees rather than to my ankles, and skedaddle in my Oxfords to the parkette on the corner of Stolzenthalergasse and Pfeilgasse. Whipping the "liberated" letter opener out of my coin purse, I slash open the envelope and devour his words like a locust.

Dear Frau Milena
When I took the manuscript from the large envelope, I was almost disappointed. It was you I wanted to hear from and not the all-too-familiar voice from the old grave. Why did it get between us? And then I remembered that it also acted as a mediator between us. The fact that you like the story gives it of course some value. What's more, it's incomprehensible to me that you've taken upon yourself this great labour, and I'm deeply moved by the faithfulness I wouldn't have thought possible in the Czech language, as little as I would have suspected your beautiful natural qualification for it.

And what are you going to do now that this translation is near the end? I read with great admiration your piece in the *Tribuna* about your disdain for the Viennese soup kitchens. Why don't you leave Vienna for a while? I so much wish you could be in Merano.

At present, I cannot leave Merano due to a real disease of the lung. Half of Western Europe has more or less faulty lungs. I live here pretty well, more care than the mortal body could hardly stand. I get endless sunshine from my deck chair overlooking the overgrown shrubs and strange vegetation. Formerly part of the Empire, the Dolomites have a warmness I miss when the puddles in Prague freeze over.

I'm not going to write anything else about today; there's nothing of greater importance I could talk about. Everything else tomorrow, including thanks for the manuscript which touches me and makes me feel ashamed and sad and pleased.

Yours,

Franz K

His words treat me to a deep sweetness, like plum-jam turnovers. I don't know how he does it with his words—the power of going out of himself and seeing and appreciating whatever is noble and loving in another. Trams peal by, a woman drops her parasol, the colliers and the coal merchants rattle by on their ramshackle conveyance, the cobbler hammers away at a boot in his shop window—the world carries on as if it hasn't just been capsized by a letter.

Bolting from the park bench, I run through the back streets and trot over to Demel's on the Kohlmarkt next to the Manz bookshop. Pushing through the wood-box entrance with lime marble slabs that stand sentry in each room, I am greeted by the ladies in the verdigris dresses and the wineskin-stained lips. They know my favourite—Sachertorte, and a couple of sheets of crisp stationery. I love these girls; whenever someone misbehaves, they scold the ruffian with, "What would the Empress say?!" It always calms the tempest. They lead me alongside the long, mirrored bar and push through the French doors beyond, entering the rear salon with walls the colour of a courtesan's ribbons. Pulling my fountain pen out of my coin purse, I sit at a marble table and compose my reply.

Sending a letter is the next best thing to showing up personally at someone's door and kissing them. I mark up the page with traces of myself and proclaim it his territory. My hands fondle the paper; my saliva seals the pre-gummed envelope. Everything from penmanship to an ink-smudged fingerprint to a lipstick-kiss by the signature reveals character. Motivation. Intention. Desire. Something tangible from my world becomes part of his world. Like young summer lovers, my letter is carried over his threshold like a newlywed.

Ernst and I only ever exchanged a few letters. There wasn't really time in those days, when we ran about the streets of Prague like urchins, escaping my father's menacing looks. It wasn't fit or proper for a girl of my station to attend the opera or accept an invitation to dinner without an escort, but we were fighting for the right to vote; the old ways of doing things had to play second fiddle. There wasn't time for courtship correspondence when I was sneaking away at night with the master key to Prague in my pocket and creeping back into my bedchamber before the lark could herald the dawn.

Now, perhaps, I have a chance at redemption. To do things properly. To find out if Franz is the man I hoped Ernst would be. I want to do something bad right now, something that necessitates getting caught.

My dear Kafka,

Because I wasn't born a boy, I was afraid of my father. When I was a little girl, I remember, my mother bore a son. I have a brother and his name is Jan, like my father. But my mother was feeling poorly and couldn't give the boy her breast. She cried for a wet-nurse, but my father said, with spite and hatred, that if my mother couldn't nurse, then she shouldn't have children. Jan died after a few weeks. They buried him in our family mausoleum. I have always been looking, ever since then, for the brother I lost. Is that you?

It pains me to read that you are feeling poorly. The literary salons and circles whisper in their gossip-mongering fashion that the Merano spa where you stay specifically treats those with consumption. It surprises me that someone as ascetic as you might be ill. I hope your heart is not aching as well and you find some gold bullion in your future. You have so much to offer. I miss the high I experienced in your company.

That day at the Arco, there was no imbibing of a rich, heavy hot drink or sugary confection. Imagine patronizing a coffee house with no coffee, I told myself. You had fruit and milk—how would such a strict regime satisfy the blood coursing through your long legs?

My long legs have come in handy, apart from carrying me everywhere I go. But were I deprived of the fine sweets from Prague's finest cafés as a child, I wouldn't have used these flashy gams to jump into the Vltava River and swim to the other side when I was late for an appointment! You will no doubt have heard of my exploits as an adolescent, and most days, I still entertain my streak of rebellion. There is nothing so intoxicating as a drink from the upheaval fountain; I hope to get drunk on it. This level of inebriation has landed me in hot water, or rather, rooms that empty quickly as I enter. But, as Swedenborg once wrote, the more angels, the more room.

Your invitation to Merano appeals to me greatly. Vienna is absurd, and so is my husband. But it is an awful feeling to want to go away and to want to go nowhere. And then there is the most dangerous risk of all—the risk of spending your life not pursuing what fulfills you.

I am delighted to read that you enjoyed my "Stoker" translation and my piece in the *Tribuna*. What praise! You will forgive me if I refrain from personally sending my feuilletons. How galling such an act would be to me. Writing is new to me, but the urge to, as Hamlet said, "unpack my heart with words" is overpowering. Yet, the more life you live, the less easy it is to write! Writing is all about the non-life.

Perhaps I sound altogether too sensitive here, not tough enough for this new post-war world. But remember that long after roses have bloomed and dropped their petals, the thorns remain.

Yours,

Milena

I twirl my fountain pen between my fingers, then bite the end. I once read that Pythagoras theorized on the state of carnal appetites, saying there is a good principle, which created order, light, and man, and then there is an evil principle, which created chaos, darkness, and woman.

I feel the chaotic dark. My lust for a newness has sponged up another person and detonated into single cells. Into molecules. The afternoon is balmy. Lovers are ducking into photograph booths, making goofy faces at the camera in between delicately placed smooches. I run out of Demel's faster than fast, thighs burning, lungs choking. I run and I run and I run, waiting to crash into another person.

AS I RIP KAFKA'S reply clean from the envelope, I notice that he has changed tones. He is no longer using the plural *sie*, the form of address that is formal, proper, and reserved for those you do not know well. Instead, he is using *du*. That is how you address a close friend, family member, or someone who has known you your entire life. It is strangely intimate, and my eyes break across each line as though it spits red flames.

> Dear Frau Milena
> You are very strange, Frau Milena. There you live in Vienna, have to suffer this and that and still have the time in between to be surprised that others, I for example, am not feeling particularly well and that I sleep one night rather worse than the one before. My three sisters have a more sensible attitude; they want to throw me in the water at

the slightest opportunity, whether we are near the river. Would it surprise you also to learn that I, too, once swam in the Vltava? These long legs are good for some things, faulty lungs be damned.

Your relationship with your father is akin to mine. If you ever want to know what my early life was like, I'll send you from Prague the gigantic letter I wrote my father about six months ago, but which I have not yet given to him.

Another peculiarity I think we have in common, Milena: we are so shy and anxious, almost each letter is different, almost each one is frightened by the preceding letter and even more so by the reply. You aren't like this by nature, that's easy to see, which is why your letter dispels many an uncertainty. I see you clearer, the movements of your body, your hands, so quick, so determined; it's almost a meeting, although, when I try to raise my eyes to your face, then, in the flow of the letter, fire breaks out and I see nothing else.

Of your husband I had made myself another picture. You know, Milena, when you went to him, you took a large step down. You are a whirling dervish of passion, drive, and unparalleled grace.

But if you come to me, you'll leap into the abyss.

Yours,

Franz K

P.S. Can I get a letter by Sunday? It's crazy, this passion for letters. One leans far back and drinks in the letters and is aware of nothing but that one doesn't want to stop drinking. Explain this, Milena...teacher! Your last letter arrived late in the evening, and I actually said to myself: Enough, you can't read this tonight, you must get some sleep. But

I read it and the tension of not hearing from you all day dissolved itself; almost as if you were here and I could have laid my face with a sigh of relief in your lap.

I inhale sharply and hold his letter as though I'm cupping a jackdaw.

A Danubian spring has found its place in Vienna, making very fine weather in the daytime, but we still wear our coats in the mornings and evenings. The clearness of the sky and the olive colour of the leaves suggest so many thoughts and feelings. The Burgtheater is winding down the season into nothing. The last play on the bill is halfway through its run, but I haven't made an effort to attend, so the days feel dryer and longer than the deep state of July.

I tuck Kafka's latest epistle into my new satchel that I bought in Josefstadt, finding my coin purse too impractical. My deliveries, letters, packages, carbon copies, and contributor copies can all now mingle nicely with my notepad, pens, and letter opener. I point my feet in the direction of Kettenbrückengasse and walk over to Café Sperl, with the mahogany accents and the velvet buttermilk drapes cascading down the two-storey windows. I sit in a booth in the left salon with vermillion brocade cushions. Sachertorte and Haselnusstorte slices lounge under glass domes at the server's station with stacks of commemorative matchbooks left over from Kaiser Franz Joseph's funeral.

The head waiter eyes me as I heave my satchel disdainfully atop the marble table. Probably named Florian, Anton, Emil, or Ulf (almost all head waiters bear these names), he takes my order: a caffè latte and a slice of Linzertorte. Yet after I've said my thanks and turned to my satchel, he leans in.

"Frau Pollak, I couldn't help but notice your satchel."

I look up at him, and he immediately straightens his back.

"Yes?"

"It is—" he chooses his words carefully "—not often we see ladies porting satchels in our establishment."

I smirk. "Don't worry, my dear, I never port it on Sundays."

"No," he smiles, "of course not."

I return to my satchel, only for him to lean in once more. "It's just that it's not something that respectable ladies are known to have."

I give him a look that I found in the rubbish bin next to his commentary. "When you find a lady that meets your respectability standards, we can ask her. But I'm afraid I wouldn't know what your respectable lady might or might not have."

He motions to the barmen and barflies crowded around the server's station near the entrance, all straining to hear our conversation. "Yes, we've all heard of your exploits." No doubt my legal matter in the autumn was all these crones and cronies could yak about. "However, it must be said that your attire isn't everybody's cup of tea."

I glance about the salon. Women in straw hats with elaborate feathers whisper with hunched shoulders. Men fiddle with their watch fobs. An elderly gentleman with whiskers and a cane has lost all sense of propriety and stares unabashedly at me, maintaining his expression of displeasure even after I've narrowed my eyes at him. I catch my own reflection in the mirrored fireplace at the far end of the left salon. My face is so tense I look as if I could quite easily bite off the end of a cigar. Clenching my jaw, I have half a mind to gather my things and storm out. I am well aware that I dress like Isadora Duncan, but this is 1920, for pity's sake! Women can vote, women can drive, women can own property, and as the Great War proved, women can work.

So, I compose myself and coolly say, "Thank you for explaining so thoroughly, but I'd much rather be somebody's shot of whisky than everybody's cup of tea."

Anton or Emil or Florian or Ulf swallows hard and then folds his hands behind his back as he steps away. I roll my eyes. Men are so lucky we even let them leave the house.

I turn back to Kafka's letter and begin to compose my reply. The post has become a rather reliable service since the war ended. During the war, telegraph wires were severed and postal offices were mortared out of existence. We had to rely on expensive messengers who would run frantically from site to site to deliver mail. Now, my letters and telegrams with Kafka are crisscrossing each other in transit. I imagine my letter brushing up against his as they pass each other in the carrier's sack, holding each other close for a kiss before parting.

Touching my fountain pen to the page, I think of his use of the informal *du*. I bite my lip. How scandalous. The Viennese café society is willing to overlook a lot of bad behaviours from great men, but the same is not true for women. Or rather, married women. Married women with a history of thievery. But the more I correspond with Kafka—thinking of his hooded brows, his long frame, his asceticism, and the way his eyes lingered on my legs—the more I realize that I don't feel an ounce of guilt or impropriety. The instincts that allowed the Affable Thief to flourish are the same here. And besides, as Baudelaire once wrote, "The sole pleasure in love lies in the knowledge that one is doing evil."

A thought occurs to me as my hot drink and pastry arrive at my table with a thud: What exactly are Kafka's intentions? Is he trying to steer me toward recklessness? He's a noteworthy man who works in insurance, and Christ, he runs in all the same social circles as Ernst and I. Perhaps he is more like Gregor Samsa than I originally thought. What was it he cautioned at Café Arco? That he might truly be a misanthropic demon in disguise? Maybe I need to press a finger to his teeth and see where his sensitivities lie.

So, as a precaution, I do not use *du*.

My dear friend,

Do you think this a cold way of beginning?

I haven't forgotten or forsaken you. You live on in my imagination and memories. You are a beacon of inspiration on all fronts. I do not know how men fall in love, but I cannot grip any love between my talons without first being a friend. Is there anything better than a limitless friendship?

It is fashionable these days to say that naturally the best women are sure to find husbands, thus attaining the security for a full life. But I, a married woman, know everything is temporary, including wedded bliss. There are many wonderful women who come to know quite early in life that marriage is not for them. In these cases, friendship is all that remains when the fantasy of matrimony fades away with the first glimpse of reality. Friendship is the greatest love they will ever have. And what a fine and tidy wealth that is. Romantic love is a poverty.

Do not misunderstand me. Ernst is a great love. I find I could never leave him. The many secrets we kept together in Prague cemented our love, things I could never repeat on paper, but suffice it to say, despite what he puts me through as of late, I am loyal to him above others.

That sounds awfully tragic, doesn't it? Almost pitiful. I always give the benefit of the doubt to the most caustic of men. What's wrong with me?! Why, Beelzebub could introduce himself to me and I would straightaway compliment the way the flames from his pitchfork melt the ice in my gin and tonic or the way his scythe makes tidy work of neatly severing my arteries.

Yet, I owe Ernst more than my own father. I have very little money—Ernst doesn't share much of his wages with me, and if one were to choose to wait for a magazine to pay a writer on time, one would wait a rather long time. Vienna is a gurgling cauldron in one little corner of hell, and where I once had many people with whom to cavort, right now there is no one but you. I'm not looking for much in life anymore on that front. But I feel like I need some companionship, or I'll go too far into myself.

When Ernst is actually home for a long period of time, I find I can work even more, as long as he's working too. Back in Prague, my best girlfriend Staša Procházková and I had a great literary salon, just the two of us. We'd read in different parts of the house, and I'd cook one-pot meals. They would simmer all day and release lovely smells, and then at the end of the day we'd drink wine and eat and discuss our books. It was heaven. I was hoping for more of that here in Vienna, but everyone is busy and tied down, trying to survive, and no one I know who lives in Prague ever leaves. Or can leave. I was once the same way. I've pretty much given up on the Viennese crowd.

I'm looking for something in my life...a new situation, a new preoccupation...I don't know what it is yet. I need to step outside of my old box.

Might I ask about your status? I would think a man like you would have a wife, at least a fiancée. I do wonder what she might be thinking about your correspondence with me. If we are true friends, then I must make you do all you can in these matters to be honest. How beautiful is your love for her? Do you tell her you love her as you read my letters in secret?

What do you know of love?

Which makes me wonder what you want in me. A friend—I should hope so. A lover? Or do you simply need an audience?

Yours,

Milena

"FRAU POLLAK, YOU'VE BEEN counting your coins for five minutes now. Do you want to send this letter or not?"

The clerk at the post office is at her wits' end. It's true. I have been prevaricating for almost an hour. Should I indeed send it? Am I too forthright? It is a full-time occupation, navigating men's feelings. Would I gravely offend him? Or would he take the chance to respect my genuine concern? There's only one way to find out. But I've been counting my coins at the desk without haste, waiting for a sign, any sign.

"I do apologize, I just . . ." I look to the line of impatient men behind me itching to send their telegrams. "I'm having a crisis of consciousness."

She rolls her eyes. "If you're looking for therapy, Dr. Freud's office is in the ninth district." It strikes me that the post must witness all the vices of the Viennese. Secret lustful telegrams. Final notices from the bank of foreclosure and repossession. Mournful death notices sent to mothers from the War Office. Care packages of bread and cheese from the outer provinces. Vials of opium and cocaine. And then there are my letters to Kafka.

I lean in. "Might I pose a question to you?"

She blinks. "Me?"

"Yes, what is your name?"

"Fraulein Bettina," she replies, as if it might be the wrong answer.

"Fraulein Bettina, I ask you, what would you do if your husband was putting words in your mouth while a friend was putting thoughts in your head?"

She pauses for the length of the Old Testament. "I beg your pardon, Frau Pollak?"

"Wouldn't you want to know where you stand? Wouldn't you want to know that you're not insane for reading between the lines?"

I drop my head in my hands. Through the lattice of my fingers, I see Fraulein Bettina look over my shoulder at the line of men in bowler hats and trench coats shuffling their feet and sighing heavily. I expect her to throw me out and ban me from the premises. But rather than treating me like the neurotic that I am, she leans in and places her hand atop mine. "Frau Pollak, I'm not sure I understand what you're asking of me."

Compose yourself, for pity's sake. "No, of course not." I touch my cheeks to cool their redness and smooth the sleeves of my woolly sweater.

But then she whispers, "All I can tell you is that ignorance is the only slavery."

I meet her gaze. She lowers her eyes, quickly counts my hellers and remaindered coins, takes my letter, franks it with postage, and drops it in the sack behind her.

AS WARMER CLIMES DEVOUR the remains of winter, the world seems to be finding its footing again. There are free and fair parliamentary elections in Czechoslovakia, a surprising sign of stability in such a new country. The Social Democratic Worker's Party takes both the House of Deputies and the Senate, with a sizable turnout, though not a majority. However, a new party that only formed a few months ago is on everyone's lips; it's all Ernst, Werfel, and Blei can yammer on about at the Herrenhof while they sip copitas of port and haggle over the bill with head waiter Anton. The German National Socialist Workers Party. They were elected to a considerable number of seats. Of course, we all know it is due to the ethnic Germans who have always lived primarily in the Sudetenland. I do wonder if Kafka might have been swayed by their fiercely German rhetoric. Surely not. Their leaflets and gatherings have been reported as strangely antagonistic—what a tactic to take for a people's party. Nevertheless, we all sit at our regular table and toast our absent comrades and countrymen. How I miss my beloved Bohemia, where on every balcony you can find a woman who looks like me, smiling. I wish I was among the crowds in Wenceslas Square to celebrate this news, the turning of the tide, the arclight of the future that shines so bright upon the Czech people. This longing guts me.

There are some setbacks, however, and the world is quietly advancing and forgetting about the Viennese. The *Neue Freie Presse* publishes a damning report that the coal yards by the train stations in Vienna can only provide enough for one day's operations. Any blockage, snowfall, or other unforeseen event, and the trains cannot travel. Vienna is cut off from the entire world, with food and fuel shortages, no warmth and no light. We are two million people who starve together, freeze together, and lose our equilibrium. Together.

Surprising even myself, I have hope for this little metropolis that goes round and round in a circle like a gust of leaves. Men *and women* who have reached twenty years of age can vote, and what's more, their votes are worth the same and, moreover, secret. Child labour is quickly abolished. The Republic enforces a ban on overnight work for women and youngsters. Conditions for house staff such as maids, servants, and butlers are improved. Now, factory workers only have to toil for eight hours. The bills certifying the right to holidays, the right to unemployment benefits, and the right to unionize and arrange collective agreements pass. We read about each new progressive advancement like locusts feeding on corn. We huddle around the newspaper rack at the Herrenhof, grabbing copies of the *Wiener Zeitung*, the *Wiener Journal*, the *Volksblatt, Die Presse*, and the *Kronenzeitung* when Professor Freud publishes a stirring, albeit cryptic, statement: "I do not wish to live anywhere else. Emigration is out of the question. I will continue to live with the torso and pretend that it is the whole body." How about that. If Freud can still find joy in Vienna, maybe I can too.

And then the greatest day in April arrives—the 22nd—when *Topič* is published in *Kmen*. I send telegrams to my dearest girlfriends Staša and Jarmila in Prague, and to my father at his oral surgery in Nové Město. My editor, Neumann, sends me my contributor's copy, and Fraulein Bettina behind the clerk's plinth hands me the package with "Here's your tree trunk" and a coy wink. But there is still no reply from Kafka to my last letter.

I burst through the doors of the Herrenhof, where Hermann Broch has joined Ernst, Werfel, and Blei at our regular table. "It's here, boys!" I wave the package in the air.

"Milena?" Ernst asks.

"*Topič*! It's published, it's finally published!" I rip open the manila envelope and pull from it a pristine copy of *Kmen*. I push everyone's plates of cake and strudel away and slam the magazine down in the centre of the marble tabletop. Ernst nods to the waiter to clear the dishes. I flip the pages until I see it. "There!" I slap the page with the back of my hand.

In big black lettering with lightning bolts surrounding the headline, the glorious majesty of the written word is displayed for us to read out loud in unison: "Franz Kafka: *Topič.* A fragment. Translated by Milena Jesenská!"

"Anton!" Ernst calls the waiter back.

"My name is Moritz."

"Anton is a better name."

"Mein Herr?"

"A big frothy glass of glühwein for my wife!"

Anton-Moritz bows his head. "Right away, sir."

"Milena, what an achievement!" Werfel, who is normally miserly with his praise, pats my back and pulls out a chair for me. I sit with a big exhalation. Blei leans over the copy—two huge columns adorn each page of my translation—and reads with a bemused look on his chubby face. Even Hermann Broch, whom I must admit I do not know well, smiles with glee and eyes me up and down as though I were a trophy.

I take my glass of warm mulled wine in my hands, but before I can take a muchneeded sip—

"Gentlemen!" Ernst stands and raises his pint of beer, and the boys all do the same. "To my wife, who couldn't even speak a word of German two years ago, and now it kneels before her like a servant. To a truly accomplished gentlelady, and not your regular hausfrau!"

I gasp, "Ernst!" and elbow him in the ribs.

"See what I mean?" Ernst shrugs and the boys laugh. "To Milena. Prost!"

"Prost!"

I stand once more to clink glasses, and as we all take huge, celebratory gulps, I notice Hermann's eyes lingering on the cello of my hips. When he realizes he has been caught, he does not look away. Rather, he meets my eyes and finishes his drink.

Werfel is easily exhausted and takes his seat first.

I turn to him. "Oh, come now, Werfel, aren't you going to read it?"

"Milena, my dear, maybe later. It's quite a long piece. It would take me more than twenty minutes to get through it."

I bring my glass back up to my lips. "My condolences to Alma Mahler if you can't endure twenty minutes." I take a big swig of my mulled wine.

Werfel's mouth hangs open and Ernst nearly chokes on his drink. "Milena!"

Hermann covers his mouth to stifle his laughter, but his eyes shoot bolts of lightning in my direction. I raise an eyebrow and my glass to him. We hold our stare. I want to burst into flames.

"I should probably go." I slam my empty glass down, droplets spurting onto my fingers. Stuffing the issue of *Kmen* into my satchel, I lean down to Werfel and say straight to his stupid, avuncular face, "Now who's looking like six volumes of Dostoevsky?"

I stomp to the glass doors and aggressively push through them, leaving a wall of silence behind me that blows like tumbleweeds. A satisfaction so deep and profound takes hold of my body that I can feel it tingling all the way down to my toes. As I trot along the cobbles, a giggle escapes my lips.

"Milena! Is that you?" Glancing over my shoulder as I turn a corner onto the Ringstrasse, I see a figure running toward me, trench coat lazily undone and bowler hat in hand.

"Max!" I exclaim as we kiss cheeks. "What a surprise!"

"I'm in town briefly for business." His cheeks glow with the rush of his gallop. "I thought I might see you at the Herrenhof with your husband."

"I just left, but Ernst is still there." I look over his shoulder. "Is Doktor Kafka with you?"

Max's lips curl at the edges like a tortoiseshell hairpin. "No, he's still in Merano." He pauses before adding, "As you will no doubt have heard."

I swallow hard. "Yes, we have been corresponding."

"To say the least." His forehead crinkles.

"It's for the translation of 'The Stoker'—which was published today, in fact!"

Horses whinny as they trot by, pulling conveyances of potatoes and onions. Chauffeur-driven automobiles overtake them, not leaving enough space between them and the oak-trimmed trams. A man in the Volksgarten sets up a tripod with a Goldmann Spreizenkamera: a strut-folding camera the shape of a small black box with a focal-plane shutter. He sinks down to peer through the viewfinder and squeezes an air pump not unlike the one found on the end of my Claudine eau de parfum. The Viennese in their Tyrolean suits and Oxford brogues walking the sidewalks stop to stare at the photographer as he pans from left to right. I notice all this in my attempt to escape Max's gaze. Maybe the city will swallow me whole.

But Max smiles. His spectacles don't hook behind his ears, and with his bulbous nose, big ears, and frankly oafish chin, he looks one lens away from being cross-eyed. "Milena, Franz is one of my most trusted friends," he says.

"Yes." I lower my eyes.

"So don't talk to me as if I'm other people."

"I beg your pardon?"

"I know how much he means to you"—he adjusts his collar against the warm breeze blowing along the Ringstrasse—"and how much you mean to him."

I throw my hands up and shake my head, turning toward the nearest bench in the Volksgarten not fouled by pigeons. Max follows me into the garden and we sit, but we do not dare look each other in the eye. I sigh like a poisoned lark as we watch the city move by.

"Max, I don't know what I've done wrong. I've written him and he hasn't responded in days. Normally, our letters and telegrams criss-cross so often that I have become friendly with my post office clerk, by heavens! Now he falls silent when I simply wanted to know ..."

"Yes?"

"Well," I say, folding my hands, "men seem to assign little substance to their friendships with women. However big a man's capacity for friendship, the beauty of it does not fill his horizon. It does not satisfy him. He is impatient with the mere mention of the word."

"Is that what you want? Friendship, or—" Max crosses one leg over the other "—something with a little more ... nectar?"

"I don't know. I truly don't. It's so hard to tell on paper. I toiled into the night on his translation to reach his level, but how can anything so pure and thoughtful on the page ever translate to reality?" I watch as young families in the distance enter the Kunsthistorisches museum to see the exhibit on the Dutch masters, while those exiting run toward the Grillparzer monument where the man selling roasted chestnuts has set up his cart. The monument has reliefs named Sappho, Medea, a Dream Is Life, and the Waves of Sea and Love—things I have been accused of in my life, or things in which I am so often trapped.

"My dear," Max says, breaking the silence, "you are a married woman. Letters are one thing, but you must think of your husband."

"Oh, what about him?" I scoff. "He's perfectly fine. Ernst has a mistress—everyone knows this."

"It's different for men."

"Yes, don't I know it." I cross my arms. "Men are allowed all the fun, and women have to grin and bear it. I have to manage everyone's feelings—Ernst's, Franz's, my father's, even yours! When do I get to be concerned with my own?"

Max looks down at his lap. "What do you think would be best? You couldn't possibly—"

"I think," I reply, cutting through the nonsense, "the best course of action would be to see him again. It's been months since we encountered each other at the Arco."

"You want Franz to come here?" He lets out a siren-like humph. "You don't know him very well, do you?"

"I could go there."

"He would like that even less."

"I should have remained in his company longer when I saw him in Prague. Merano and Vienna are no substitute! The Viennese are all philistines, my husband is a libertine..."

"And you are a lovertine."

Feeling my nose sting and my jaw begin to tremble, I put a finger to my lips to gather my composure. "In my utterly inconsequential opinion," I say, "a woman who lives without folly is not as bright as she thinks she is."

Max lets out a throaty laugh; it is an ode to joy that breaks my melancholy. We can finally look each other in the eye and smile.

"Listen, my dear," he reaches into his breast pocket and pulls out a folded piece of paper, "a letter arrived this morning from Franz."

"Oh?"

He nods.

"Is he ... well?"

"It would appear so. He wasted no time in telling me his opinion of you."

"What does he say?" I ask a little too quickly, looking between him and the letter, which he holds with an iron grip.

"I think it might be impertinent to—"

"Oh, come now, Max, he'll never know of this small lapse in confidentiality." I give him my best Gloria Swanson smile. "Besides, I just want to read the part that concerns me!"

Max unfolds the letter and there is Kafka's unmistakable scrawl. The lazy *l*s, the absolutely oppressive *g*s, the double *t*s that stand like sentries, and the uppercase *Z*s shaped like charmed pythons rising out of a basket.

"Milena, I don't think—"

"Bloody hell, just give it to me." I rip it from his hands so quickly he recoils as though he's been burned.

"Or I can just give it to you, that's fine." He sucks his finger pads. I ignore him as I race through the text until I find the passage in question.

> I would be doing well, if I could sleep. One of the reasons for that is my correspondence with Vienna. She is a living fire, the likes of which I have never seen before, a fire, by the way, that only burns for him. At the same time extremely gentle, courageous, intelligent, and she hurls everything into her sacrifice, or has, if you wish, gained it by sacrifice. What sort of man could cause that?

I cover my mouth as a hot tear rolls down my cheek. "He's referring to Pollak."

Max yanks the letter back, refolds it along its demarcated lines, and nods. "I dare say, he is rather envious Pollak got to you first." The letter disappears inside his inner breast pocket.

I wipe away my tear. "Oh, why the devil hasn't he written me back yet?"

"Franz Kafka is infamous for keeping his feelings to himself, but in your case, Milena," he takes my hands in his, "I think he struggles to decide on the right language to describe them."

WHEN A WOMAN SAYS she has sinned, it can boil down to only three things: prurient thoughts, inflicting pain, or sexual deviousness. These things always happen in threes.

She is a living fire.

It's true. I do burn. I singe everything in my path; I leave nothing but scorched earth and scarred flesh. But, oh, the light I give off. You could read by it.

Excitement courses through me tonight. The joy of *Kmen*, the spark of Hermann's eyes as they took me, the pleasure of Kafka's words. He wouldn't say such things about me to Max if he wasn't in love with me. Or maybe it's lust.

I open the door to our lavatory, where Ernst is bathing in the porcelain tub with the lion cub feet. He has poured suds in the bath and drizzled the water with lavender oil. A wet washcloth is draped over his eyes, but when he hears the door click, he whips it off and jerks his head up.

"Oh," he sinks back down, "it's you."

"Not quite the reception I was hoping for, my darling."

"Well," he grabs the bar of lavender castile soap and passes it over the washcloth a few times before seeing to his arms and shoulders. "You know how much I admire and esteem Werfel."

"That popinjay? Come on now. He's a big boy. He shall live to see another day." I stand directly over him.

He looks up at me with skewered eyes. "What do you want, Milena?"

I see his naked body beneath the soapy sheen of the water's surface. His eyes follow mine. He notices what my eyes gaze upon, and his body reacts. "I want to take a bath."

"I'm almost done." His voice betrays what is happening to his body. "I can leave the water for you so you don't have to refill the tub."

"Or," I say, grabbing the hem of my negligée with both hands, pulling it up over my head, and tossing it aside, "I could just get in with you."

Ernst looks at me like I am reborn. "Before, you were treating me like the stepfather of discipline, the bane of body and mind," he says, without looking away from the curls between my legs.

"Yes, well," I say as I touch his chin and pull his eyes up to my face as I climb into the tub, "no romance goes unpunished." As I break through the water, it surges and sploshes over the sides. His knees come to his chest as I force myself opposite him. He can see what's in my eyes. I can see what's happening four finger-widths below his bellybutton.

"And now you welcome me with open arms?" he asks.

"Mm-hmm. Might I also welcome you with open legs?"

His cock breaks the surface of the water as I spread my thighs before him.

"I thought that kind of sport didn't agree with you."

I move closer. "I've developed a stronger stomach."

As I wrap my legs around his waist and push my pelvis up against him, feeling him throb against me, he looks up at me in sheer wonderment. "Mischief is the devil's vice, Milena."

"Darling," I take my thumb and put it in his mouth, "I am the vice."

8

You Must Be a Great Lover

VIENNA

1920

The hours drop like stones in a ravine as the gauze of morning fades. I sink off the mattress in my bedchamber, my naked body unstable, muscles failing, stretched and pinched from last night. My feet might give way, but my toes somehow keep me upright. Like a skeleton, I drape myself gingerly with my white lace negligée and silk brocade robe. Paní Kohler isn't in until midday, so I tiptoe out into the pantry. Ernst has already left for the morning, and I am glad for the moment alone. Fingers rapid with nerves like a sacrificial swine, I ignite the gasring burner with the snap of a match. Blue flames tickle the iron as I place the tea kettle over it. From the rear balcony, the back courtyard of the Alt Lerchenfelder parish is the colour of peach marzipan and clotted cream. The balcony is just large enough for me to snatch a quick breath of crisp morning air as I drink my verbena tea in my robe; Ernst is always chagrined when I do this, yet neither my watchful neighbours down Mentergasse nor those taking their poodles and schnauzers for a stroll through Josef-Strauss Park seem to mind.

I collect the *Wiener Tagblatt* from outside our door and sit at the table with my tea and sticky bun. How Viennese I've become, I realize, as I flip immediately to the theatre and opera repertoire section, rather than the front-page headlines about parliament, world affairs, and politics. Perhaps this city is like an ostrich—more concerned with all that is pretty and appealing rather than grounded in reality. Daily happiness can usually be found in forgetting all that one can. Happiness is a long life and a short memory. But I am writing an essay for the *Tribuna* about the harsh facts of war profiteers who continue to milk the eighth district of all her worldly goods to then resell at inflated prices. We who have to eat black bread made with double the yeast so it will rise quickly, and who can't afford more than a dozen potatoes a fortnight, know quite well the nature of our reality. The boisterous crescendos of the *Blue Danube* waltz that once carried us across the dance floor have now dissipated, and all that's left is a sonorous, tremolo denouement, punctuated by cymbal crashes.

I dress quickly and leave the apartment, torturing myself as I walk to the post office on Bennogasse. I still haven't heard from him. I take my place at the back of the queue, but Fraulein Bettina spots me and calls me forward.

"Frau Pollak!" She hands me a letter. "I was hoping you'd come in today."

The postage says Merano, Italy. "My dear girl," I grab her hand, "one day people will write folk songs about you."

The line of men in hats starts to huff and shuffle with annoyance. Bettina turns back to them and their urgent telegrams, but not before saying, "I hope this answers your questions." I glide out the door on her smile and knowing glance as if they were wings.

Dear Frau Milena

This mode of address is becoming tiresome. You are a castle with mighty high fortifications. So, I know it is absolutely useless to write you a pandering, conciliatory note of my affections. No, that would be furthest from my goal. I'm wondering whether I said too much in my last letter. Even so, I can't take back what I mentioned about my feelings for you. Please understand, Milena, that I am indeed trying with all that I am to face the facts—that is, to be realistic and not to dream or be sentimental. Yet I think you know by now that only a bit of your soft presence in your letters gives me great comfort. You underestimate the effect of your letters, Milena.

You ask about friendship. I have heard men run down the friendship of women as having very little substance. Those who speak as such have never known a real woman's friendship. To be fair, I have never corresponded with a woman as I have with you—this new territory I gauge with shaking feet. There is no other such as Milena. So do not doubt that I hold our friendship in the highest esteem.

By the same token, do not for one moment infer that this situation is merely of my making. For instance, you could have told me nothing about yourself, but then you would have deprived me of the pleasure of getting to know you and, what is even more important, of the pleasure of testing myself on it. This is why you didn't dare keep it from me. You could have kept a number of things secret, or glossed over them, and could do so even now. If you will permit me: since when, and why, do you have no money? I can understand how you must be weary of the constant scramble to survive. Those without means are often set as rats upon the pile. At least you have beauty, brains, and talent to accompany you. Why did you at one time see many in Vienna and now no one?

You ask about my engagement. I've been engaged twice (three times, if you wish—that is to say, twice to the same girl), so I've been separated three times from marriage by only a few days. The first one is completely over (I hear there's already a new marriage and a small boy), the second is still alive but without any prospect of marriage. Her name is Julie Wohryzek, a dressmaker. I have affection for her, naturally, as there is boundless sweetness that comes with her hand. But the same can be said of a Labrador.

There is a fear—a dread. It is a strange bedfellow that keeps me awake at night, beyond the issue with my lungs. It triggers a cannonball that lands upon my chest whenever a woman looks at me the way Julie did the night we announced our engagement. Or the day you looked to me as I scrambled at your hemline with the shards of a broken glass.

It's terrible for me to see you in the overheated oven in which you live. You have done very well for yourself; you are filling up your glass as an artist. Travel and love are just what you should be doing. Don't panic, it's all leading somewhere. Enjoy these juicy nights and days. Writing is the finest of drugs. It can't be beat.

Yours,

Franz K

P.S. Please say *du* to me just once.

Jackdaws swoop and swirl overhead; one flutters to the ground, hopping around on one foot. I make a mad dash home, letter pressed against my breast like a suckling babe. As I wind through the streets of Vienna, lovers nap curled up on the grass under the hide-and-seek sun. Children giggle and do cartwheels. Dogs nuzzle each other as they wiggle around in the greenery. As the sun moves across the sky, fresh colours turn into new shapes; mauve with hints of gold stuns me with undying beauty. Shocks of red, burgundy, yellow, and alabaster. The scent of the Danube drifts up to me. Single men ride bicycles, but there's always a woman on the back, skirt dancing in the air, arms wrapped around him, holding on tight.

I burst through our front door; I cannot wait to reply to his incredible letter.

"Milena, there you are!"

I whip my head around to see Ernst emerging from his bedchamber.

"Judas!" I screech.

"Did I startle you?"

"Did you ever!" He approaches as I clutch my heart and places two plush kisses on each of my cheeks. "What are you doing home at this hour? I thought you'd left for the bank."

"I finished up early." He rubs his hands over his belly like a child with the most cake. "I thought we might spend the day together. What's that you've got there?"

I am still pressing the letter my breast. "Oh, this?" I toss my head cavalierly. "It's nothing, just a letter from Franz Kafka."

"Well, give it here!"

"It's not for you." I shove it into my brassiere. "It's for me."

"For you?"

"It's about my translation of 'The Stoker.' He read it in *Kmen*, naturally."

"Yes, of course."

Approaching my husband and placing both hands on his cheeks, I cup his face. "Now, my darling, what shall we do today?"

He pulls me into a hug. I freeze at this sudden show of affection. We haven't hugged in ... goodness me, I cannot remember the last time. His arms envelop me like a worn, old blanket. I slowly sink into him and smell pipe tobacco and eau de cologne on his shirt collar. I breathe it in. I can feel his pulse throbbing against my cheek. It syncs with mine. Opening my eyes, I am staring directly at his gingham cravat. Love is much like knotting a cravat—you have to relax it and tighten it. And sometimes, you have to start again with a new knot.

AS EARLY AS FIVE o'clock in the morning on Saturdays all sorts of conveyances, from hand-pulled trollies to horse-drawn flatbed carts and even petrol-fuelled automobiles, pile into the Naschmarkt. The 250 acres of land sandwiched between neoclassical buildings, prodigious in size and rich in architectural style, with the Danube running along the south side, becomes a marketplace for live poultry, caged cattle, sheep and pigs, cured herring in barrels (gutted or ice-packed), sugar beets, yellow potatoes, and beautiful garlands of fresh flowers woven by the women of the Garland Weavers Society. Their chaplet wreaths are so elegant that one cannot but regret that they are perishable. Their stand is the only one that remains past eight o'clock in the morning, when the Naschmarkt turns into a peddler's market, attracting bargain and curio hunters from all parts of the metropolis.

The variety of wares for sale is extraordinary and the crowd of buyers and spectators hardly less so. Men in bowler hats and suspenders leave their jackets at home on this balmy early June day to buy world globes, magnifying glasses, and road maps of Galicia, Transylvania, and Silesia. Women in loose-fitting tan blouses and square-hipped azurite skirts that rise perilously above the knee buy picture frames, remaindered silver, and glassware.

Across from the Naschmarkt, the building façade that Koloman Moser designed shines brightly in the sunlight—painted red roses and geranium bouquets encircle each window in a labyrinthine wreath. Goethe once said that architecture is frozen music. Vienna has many problems, but music and architecture are not among them

Nowhere is Vienna more visibly alive than at the Naschmarkt. Everyone bargains and haggles for the best deals; an argument over mere hellers always ends in a handshake and a pat on the back. I don't buy something very often; there's not much we can afford these days.

Vienna may be rebuilding herself, but the rate of inflation is beyond repair. Three years ago, a coiffure at the hairdresser's cost four crowns. Now the price has jumped to ten, and it will only go up. Even here at the Naschmarkt where bartering is expected, notebooks in cardboard boxes are five crowns, bags of cigars are fifteen crowns, picture frames are thirty crowns, and an oak armchair will run you a hellish fifty crowns.

Sometimes, when I'm walking down the Herrengasse to Café Herrenhof, I can hear the drone of the Austrian National Bank's printing presses, churning incessantly, day and night, to produce new banknotes. Soon, there won't be a single thing one will be able to buy with the one-crown coins, and they will simply stop minting them. They won't even be fit for beggars.

Today, however, I am in the market to buy. Having squirrelled away some savings from my *Tribuna* column, which has now become an almost full-time position, I feel the need to show my love and gratitude to someone. As a schoolgirl, I would pluck the pasqueflowers from the cemeteries and gardens and hand them out to my classmates. If someone in the neighbourhood fell ill, I would slip unnoticed into my father's dental surgery and dip my fingers into the drug cabinet, taking whatever opiate or barbiturate I could find. The Affable Thief started her work from a young age, albeit with a more altruistic motive. As much as the ease of thievery still appeals to me—why, looking around this market, how simple it would be to slip an item or two into my satchel without anyone the wiser—I am working hard to suppress those urges.

I am endeavouring every day to be the woman Kafka thinks I am. I tell myself that with the right attitude, society will give me more latitude.

As I approach a jewellery and wristwatch vendor, I am greeted by Herr Karl Reifmann, the son of a veterinarian who opened his shop on the Judengasse near the synagogue. When strolling past to reach the Danube, I have often noticed Reifmann's shop while asking Ernst about his lack of attendance at synagogue. Ernst, without fail, shrugs and changes the subject. He's always been an in-between Jew, as I call it: not enough of a Jew to pray at temple or observe the major holidays, but enough of a Jew for people like my father to call him a Shylock and a scourge upon gentile society. If this bewildering treatment has ever bothered Ernst, he has yet to express it to me.

It is Ernst I am thinking of as I pick up a square Jugendstil silver locket from Herr Reifmann's table and pay the man a kingly sum of sixty crowns—the same price as an orchestra seat at the opera. Perhaps I won't be able to buy my daily bread for the next little while, but this, by God almighty, will feed me more.

I walk back to the stall that offers every typewriter imaginable and ask the man if I might sample the new Adler. *Clackety-clack-clack-clackety-clack-clack-clack.* I rip the page from the platen, shove it into my satchel, shouting cavalierly over my shoulder, "No, this model is no good for me. Many thanks!" and disappear down the next row of market umbrellas and hordes of punters. Approaching the stall sporting seamstress and tailor supplies, I quickly lift a pair of fabric scissors off the cotton tablecloth. *Schip-schip-schip-schip-schip-schiiiiiiip.* One, two, three—drop the scissors—four, five, six—run down the row and disappear around the next corner before anyone has noticed what I've done.

Leaning against a buggy, I take the typewritten phrase that I've cut into two small, neat and clean squares and slide one into each frame of the Jugendstil locket. I hold up my handiwork to let it sparkle in the June sun.

Your

Skin

Against

My

Skin

Skipping across the cobblestoned piazza to the Kettenbrückengasse Stadtbahn station, I make my way to the Photoautomat booth just outside the entrance. Having adjusted the seat and chosen a white background from the options of white, black, or striped, I drop in a coin and strike a pose in profile. *Flash.* Smile. *Flash.* Pucker my lips. *Flash.* Hands together in prayer. *Flash.*

I whip back the curtain and listen to the machine *whirrr* and *chunga* and *skreeeee.* Finally, out pops a long column of four monochrome portraits into the metal courtesy slot. Blowing on them to set the picture and prevent bleeding, I take out the locket once more. Carefully folding and tearing each picture from the column, I place the profile exposure and the puckered lips exposure into either side of the locket, covering up the typewritten phrase. *When he finds the words, that will be a nice surprise,* I tell myself.

I can feel a change in Ernst's attitude toward me lately.

There is a reverence where none existed before. I think perhaps he once thought of me as a blemish he had to cut out, but I stayed beneath his skin, and every day I have inched closer to his lungs. Now he is breathing me in, and I adore being inhaled in this way.

I AM LYING NEXT to Ernst in his bedchamber. His chest rises and falls in deep sleep. I cannot remember the last time I was invited to share his bed. It feels unnatural, but also—how I've missed this. The radiator hums and ticks against the wall; it's the faintest of sounds, but I focus on its rhythm. The midnight tram rattles by on the street below and shakes the glass in the window and the books on the shelves. The scent of sauerkraut and blood sausage stew wafts from the flat next door. Frau Volker must be making a big pot to feed her sons for the week. Somewhere in the distance, a radio buzzes with the fuzz and snap of electricity—someone in the quarter must have left their window open. The Alt Lerchenfelder church bells are quiet for the night, but the roar of the Stadtbahn trains on the elevated tracks as they pull away from Josefstädterstrasse station heralds the hour.

Grabbing my dressing gown off the bedpost, I tiptoe out of the room and over to the study. I can wait no longer.

My dearest Franz,

I wish I could talk to you. What would I say? I would listen. I am grateful to you for sharing your life with me. I wish I could help you not feel so much dread, but dread is part of life when things are going well. I always lived in terror when my late mother would tell me how well she was feeling, how lucky she was to receive such care, how our little family was thriving. I knew that the end was nigh; that a bad time would surely follow. By doubting and fearing and dreading, we all feel two things simultaneously...opposites.

I feel dread too. It must be connected to my father. I can't understand why Ernst stays and holds on to me when he knows the real me. What is the real me? Even I don't know; it changes. I'm sure you don't know. And when the day comes that you win literary prizes, they'll want to give you a visa to Britain or America or Italy, and this—whatever it is between us—will stop.

You are still in the lap of luxury in the Dolomites, I see. When can I persuade you to visit me in Vienna? We could make elegant work of this city. Those Italians cannot possibly know more about spirit, resiliency, or courage. Two Bohemians running about the former seat of an empire—it's like a scene out of an opera: Lehár's *The Merry Widow*, even.

A Neapolitan woman passed me on the street today and I thought of you. She had the most beautiful scar on her cheekbone. Tonight, over dinner with Ernst, I thought how I might scar you—by boring a blade across your skin. But now, after waiting impatiently for a reply, and then receiving your letter, I see there already exists an open wound upon your flesh, profound and cavernous. I've touched bone.

I press my fist into your cheek, my dear Franz. You are wincing and gritting your teeth as the pain slices deeper. I prod again and again.

You are going to miss this welt when it's gone.

Yours,

Milena

I give the letter a once-over with a satisfied smile before slipping it into a pre-gummed envelope. How Franz will love this. How his body will react. How my letter will touch him. How thoroughly I've used *du*.

Later in the evening, after a full day of pacing up and down the carpets of the apartment, fretting that perhaps I've revealed too much, that he will put me back in my place, the one where I truly belong, that word will spread and I'll lose my column in the *Tribuna*, that Ernst will leave me penniless and alone—his reply comes.

Dearest Milena

You must be a great lover...

I drop the letter opener and it makes a *ka-chunk* on the floor.

"What was that?" Paní Kohler pokes her head into the sitting room from the larder.

I toe the letter opener under the rug by the davenport where I sit. "Nothing."

My shaky voice betrays my eager smile. She eyes me curiously but returns to the larder. I go back to Kafka's letter. *Yes, Milenka, you read that right.* I bite my lip and continue.

You must be a great lover. You love so grandly, so obsessively, so colossally. You are a brave and honest woman—a woman with many lovers yet to come. Ernst is an oasis, so sit, drink the water, feel how much he cares for you; you don't have to drive him away, for you so obviously own his soul.

Here's an idea for your next story—write about a woman who finds what she's looking for and subverts it. That story will protect you. Live your doubles through fiction—you're so good at it; you imagine with such incredible details. Your art, which is alive in you, is building and growing, your experience and pain make your heart larger. Keep your art close; it is your true lover.

Fast courtships often create vacuums of doubt, and we're never sure what they were exactly. Is lust transient? This man is besotted with you, Milenka, the ups and downs don't matter.

Be careful with the *Tribuna* feuilletons, however; I'm always afraid you will reveal too much in them and endanger yourself. I feel your column is a kind of dark version of you that you use to punish yourself. I haven't read it this week; I have to catch up. I prefer hearing from you one-on-one, and then when I read the column, I know the subtext, or some of it, but you always surprise me. You bring the moods of your life to it, even more than in your letters.

Strange how your letters dazzle me, Milena. I sense you are now in the most beautiful time of your life—not happiness and peace and all that other folly. No, you are going to have about twenty more years of the flesh where your beauty will grow and increase and your mind will follow your beauty around and wonder, "What is this? Can I trust this? I don't feel like the person they see..." For you see yourself as someone who was betrayed, you see the marks. Others see the future—your glorious energy and compassion, your fairness, your love of humanity, it's all colossal. You really do like people and the world. You care about it.

I know you're selfish too.

I must end here. More tomorrow.

Yours,

Franz

P.S. Do me the favour of burning this letter upon receipt. I do not want to create a situation where explanations must be made to a furious husband—from you or, even worse, from me.

I look around the sitting room: the glass liquor trolley with the gilt edges, the silk brocade armchairs with medallion backs and cabriole legs in the French style, the white ottoman with the secret storage compartment, the solid oak credenza with the starburst carving—an embarrassment of riches.

I grab Ernst's lighter from his dinner jacket pocket, walk into his study, set the oil lamp alight, and slowly burn Kafka's letter. It drops into the copper waste bin at my feet slowly, hitting the bottom and scattering into a million scorched, inky-black pieces.

THE NEXT DAY, AFTER a long constitutional, I climb the spiral staircase to our flat to the sound of shuffling and muffled voices coming from underneath the doorframe. On my opening the door, Paní Kohler greets me not by offering a glass of lemonade or taking my satchel, but with the words, "I am sorry, my dear, I had no hand in this and couldn't prevent it."

"Prevent what?"

The hushed voices and creaking floorboards are emanating from Ernst's bedchamber. I won't start counting until it hurts.

I look at Paní Kohler. She closes her eyes and shakes her head.

Five.

I drop my satchel with a thump and fly across the flat as though I were on a witch's broomstick.

Four.

I swing open his bedchamber door.

Three.

Ernst stands next to his bed in his dressing gown. Buttoning her waistcoat and smoothing her hair in the mirror, Mitzi puts some grease onto her pinky finger and smears it across her lips.

Two.

Mitzi walks right up to my face, looks me in the eye, and then brushes past me toward the door, bumping my shoulder as she passes.

One.

The door slams behind her. The locket burns a hole in my fist. Ernst sits on his bed and finally meets my gaze.

"Get out," he says.

Zero.

9

An Invitation to Vienna

1920

The long bar at the Hotel Metropol is one of the only places in all of Vienna with central heating. Overlooking the Danube from Morzinplatz, its elegant ladies' salon, hairdressers, and typewriting facilities make it one of the few places I am unlikely to run into any of Ernst's crew, or the man himself.

Trams rattling by outside shake my sherry cordial, which is mediocre at best. The place is raucous this evening, as it is almost every summer evening, with its reputation for hosting all kinds of soirées and balls in the festival salon. At least with this hubbub I can go unnoticed. I won't have to hide my face from prying eyes, as everyone is too busy to notice the twenty-three-year-old going on sixty, with a fictional marriage and a buffoon for a husband. I cried all the way here, but now, as I nurse my second-rate drink and my third-rate blues, all I feel is anger. Not at Ernst. I knew who he was when I married him. How laughable it is, this business of men; they are a currency I know not how to spend.

No, I am furious at myself for loving him so much, for all that he has done for me, for all the gratitude and obligation I feel for him even now, for my debt to him, which I fear I may never be able to repay. I run my finger over my scars, tracing the lines that go nowhere. What he did for me back in Prague ... It will always ensure he owns prime real estate in my heart. Even now, despite the obscene, disgraceful, undignified manner in which he betrayed my loyalty, and then scolded me, I cannot hate him. All I can do is hate myself. It is one thing to recognize you've been a mug. It is quite another thing altogether to recognize you'll be a mug for the rest of your life.

"Milena?"

I raise my head from my drink to see Hermann Broch approaching from the banquet hall in a tuxedo, a copita of port in his hand. His hair is slicked back with brilliantine, and a vermillion boutonniere is the only flash of colour in his monochrome attire.

"Hermann?" I exclaim as he kisses both my cheeks. "What's the occasion?" I nod to the banquet hall swirling and swinging with brilliant sashes, gowns, coattails, spatterdashes, and cummerbunds.

"You know the psychoanalyst Freud?"

"Who doesn't? His papers on the id, ego, and superego were all anyone could talk about for weeks in the coffee houses."

"Well, he is going to be a grandfather."

"You don't say!"

"Yes, his son Martin and daughter-in-law Ernestine are expecting."

"What a blessing."

"Isn't it just. However, Freud's daughter Mathilde is barren, and I think this news is a great strain on her and on the festivities in general."

I think of my own lack of children and thumb my glass. "Well," I raise my drink, "mazel tov to the Freuds."

His glass clinks with mine. "Prost."

"L'chaim."

We drink, but it is his eyes that imbibe all that they see as they rise and fall along the length of my body.

"I didn't think you were much of a dancer, Hermann."

He sits next to me at the long bar and angles his body in my direction. "I'm not. The gents are playing bridge in the billiards room. In fact, I carried my hand out here with me." He withdraws thirteen cards from his breast pocket and fans them out in front of me.

"Why did you walk out with your cards?"

His lips curl and a knowing glint appears in his eyes.

"Why you little charlatan," I gasp.

"I wouldn't ordinarily cheat, Milena, but someone needs to teach these Jews a lesson."

I recoil. "I'm terribly sorry, but you are a Jew, are you not?"

"*Was*," he corrects as he finishes his port in one gulp. "You're looking at a Roman Catholic convert."

"You do know I am married to a Jew?"

He slides closer to me on his barstool. "Yes, and how is that working out for you, Milena, dear?"

I look down at my drink, my stomach in knots. "What do you mean?"

His thumb caresses my chin and lifts it up, forcing me to face him. "What else can I mean? What would you be doing here at the Metropol all alone on this gorgeous June evening were it not for a disappointing husband?"

"Are you a student of human behaviour?"

"I am a writer," he retorts. "It's the same thing. Besides, everyone knows what they're like. I think they give too much credence to their holy books. Why, according to the Torah, you're nothing but property to be bought and sold."

I smack his hand away from my chin. "That's rather fascinating because I come from the Church of the United Sisterhood of I Don't Give a Damn What You Think."

"Oof, there's the Milena moxie I like," he sneers.

I am fresh out of things to say. I keep trying to turn my body and my eyes away from Hermann, but he keeps bringing me back to his moving lips, his strident words, his body inching closer. "Look, Milena, your husband is a banker. The only thing he cares about is money and fornicating. I'll wager he'd combine the two by fashioning a billfold out of foreskins taken from the local mohel."

"You're disgusting, Hermann."

"No matter what you rub—him or his billfold—it doubles in size!"

"And you're an obscene lush."

"Look at what the bankers have done to Vienna! Can you even afford that drink? This rate of inflation will be the death of us all."

"What do you want?"

He grabs my shoulders and pulls me in. When he seals his mouth over mine, his hot lips sear my skin. His tongue prods and invokes mine. He wraps me up in his arms and soon his hands are in my hair and mine are drawing him deeper and deeper. Arching my back, I almost fall off my barstool. There is a throbbing between my thighs. I can feel what he is doing to me. A surge and a gush.

The hotel spins. I wrench my mouth away and push his hands off me. Wiping my mouth with the back of my hand, I slide off my seat and regain my footing.

"Come now, Milena, this is Vienna!" he fumes, as I drop a few crowns on the long bar and take my skirt in hand. "Don't be such a loathsome Victorian about it all."

I stop and look him dead in his cold eyes. If my stare were daggers, he would fall like Caesar. He staggers back as I approach him once more, reach for his thirteen playing cards, find the card I'm looking for, and slap it against his chest. "You may think of yourself as some kind of king of hearts, a Casanova to woo all the distraught ladies in the night. But you're going to lose that game, no matter how hard you cheat."

"The game of seduction or the game of bridge?"

"Both."

"What would you know about either?" he shoots back.

I smirk. "I can tell you've never actually taken a really good look at the face of the king of hearts, because if you had, you would know that he's stabbing himself in his own head."

Hermann looks down at the card. By the time he looks back up at me in shock, I am long gone. I run through the night along the Franz Josef Quay. I have no problem taking a lover. I do have a problem taking a lover who isn't Kafka.

* * *

FIRST AUSTRIAN REPUBLIC NATIONAL TELEGRAPH

DOKTOR KAFKA, MERANO-UNTERMAIS,

PENSION OTTOBURG

MORNING

I AM GOING TO HOLD ON TO THE SCENT OF YOUR LETTERS TO MAKE SURE I BREATHE ONLY LIFE, AND AFFECTION, INTO MY LUNGS. COME TO VIENNA. DESPITE YOUR FEAR, YOUR ILLNESS, COME MEET ME.

~MILENA

KINGDOM OF ITALY ROYAL TELEGRAPH

FRAU JESENSKÁ, POSTE RESTANTE, POSTAMT 65,

BENNOGASSE, WIEN VIII

AFTERNOON

I DON'T BELIEVE WHAT YOU SAY, MILENA, AND THERE'S NO WAY IT COULD BE PROVED TO ME. I DON'T DARE OFFER YOU MY HAND—THIS DIRTY, TWITCHING, CLAW-LIKE, UNSTEADY, UNCERTAIN, HOT-COLD HAND.

~YOURS

(NOW I'VE LOST EVEN MY NAME; IT HAS BEEN GROWING SHORTER ALL THE TIME AND NOW IT IS: YOURS).

FIRST AUSTRIAN REPUBLIC NATIONAL TELEGRAPH

DOKTOR KAFKA, MERANO-UNTERMAIS,

PENSION OTTOBURG

EVENING

WHY WOULD YOU SAY THAT TO ME? HAVE I NOT PROVED TO YOU WITH EVERY OUNCE OF MY LINGUISTIC CAPABILITIES THAT YOU ARE THE FIRE AND I AM THE PYRE?
~MILENA

KINGDOM OF ITALY ROYAL POSTAL SERVICE
FRAU JESENSKÁ, POSTE RESTANTE, POSTAMT 65, BENNOGASSE, WIEN VIII
DEAR MILENA,
WHY ERNST OF ALL PEOPLE? WHY DID YOU MARRY ERNST AND NOT SAVE YOURSELF FOR ME? YOU MUST CONSIDER, MILENA, THE KIND OF PERSON WHO COMES TO YOU, THE 36-YEAR JOURNEY LYING BEHIND ME (AND SINCE I'M A JEW A MUCH LONGER ONE), AND THIS IS WHY MY 36 JEWISH YEARS, FACED BY YOUR 23 CHRISTIAN ONES, SAY: YOU ARE 36 YEARS OLD AND AS TIRED AS ONE CAN PROBABLY NEVER GROW THROUGH AGE. OR MORE CORRECTLY: YOU AREN'T REALLY TIRED, BUT RESTLESS, AFRAID TO TAKE A STEP ON THIS EARTH. AND NOW MILENA CALLS ON YOU WITH A VOICE WHICH PENETRATES YOUR REASON AND YOUR HEART WITH EQUAL INTENSITY. BUT SHE DOESN'T KNOW YOU. A FEW STORIES AND LETTERS HAVE DAZZLED HER. BUT THAT YOUR ACTUAL PRESENCE WILL NO LONGER DAZZLE HER IS SOMETHING YOU CAN BE SURE OF.
~YOURS

FIRST AUSTRIAN REPUBLIC NATIONAL POSTAL SERVICE
DOKTOR KAFKA, MERANO-UNTERMAIS,
PENSION OTTOBURG
DEAR FRANZ,
I MARRIED HIM BECAUSE IT WAS A STRANGE AGE, WHERE

WE FOUGHT SECRET BATTLES WITHOUT UNDERSTANDING WHAT WE WERE FIGHTING FOR. ACCORDING TO THE LAWS OF YOUTH AND IMPETUOUSNESS, I SWORE TO REBEL. I KNEW WHAT I WAS RUNNING FROM BUT NOT WHAT I WANTED. REVOLUTIONS ARE NOT WON OR LOST; THEY SIMPLY PASS INTO NOTHINGNESS. AND THE WORST REALIZATION ONE CAN HAVE IS—I AM NO REVOLUTIONARY. AND I DO SO WISH YOU WOULD STOP TALKING ABOUT YOUR JEWRY AS IF IT WERE A DETERRENT OR A HINDRANCE, RATHER THAN AN INCENTIVE. SO I ASK AGAIN: COME TO ME IN VIENNA.
~MILENA

KINGDOM OF ITALY ROYAL TELEGRAPH
FRAU JESENSKÁ, POSTE RESTANTE, POSTAMT 65, BENNOGASSE, WIEN VIII
YOU SHOULDN'T ASK ME ABOUT VIENNA; I WON'T COME, BUT EACH MENTION OF IT IS A LITTLE FIRE WHICH YOU HOLD AGAINST MY BARE SKIN; IT'S ALREADY A SMALL BONFIRE WHICH WON'T BURN DOWN BUT CONTINUES TO SMOULDER WITH THE SAME, INDEED WITH INCREASING, POWER.
~YOURS

Hopping on a tram headed toward the epicentre of the city, I see everything around me magnified as though I am a fish in a tank. Whether you go clockwise or counterclockwise along the Ringstraße, the builder is the most common person to see in Vienna. Villas and many-storied houses are being erected now that the war is becoming a memory. Infant neighbourhoods are being born, and neighbourhoods that have come to maturity are expanding upward and outward.

As the scenery whisks by my tram window, all I can do is reflect on the mess in which I've found myself. I have destroyed a beautiful relationship with my exigent need to have Kafka here by my side. Why, we had a perfect relationship, because we existed almost entirely in each other's minds. A letter is the best way to build a fantasy around a person based purely on your interpretation of their words, intentions, desires, and motivations. I can deduce his character from an ink smudge; I can summon his faults and his fortes simply by the amount of pressure with which he placed the nib of his pen to the page. But the cardinal sin I've committed is begging him to be real, to split my fantasy in two as though I were coring an apple.

I haven't replied to his last telegram since Sunday. Enough of these bloody things anyway. The real question is, if I tell him everything that Ernst has done for me, will he turn my weaknesses into his target? Or turn me into a distant friend with whom he once carried on a correspondence?

At the Stubenring stop, a pregnant woman boards the tram, easily six months along. The men bury their heads in the folds of their newspapers and pretend not to see her. It is the women who jump up and vacate their seats, guiding her by the sleeve or elbow. The pregnant woman catches my stare, and I offer her a weak smile. She smiles back and nods. The tram jostles and jolts along, and we pass builders on their knees replacing the cobbles by the tram rails, snatching their fingers out of the way just in time, and then resuming their work as if they had not just been inches from a deformity.

As we pass the wide Schwarzenbergplatz, it disappears from beyond the window, and suddenly I see Prague's old city square, cobbled, expansive, and loaded with coal merchants, ironmongers, blacksmiths, and other men of the earth. In my memory, the astronomical clock casts a silent afternoon shadow upon everything.

I AM TWENTY YEARS old, the Great War is two years deep, and I am with child.

And I already know what I have to do.

Ernst already knows too and has begun to make enquiries. The night I told him, we held each other on the davenport in his sitting room with barely enough room for two, clinging to one another as if our tears and wails might somehow separate us. It was a devastating blow when the truth of the matter was laid before us—not now. Not yet. We aren't married. We are carrying on, much to the chagrin of my bourgeois father, who is embarrassed by my fondness for a Jew. Perhaps if we were already affianced, we could throw together a hasty ceremony and keep the child, fudging the dates a bit. But this simply won't do.

Despite his many contacts, Ernst's enquiries have not come to fruition, so he suggests I ask my father for help. When I do, my father smacks me across the face, but then immediately sets out to the postal bureau to make some telephone calls on my behalf. Ernst is waiting for me out on the street as I emerge from my apartment block, face ruby as a pickled turnip.

"That's going to leave a mark." He runs his fingers over my raw and throbbing cheek.

I look up at him. "Doesn't everything?"

He wraps me in his arms and cradles me through the streets, back to his flat, to wait for news from my father.

The procedure is common enough, but the stigma surrounding it even more so. Discretion overrides everything, considering its illegality. But my father comes through and makes sure I receive the best care. He even takes charge of my recovery.

I know it's the right decision for me at this time, but I also feel the smack of gossip in my face, more than the smack of my father's backhand. What I could normally ignore or brush off, I take to heart. The war wages on, and men are coming home with faces unevenly stapled and sewn back together; those who are missing limbs can still feel them tickling. It is all too much.

THE TRAM BELLS RING, announcing the next stop, and the whole carriage jerks me back to the present. Catching my breath, I take the stairs two at a time and run across the Georg-Coch-Platz to Biberstrasse, making a beeline for the Austrian Postal Savings Bank. I push through the towering rotating doors at the front entrance, where I find myself on a red-carpeted grand staircase with grey marble highlights on either side. To the left, a dedication to Kaiser Franz Josef, which already feels so dated, and the architect Otto Wagner, who redesigned this building about fourteen years ago. Swinging oak doors lead into a great skylit hall. The floor panels brighten when the sun begins to set. Each wicket is numbered and illuminates when in service, with a sliding glass window, rather than the usual wrought-iron divider. This truly is a post office for modern times and, dare I say it, the future.

I take out the small package no larger than a typewriter ribbon tin. Inside is the locket. Using the courtesy stationery and fountain pen, I include a small note, echoing my mother's words:

> All I will say is this—there are two possibilities in life: to accept one's fate, or to seek one's fate.
>
> Milena

Slipping the small card in the package, I wrap it in brown paper and secure it with twine. When I reach the front of the queue, the clerk asks the postage destination.

"The Dolomites," I say. "Merano."

IT IS THE LAST day of June. There has been no response to my package. Why does he not respond? I have spent the entirety of the morning pacing the apartment. Ernst left before dawn to see to his business affairs in Prague. Normally, I would accompany him, if only to see my old friends Staša and Jarmila, but the prospect of even a few hours alone with him in a train berth was too dire a thought to bear.

Today I have dressed myself—without any help from Paní Kohler—in a cerulean blouse with white polka dots and a massive pussy-bow at the neck, a tightly-cinched belt at my waist, and a long flounced skirt. I told Paní Kohler that I will no longer wear a corset, not even those "healthy" corsets they have begun peddling, promising no bones, no lacing, and adjustable shoulder straps. No, thank you. I now wear a wristwatch—a sign of a serious approach to life. My coiled ashy brown hair is parted in the middle, the curls tamed with hairpins, and the tresses tucked behind my ears and gathered into a neat bun at the nape of my neck. I've even managed to sneak in a beaded necklace at my collar that flops out over the pussy-bow. I will be taken seriously as a writer, even if I have to cut off all my hair and bind my breasts and dress as a man. This is a start.

Overlooking Lerchenfelderstraße from my window, I see the district children yelling in Josef-Strauss Park, posturing teenagers exchanging Virginia cigarettes and automatic lighters, and old men snoring on benches. Pigeons frolic like lovers. Young people are everywhere, filling the trams and the gardens, playing instruments, drinking beer from bottles. Babies in strollers reach out and up to the sky. Low-flying jackdaws and dandelion seeds are woven into the fabric of the breeze. Sun made of linen. Clouds of heavy wool.

Two young girls, not much older than fifteen I'd wager, come into view as they sit on a bench. One breaks her flaky butter croissant in half and hands a piece to the other. They embrace, holding each other longer than normal. There is a whisper in an ear, a kiss on a cheek, a far-off look in their eyes. Their foreheads rest against each other. In my school days at Minerva, my classmates whispered that my closeness with my best friend Staša went beyond friendship. Staša and I laughed and laughed. Let them whisper.

In fact, there was once a stage actress that I so adored that I rang her doorbell with a bouquet of pasqueflowers. I don't know what came over me—a sort of bacchanalian or erotic hysteria. I was led up into her flat that overlooked the Old Town Square and, to my surprise, she invited me to sit with her. I must have been fourteen, but she gave me wine and a fizzy drink. She looked me up and down in a manner that made my thighs tingle with heat. She said, *My, what a pretty girl*, and *A pretty girl should always have another girlfriend*, and *Is she pretty like me?* It could have been the wine, it could have been my pulse throbbing in my ears, but I wasn't sure what to say. It was only when she tried to kiss me that I managed to gather my wits and bolt down the stairs. I laughed the whole way home.

Now, the overwhelming good mood of everyone makes me want to buy an ice cream cone from the soda jerk just so I can ram it up their nostrils. Like bashing in your neighbour's rose bed just to destroy something colourful.

It is not yet noon when Paní Kohler pokes her head around the doorframe of my bedchamber. "This telegram just arrived for you, ma'am."

I dash to her side and rip the envelope from her hands so quickly she jumps back as though she's been stung by nettles. She scuttles away as I slash it open.

FIRST AUSTRIAN REPUBLIC NATIONAL TELEGRAPH

FRAU JESENSKÁ, LERCHENFELDERSTRASSE 113

WHAT KIND OF COCOA IS THIS? WHAT KIND OF PASTRY? IS THIS WHAT YOU LIVE ON? I ARRIVED AT THE SÜDBAHNHOF

TWO HOURS AGO AND MADE MY WAY TO CAFÉ SPERL ON THE GUMPENDORFER HAUPTSTRASSE. CARE TO JOIN ME? ~YOURS

I knock over a chair as I fling myself toward the front door. It goes *ker-smash* and Paní Kohler calls out after me in a panic as I slam the door behind me. I dart out of the building, sprinting through the winding streets. The sun blazes like Beelzebub's cauldron; my hair sticks to the back of my neck.

Gumpendorfer haupstraße is only seven blocks away! The streets fall behind me like rooks under the movements of the Queen. Burggasse, Siebensterngasse, Lindengasse … I am dissolving the distance between us, yet somehow, I am still caught between the folds of this dark, fishhook city.

As I cut across Windmühlgasse, past the Phonopolis victrola music shop and Dr. Reifmann's veterinary clinic for feeble and infirm house pets, my shoes start to give way. I wrench them off my feet, hold both in one hand, and run barefoot. Motorists blow their horns and men in hats fold their arms and guffaw—I left the flat too quickly to put on my hose.

Lungs bursting, I can see Café Sperl in the distance, becoming larger as I sprint. Then I notice a figure stepping outside its doors: endlessly tall and endlessly lean. Senselessly long legs, sunken cheeks that are pale one moment and crimson the next.

My eyes are jesters, surely. Always fooling me. The figure shoves his hands in his pockets but looks up as I bolt across the street. We come face to face. He is standing before me. He breathes a bit, burnt-umber eyes ablaze. My reflection scorches his retinas.

"Milenka ..." He looks me up and down, to the shoes in my hand, to my bare feet on the stone slabs of the sidewalk, and a smile breaks across his face. "You found me."

One hand wrenches free from his pocket; in it, he is holding the locket.

My chest rises and falls rapidly. "*You* found *me*!" I reply, and leap forward. I wrap my arms over his shoulders and press him to me. His hands encircle my waist, and we stand there, holding each other, defying scornful stares and tongue clicks.

The chestnut trees are in bloom. The sky above Vienna, illuminating every last silver speck and glossy sheen of the city, capsizes with the weight of the sun. It warms our skin like an unforgiving supernova. In this moment, there are only four elements on earth. Flesh. Pulses. Nerves. Blood.

10

Day One

The Austrian peace treaty is in the French Senate!
—Innsbrucker Nachrichten *newspaper, July 1, 1920*

Franz sits across the marble table from me in Café Sperl and we are both grinning like fools, shaking our heads in disbelief. As the espresso machines buzz and hiss, cutlery clacks against dishware, hushed voices order hot drinks then chat about the cost of inflation, and waiters' leather-soled shoes squeak against the linoleum floor, we feel the need for propriety. We cannot display reckless affection as we did just now on the street. So his hand gently creeps across the table, as if to cup his glass of hot milk, but his fingers caress mine, hidden behind a saucer. My shoes, now back on my feet, find a way to mingle with his calf.

"I can't believe you came," I say, blinking back my shock. "What a surprise."

"Do you like surprises?" he asks, eyes hooded under that brow of his, but full of joy.

"I like *your* surprises," I reply.

"I almost didn't come," he admits, sucking in his lips for a sheepish look.

"Don't I know it!" I say. "The amount of convincing in my telegrams was colossal."

"No, I mean to say," he leans in, "my train was headed for Prague, but I decided at the last minute to alight in Vienna. Barring any further rail strikes or electricity cuts to the rail line, I am sure Prague will still be there in a few days."

"What was the impetus behind your sudden decision, then?"

"You invited me, Milenka." He says our private term of endearment and I feel like administering some sin upon his flesh.

"You could have said no," I press.

"Say no to Milena Jesenská? I think we both know that is an impossibility." He winks as he brings his hot drink to his mouth.

After all these months of correspondence, of translating his deeply personal words into the language of Czechs and Slovaks, after thinking endlessly of our brief encounter in Prague, of daydreaming of him coming here and whisking me away, here he sits before me in all his splendour (with a hint of rancour), and I can't help but wonder, what is this life? It is many things, but Lord help me, it is never dull.

He looks about the café and, as if his eyes were photographic lenses, notices details I have overlooked. "My word, there are a lot of watercolours hung on these walls, are there not?"

I follow his gaze. "Oh. I suppose so. I never paid them much attention."

We look about. Watercolours and charcoal sketches of the Rathaus, the Art Academy, the public squares, the fountains, even some of the townsfolk: the pedlar who sells wooden dolls along the banks of the Danube, the vicar who rings his bell and beckons the faithful to Sunday Mass at the Stephansdom, the rare and used bookseller on Klosterneuburgerstraße, even a few of the black-market sellers I met on the Pohlgasse when the Affable Thief was in full swing.

"I don't know if I like them," I admit.

"No, they are definitely unskilled," he says, "but maybe one of these artists will grow to be the next Klimt one day."

The waiter pushes the pastry cart by, and I call him over.

"A slice of Sachertorte, meine Dame?" he offers.

"Tell me, Ulf," I say, not entirely certain Ulf is his name, and not caring in the slightest. "Why all the watercolours and sketches?"

"Ah so," he gestures like a guide, "it's a longstanding tradition here at Sperl. The Art Academy and the Secession are not far from here, so we get many an artist sitting for hours at our tables but, times being what they are, unable to afford a drink. So, in exchange for a watercolour, we offer a free cup of coffee."

He pushes his squeaky-wheel pastry cart to the next table, and I lean over to Franz. "Don't think him too generous. There is always an ulterior motive among this type of proprietor."

Franz folds his arms and a glimmer of amusement flashes across his eyes. "Oh, really? Are you, what they call, street savvy?"

"All I know," I whisper, "is that the army requisitioned Café Sperl early in the war and used it as a stable for their horses. Much damage it did to the establishment. And seeing as how nobody can afford repairs, these totally unremarkable watercolours are undoubtedly hiding bullet holes or hoof imprints."

Franz looks at me, his darkish eyes, shaped like bricks, bright as mud, and I can tell he's working something out in his head. "What else do you know about cafés that the rest of us do not?"

"A challenge?" I raise an eyebrow.

He nods, licking his bottom lip.

"I've always welcomed a challenge," I warn.

"Then, by heavens, don't back down now."

"Ulf, my dear," I call over my shoulder, and the waiter scuttles back with his squeaky cart.

"Meine Dame?"

"I have a dozen trucks with coal, flour, candles, condensed milk, and oranges," I say to him in a hush, keeping my eyes on Franz, who looks confused. "To whom should I sell?"

Ulf doesn't answer immediately, so I slip a twenty-crown note into his pocket.

Like the seventh minute of boiling an egg, Ulf suddenly becomes ebullient. "The gentleman in the corner at the table on the right will buy it, perhaps half today and half tomorrow when he returns." Ulf tucks the note deeper into his pocket, bows, and pushes the cart away.

"You see?" I say to a wide-eyed Franz. "Even in such low times, the black market of the cafés operates the same as it ever did."

"Do you have a dozen trucks, Milena?"

My lips curl like a sugar spoon over a blue flame.

"Why you little storyteller." He lets out a gasp but quickly covers his mouth. "And where did you get a twenty-crown note?"

"I liberated it from Ernst's billfold."

"You mean you stole it."

"I pick his pockets when he's bothersome, loud, or irritating, which he is constantly." This is the most freely I've spoken about the Affable Thief with anyone, and I don't dare elaborate.

"God in heaven."

"Have I impressed you, Franz?"

"I think," he nods a few times before continuing, "that I have lived a rather sheltered life in comparison to you."

The tip of my shoe slides higher along his calf, then back down again, as though stroking a feline. His fingers lace with mine, and his long thumb caresses my index finger, stained azurite-blue from my fountain pen.

"Why do you always write to me in German?" he suddenly asks. "Even now, you speak to me in German instead of Czech."

"I suppose..." I search for an answer, "I wasn't sure about your Czech skills. It is a notoriously unforgiving language."

"German may be my mother tongue, but I am a Czech man, through and through."

"Are you now?"

"And I find it much more intimate."

"Are you trying to make me blush, Franz?"

"Would you like me to?"

"You wouldn't dare."

"You see," he smiles as his fingers grip mine with a deeper need, "your German is masterful, and even when you make the odd mistake, it still seems to work for you. It's as if the language lies down before you like an unworthy palace slave."

"I'm not sure what to do with such high praise."

"You could write to me in Czech," he says. "I only want to speak to you in Czech, because only within it, the true Milena is found."

My eyes drop to his lips. His lips part. I squeeze my legs together. We lean toward each other and he places the slightest kiss, breathy and tingling, on the top of my hand. As the blotchy warmth of a blush crawls up my breasts and peeks above the collar of my blouse, I bite my lip.

"So," he breathes. "Czech. Please."

Ulf saunters by with his cart and I reach out to grab his arm, plunging my fingernails into his skin. "Cheque, please!"

FRANZ AND I WALK silently through the winding, narrow corridors that act like veins to the artery of Vienna. Light rain, slow drizzle, and then blistering sunrays meet us every few minutes. Pause. Long silence and more pauses. I'm hoping he'll say something first. Lines of trolleys and trams drop off mixed crowds of school children and the elderly, all gleeful, as they step lightly toward the Kunsthistorische museum, buying souvenirs and postcards.

I am looking at Franz, willing him to look back. He does not.

We pass rows of three-storey houses all in white with Greco-Roman portico columns and flat windows. All rebuilt after the war. Franz runs his fingers through his thick, rich hair like it's the only thing keeping him together. He finally looks at me with his dark eyes. I meet his stare like I can make him disappear with one giant blink.

A nebula hangs between us. I could touch it, but like a cloud of smoke it would curl around my finger before dissolving completely. What it is exactly that floats in the space between us is unable to solidify. I feel like a foreigner in adulthood.

Franz has a look on his face like he's in exile. "Do you ever fall asleep to the music on the wireless?" he suddenly asks.

"Often," I say.

"Does it disturb you?"

"Disturb me? How?"

"I am famous for my insomnia, and I keep waking up in the middle of the night, hearing clips of songs in my dreams."

"Clearly, you are insane," I assure him.

"Why thank you." He smirks.

"Why am I not in your dreams?"

"Clearly I'm not that insane," he says.

I guffaw and pinch his arm.

We saunter across Mariahilferstraße and I realize that I have been leading him northward: to the beacon that is Lerchenfelderstraße.

"In all honesty," he cuts through my train of thought, "you have been in my dreams."

"Have I?"

He nods with a faraway look in his eyes. I put one foot in front of the other, trying to walk through this feeling. "I'm sorry. I have no business being there."

"Nonsense." He waves a hand in the air. "As a matter of fact, I had a dream of you this morning, which I found almost entirely impossible to extricate myself from. It held me by the tongue."

He clasps his hands behind his back, and I clasp mine in front, holding myself close. "Tell me."

He looks at me sideways, a glint in his eye. We pass by the entrance of Herr Tešarek's poulterer, and the tang of dead game, fowl, and turkey greets my nose.

"Well, it was here in Vienna. You were on the street with me, much as you are now. You were standing on the pavement, I with one foot on the road. I held your hand, and then a senseless, fast, short-sentenced conversation began. It went tit for tat, and lasted almost uninterrupted to the end of the dream."

We descend the quiet cobbled square that abuts Saint Ulrich's and turn onto Neustiftgasse, our footfalls clicking like the clop of horse-pulled carriages.

"That sounds very much like the afternoon we've already had, don't you think?" I smile up at him.

"It does. It reminds me of something I once read

somewhere that went vaguely like this—" he clears his throat—"'My beloved is a fiery column which moves across the earth. Now it holds me encircled. It leads, however, not to those encircled, but those who see.'"

The cold drizzle on my skin matches the cold air swimming down my throat. Bicycle bells ding. The day is ultra-yellow, the air hot with the scent of stews and meats and pastries. The bells of St Ulrich ring out the quarter past.

I take his hands in mine.

"I have a feeling," I say, "that you and I are going to enjoy each other's company immensely."

"Yes, but," he looks up at the sky, "I'm sure God will find a way to make us pay for it."

WE BUY PAPER FANS from an Asian vendor. Franz says he likes women with large feet. Women are like brown stallions, he says, galloping along at breakneck speeds. "This requires a good hoof. And if she can run faster than me, I know I've found my wife."

He buys a couple of Chinese pears. "Where did you find such a lovely lady?" the vendor asks in highly accented German.

"They're just wandering around the Ringstraße," he quips. Man alive, he speaks like death could not touch him.

He passes me a small fruit that tsunamis my inner cheeks with juice and membranes, falling apart in my palm with unstable softness, forcing me to stuff the whole thing into my mouth. He smirks at me, like it was his plan all along to watch me fumble. He rubs his thumb over my bottom lip and chin, catching the overspill. My lip swells as it retakes its shape, and I suck it into my mouth to tongue the stickiness away. Eyes lock. Nervous smiles. A small flash of teeth and joy.

"You're so beautiful," he says, as if he wishes I weren't.

He clamps down on a pear and shoves it past his teeth, cheeks filling out like two tennis balls. I snicker. I feel his hand soft on my hip, sliding up to my wrist, and then shyly reaching for my hand, almost like an adolescent. His hand creeps into mine. It is big, a bit rough, clammy and calloused, but he holds mine gently, almost nervously, as though he's scared it might break. He thumbs the rise and curve of my palm as though he were a palm reader. He traces each line like it's a Braille map to treasure. *X* marks the spot. My heart bursts.

I have decided I will sleep with him. He doesn't know it yet.

LERCHENFELDERSTRASSE IS CLOSING IN on us. Walking up to the street entrance for 113, I squeeze Franz's hand and give him one of my dazzling Gloria Swanson smiles. But as I open the door to our flat, a voice calls out from the larder, "Ma'am, you're back! What caused you to leave in such a—"

Paní Kohler is still here, damn her fierce loyalty and sense of duty. She sticks her head into the hallway entrance and sees me close the door behind Franz.

"Ah, I see." She grabs the dishrag hanging from her belt loop and wipes her hands.

"Paní Kohler, this is Franz Kafka."

She looks at me, eyes wide. "The novelist?"

"At your service." They shake hands and she blushes.

"I would offer to take your hat, but I see you are not wearing one," she blusters.

"All the better to see you with, my dear."

Paní Kohler lets out one of those nervous laughs that shocks you at first with its penetrating boom, and then very quickly tapers off into fidgety gurgles that could easily be mistaken for hamster squeals. "Very clever," she titters. "My, you're clever, awfully clever. Well put."

"Paní Kohler, why don't—"

"Yes, I have a million things to do around this flat, no rest for the weary, as they say. Ha ha ha." She looks about the floor as if she has left her equilibrium there. "I'll just be in the—" she points to the pantry and quickly scuttles around the corner. We hear the sounds of spoons clacking and tins stacking.

Franz looks at me. "'Paní' just means 'Mrs.' in Czech. Why not call her by her first name?"

I give him a look.

"Does she have a first name?" he presses.

"I wouldn't dare call her by her first name any more than I would my own mother, God rest her soul."

He takes a few steps into the flat and peers about the sitting room, the large windows overlooking the street, the two bedchambers at opposite ends. "So this is where you live. Where all your letters and telegrams originated."

"Does it fit my character?" I follow behind him and try to match his gaze.

"I haven't decided yet."

He walks straight into Ernst's study. Inspecting like a Pinkerton with a case, he lifts scraps of foolscap, sniffs at the nib of a fountain pen, runs his fingers over the keys of the typewriter, leans in to read the titles of books running up the red-bound spines. As he picks up one book, a stack of his letters and telegrams reveal themselves beneath.

"Is this your workstation?" He picks up one of the first letters he sent me, scanning his own penmanship.

"I commandeered it from Ernst. I don't think he's used it in months."

"Aren't you worried he might find our correspondence?"

"Please, he can't even find his own correspondence most days and sends Paní Kohler into a frenzy trying to locate it. I doubt he cares to rifle through mine."

Flipping through the array of documents and titles, he comes across my issue of *Kmen*. "You wrote the translation here?"

"I did."

He places his hand atop the table and closes his eyes, like it's a blue flame from a well-lit hearth and he's basking in the warm glow.

I walk up to him. So close, his breath ruffles my blouse and whistles past my ears. "Milena, you are like the sea." He opens his eyes and looks down, his gaze tender, echoing the words from his telegram.

I reach up and caress his cheek. "Be careful not to drown."

WITH NO PRIVACY OR peace, my plans to seduce Franz at home have crumbled like a day-old croissant. So I take him to the Burg Kino on the Opernring. It's one of the few cinemas in Vienna where there are several shows per day on the even hours. I like to sit there sometimes and see a picture two or three times. For a few hellers, I can escape the noise of the Ringstraße, or even just the constant echoes inside my head, and simply let the story wash over me in the silver light.

Franz and I enter the groß salle of the Burg Kino and take our seats in the balcony, curved like the lunar crescent. We sink down into the plush red velvet seats with oak arm rests, and warm our hands on the hot roasted chestnuts we bought from the vendor in the Burggarten across the street, waiting for the show to start. Today, the marquee boasts the Soviet film *Journey into Life*, the American film *I Was Lynched*, and the French film *La Grande Illusion*.

I thought this excursion might be to his liking, but something in his air has changed. He won't look me in the eye; he won't open his mouth to speak. Most of the men I've known, from my father to Ernst, have had a churlish, taciturn streak. Men love to throw a tantrum at the slightest excuse.

But we are together, at last, in Vienna. The locket I gave him is tucked into his breast pocket, and not once has he reached for it. I look down at my hands. I'm squeezing them, clenched fingers interlocking. Red patches blossom in my palms where blood vessels and veins are constricted, and white where no blood flows. I am tensing like the moment I walked into the Commissariat and confessed my thievery. I brush my fingers against my lips, as though each digit belongs to someone else. I pretend Franz is kissing my hands.

"Is anything the matter?" I finally say, when I can no longer stand his brooding.

"No," he says, looking down at the chestnuts in their brown paper bag.

There is a pause the length of a Victor Hugo novel. Couples file into the cinema with large buttery pretzels and bags of salted popcorn in their arms.

"It's just that there seems to be something wrong," I prod again.

"Why did you bring me up to your apartment?" he says before I've even finished the last word.

"Why do you ask?" Please don't make me say it.

"Ernst was all over that apartment." He fingers a chestnut but doesn't put it in his mouth. "I could see him in the rolltop desk, in the cigarette caddy, the Persian rug underneath the davenport. I could pick up his scent on the drapes. If I had his taste, I would kill myself... or go to America, which is essentially the same thing."

"I—"

"I don't say this out of jealousy, Milena," he cuts me off. "I'm not jealous."

"No, of course n—"

"But how am I supposed to find my way between these two facts: that you have your own bedchamber, but you often share one together?"

I do not tell him about why I am so devoted to Ernst. Or why I could never leave him. How could I? How would I ever get him to look at me again if he knew what I'd done? A young couple in the row in front of us exchanges a look. I've been embarrassed before, but by men who meant nothing to me. I feel my anger boiling like a pot of glass noodles.

"You've always known I was married." I pop a chestnut into my mouth and chew it crudely, speaking through mouthfuls to show him my disdain. "I've never lied, and I never made any secret of it."

He finally looks at me from under the hood of his misanthropic brows. "That's not what I mean—"

"No, you just mean that you've never had to deal with a woman who wasn't virginal." I punctuate the last word with the chomp of a meaty chestnut.

"Perhaps I assum—"

"That what?" I snort through mouthfuls, dropping crumbs and slivers onto my collar. "That my marriage was unconsummated? I've been married for two entire years, Franz."

He looks back down to his chestnuts, eyeing them as though they are a poisoned chalice. "Yes."

"I am entitled to my share of happiness, just like anybody else. And unlike you, I've actually committed to one person and given it my best shot. I'm not consumed by doubts and accusations that I allow to fester and rot inside my mind. I don't overthink how I feel. I just feel. You could not for one minute fathom such an existence without weighing the long-term benefit to your present-day happiness."

The couple in front of us gets up and changes rows. Somewhere behind us, a coin purse drops with a clang and an usher slams their flashlight against an arm rest.

I swallow what's in my mouth, and what's hanging in the air. "I'm sorry," I lower my voice, "I shouldn't have said that."

"No, you should have." He finally jams his hand into his paper bag and comes out with a palmful of chestnuts. He eats them one at a time; the look on his face says he's not even sure he likes chestnuts. "Our letters created an entire realm, a planet that made me forget there are other factors, other people. That realm scratches at the surface of my bitterness and jealousy just hiding beneath the water's sheen. Either this world is so tiny, or we are so enormous; in any case, we fill it completely."

"Well, if this world of yours doesn't fit me, then I'll carve a hole in the world and make it fit."

He is silent at that.

"Ernst isn't here now." I touch his arm and lean in.

"Yes," he says between munches.

More insufferable silence. I'm uncertain whether I've put his fear at ease; perhaps instead, I've merely doused the flames of his unendurable second-guessing and prevaricating.

"I suppose," I say, "this is why I like the cinema."

He looks at me. "How's that?"

"Well," I begin, "situations in movies are always either black or white, much like the picture itself."

He furrows his brow.

Taking his silence as a sign that I'm making headway, I go on. "In real life, people are complex, both good and wicked. We can be simultaneously trustworthy and suspect. Cowardly and heroic. Every soul is multifaceted, our struggles and our journeys always unpredictable and bottomless. But on the silver screen," I put my hand atop his, "we can give our minds a much-needed respite from our daily difficulties. Cinema makes life easier to bear."

"In that case," he places his free hand atop mine, so our hands become a tower of fingers and palms, "I am thankful you brought me here."

The lights dim on our smiling faces, and the feature presentation begins. As it turns out, Burg Kino is also showing the new Swedish film *Erotikon*. It's a comedy by Mauritz Stiller about a married woman named Irene who cannot decide if she'd rather have an affair with an aviator or her husband's best friend. Meanwhile, Irene's husband wants to leave her to marry his own niece. The film is sexually audacious to say the least, and I can tell Franz is a bit unnerved. Is this the fear he was alluding to in all his letters?

"It's quite a chaste and pure picture, don't you think?" I whisper to him.

He snorts. "Indeed."

"I mean, pure in thought."

"Milenka, my dear, the only thoughts this movie has are impure ones."

In the darkened cinema, I reach over to him. He moves as though I'm going to put my hand atop his and lace our fingers. But instead, I place it on his thigh. He instantly grows excited. He looks at me, but I keep my eyes on the screen; my free hand dives into the roasted chestnuts and comes up with fistfuls of sweet, round nuts.

The chestnut trees are in bloom. Blue pockets of sky play hide-and-seek with the slowly rising moon. The evening is balmy and temperate. The jackdaws swoop and sing from their perches. As Franz uses the lavatory, I walk outside the cinema and stand under the marquee, the drizzle spattering just inches from my shoes. I pretend the night is a woman who is crying because she is happy.

I inhale one more sharp breath of fresh rainy air when an automobile drives by along the Opernring. One of those new automobiles from Munich: a Bayerische Motoren Werke. The silver sheen of its finish and the glare from its headlights make me blink until all I can see is halos of light.

Franz joins me and we sprint through the streets, ducking in and out of doorways to stay dry. The rain can't make up her mind between a light peppering and a tempest. Motorists fend for themselves. Moths don't know where to go. An eerie calm settles in, and the sky opens up to reveal burning stars. The city is down for the count.

We finally reach his train station hotel: the Riva. In the dimming evening shade, the antiquated hotel before me looks like a ghost from centuries past. Up and down, the ends of the street are occupied by wretched blocks of flats and apartments, dilapidated tenements, and condemned houses. But this hotel next to the South Station stands out like it was meant for a Dickens novel. Bright-red brick with green, gold, and white trim. I can almost hear Napoleon's army just by looking at it. I came all this way, and now the universe is sending me a sign not to go any further or face the wrath of the night gods.

"It's all I could get on such short notice," Franz says, noticing my expression as he leads me up to his room. He tells me he usually stays at the Golden Jägerhorn Inn in the centre of town. There he has a single-pane room on the fifth floor, fully furnished as if they know his personal taste, he says.

At the Riva, he has a simple room one would expect for frequent and frugal rail travellers. A wretched bed on a box spring. A nightstand with a small gas lamp. Vermillion drapes with tassel-edged curtains. Satin linen.

Lamplight the colour of dull gold. Verdigris rugs over stained hardwood. On the basin sits a porcelain water pitcher with lapis lazuli highlights in the Dutch style. His valise remains unopened at the foot of the bed, like he threw it there without a care for his belongings.

"Aren't you going to unpack?" I ask.

"Unpacking squanders time. It is a bourgeois indulgence," he says with a sigh.

"My word," I raise my brows, "I had no idea the kind of self-loathing only unpacking could release."

As he drops his keys and coins on the nightstand, I cross the floor and look through the window to see if I can observe any movement. Anyone who might recognize me. I see Arab coffee houses where no women are to be found, Italian waitresses in the Hungarian public houses, laundry hanging on the line where balconies and windows should be, and old women struggling with large parcels. Trams and trolleys jostle by.

The Foehn passing under the glass pane cools my flushed flesh. The tenth district is all brick at night. The granite sheen of the houses, streets, walls—everything in rich dirt colours soaked by the showers. Leaves mulch in puddles of deep bamboo hues; the people dress in soft mahogany. I see earth and straw and tree bark and chocolate and coffee in everything along this district of south Vienna.

Through the walls of the hotel, I can hear the faint hum of electric light fixtures and the coo of voices. As Franz's footfalls approach behind me, I inhale this moment, the last moment before everything changes. An ache and a throb pound in my belly. A poltergeist. He stands shoulder to shoulder with me in the window, and we look out as the imported lagers clink with sparkling gold cognacs inside the lively public house across the way.

"I'm afraid I'm not very well prepared for this," he says quietly. "I don't have much knowledge of the world, in contrast to you."

"Still," I whisper back. "You found me."

"I wouldn't have suspected that you could be found." He looks down at his hands on the pane before turning to face me. "But I thank you for it."

He places a kiss on my shoulder and electricity shoots up my neck. I shudder and gasp. He pulls back to look into my eyes. His gaze forces my mouth open. He kisses me slowly. His eyes close, but I keep mine open because I don't want to stop looking at him. If I do, I'll miss something. I missed so much of him all those times he made me so nervous that I looked away.

He pulls his mouth away from mine and a droplet of his saliva jewels my bottom lip.

"The beat of this music is too fast for my lungs," he says suddenly, with a gasp and a cough. I don't know what music he's talking about. It's a quiet evening. There must be something he knows about kissing that I don't. Perhaps the more you kiss, the louder the music in your head gets. I'm going to have to start kissing in larger and longer quantities.

He stumbles and sits on the bed, wheezing a bit. I pour him a glass of water and kneel by his side. He only sips at it, barely taking it in. But his chest rises and falls with laborious breaths. I put my fingers to his temples and rub them rhythmically. Perhaps there is music after all, because I seem to massage his temples in a four-four time signature. My thumbs press across his flat, wide forehead and his eyes close. His blanched knuckles gripping the glass of water loosen and a salmon-pink colour returns to his skin.

With one long exhalation, he opens his eyes again. "Your hands are blessed," he says, reaching up to my wrists. He places a kiss on one wrist, but as he pulls away, his eyes remain locked there like they are tethered to my arm.

I follow his gaze. He has seen the scars.

"Milenka..." His voice trails off.

The scars are a faded mottled ash with lines of purple. Fine and narrow, hastily patched together by my father with horsehair and thread. Suturing was never his strong suit. I yank my arm back and cover my wrist with my hand.

"Milenka," he repeats, this time with greater urgency. "What did you do?"

"I can't tell you," I breathe.

"Why not?"

"Because if I do, you'll never look at me the same way again."

He thinks about this. "Maybe I want to look at you with new eyes," he replies. "Maybe I want you to look at me differently too."

"You'll judge me." I grip my wrist.

"I'll take that risk if it means knowing you better."

There's no way that I can lie to him now. He'll find out eventually from Max or Werfel, or even by asking around the Arco when he gets back to Prague.

He pats the bed. "Come. Sit. Tell me."

So I explain to him, finally, why I am forever obliged to Ernst. When I was young and sprightly and had my pick of many bachelors, I thought Ernst was lucky to have me. But after the termination, and my brush with death, I realized how lucky I was to have Ernst. My father called it a cry for help, just another example of my amateur dramatics. But it was Ernst who found me, who listened to me wail, who held me as my father stitched me up, and who defended me to everyone who spoke about me as if I had been raised in a garbage scow. I could never again forsake him or speak ill of such a brave and bold character.

It wasn't long after that my father confined me to an asylum for the mentally infirm. But it was Ernst who hatched the plan for my escape. It was Ernst who waited for me at the other end of the field that night with a coach as I broke out of my quarters. It was Ernst who married me, willfully and gladly, after all the trouble I had caused, and took me away from my father and a city full of gossip. It is for all of this, and perhaps more, that I love my husband. Despite everything that has happened since, I cannot help but love Ernst. No matter what happens, I will always love Ernst. I owe him my life.

Franz stares at the corners of my eyes like he's waiting for the stone-heavy tears to tumble down, but he does not offer me his shoulder. Or a hug. Or his handkerchief. He stares into my brokenness and absorbs it.

"It seems fairly obvious to me that you don't owe him anything," he finally says.

"I couldn't have seen my way through that mess were it not for him ..." I press all my pain into the extremities of my wet lashes, the tip of my stinging nose, the stem of my collapsing chin.

"Yes, you could have."

"How can you say that?"

"He shouldn't be praised for being a decent human being. That's the lowest bar he could have reached. Milenka, there is so much more to love than what he has offered you."

"What do you know of love? You've never been persuaded to matrimony—"

"The question is, what do you know?"

I walk over to the basin, pour in some water from the pitcher, and splash my face. Cold. My face is hot and puffy. The water sets me steaming. I wipe my eyes with the sleeve of my blouse, but I leave my cheeks wet. Droplets collect at my chin. I let them.

"To me," I finally say, "love has always seemed very much like a soup—the first mouthful is very hot, and the ones that follow become gradually colder."

"Milenka..."

"Am I wrong?"

"Yes."

"How would you know?"

He gets up and stands three finger-widths away from me. His shadow falls over my eyes. I can hear his heart beating. Or is that mine?

"I'll tell you some other time."

Popping open the buttons of my blouse, he snaps off my underthings so quickly it burns. Dissolving the planet between us, he smashes his mouth over mine in swollen passion. My hand slams the back of the nightstand as I trip backward. Franz grabs my shoulders and I lurch forward into his arms. We jump up and down in a sweaty frenzy as we undress. I smack his bottom as his trousers and briefs drop like a moat around his ankles. He grabs the pitcher from the wash basin and douses me with water as I whip my skirt at him. He backs me up against the wall as I laugh manically. He brushes the wet hair from my face, staring at me with a fond memory in his eyes. I yank his face down and shove my tongue down his throat; he slides his fingers between my legs. I move my body along to the measure of his fingers. Knead his hair. He swells against my hip, and I wonder how much longer we can both wait. His nipples tickle mine. His toes are a bit crooked. The friction of skin against skin feels like a sweep of ocean water dousing a fire. We clumsily find the mattress and I wrap my legs around him. He pushes inside me and I look up at him and wonder about the minutes. The individual seconds, even. Come. Come. I bite his shoulder as he slumps forward on my collarbone. We lie like that for a few hours, sheets lumped at the foot of the bed like a dead body, taxis honking below at the hotel guests for a fare.

11

Day Two

Cessation of rail transport with Hungary.
—Neues Wiener Tagblatt, *July 2, 1920*

A day with Franz in fragments:

DAWN—I awake, the hum of electricity in the corridor flickering beyond the door. I peel my lids open, light splits my brain, I doze again.

I rub my blotchy morning face. Franz is next to me; I can feel the rise and fall of his breathing on the mattress. He is atop the sheets, me beneath. Scratching my shoulder, I feel like my body is aflame. The itch becomes exigent. Tilting my head, I see little red bumps, raw and seething, forming a line. This infernal hotel has goddamned bed bugs! I yank the sheets back and jump out of bed, jabbing the mattress with my foot as if I expect to see millions of microscopic beetles tumbling out of it like gymnasts. I slide the window up, run my fingers over the sill, thumbing the dust. Across the way, the public house is quiet and still, as if the raucous gathering from last night was all imagined.

Franz is awake and looking at me. Dark circles around his eyes, dark skin—blinking me in. The expression on his face is one of bemusement.

"What?"

He smiles but says nothing.

"Come now, what is it?"

In a raspy morning voice, he says, "I heard bits of a song in my dreams again."

"What was it?"

He clears this throat. "They say that I should beeeeeeee in the follies! Hot tamales! They say that I've got a pair of eyyyyyyyyyyyes just like all Svengalis! I could make a music master drop his fiddle! Make a bald-headed man part his hair in the middle..."

Listening to him sing this peppy song without any respect for tone or key is like being trapped in a very one-sided conversation.

I sing the chorus over him, "'Cause I'm a red-hot mama!"

There is a loud knock—likely a broomstick—on the adjacent wall and we cover our laughing mouths.

"I know that song too," I say. "I've heard it when I tune the radio to the foreign stations."

"It's an American jazz singer, the woman with the deep voice from the Ziegfield Follies," he says. "But it's too early in the morning to remember her name."

"You should get out of bed, in any case."

"Why?"

"I think the mattress has creepy crawlies ... my shoulder is red with bites."

He leaps off the sheets, rubbing his face, arms, and hair as though he's in an ice-cold shower. "These wretched station hotels," he mumbles. "Well, that settles it."

"What?"

"We're going to have to burn this whole place to the ground."

"I'll get the kerosene." I scratch my shoulder. "But before we commit to arson, perhaps we should go out and spend the whole day outside trying to remember the name of that jazz singer."

"That doesn't sound like much fun."

"It can be if you want it to."

"Does anybody ever tell you no?"

"No one who lived to tell the tale. You know, mein liebe Doktor Kafka, you have an uncanny ability to make every prospect of fun and merriment a chore."

"And you, meine gnädige Frau Pollak, have an uncanny aptitude for compliments."

"Sounds like you're the lucky one in this outfit."

Outside the hotel window, the city of Vienna swelters, teeming with life: the dirty streets, the strong aromas, the overwhelmingly snarky attitude, the bicycles and their bells. Everything here, from the architecture to the people, is a memory of a memory. Wreckage upon wreckage. Disaster upon disaster. Pigeons and trams and Danube boat excursions. Vienna burns like brimstone and I am a moth that can't stop scorching itself in the flames.

I reach over and tug on his thumb, pawing at his skin. "Come now. Let me show you how to truly live."

NINE O'CLOCK—We borrow bicycles from the hotel concierge, a man named Herr Emil who is constantly checking his teeth in the reflection of his watch. I expect he is waiting for a certain guest to descend the stairs so that he might pay her more attention than the others.

While Franz is tinkering with the height of his bicycle seat, I ask Herr Emil if he might have an extra pair of slacks in the backroom.

When I finally join Franz outside with the bicycles, his gaze lowers to my legs. "What are you wearing?"

I take my bicycle in hand, straddle it in one swift move, and push away from the curb. "Women's clothing is too restrictive for the act of bicycling!"

"Don't you think you should dress more conservatively?" he calls to me.

"I would, but I don't own anything made of pistols, doctrine, or jingoism!" I call over my shoulder.

He peddles up next to me as we move along the Recht Wienzeile promenade toward the outer hills. Riding next to the deserted Stadtbahn tracks, we pass Margaretengürtel, Gumpendorferstraße, and then underneath the elevated rail tracks. We cycle faster and faster, the sun on our backs and shoulders, wind making our hair flutter and flap like full-mast flags, heading toward Hietzing and Ober St Veit until we reach the Schönbrunn gardens just outside the city: lush green inclines, lavender sprigs, crystal ponds where lily pads mingle with bulrushes. Cows dawdle along dirt paths, past châteaux with triangle-latch roofs.

We lean the bicycles against the entrance. Franz is breathing heavily but not wheezing, gasping, or coughing. There is crimson on his cheeks and sweat dotting his brow and upper lip.

"Am I truly living yet?"

I grab his hand and lead him upward. "Not yet!"

TEN O'CLOCK—The gardens surrounding the palace have always been open to the public, though even without a Kaiser, the palace itself is still off-limits. The war-time orphanage that was housed here is gone, but the old guards and mounted servicemen still sentry the palace as though the Kaiser might return from exile any day now. Franz and I circumvent the colonnade arcade entrance where hordes of sojourners crowd the pathways and enter via a side entrance, walking along row after row of blossoming trees, until we stand before a pond leading to the Romanische ruins—a perfect oval heralding the intersection of the dusty paths that form a constellation. A petroglyph woman sits atop an oasis and bends to the aid of a water cherub and a quacking stone duck.

We inhale the scent of pinecones and strong spiced wood, filling our lungs. Beetleheads and bats appear in the periphery, among spotted toads, magpies, malt worms, and pigeon eggs, while pigs squeal distantly through the bush and fallen logs in their weedy mating rituals. I feel a relaxing warmth rising up my thighs, vessels engorging in my pelvis, swelling until I'm sure my capillaries will burst.

Franz stares. I stare. I will him to speak first, before I unravel the fabric of the sky, tearing and slicing away at it until we are crushed underneath.

Ruins of Carthage come into view as we walk forward—the river gods Danube and Enns in a rectangular pool, flanked by columns, reliefs, a frieze of Roman mythological characters, and framed by a proscenium arch that is supposed to suggest the entrance to a castle long crumbled and lost to the earth. These aren't real Roman ruins, they're only about 150 years old, but they capture the imagination, nonetheless.

We begin to climb the steep path toward the gloriette. Franz trails slowly behind me, his white collared shirt undone to his chest cavity, his neck red from the sunrays. Something about the dark solitude, the quiet, the lack of echoes, where the distance is buried behind a cornucopia of brown and green—it all feels so warm, like a hug from the inside. It's freeing. Nothing amber or luminous, like a façade or a monument, to draw your attention away from the liberating seclusion of the woods.

The deep darkness of the shrouded forest beckons me. I wander off the stone path, round the first collection of Austrian pines, and dive headfirst into green. Franz follows me silently at first, but then, as I push forward into the thick brush, I can hear his laboured wheezing behind me. He clutches at his already-loosened shirt, gripping the stiff buttons all the way down, tugging them to release, as if he has been garroted.

I rush back to his side. "Oh, darling, is it the climb?"

He shakes his head as he fights to suck in air.

"Is it . . . the two of us? Alone. In the woods?"

He meets my gaze. He nods only once.

I sit him down on a tree stump carpeted in mulch and rub my hands together for warmth. As he gasps, I massage his temples as I did last night. He closes his eyes and concentrates on his breathing as I push the fleshy flat pads of my thumbs into his skin, massaging from brow to bone. His hair is shaved from temple to nape, and white stubble mingles with dark velvet charcoal strands. His dinner-plate eyes suddenly look small, like two quotation marks on a blank page.

"Darling, there is no need for this fear," I whisper. "It's just me. It's just you and me."

Pigeons maraud on the stones and mulch at our feet. Patrolling for crumbs. Eavesdropping. He reaches up and grasps my wrists; his large hands, his long fingers, encase my flesh with ease. Pulling my thumbs gingerly from his skin, he finally opens his eyes; they are wet. Our faces are so close, our eyes locked.

A pause hangs between us like fruit from a tree. Eventually, he is going to have to speak to me. A word has to crack through the voluminous stillness.

He is eyeing my mouth. I think he might kiss me, but instead he says, "I love the whole world."

My surprised gasp turns into a smile. "You do?"

He nods. "And that includes your left shoulder."

His eyes travel down. I am being investigated. An inventory of who I am. Notes taken, catalogued, and checked. My mouth to my eyes. My forehead to my hairline, trickling down the side of my face. My chin, across my collarbone, past my clavicle and to the round softness of my shoulder barely visible beneath the soft fabric of my blouse. I follow his gaze, and then I meet his eyes again.

"It does?" I breathe.

"Mm-hmm," he murmurs. "Would you be so kind as to pull your blouse down?"

His eyes are a lighthouse and I cannot see anything but his beacons. My breaths are deep and shallow all at once; whatever is coursing through me is sending blood rushing to my forehead, dizzying me. I reach up and hook my fingers around the neckline of my blouse. I slowly reveal my shoulder.

He bends to kiss. My burned lips scar under his. I squeeze myself to him. His lips glide away, but our foreheads lock tighter than a kiss. My mind throbs against his. Temple to temple. *Stay in my temple. Worship me and sing my praises. Fall on your knees. This is your altar. This is your body. Turn me into wine.*

His lips travel across my ear, along the length of my neck, sending shockwaves across my spine and evoking a shiver. He hovers over the curve of my shoulder before finally blessing it with his tongue.

My face is above his in these woods, but suddenly he grips my waist and rolls me to the soft earth. "I have no fear at all," he whispers.

"Squeeze me," I tell him. He does. My ribs will break. *Keep squeezing, harder, until I can't breathe. Wrench it out. Exhale, don't inhale.*

I slide down the length of Franz's body and open my mouth. Hands fumble in the shadows. *Quiet, or someone'll hear.* The hill is dark, but life stirs in her yet. Sounds of beetles below in the grass and swallows above in the hollows of trunks. Wind-disturbed leaves. Lips travel across skin. *Shhhh.* Body parts falling out of clothing. With my tongue on his nipples, I spell out insults about his fiancée.

He jerks, grabs my shoulders and pulls me back up.

"No," he says.

"No what?" I breathe.

"Don't."

"Why not? No one's watching."

"Not here. Not like this."

"What's the matter?"

"Is this what you want?" He motions to the ground, grimy with moss and decomposing bark.

It really is what I want, or at least it was, right up until he said that. I've never had anyone deny me before; I don't know what to say.

"Are you mocking me?"

"No, Milena, but I am not joking."

"Oh. I'm sorry, I thought, I mean, I assumed you—"

"Don't be silly, of course I do. But not here. This isn't special."

"No, I guess not." Even though I think it is.

"Come here." He folds his arms over me.

I am wrapped up in something, but it's not Franz. It's not me. What am I doing to myself? I don't even know anymore. My head is somewhere far-off. Somewhere gone. I don't care about writing or Ernst or my father. I don't care about thieving or fancy frocks. I'm fixed up here like a fresco on some ancient ceiling. I can't picture my life anymore without picturing serpent tails.

He gets up suddenly, tucking his shirt back into his trousers and flicking off the dried leaves.

"Won't you sit?" I look up at him, still caught in the moment that is already gone.

"I want to stand."

"Why?"

"If I can't be erect, then I'll be upright."

I let out an exasperated sigh; I could cry, but I am still too stuck in a trance to really do or feel anything.

He kneels back down to me. "Listen to me, my Milenka."

I meet his gaze; my nose is stinging, but I force myself not to well up.

"We are already one, of that I have no doubt." He rests his head on my almost bare bosom. We are two needles passing through layers of skin, but he has found my heart and sewn it taut as a drum.

I clear my throat and he rises away from me. I button my blouse and shake Herr Emil's trousers to free them from the twigs, grit, and burrs. "The Hietzing cemetery is just on the other side of the gardens." I motion westward. "We could go say hello to Klimt, Koloman Moser, and Otto Wagner, if you like."

He tilts his head as he looks at me. "Let them sleep. I think I'd much rather stay among the living with you."

I nod, but I stay silent.

"I think you might have been right," he says.

"About?"

"I do feel like I am truly living here." He breathes deeply. "I wish I could live here forever. It's a pity I'm only mortal."

I smooth out my garb one final time before pushing past him and back out onto the stony pathway. "Speak for yourself. I plan to live forever, even if it's the last thing I do."

* * *

MIDDAY—The thoroughfares we follow to reach the gloriette—both scattergun and ruttish—are quiet, deserted. We approach the magnificent structure overlooking the gardens and the city, erected by the Kaiser and Queen Maria Theresa, and we climb a staircase flanked by two alabaster Roman sentries, lion's heads at their feet. The colonnade pillars hold up the vaulted pediments and pilasters. Spread out before us on the horizon is the butter-coloured palace, and beyond, Vienna peekaboos from behind each baluster.

A café is nestled inside the gloriette. Sculpted eagles with hay in their talons are positioned underneath the Habsburg royal crown. Four pilasters are wedged between two vaulted windows as tall as ivory tusks, and the bright and sunny salon is smartly decorated without drapes, but the oak tables, red velvet seats, and little booths are tucked below the panes of glass. The servers are all male, in ridiculous black tuxes and mismatched loafers, their waist-pouches filled with hellers, crowns, ticket orders, and chewed pencils.

We sit by the streaming light of the windows and order two café lattes with extra Schlagobers. Franz also orders a bottle of Apfelschorle, for which he developed a taste during a short stint in Berlin. I chatter nervously to fill the silence growing between us; I'm like a hyacinth macaw in a gilt cage. I talk about the long arduous process of translating and of my role as fashion correspondent for the *Tribuna*. Franz says he has read all my columns with interest and admiration. He tells me he wrote "The Judgement" during one long night in 1912, and that the letter to his father—which he wrote last year but never sent—is more than a hundred pages long. It would seem words flow out of him like sudden snow squalls. The difference between our methods forces a long swig from each of our tall, steaming glasses.

The differences are suddenly all we can see.

As the tedium grows, we are temporarily distracted as a war hero takes the table next to us with a young girl I assume is his daughter. The man is missing one leg below the knee and three fingers on the opposing hand. One ear seems to have melted, because the side of his scalp bears skin like the smooth ripples of a waterlogged rock. A tiny hole is all that is left of the cartilage and lobe. The young girl is wearing a feathered fascinator in her bobbed hair and a formless dress—no sash, no belt across the waist—signalling that she is deeply attuned to the changing fashions of the times. She helps the man take a seat and holds his crutches for him as he settles in. His voice is raspy from the mustard gas attacks of the trenches, but he can still order his own damn drinks, thank you very much. When his daughter asks if he can see the palace just beyond the valley, he snorts that his eyesight has never been better, he'll have you know. Franz and I exchange glances as the man, increasingly agitated, raises his voice to describe the colours of the horizon over Ypres each time a Minenwerfer mortar exploded on target, levelling the city to the ground. Grey plumes meant pulverized stone. Brown plumes meant upturned earth. Pink plumes meant vaporized bodies.

I have to look away; I cannot hear any more horrors today. I turn back to Franz and notice his face is coated with the patina of memory. He pats his breast and pulls the locket from his vest pocket. He applies pressure to the clasp and it opens gingerly.

"They are very fine photographs." He grins.

"The Photoautomat did all the work," I say.

"Nonsense." He gives monochrome-me one last smile before secreting the locket again close to his heart. "Although I do wonder why you'd send me your photograph. You have a beauty that I could not soon forget."

Thinking of the hidden note, among other things, I say, "Perhaps it is what's underneath my beauty that counts."

He nods, and we both look out the window, watching families picnicking down the valley, until the server comes to settle our bill.

TWO O'CLOCK IN THE AFTERNOON—"My father is said to have participated in the last reported duel in Prague."

"Oh?"

"With a sabre instead of a pistol."

"Sounds like something a hot-blooded Jesenský might do. What was the impetus?"

"A literary dispute, said the rumour mill. But it could have easily been about an impropriety with a married woman."

Franz gives me a look.

"He would take his colleagues' wives for walks in the woods of Petřín Hill."

The woods around us seem to be listening as we pass through the quiet stony paths of Hietzing shrouded by hanging branches and muddy nests. The sanctuary is almost hissing at us.

"That must have been a great strain on your mother."

"She was ill. And he was a beast."

"Milenka—"

"She was no shrinking violet either, mind you. I accompanied her once to a spa town for treatment. At one point, we lost each other. I searched for her in the public bathhouses and tonic steam rooms and whirlpool mist therapies and Turkish massage. I dashed out into the park, and there, on a bench overlooking the valleys, I saw her in the arms of a man I did not recognize."

"Why are y—"

"Because I have always believed that tall trees embolden loose morals."

He clasps his hands behind his back as we walk and keeps his eyes on the trail. I fold my arms as though there's a chill, but there isn't.

"What do you think you'll do first once you return to Prague?" I ask.

He furrows his heavy brow. "Pay a visit to my mother, that's for certain."

"You sound like you don't have a choice in the matter."

A small grin appears at the tips of his lips. "As Alexander the Great once said about his mother, Olympias, it's a high rent she charges for nine months' lodging."

We chuckle a little. Our shoes—my heeled Nil Similes and his Oxford brogues—make the only sound now. Crunching along the stony dirt path, the occasional twig or pinecone afoot. My heart is in the stones it feels like. Maybe I've put it there. But I cannot leave well enough alone.

"Do give my love to Julie when you arrive."

"Milenka, please—"

"And if you would be so kind as to drop in on my dear friends Staša and Jarmila, I would be ever so grateful. I miss them dearly."

"You cannot ask that of me, surely."

"Why not?"

"Whenever I want to imagine hell, I think of Staša."

I raise a brow. "God in heaven, you have got to learn to form an opinion, Franz."

"My good opinion of her was lost when I witnessed her obnoxious, loud, overbearing tirade inside the Obecní Dům café over the price of a hot breakfast."

"Hmm. That sounds like something she'd do."

"And as for Jarmila, well!" He snorts and points his palms to God.

I think I know what's coming next, but surely there's no way he knows about—

"Word travels fast among our little literary circles. Jarmila was all anyone could talk about in February."

"I know she has made some mistakes—"

"Max told me all about it."

"What did he say?"

His eyes are coal bullets. "She was having an affair with Willy Haas, and that's why her husband killed himself."

We have stopped walking. Our bodies are turned away from each other, but our faces are red, heaving. I cannot tear my eyes away from him anymore than he can me. A shadow is cast upon us.

"Jarmila also works as a literary translator from German to Czech," I whisper.

"And Willy Haas, wouldn't you know it, is a writer who trained as a lawyer." Franz's eyes glisten as his anger fades.

I grip his collar and pull his face to mine. My eyes are pools and he is drowning. "They're not like us, Franz."

He circles his arms around me and I bury my face in the nook of his neck. A very real fear is penetrating both of us now. Before, in letters, the reality of our predicament could be ignored, but in person, the consequences seem to be hunting us from the shadows. I think of the times in my childhood when my father would take me to see the wax figures at the circus sideshows depicting famous murderers and martyrs of Bohemia. They would give me the most torturous nightmares, but I always begged him to take me back. That feeling of being thrilled to my core was addictive. Of losing my footing on purpose. Of rocking a fragile boat until everyone and everything had capsized.

EIGHT O'CLOCK—There is an underground cabaret behind the Prater. I drag Franz by his shirttails, and we pay the buffoon in an Arlecchino mask at the box office eight crowns each for admittance, and descend a smoky, musty set of stairs to the small black box theatre where one Fresnel hot light is aimed at the elevated stage. Men in top hats and women in short skirts lampoon the mayor and his ridiculous spending, or the new banknotes not worth the paper they're printed on, satirizing the scandals of socialites and debutantes, their affairs with portly, moustachioed men who are wider than they are tall. Drinks are cheap and flowing; entertainment is hilarious and always colourful. Dancing is encouraged. In the audience, the gals wear makeup and the men are soldiers of fortune.

After the final bow from the master of ceremonies, a small jazz quartet—a pianist, trombonist, clarinetist, and percussionist behind a kick drum and hi-hat cymbal—strike up the chords. A red light hangs from a gable. Short hems, fishnet stockings, bobbed hair, boyish dresses, coat-tails, white spats, and buckled shoes flash by us in a blur and descend upon the sparkling dancefloor. It's a new song and a new dance craze that has taken America by storm. I've heard it several times on the wireless.

I lock eyes with Franz. "The Charleston!" I squeal, and I gather his hands in mine, leading him down to the dilapidated floor.

"No, no!" His eyes flutter wildly about. "Not in front of everyone!"

"Come on, I want to dance!"

"But I'm not very adept at—"

"You'll do fine!"

"I can only spin around three times before I vomit," he says, to which I laugh. "Everyone will see."

"Oh, no one is watching you, Franz! Look!" I motion to the gaggle of heads already bobbing up and down to the music, as chairs and tables are still being pushed against the walls. "They're here for joy, not judgement!"

"Milena, I just don't think—"

"Franz," I pull his face close to mine, lowering my tone to that of a strict governess. "I want to dance. I want to dance the Charleston. And I want to dance with you."

His furrowed brow relaxes a bit.

"Can you do that for me, my darling?" I ask. I climb

on my tiptoes and place a kiss on his lips—a fat, plush one that leaves him swollen and red in the face.

His eyes nod yes before his head can.

Eyes a-glimmer, I swallow my dance partner in the swivel of my ankles that roundhouse across the floor. My knees pump up and down and then shimmy side to side. Feet and hips jazz it up, turning in and out. I dance all around him, for gyrating is an ancient mating dance. There's a scent of burning sugar—I can smell it off him as he pants along. I can feel myself becoming the trumpeter as he hits a crescendo like a thorn bird swelling in heat. Full throttle as we go, Franz's hands reach for my hips, feeling them up and down, pounding closer to his. The drums and clarinet are dripping angry juices all over the room. Dizzy in a spin, Franz is a floored jaw.

The room hoots and hollers, wildly applauding the band. I take a breath of satisfaction and wipe the sweat off my brow. Franz dips his head to me and I wipe his brow as well, a smile frosted on my face.

The music kicks in again; this time it's the famous "Tiger Rag," and the crowd suddenly blends into an inferno of revolving bodies. Franz and I press our foreheads together, laughing at them in a dizzy sort of daze. The pungent burning sugar aroma is Novocaine for my brain. I smile up at him. "Just like joy, dancing is an elixir and absolutely essential!" I say over the music.

He looks like he wants to respond, but then a familiar look crosses his face and his gaze droops. "Franz?" I tuck my head so I can look at his face, but he pulls away like I've stolen his breath. His hands rise to his chest and his mouth hangs open, trying to suck in air, but the ridiculous lung just won't inflate. He begins to cough, whipping his silk handkerchief from his pocket and holding it to his mouth. When he pulls it away, it is spotted with red droplets. He tries to push through the crowd, but I put my hands on his arms and pull his eyes into mine. Forehead to forehead, we are lost in suspension. Everything goes quiet. Time slows down. The room is forgotten; the people are phantoms. The music is underwater, muddled and caught behind a wall.

"Just stare into my eyes, and it will go away," I say.

I inhale as he does. We exhale together. Inhale. Exhale. His big brown eyes are lined red as though they're packed with sulphur. Tears tumble down in frustration. Inhale. Exhale. The drained colour of his cheeks slowly returns to normal. Scott Joplin's "The Entertainer" is playing somewhere in the distance, and as we breathe together, it slowly grows louder.

"It will go away," I say again, running my fingers through his hair.

And it does.

MIDNIGHT—His wretched mattress at the Riva has been flipped and turned down. Bed bugs be damned. We don't have a care. Removing my underthings, a finger slips in, eliminating my throbbing walls.

I want to be swallowed. Like the field mouse pierced and severed by the eagle's talons, flying apart in the sky as I'm carried to the feeding nest. Eaten by young ones. Vicious and real.

Damocles's sword is scratching my carotid artery. My writings will be famous one day, he insists. With this sex act, all I can hear is the delicate jangle of his gilt Star of David falling down the chain around his neck. "Worship what enters your womb," he says. Like Sunday eternal.

Shards from inside me tumble forth. The smell of our still-human bodies. Turning cold and into primates. Gobsmacked. Petting.

Menses remnants are left on his fingertips. Red and fragrant. Circles and curves of red. I want to be stricken down until love oozes out of me. Until it seeps out of every pore along with the blood. No matter what, I always want to be within its striking distance.

Across the alleyway in the Hungarian public house, wine sours. Down on the street, dogs madden. Above the city, air fouls. The crescent moon hangs low.

12

Day Three

At the conference of the International Women's League in Salzburg: The first doctor of Austrian state science—a woman!
—Die Frau, *July 3, 1920*

As the sky turns deep blue with a wide purple channel through it, the morning comes flowing in. I am lying in his bed, but it's as if I am orbiting the earth—a clairvoyant perhaps. I think I'm ridding him of this fear, this terror of his, simply by naming it.

The morning sunlight is fresh as I crank my head to see him sleeping like a seahorse beside me. For all his claims of insomnia, he sleeps deeply next to me. Black hairs swirl up his legs, over his knees, creeping across his thick thighs. Gathering into a triangle where I have deep throated and salivated. His belly flat, hair calligraphies up his torso. His jugular. The jut of his chin. I feel something new rising underneath my skin, a dawn or a melody. We never fall in love the same way twice. Even desire has its shades.

After waking and washing our bodies with a damp cloth in the basin, we dress quickly. At Café Korb in the heart of town, just behind St Peter's Basilica, we order croissants and butter tarts wrapped in wax paper so we can enjoy them al fresco in the early July sun. As Franz pays, cutlery all around us clacks into glasses. Espresso machines grind and hiss. Across the café, a young flâneur fumbles for a cigarette and tosses it between his lips, but the automatic lighter does not ignite. There's a snap of his thumb on the lighter, trying fruitlessly to make it flame. The liquid at the bottom jiggles, sloshes up the sides. His thumb snaps and snaps, but still no flame. As we head for the Volksgarten, he tosses it down, ejecting it from his palm as though it wasn't worthy of his touch in the first place. As early as a few days ago, I was that automatic lighter, unable to ignite. Now I'm aflame.

The morning is balmy and still hazy, as I suspect we both are. The Volksgarten is still quiet at this hour. Midday is when the buggies and the screaming children chasing dreidels and balloons populate the benches and green expanses. We sit on the steps of the Grillparzer monument and bite into our pastries.

"Have you ever read Franz Grillparzer?" he asks, nodding up at the curved sculpture of the author.

"I don't believe so," I say through mouthfuls, crumbs falling into my décolletage.

Without hesitation, Franz reaches over to my breasts and brushes the crumbs away like it is second nature.

Like we do this all the time. I would blush were I not so comforted and eased by his touch.

"I'm going to send you 'The Poor Fiddler.'"

"Is it of great significance to you?"

He rests his elbows on his knees and gazes out at the Burgtheater brushing the skyline. "No, though it once was. It's just so Viennese."

Pigeons flutter above our heads, and the trams ding their bells as pedestrians dart in front of their rails at the last moment, narrowly avoiding disaster.

"I was thinking—"

"Now, now, what would the Empress say?"

I pinch his shoulder, and he lets out a "Yeowch!"

"You had it coming."

"Fair point." He grins and rubs his skin. "Do go on."

"Would you be averse to me translating more of your works into Czech?"

Chewing on the last of his flaky pastry, he crumbles the wax paper loudly into a ball and then squeezes it tightly in his fist.

"The last one turned out quite nice, don't you think?" I continue. "And my editor at *Kmen* received some rather fine praise from readers. I'm sure it would—"

"Which works did you have in mind?" he interjects.

"Well," I let him take my empty wax paper to mingle with his own. "'The Judgement,' perhaps. Definitely *The Metamorphosis* ... that goes without saying. And I think *The Meditation* might be a fine addition."

He trots to the waste bin and back again. "I'm sure whatever you do with the translations will be fine indeed."

"Truly?" I ask. He nods and I clutch my hand to my bosom. "Thank you," I say.

"Bah." He waves a hand, shooing away any praise. "It's a pity they aren't more precious to me. Then I could really express the confidence I have in you."

I link my arm through his and we sit for a moment, entwined. But he has two looks on his face simultaneously: one is wonderment, the other worry.

"What is it?"

"You'd be excused for thinking me insane, but this is all new territory for me."

"Territory?"

"You," he says, crimson rising up his ears, from lobe to cartilage. "I've never known a woman like you. The women of my life have been domestic, happy, traditional..." he lowers his gaze and his voice, before adding, "...erotic."

"Am I not those things?"

"Yes, but very rarely has their intellectual prowess come into play, Milenka. Not like this. Not like you." He averts his gaze. At the other end of the park, a baby in a pram shrieks in an all-consuming fit.

"You hear that, Franz? That's my internal monologue right now."

"Look, I devour everything you write. I love your style; I am constantly clipping your feuilletons from the *Tribuna* and pasting them into my scrapbook. I have praised you to Max up and down the length of the Danube. I truly get a kick out of the way your mind works."

"I can feel a 'however' coming," I say.

He meets my eyes. "*However.* You have a strong streak of independence. What can this mean for our future?"

"You think that because I'm clever I'm incapable of fidelity?"

"No."

"Then what?"

"Not for nothing, but I was engaged for a long time to Felice. You know this."

"Yes."

"And it all fell apart the moment she lost interest in my writing. I stayed up all night writing 'The Judgement,' and she wouldn't take the time to read it. She couldn't have cared less. But you. Not only have you read all my words in such precise detail, you want to translate them! It is unprecedented for me, especially since you're a woman. This shakes me to my core, Milenka. Felice, like Julie, was a combination of domestic and sexual. To add another level—of authoress, of writer, of intellectual equal—is so very new to me."

"Are you punishing me for being accomplished?" I can feel anger boiling inside me like a powder keg.

"Certainly not."

"No wonder you so greatly admire Ernst." My voice betrays my mind screaming at me to calm down. "You think just like him. Despite what you wrote in your letters, you are on his side. You admire his ability to type at lightning speed, to maintain his reputation, to keep several mistresses, all while being beholden to no one. You think women should be *obscene* and not heard."

"That's not what I mean."

"No? Name one female author whom you enjoy reading."

He blinks.

"Not Božena Němcová?"

He shakes his head.

"Not Eliška Krásnohorská?"

He purses his lips.

"Not even my aunt Růžena?"

"I haven't had the privilege, no."

"God in heaven!" I raise my hands as if Christ might smite me where I sit. "What did you even love about Felice anyway?"

A dreamy smile curls on his face, and his eyes gleam in admiration. "She was good at business."

The line between passion and revulsion is a thin one, and I am toeing it. If I follow this line, there might be more to lose than just my way home.

THERE IS A STATIONERY shop next to the post office on Bennogasse. "We could buy ink vials, typewriter ribbons, and postcards," I suggest, "and then read the penny dreadfuls right off the rack."

He rubs his chin. "I *would* like to send my sister Ottla a postcard."

"Great." I head for our bicycles locked against the iron fence.

"Wait." He comes up behind me. "Why don't you just hop on the back of mine?"

"You mean …"

"What better way to see the city?"

I glance nervously between him and the bicycle he's already mounting. I hate the feeling of overloading a bike, of taking sharp corners and dipping so low that my knees hover inches above the paving stones. But I smile dutifully and climb on behind him, gripping his lean torso. My legs spread; he scoots up to sit between them. My bosom presses into his back, my palms gripping his ribcage, my chin on his shoulder blade. He shoots us off down the street and I squeal as the morning air whizzes by my ears.

At first, I am petrified, the cobblestoned streets precarious. At any moment their instability threatens to launch us midair into a collision of my worst fears. But as we move in and out of thoroughfares rebuilt after the war, I get used to the feeling of the cobblestones conveyor-belting underneath us at breakneck speed, of the wind blasting through my hair. I want to rocket through the streets, eyes up to the sky, never looking back. And like a child's, my squeals morph from fear into delight. I throw my arms up into the air like I am soaring.

We pass the Rathaus, pass the picketers and police forces squabbling outside the parliament, circle the Volkstheater, mount the pavement as we pass the Hotel Höller, and flow with the cool breezes that are pushing us up Lerchenfelderstraße. The tram rails prove to be a little dangerous for our small wheels, so we swerve up side streets, under archways, through parkettes and dead ends. When we get lost, we stop to ask some old men drinking Kir on the steps of their sundries shops the way.

Franz increases the speed like neither the sun nor his lungs could stop him. I lose myself in the rhythm of his body.

We screech to a halt outside the stationery shop on Bennogasse, giggling, cheeks aglow. We hop up the steps, and the overhead door chime noisily announces our arrival. We peruse wax letter-sealers with wooden handles glazed with a maroon or vermillion stain. There are long red sticks of wax sold by the bunch, bound with twine. Pre-gummed envelopes are also sold by the box, as well as paper cardstocks of varying thickness and weight. Fountain pens are sold next to dip pens and even the outdated but rather quaint pre-sharpened quills. Rotating racks of city postcards feature the Stephansdom tower, the Graben filled with parked automobiles on a Saturday, the Michaelerplatz filled with British and French tourists in white espadrilles, the Hotel Metropol with the Danube promenade winding in the background, and a nighttime view of the Palais Pallavicinni's ornate entrance. As Franz decides on a postcard, I flip through the shelves of penny dreadfuls and pulp fiction featuring femmes fatale with red lips and Pinkertons in fedoras who always get the crook to confess in the end.

When Franz finally purchases a postcard featuring the haunted hallows of the Molker Bastei with its deserted cobbles high above the city, we skip next door to the post office.

"Frau Pollak!" Bettina greets me from her telegraph desk. "It's been quite a few days since I've seen you around here. Normally I expect you before midday, and then again before supper."

"Hello, Fraulein Bettina." I wave as we move past the line of men in hats grumbling about the urgency of their telegrams.

"Don't worry, Frau Pollak, your absence curiously coincided with no new arrivals at your Poste Restante address." Bettina ignores the man in front of her who loudly clears his throat and waves his telegram text at her. "Nothing from Merano today."

Franz looks at me with mouth agape. "Does she—"

"Of course not." I smile at him. "I'm here all the time, is all."

He shoves his hands in his pockets; the locket in his vest jangles. "I guess I just assumed..."

"Yes?"

"What with your husband and all... Well, I just didn't figure you for a gossip."

I narrow my eyes. "You're not well acquainted with many women, are you?"

Franz scoffs at my silly poke and goes to write a note to Ottla. I'm not sure why he wants to send this to her—he will arrive back in Prague before the postcard has even made it across border inspection. But as I'm pondering this, I witness something strange.

Franz can't decide in which wicket he would like to write. He keeps prevaricating, until he chooses the wicket with the largest window. *Awfully nervous*, I think to myself, *especially over such a small decision*. It's rather odd. Once the postcard is completed, he starts labouring over his coins, counting and recounting his crowns and hellers. Then he finds his place in line, but he steps in and out several times, like he's forgotten a heller or to dot an *i* or cross a *t*. Finally, he reaches the front of the queue and gives Bettina his postcard and coins. As luck would have it, the price of postage has not risen significantly with the rate of inflation, so he overestimated the cost. Bettina returns his change, but we cannot exit the premises until he has spent several minutes counting and recounting the coins.

This is tiresome, I gripe to myself. What is going on with him? His hands shake, his eyes flutter, his jaw clenches. Suddenly, he concludes that Bettina has given him too much change, so he waits in line again, for heaven's sake, just to give her back a coin. Finally, when we exit, he realizes Bettina was correct all along and he has in effect short-changed himself.

He turns to go back inside the post office, but I grab his sleeve. "Franz, my darling, enough. Let it go."

"What?"

"It's just a coin. And I'm anxious to spend more time outdoors. Let's not belabour this point any further, all right?"

"Let it go? But now all day I will be without money that is rightfully mine."

"Darling, it's not twenty thousand crowns! It's just a heller!"

"But it's *my* heller."

"Are you really going to spend all day vexed about one little coin?"

Franz stands there; he rubs his chin covered in five o'clock shadow. "Hmmm."

"Oh, for heaven's sake, Franz!" I cry and storm off down Stolzenthalergasse.

"Milenka!" He calls after me, but I keep marching toward Pfeilgasse. I can hear him fiddling with the bicycle pedals, and then the *clink-clink-clink* of the poorly oiled chain coming up behind me. He slowly cycles next to me as I practically goose-step down the street. Reaching a round parkette, I sit on a bench with a dramatic sigh and cross my arms. I frown at him as he hops off his bicycle, leans it against a bench, then turns and looks at me. He shoves his hands in his pockets.

"You're behaving as if you're naked and everyone else has clothes on, you know that?" I bark at him.

He looks at his feet as he steps toward me. I cannot help but notice that he is endlessly tall, endlessly lean, and in some ways, endlessly weak. His senselessly long legs, his sunken cheeks that are pale one moment and crimson the next, his small voice that is quiet, gentle, broken: it's as if he is someone the world has injured.

He sits next to me, heaving one long shank over the other, and folds his hands in his lap. We sit in silence for moments that burn like the last dying embers of a cigar. I cannot understand why he makes me so angry yet evokes such strong passion. Sometimes I can't decide what I want from him: sexual intercourse, or the permission to shoot him out of a cannon. I'm sure both would elicit quite the satisfactory afterglow. The longer neither of us speaks, the more I start to feel ashamed for my outburst. But instead of scolding me, he just sits quietly, which makes me furious all over again.

"Why are the simplest of things so mystical to you?" I ask, exasperated. "Money, social order, currency exchange, even typewriters. You look at them like a child looks at a locomotive."

A cyclist rattles by on a Dutch-framed bike with a wicker basket of flowers hanging off the front handlebars. Her espadrilles are the colour of sandalwood, and her blond hair dances with the melody of breeze and sunlight. We both stare after her down Pfeilgasse until she becomes a dot.

"Let me explain it to you as best I can. When I was a little boy, our cook, a sturdy woman who never suffered fools or children gladly, would walk me to school every day. Our house was on Malé náměsti—you know it well, I'm sure, it separates the small town square from Old Town Square."

"Yes, of course."

"As an adult, I see now the walk was nothing, but as a little boy, it seemed like I was hiking the Camino de Santiago."

I snort.

"She'd walk me through the Old Town Square, past the astronomical clock surrounded by onlookers crowding its base, through the marketplace where the coal merchants, cobblers, glazers, milliners, and poulterers loudly announced their prices. Then we'd pass through the tiny alley next to the Our Lady Before Týn, and before us would be a selection of arcades, arches, and underpasses. Everyone would go for the far right arch where the public houses and brothels were located, but we would pass under the far left, which was always quiet and deserted, and led into Týnská street. Winding upward, I would hear the bells of Jakob's Kirche just to the south as we turned onto Masná street, which smelled like a butcher's bathtub. After what seemed like hours, we would finally arrive at my school."

"Yes, Franz, I know Prague like the back of my hand. Why are you telling me this?"

He gathers his breath before continuing. "One morning, as she was walking me to school, I saw an old beggar woman in the alley beside Our Lady Before

Týn. She was on all fours, head down almost in a puddle, holding a small cup above her head, praying for coins. I couldn't have been more than seven or eight years old, but I felt a kinship with her. I knew I had to give her something. I tugged on the cook's skirt hem, but she wouldn't let me stop to give her a Sechserl—it was ten kreuzers at the time. I realized then that maybe stopping was showmanship. It was perhaps drawing attention to what should be ignored, and I felt like a fool. Later that afternoon, as I was coming home from school, I broke the Sechserl down into ten coins at the Tabak. The old woman was still there, on her knees. So I gave her one coin, but I didn't stop for her to thank me. I would rather have died on the spot. Instead, I ran around the entire church, up Celetná street, where my father had a haberdashery shop, circled the rear, and went down to the beggar again, where I dropped a second coin into her cup."

"You didn't!"

"I did that ten times: dropping a coin, running around the corner, coming down the back bend, full circle, just to give her an entire shilling. Then I went home and cried into my pillow until my mother replaced the Sechserl."

"Franz." I place my hand on his forearm.

"So you see, as a child, I developed microscopic eyes, and once one has those, one is completely at a loss. Things roll around in my head, taking on a significance they shouldn't, until they don't make sense anymore."

"Darling, I know that. Don't forget all that we've exchanged in our letters. I know you. It's just that today... today you seem to be having a more acute attack of nerves and analyses, don't you think?"

He finally turns to look at me, placing his large square hands atop mine. "My dear, today is my birthday."

My mouth hangs open. "It is not!"

He nods. "It is."

"Why didn't—"

He looks away. "I didn't want to make a fuss."

"But—"

"Who over the age of sixteen actually enjoys birthdays anyway?" He waves his palm in the air as if to shoo away a birthday celebration. "Thirty-seven." He looks to me with eyes expecting revulsion. "Thirty-seven years old. My word, when I say it like that... It's sobering to think that when Mozart was my age, he'd been dead for two years."

"Hear, hear!" I cheer, and then pat his back when a tiny cough escapes.

"How old are you again?" he asks.

"Twenty, if you don't count Saturdays and Sundays."

"And if you do?"

"Almost twenty-four, but I still feel like I'm fourteen. That is, until I spend any time with fourteen-year-olds, then I realize that, no—never mind—I'm twenty-four."

He chuckles. "You are so silly, Milenka."

"I rely solely on caffeinated beverages and my silliness to get me through the day. Now, we must do something to celebrate."

"Oh, please, none of that, really." He holds up his hands.

"Pish posh." I look over as a hot car selling grilled bratwurst on a stick sets up near us. "What a delicious aroma." I inhale deeply the scent of cured meat and peppercorns. "Would you like one?"

"Oh no, I'm a strict vegetarian."

My, how I'm learning so much about him today. "Oh. How ... ascetic." I choose my words carefully. In these days of food shortages and hunger, he would deny himself even more. "Why?"

"It's a choice I think everyone has to make for themselves," is all he says. He has a look on his face, like he's been asked this question many times before and it grates on him.

"Is it easy to give up the temptations of—" I think of the most apt word "—of flesh?"

He looks at me. His eyes spike like the overture of *The Barber of Seville*. "It's easy for vegetarians, as they eat their own flesh."

I ponder that thought for quite some time, almost certain that we had never been talking about meat in the first place.

AS OUR SINGLE BICYCLE rolls along, we take the turn by Café Central rather sharply, bouncing and squeaking past the Herrenhof, Michaelerplatz, the Albertina and the opera house, until we're suddenly on the other side of the Ringstraße, racing around the verdigris patina of the Schiller monument in Schillerplat, and sputtering past the Secession Building. Traffic slows to a halt in front of the Secession Building every time. Even the horses pulling carriages and conveyances cannot help but admire it: the goldleaf dome that harkens back to Klimt and his portraits, the Ver Sacrum nameplate off to the side, which was the name of the Secessionists' magazine, and above the entrance the motto *Der Zeit ihre*

Kunst. Der Kunst ihre Freiheit—"To every age its art. To every art its freedom." The three gorgons of painting, architecture, and sculpture adorn the entrance.

We take the sharp turn by Karlsplatz and cut across Resselpark with the merry-go-round humming in the distance to its organ-grinding jingle. I say into Franz's ear, "Let's rest here for a bit," and the bicycle screeches to a halt. He leans it against the massive fountain pool in front of Karl's Kirche, and we buy two cones of flavoured shaved ice.

Franz holds my hand delicately as we walk under the side arches of Karl's Kirche and come out on the other side. His grip tightens as I take mouthfuls of my shaved ice. He brings my hand up to his chest and holds it. Holds it. Holds it. My fingers feel his cavity thump. I can't think of anything now.

The clouds are the brightest thing in the sky: milky, drifting in and over the city, dream-like. We are absolutely alone everywhere. I feel as if I can finally call this sprawling metropolis my home, finally map myself in this large, open space. Standing here with the city spiralling all around us, I cannot look at these massive estates and this towering domed cathedral without thinking, *What a good place for sexual intercourse*. I think I'm going through a temporary obsession. Temporary, even if it might last a lifetime.

As we stroll down Alleegasse and pass alongside a lengthy two-storey palais with massive windows flanked by pilasters and supported by colonnade balustrades, Franz stops to gawk. "Do you know what this is?" His eyes light up.

I shake my head.

"It's the home of the Wittgensteins."

My neck cranes to take it all in. "You don't say! They're the richest family in town."

"Them, and the Rothschilds."

I suddenly recall a bit of gossip I heard winding its way through the Herrenhof a few months ago. "Did you hear of the suicide of their eldest son, Karl?"

"No."

"He was an officer in the war," I lean in and whisper, "and his troops mutinied, so he shot himself in the head. A couple of weeks later the war was over. It's a tragedy."

"Didn't his brothers—"

I nod. "Yes, two of them. That makes three to die by suicide."

Franz looks up at the massive entrance portal before us. "Then I suppose it's true what they say—wealth can't buy happiness."

"Well, I'd give them an entire slice of my happiness just to spend an afternoon living in a palais like this. Can you imagine what it must look like inside?"

"Mmmm." He nods his head, looking up at the windows for any movement behind the curtains. "I have a hankering to see it."

Brilliance flashes before my eyes.

"What's that look?" he asks.

I take his shaved ice from his hand and dump it with mine on the sewer grate.

"Hey! What are you—"

I reach into my coin purse and bring out my ring of keys. I count the keys to my apartment block, to my apartment door, to the rear gate of the courtyard, and to the door to the roof, until finally—aha! The small brass key. "You want to see inside? Well, let's go in, shall we?"

"What in God's name—"

I lean in to inspect the buzzer panel. At the bottom is a small keyhole. Perfect.

"Milenka!"

I slip the key in the slot, jiggle it a bit to the left, and the front door buzzes automatically as it unlocks. "Shh! Come on!"

He grabs my extended hand and I yank him inside the front corridor, pushing the heavy door closed behind us. The corridor isn't lit, though a little light peeks in from the small stained-glass window above the door. The corridor leads to another door, presumably where the entrances to the palais and the servant's cottage deviate. The smell of baked bread and the echoing clanging of pots and pans suggest the palais kitchen in the basement is in the middle of a service. The squeaking of cables behind the walls is the telltale noise of a dumb waiter ascending and descending by rope and pulley. A few rows of letter boxes extend from the wall before the second door.

"Milena, where on earth did you—"

"Oh, this old thing?" I raise the key and an eyebrow. "Why, it's the master key to the city, my darling."

"How did you get it?"

"Haven't you ever wondered how the postman enters each apartment block to deliver the mail? They have a master key. It's the same in Prague. Every building, from tenement to villa, has been fashioned so that the postman can enter using the same bloody key. During the war, when we all fell upon hard times, and morals were somewhat looser, someone had the smarts to bribe a postman to borrow the key for a few hours. A copy was made. And then suddenly, the key spread across the city. Almost anyone with the merest degree of street smarts now has a copy."

"Including you."

"I can be very persuasive when I want to be, darling." I dance a brow up and down for effect.

"Of that I have no doubt." Franz looks at me with wonderment the size of the Arabian Desert. "Milenka, you continually surprise me. Your savvy doesn't end with the black-market café scene, clearly."

If only you knew the Affable Thief, I think, to my own amusement. I sneak my arms around his neck, and like an instinct, his hands find my ribcage, pulling me toward him.

"Happy birthday, Doktor Kafka," I whisper, and his mouth smashes over mine.

There is another world waiting between our bodies. A planet within a kiss. Pleasure and torture, sewn with the same thread. The joy of bodies together. I can feel his four fingers through mine. Cold, long, slender. His hand has been brought to me on a platter of lips and kisses. This is the moment all my scheming and seducing has been for; these four fingers are mine for as long as I please. I kiss them.

Our lips part and he catches his breath.

What I wanted in the forest yesterday was clandestine, pure, and innocent, but he wanted no part of that. What he wants is for his hands to be covered in grease from the bicycle chain and grime from gripping the handlebars. He wants a desolate entry corridor where opposing odours linger. He wants to smear his dirty fingerprints across my cheek. I see it in his eyes: the chance of being discovered, of being charged with an obscenity. The promise of disgrace quickens his pulse.

We cover each other's mouths, for what we are doing is creating enough echoes. His body is jolting, shivering, ticking. I tighten as he fattens. We stiffen, heads up in the air, legs weakened—suspended between skinfolds, softer than tongues, teeth, fingers. Flesh-deep.

I work my hands through his hair like they're tortured animals. I want to destroy him while he's inside me still. Riding upon his body to kill all girls he loved before me. Moving warrior-hard and hurtful. Wordless. My lover tastes of burned-down houses, loud symphonies, of first and last things.

Capsized. Flipped. Collapsed. His forehead soaks into my shoulder.

I am a destroyed woman. There is no point in writing another feuilleton anymore. I quit! No Ernst. No father. No dead mother and brother. There is only the aftermath of the war, Vienna, and Doctor of Law Franz Kafka.

13

Day Four

Warsaw under threat? Piłsudski's cry for help to Foch.
—Neues Wiener Tagblatt, *July 4, 1920*

The curtains beyond this bed bring shade and softness to his appearance. Light dances. Our bodies are pretzeled. He is one end of the wire and I am the other. One can't pull one without the other moaning. His skin carries scars like calligraphy, his fingers dented. I am fond of these things. Like corn in a husk, I want him to bite me so I can glisten in his teeth.

The sky beyond the window is filling with light, and from distant balconies comes the throaty rumble of pigeons settling and trams accelerating. We adjust to the light so we can doze another quarter of an hour, and he puts his arm around me. Legs intertwined. Fingers woven through hair. Pupils dilated. We're still now.

There is a power to standing still in a moment. I think

of that time when I was a young girl and we lived in the building on Na Příkopě at the base of Wenceslas Square—the former credit union building with the ungodly busts of men peering out from underneath the balustrades. From the balcony of our attic apartment, every sort of skirmish, gathering, scuffle, or, on this particular day, massacre could be witnessed. On Sundays, the Czechs and the Austrians were always milling about Wenceslas Square, but for the most part, they kept to their own. From opposite ends of the thoroughfare, they would mingle among themselves, share gossip, smoke cigars, buy roasted chestnuts, wolf whistle at a woman with a plunging décolletage, and sing folk songs to taunt their rivals.

My mother used to beat her carpets on our balcony; the *frap-frap-frap* was so constant you could dance to it. On this day, her *frap-frap-frapping* slowed to a halt, and my heartbeat did the same. I joined her on the balcony to see a group of Austrians marching along Na Příkopě from the Powder Tower at the far end, arms linked.

"What are they chanting, Mama?" I looked up at her, but she shook her head in confusion. She never learned to speak German.

In the street, the Czechs began to march from Wenceslas Square. Turning the corner from the Koruna palace, they hurled obscenities. Both sides had raised fists; both had bullets for eyes, spears for legs, cannons for voices. The gendarmerie suddenly appeared between them near the entrance to the old casino as each faction inched closer and closer to fisticuffs. The coppers told the Czechs to halt, but instead, the two groups continued forward. They were going to clash; it was inevitable. I gripped my mother's skirt in one hand and the iron baluster of the balcony with the other, smushing my face between the bars to see.

Shots fired. The coppers were firing into the crowd! They charged on their horses and beat down the Czechs with their batons. Screams flooded the high street; horror and fear bounced off façades, echoing toward us. We watched, helpless, from the balcony, as the streets emptied quickly, and all that was left on the cobbles were two figures. One was a man, shot down, crumpled on the ground like a discarded washcloth. The other figure was—I will always remember how my mother and I stood petrified with worry on the precipice—

"Papa!" I screamed, but my mother quickly wrapped my mouth with her palm and held me close.

My father stood calmly, as if he had been out for a stroll, as if he wanted to enjoy birdsongs and wind rustles for a moment longer, arms at his sides, for what felt like the length of a cold January. The coppers on their horses paused. The Austrians and their taunts fell silent. The Czech screams and scrambling feet were suddenly reduced to pitter-patters. My father then, as if blind to the melee around him, bent at the knees and began to wrap the wounds of the fallen man—more like human wreckage—in his cravat and handkerchief.

My mother cried and hugged me tight enough to crush my bones while we watched my father gather the man up in his arms and carry him inside his oral surgery on the first floor of our building. Relations between the Czechs and Austrians had always been fraught under Empirical rule, but for one still moment, compassion was the order of the day.

Franz stirs beside me, the light creeping up his face, the stillness broken, and his head lolls on the pillow to look at me.

"Milena," he whispers into my ear. I turn to him. "I have to get back."

"MILENA ... MILENA ... Milena." He repeats my name in a mumble as we walk toward the Westbahnhof.

I look up at him.

"Today, I can't say anything else," he says. "How could I? I have seen the future and it is Milena."

"I hope the train never comes," I say, as we cross the station's great hall and take the stairs to the platforms. July sunshine pours through the massive glass barricades and skylights. Steam billows from engines, whistles blow, men with parcels under their arms run after moving carriages. A man drags a wooden dolly across platform 9, filled with leather valises, hardshell suitcases, round hat cases, all adorned with tourist stickers: skiing in Innsbruck, canoeing in Salzburg. There is so much happening around us, and even more inside of us.

"Damen und herren!" the station attendant bellows from his soapbox, and we strain our ears to hear over the squeal of locomotive breaks and footfalls clomping across the marble hallway.

"Track 5," I repeat after the announcement. "For Prague."

He puts his suitcase down at our feet and takes both my hands in his. We look at each other, eyelids dancing.

"How long until you get home?"

"About sixteen hours. We will have to alight for a few hours for control inspection at the border. Usually in Gmünd."

I nod and nod and nod. I cannot seem to do anything except nod and die inside. "I don't know when I'll see you again." I bite my lip to keep my voice from shaking.

"In truth, neither do I." His fingers rub my palm—those long goddamned fingers. "I must have a chat with Julie..."

"Yes, of course." My nose stings.

From somewhere deep inside the station tearoom, where travellers order hot drinks, salty pretzels, and sweet cakes, and organize black-market trading, a piano is playing Chopin's "Nocturne No. 15 in F minor."

His low voice cuts through the nocturne. "These four days have been—"

"Yes."

"More than I ever—"

"I know."

"I don't know when we can—"

"No."

"But," he says as his fingers reach up and lightly caress my lower lip as it trembles, my eyes glossy, vision blurry, "in spite of everything, I cannot help but believe that if a person, designated to die, can stay alive through happiness, then I will stay alive."

Hot tears fall from my eyes like stones. They speckle my face, tracing lines down to my chin, where they collect in diamond droplets.

"Milena," he repeats in a low moan, and pulls me into

a kiss. Our lips are soft at first, grazing each other, but then something bursts aflame inside me, and my body arches into him, my hands gripping his collar. His hands are at the small of my back, pulling me in, snuffing out any air between us.

I gasp as our lips break, everything is dizzying. People push past us, clambering to track 5. The platform conductor bellows the call for boarding. Franz and I cannot break our eyes from each other.

"How about that," he breathes, holding my face in his palms. "Look. The sunlight dims by itself. Not because of the clouds."

Don't go! my mind is screaming, but I can't bring myself to say it to him. *Don't leave me here in this forsaken city with my hellish husband. Don't take from me everything that I cannot live without.*

He bends down to pick up his valise. "I'll write to you soon."

I nod and nod and nod. He inspects my face like a treasure map. "As I live and breathe—does Milena Jesenská finally have nothing to say?" A smile tugs at his lips.

I let out a surprised chortle.

"Stop the presses"—his finger traces the lines of my profile—"we have a scoop."

He turns on his heel, and before I can call out to him, he hurries into a gallop down the platform before the barrier comes down and disappears inside a berth. From one of the iron beams overhead, a clattering of jackdaws squawks and chirps, before spreading their wings in a flock to follow the train as it lurches forward and out of sight.

* * *

I CLIMB THE STAIRWELL at Lerchenfelderstraße with shoes made of cinderblocks. I am heaving air. I eat it like a locust. Slamming the door behind me, I drop my key on the credenza and stand in the darkness. I look into the shadows and hear the clock ticking in the hall, enveloped in the best of silences.

There is movement beyond the shadows. A figure, large and imposing, steps forward.

Ernst's eyes are the shape of bricks, bright as mud. He looks at me with boil and steam.

I match him. "What?" I snap.

Like lightning, he closes the gap between us and his hand grips my throat, thumbing my chin so I stay put. I strain against his hand, but it only tightens. My veins jut and mingle with his bones. Thoughts of choking to death. I gasp and release a wail as his fingers dig painfully into my neck. He hooks his thumb around my windpipe, strangling my throat. Lungs squeak. Eyes burst out of their sockets. Blood vessels explode. His face hovers over mine, chin above chin, eyes leering down at me. A power struggle he swiftly wins. Nightmare upon nightmare.

"I could destroy you," he breathes.

"But you won't," I gurgle.

"Oh no?"

This comment lingers. I scan his eyes for lies. For a tell. For a moment's hesitation.

"I'm sorry, am I supposed to be afraid?"

"Where the hell have you been?!"

His fingers plunge deeper, and my yelps through

gritted teeth betray my resolve. I am unable to shift from under him. His ruthlessness is infectious. It's the pain I want to feel. I want to be killed by the pain while being eaten from inside. Ernst should destroy the few remnants of humanity that Franz left behind inside me. He could torch me and all that would remain would be singe marks on bedsheets, my body outline on the alabaster stone of these walls.

But he lets go and I stumble backward. My gasping lungs tear at my esophagus. My gullet contracts and my hands go to my chest.

"Where do you think I was?" I screech when I can finally breathe again.

He doesn't move. He just stands in the corridor, his back to me, staring at the wall of doors, the china hutch, the light fixtures.

"At first I thought you might be with Hermann Broch," he says over his shoulder.

"Hermann!"

"I saw the looks between you two."

"Ernst, I hate him!"

"Yes, he confirmed as much."

"You spoke to him? What did he say?"

"That there was a kiss at the Metropol."

"*He* kissed me! I didn't kiss him back."

"Please, spare me the story of two lips that pass in the night."

"He's a bigot and a bore."

"Remind you of anyone?"

I blink. "Who are you ..." He clenches his jaw, and his brows drop to his lashes. "Is this about my father?"

His face bears the expression of a wounded toddler.

"Did my father write to you?"

"An alarming report reached me from the Favoriten district."

My eyes widen.

"You were seen several times entering and exiting the decrepit Hotel Riva. Is this true?"

There is a rat somewhere, but who? The concierge? Herr Emil? Was it the owner of the Hungarian public house across the way?

"Someone wrote to my father. Who, in turn, wrote to you?"

"Your father would rather shit in his hands and clap before speaking to a pious Jew like me, but Paní Kohler handed me this telegram this morning." He pulls it out of his breast pocket. "It seems the one thing your father and I have in common is a deep shame when it comes to your behaviour."

I jump forward. "Give it here!"

He whips the postcard high above his hairline.

"What does he suspect me of?"

Ernst raises a brow.

"What do *you* suspect me of?"

"First the Metropol, and now the Riva. What else am I to think?"

I stay silent.

"Are you whoring, Milena?"

"How bloody well dare you?!"

"How dare I?!"

"That's sickening!"

"Is that a no?"

"How could you even think this of me? I'm your wife."

"You're a thief, Milena! So why shouldn't I suspect you of being a whore?"

"Because whoring is your job."

The force of the slap slams my face against the wall. The rumble of the tram on the street shakes the whole building.

There's a shotgun in my chest. It has started beating. A spear pointed at my gut. It wants the violence, the destruction. It wants to spear me, splay me, spread me out like a black sky over churning sea. Capsize me. Beat me up so I can lick my wounds.

"Is that it?" I scoff, breath short and quick. "Is that all you have to offer? Go on, hit me again, Pollak."

His back straightens with indignance. But he doesn't strike me a second time.

"I feel sorry for you."

He turns and heads toward his bedchamber. "Be at home waiting for me the next time I return from Prague," is all he says before slamming the door behind him.

I drop to the floor; a tiny slit under my nostril fills with blood. It seethes red, mingling with a wetness that smells like sweat.

14

Scars

PRAGUE

1939

The stench of rotting horses and mules filled the air. They were a frequent target during the pogroms, so the SS piled up the putrid carcasses in the Pankrác Prison courtyard—a subtle but effective act of torture upon the prisoners. The groans of wounded women and the awful screams from the gang rapes were carried on the gales that whipped through the lower corridors. Milena's instinct was to cover her nose and ears, but she wouldn't give the Obergruppenführer the satisfaction.

"Tell me about the Veleslavín insane asylum, Frau Jesenská."

"What would you like most to hear? I can regale you with stories about the doctors and nurses and orderlies and some of the other more colourful patients, but something tells me that's not what you're really asking."

"You were confined there on the 20th of June 1917 for moral insanity."

"It's a pretty nonsensical charge, don't you think?"

"I think it's the most accurate description I've read of you yet."

"My father was frustrated with me."

"For all the burglaries."

"Thieving here and there was just window-dressing."

"What is that supposed to mean?"

"It was just a way to decorate an emptiness with fickle thrills."

"Perhaps you felt empty because you had made the obscene choice to murder the baby growing in your womb. Although considering your baby was the son of a pig, I find myself in the unwelcome position of agreeing with you on this point."

Milena rubbed the scars on her wrists and kept her eyes lowered as the Obergruppenführer pulled his Italian cigarettes out of his trouser pocket and his Zippo out of the other. As he puffed, his smoke rose up forever. As the silence absorbed the air, she glanced up, waiting for another question, but he simply sat there, dragging on the end of his smoke and staring at her. She watched as the stream ascended to the low ceiling and split apart upon contact. She tried to rearrange and tidy up the puffs with her mind.

The more he stared, the more uncomfortable she grew. Smacking his insults back at him like a volleyball over the net with a good spin was nothing to her, but silence was where the Devil finds his playthings.

"Do you know who else was confined to the Veleslavín insane asylum, Frau Jesenská?" he finally said, tapping his cigarette gently. Ash tumbled down in little clusters to the floor, warm from the bodies that had lain on it.

"Were they also accused of moral insanity?"

"No, just good, old-fashioned lunacy."

"I'm afraid I'm at a loss."

He dragged on his smoke again. "I find I'm asking myself whether to actually reveal this to you. I wouldn't want to cause a crisis of conscience."

"Why the sudden care for my well-being?"

"Because it's a name from the past."

"My past?"

"Yes."

"The past is the past."

"Ah, but that's where you're wrong." He smiled. "The past is never finished with us. It isn't even the past."

Milena tilted her head and narrowed her eyes. "What sort of hollow double-talk is this?"

The Obergruppenführer blunted his cigarette butt on the leg of his chair, leaned forward, and hissed each syllable with the pleasure of a feeding viper. "Julie Wohryzek."

"The Girl?" Milena blinked.

"After Kafka callously left her for you, she went mad." He blew the last of the smoke in his lungs to the ceiling and grinned like the Cheshire cat. "Oh. You didn't know?"

She sucked on air like a leech, but nothing came. Shaking her head no, she looked down at her scars again.

"I'm terribly sorry to be the one to break it to you."

"I bet you are," she mumbled.

"Do you know what we do with the insane, Frau Jesenská?"

"Encourage them to join the Nazi party, then lavish them with official titles?"

He leered. "We sterilize them."

She met his eyes; she couldn't tear them away. But no words came forth.

The Obergruppenführer rose from his seat, clasped his hands behind his back, and strolled the length of the room once again. "We performed this procedure on Fraulein Wohryzek, but I'm afraid even after many treatments, we simply couldn't Germanize her. And if she is incapable of rehabilitation, well..."

"Yes?" she called down the length of the room, to his back. "Where is she?"

He sauntered back like the sun was on his shoulders. "Don't worry, she's currently being taken someplace safe."

"Safe?"

"For her own protection."

Milena pursed her lips. She could feel the bile rising in her throat and the explosive temper that always got her into trouble threatening to blow. "What in God's name does any of this have to do—"

"Do you think I haven't seen the scars on your wrists?" he barked.

Without hesitation, the tears tumbled from her eyes like pebbles.

Dragging his chair by the heels right up to hers, he slammed it down and sat with his mouth hissing into her ear. "Do you know what we found when we raided your flat? We know of your drug dependencies, Frau Jesenská. The cocaine. The opiates. We even found a stash of morphine-like tablets."

"They're for my bad knee," she stammered out.

"You're feeble, mentally infirm, addicted to illicit drugs, and you're prone to fits of mania. We have a special place in the Reich for people like you."

"Please, Herr Obergruppenführer!" she cried. "I have a daughter! A beautiful daughter and she's only eleven! Please don't make her grow up without a mother."

"Honza? The daughter born of your second husband, Jaromír, who was also a Jew-rat?"

"No!" she bellowed.

"Half-breeds are just as much a threat to the Reich as full-blooded Jews. She will be done away with, just like you."

When Milena leapt from her chair, her elbow made contact with the Obergruppenführer's chin. He stumbled back in shock, but when she pounced on him again, he grabbed her wrist and kicked her in her bad knee, causing her to cry out as she sank to the ground. Slamming her body down, he found her neck with his foot. "Tiger, tiger!" he hissed in amusement. "You want a little roughhousing, do you?"

Her breath truncated, she gasped and tried to yank his foot off her jugular, but the pressure only increased. Eyes bulging, veins popping, she knew this was how she would die. Under the boot of the heel-clicking, goose-stepping Butcher of Prague.

15

The Herrenhof

VIENNA

1920

In his latest epistle, Franz writes that he has had a word with the Girl, as he refers to his fiancée, Julie. They were walking in the Karlovo Náměsti park in the heart of Prague where he told her of our time together. As he spoke of his love for me, the Girl began to tremble. She was so devoted to Franz, she said, she could not imagine a life without him and proclaimed that she couldn't leave him unless he was sending her away. Was he? He was blunt, abrupt, and just said yes. Naturally she became a neurotic wreck. She said she couldn't let him leave her, especially not for someone like me who was hopelessly in love with her husband and was just using him.

Franz alludes to some choice words she had for me. But then, the letter takes an unexpected turn. She wanted to write to me.

And he gave permission for such an inappropriate act.
No, no, no, no, noooooooo.

My dearest Frau Pollak
You can have no doubt as to why I am writing to you. It was at the behest of our mutual friend, Franz Kafka, that I seek your acquaintance. A tale of the most upsetting substance has reached me, and I thought it paramount to approach you directly, rather than let this news spread throughout our mutual social circles. Doktor Kafka is my beloved and my intended, and while I know you must hold him in the highest regard and esteem, I do hope you know that he also is duty-bound to me, as well as hopelessly in love with me. I do appreciate that friendships among those in the same profession are natural, but considering your marriage, do you not see how your time together constitutes not only a lack of propriety, but a deeply hurtful blow to my feelings and wishes?

I was engaged once before to a lovely man of the highest order, but he was killed in the war. Doktor Kafka has brought so much joy into my life, and although our engagement was officially postponed last year, we have continued our relationship despite our different social standings. This postponement is not indefinite, I assure you.

Rather than make an enemy of you, I would hope you would cease any untoward dealings with Doktor Kafka and realize that we could all be dear friends instead. I would hate to have a low opinion of you, when I have heard nothing but praise from our mutual friends, and those in Prague who read your column with fervour speak to the brilliance of your talent. But I have not yet seen such attributes in you and would not wish for this to continue.

Please do me the honour of responding at once.

From your new correspondent,

Fraulein Wohryzek.

Why that sly little tit-bag.

I don't even sit down at the typewriter or reach for a crisp piece of foolscap. I take her letter, flip it over, and write my response on the back. Let her have her own words back. Let her choke on the damn things.

Fraulein Julie,

My advice to you would be to leave him at once. He has never mentioned you; in fact, I had no idea you existed until this very letter.

I'm so very sorry to read you have such a low opinion of me. But I must admit to you, my dear, that opinions are very much like a sexual climax—once I've had mine, I don't give a damn about yours.

Frau Jesenská

I want to be cruel, to destroy all the innocents of the world, like I once was, and spare them the pain of learning these lessons too late in life.

ON THE 15TH OF July, I receive a telegram from Franz. The Girl showed him my letter and then walked out of his life. She runs a millinery shop in the Olsanska neighbourhood, and Franz has asked his sister Ottla to buy a hat or two from her—I suspect to assuage his guilt rather than out of any devotion or love for her.

It begins to dawn on me that I don't feel victorious. Revenge has a rather bitter taste, as it turns out. Instead, I am furious at Franz.

The moon is coming through the window, a silent warrior. Beyond, traffic and dogs can be heard echoing through the narrowness of the silent streets of night. The city seethes with its own wounds. My brain feels as if it has been surgically split and then sutured—yellowing rot, septic with fresh sorrows, seeps out and I cannot hide it.

As I put pen to paper, I figure our love is very much like diving into the waters of the Danube, where I touch the muddy bottom, holding myself down until my lungs burst and my neck snaps, wondering when he will join me down there, and what he will say.

My darling,

I have a bakery at the end of my street that I go to daily and there's someone there who could play you on the stage. Not a twin, but he reminds me of you. He may be a cousin. Every day, when I bite into my croissant and drink my tea, I think of you. I miss our daily communions. I don't know how I'm going to survive with you across a border. I don't know how you're going to stand it when you come back to Vienna—either to see me or for your business affairs. In either case, you're bound to be accosted. Oh Franz, how can anyone stay away from your doorstep once they've seen the steely set of your chin and the blank unfeeling cast of your face? I suppose if people—and by that I mean young girls with amorous looks and shops full of hats—set themselves up so exquisitely to be dropped and finished, you might as well get paid for doing the dirty work. You might end up unhappy. But who's happy anyway?

I love how you have disguised yourself. Love is a fight where I get a fat lip and I cannot remember if it was from a kiss or a smack. It's where I scar myself with passion. What else can I do? What else is there to do?

My husband is growing plump on stuffed tomatoes, roast hare, salmon, ground coffee, beer, open sandwiches, potatoes, and red cabbage, but I am emaciated with worry—worry that I have betrayed him. What is it about this city that makes fools of us all? In Prague I was loyal and devoted, but in this city of black bread and sauerkraut, I toss all my responsibilities.

Tell me, my darling, should I be ashamed of what we have done?

For I tell you, I know I have his love, but I would rather he told me he cared about me. "I care about you" is a declaration that you can hang your coat on—dependable, sturdy, and lasts an eternity. "I love you" lasts until the evening, when someone with florid hair takes the spotlight, and then he finds her hideous and vile the next morning when she stirs on the pillow. "I love you" can mean anything. Or nothing. What I'm saying is: I've learned after two years of marriage that loving my husband isn't as significant as caring about him, enjoying his company, and looking forward to the moment he returns from work at the end of the day.

And the problem with love and monogamy is that it doesn't solve everything. All the other follies and dalliances continue, and then we get on each other's nerves. "Why do I still want to tear the clothes off that other person who is not you?" rolls around in the brain, for example.

The best we can hope for is to not get a horrible disease, and that none of our lovers write novels about us.
Milena

There is a knock at my bedchamber door. I place the letter and the pen on to the cold side of the bed. "Come in, Paní Kohler."

The door swings open, but the figure in silhouette is far too rotund and balding to be my beloved surrogate mother.

"Oh. Hello."

"Are you well?" Ernst asks.

"Yes." I run two fingers along my lip; the bruising and swelling has receded, but I don't dare push down on the skin. It would leave an imprint for days. "Come in."

Ernst steps forward—one step, two steps—but no farther. He looks about my room and shoves his hands in his pockets. He takes in the dirty teacups, the bloomers thrown to the floor, piles of crumpled-up newspapers from last week staining the bedsheets with inky-black splotches. I could drag myself out of bed, but that would suggest something I'm not ready to admit. I cannot meet him halfway, not even physically.

"I'm going to the Herrenhof tonight," he says flatly.

"The Herrenhof," I repeat.

"Yes, the gang's all there. Werfel. Blei. Broch. Gina and Otto Kaus. The Lederers. The Zuckerkandls. Alma Mahler might even make an appearance. That's the rumour anyway."

"Okay. Enjoy yourself."

"Would you care to join me?"

The question hangs in the air between us, and it is a good one. Would I? I don't know.

I shrug my shoulders. "That would be fine." I look about the room. "Sure. I just need to—"

"Yes, of course," he steps backward toward the door-frame, "there's no hurry. Take your time."

"Before you go," I call him back into the room. "Could you lend an eye to my head?"

Ernst tilts his head. "Your head?"

"Yes, my ear, here, see?" I angle my ear toward his general direction and point at the hole. "Is my brain oozing out of my head?"

In the dim light, his eyes are almost black with anger. He can see he won't be forgiven anytime soon, and that I will make him swim in regret until his skin prunes.

"You've gone crazy," he says.

I narrow my eyes at him, staring at the mess of his eyebrows as they rise. I try to tidy them with my stare. "I was never sane."

ALMA MAHLER DOES INDEED make an appearance at the Herrenhof. She links arms with Werfel, sharing the table with Blei and his quiet wife, Maria, newly divorced surgeon Otto Zuckerkandl, art collectors August and Serena Lederer, the fashion-designing Flöge sisters, Emilie and Helene, architect Josef Hoffmann, and to my surprise, Secession artist Oskar Kokoschka. Alma seems to be doing her best not to catch Oskar's attention, focusing all she has on Werfel. Everyone knows about their once-torrid love affair that she unceremoniously put to death. Oskar, deep in conversation with August Lederer about a commission, keeps laughing rather obnoxiously, then looking in Alma's direction to see if she's noticed. Ernst once told me that Oskar is so desperately in love with her that he fashioned a life-sized doll and named it Alma. I shudder just thinking of it.

Alma, though poised and friendly, has tired eyes. Her decree nisi from Walter Gropius was finally granted, after years of her openly cavorting with Werfel, but I don't think that's what is weighing on the lines of her face, the flat nub of her chin, the black tufts of hair snowballing out of her hairpins. No, the woman has suffered a great loss. Her young son, not even a year old, died not long ago. Coupled with the loss of her first daughter with Gustav Mahler about a decade ago, I dare say Alma seems to be absorbing all the extremes of life—the beauty, the tragedy, the rapturous adoration, and the bitter disappointment. She holds tight to Werfel, as if her grip will spare him any misfortune. Looking at her, I fear that the lines in her face will soon be mirrored in mine, her pain a map to my future.

As Ernst and I join the gang, I noticed Blei and Maria looking in the opposite direction, almost as if they're ignoring me. Blei's increasingly balding scalp and massive spectacles with frames the shape of Roman coins make him look even more antiseptic and severe than usual. Gina and Otto Kraus are absent, and so, blissfully, is Hermann Broch, the ruffian. Emilie is noticeably sitting as far away from Alma as possible, as both of them were once lovers of Klimt, but neither of them can speak his name now that he's gone. Emilie and Helene are wearing the most striking kaftan-like dresses, dresses they've designed themselves for their fashion house on the Mariahilferstraße. There's not a waistline or a neckline to be seen, only bare shoulders, messy up-dos, and figureless forms that look almost boyish. They might be the future of fashion for the 1920s, but I dare say they look mighty unfeminine to me. No matter, as the Flöge sisters would never strike up a conversation with pitifully dressed little me. But Zuckerkandl and Serena and I exchange pleasantries while Ernst calls over the waiter Anton-Moritz, or whatever name he's going by these days, to order our meals.

For himself, Ernst orders pan-friend butterfish with coriander risotto garnished with saffron. For me, he orders the Wiener Krautfleckerl, which is just Viennese square noodles with white cabbage, but it is mouthwateringly seasoned with peppercorns, capers, lemon zest, and crushed kosher salt. The noodles are so thin and fine I could read Franz's love letters through them. Ernst almost never buys my plate of food, and my hunger has eaten away at more than just my stomach. I do not come up for air until I have finished the last morsel.

"Good heavens, Frau Pollak," Alma says as my plate is cleared away, "you certainly did well for yourself there."

Holding my serviette up to my lips, I look around the table to see everyone stifling a snicker or a grin. The hot flush of embarrassment rises in my cheeks.

"Oh dear, I meant nothing by it." Alma laughs and tugs tighter on Werfel's arm. "Don't look like such a terrified shrew." Once again, I am the butt of everyone's jokes.

Outside the clip-clop of horseshoes on cobbles as the animals trot around Michaelerplatz echoes up the road.

Pewter serving trays clash and clang as they are stacked inside the dumb waiter and sent down to the dish washer. An electric coffee grinder whirrs into action. Liquids of all kinds—water, Apfelschorle, black tea, cream, and white wine—are slowly poured from carafes throughout the café. Maybe if I focus on the hubbub of my surroundings, this humiliation will fade into the background.

Werfel elbows Blei and they both roll their eyes.

"Now, now," Ernst pipes up, placing his hand atop mine. "I appreciate a woman with an appetite."

"Let's hope those appetites don't run afoul." Alma grins, winking at Werfel.

"She wouldn't be my wife if they didn't," Ernst says. I look at him, utterly confused. I wish I were treated in private to this mask he only wears for the public. This is the Ernst that I so desperately need most days. "A toast," he raises his wineglass, and the table does the same, "to my healthy wife, who gave up the attentions of many men for the inattention of one."

"Pollak!"

"Hilarious!"

"I'll drink to that!"

"Prost, my good man!"

Glasses clink and spirits are raised before I've even had a chance to take in what has just happened. Everyone seems jolly, like this has been well-intentioned and good-natured ribbing after all. I'm smiling, and my husband is smiling at me. He leans across his armrest and plants a kiss on my lips, in front of our entire table, though it might as well be the entire world. He has never kissed me in public before. He has always said he finds such displays to be child's play and the talisman of impropriety. But when he pulls away, he's the cat who got the cream.

"Quick, Milena," Werfel barks across the table, "what does he taste like?"

I don't break eye contact with Ernst when I say, "A substandard Sauvignon."

Werfel slaps the table and everyone cackles.

"I dare say," Blei says, after an eternity of brooding, "it used to be that women dropped a handkerchief when they wanted a man's attention. Now they drop their necklines."

"Or in Werfel's case, they drop weight," I retort.

"I'll have you know," Alma interjects, "that I am the same dress size today as I was a decade ago."

"Oh, I didn't mean your dress size, Alma. I meant your previous marriage. You surely must feel ninety kilos lighter. Although considering you've now made your way through two husbands, that figure should no doubt be doubled."

"Milena, if there's one thing I've learned, it's that one needs to run wild in this life and open one's heart to many different possibilities."

"Oh, Milena knows all about opening herself up to possibilities," Blei counters, "except in her case, she's opening her legs."

In the next booth over, a spoon drops to the floor.

Our table falls silent, everyone's eyes linger on their drinks, and no one looks anyone in the eye. Except for Blei and me; our stare could set fire to brimstone.

"Blei, I think that was somewhat of a breach of taste," Werfel says. What an understatement.

"It comes from a place of concern." He gives Werfel an innocent shrug.

"My dear Franz Blei," I say through gritted teeth, "have you had the occasion to write to Prague recently?"

He doesn't look away. "Why, yes, I have. To many people of all shapes and sizes."

"Any of those shapely people happen to be my father?"

"As a matter of fact, yes." He folds his arms over his chest and heaves one leg over the other. "But I'm afraid he doesn't send his regards."

"Milena!" Ernst catches my chair as it almost hits the ground when I push it back violently.

"Blei, as your bald head proves, it is entirely possible to come out on top and still be a loser." I toss my serviette across the table; it skids and slides, but I have dashed to the ladies powder room before it comes to rest. I drop my knickers, sit on the commode, and bury my head in my hands. Blei is a horrible cretin of the lowest order; he has very nearly ruined everything.

And what's worse, I deserve it.

My womb swells and simmers and gurgles. I thought I'd stopped menstruating the day Franz left, but now I'm spotting. And I welcome it. I will sit here and drip into the bowl until I drain the life out. Until I can feel how my mother felt. Until I can see in the swirl of red and toilet water something resembling my life.

I lean my head against the stall wall. I will sleep here if necessary.

I stare at the blood-soaked undergarments between my thighs for a long time. The absorbed blood is arranged quite neatly. Concentrated swirls. Concentric circles.

Darker areas like shading. Contours smooth. In the lines of the blood, I see a face. A face that knows all my secrets.

And he's smiling at me.

This thought makes me rise, pull up my garments, and clamour out of the stall as though it's contagious. The vanity mirror reflects a frenzied woman with turmoil sucking her insides out. I feel clotted. My blood is now as cold and dry as the blood that once engorged Franz like a darting sea lion.

As I step outside the ladies', I crash headfirst into Ernst's chest.

"Judas!"

"I didn't mean to startle you. Are you all right?"

I sweep out the wrinkles in my blouse, and then place a palm to my forehead. "Yes."

"Your cheeks are flushed."

"I'm just hot."

"Forget about Blei, he's a miscreant."

"To say the least."

"Especially when he's had a drink or two."

"He thinks he's the bee's knees."

"I don't mean to cast aspersions, but Maria might leave him, and he doesn't care. He longs for the bachelor life again."

"Ha! I wish I had the confidence of a middle-aged bald man. I would consider myself irresistible no matter the circumstance. And you, Ernst." I look up at him; his rosacea spreads like pink ink blots across his face. "Do you long for the bachelor life again?"

He carefully raises a finger and traces the small bruise by my lip that I've mostly covered with powder and cold cream. The mottled yellow-purple lines poke out stubbornly from the concealment. "Not for the wide world."

He draws me into his arms, and I burrow my face in the nook of his neck. Perhaps there is a vestige of love still left in him. I will stay buried in his warm flesh, unable to breathe, until my lungs cannot withstand the pressure, until they splinter and flake off, leaving me bare to the world.

16

Come Back

VIENNA

1920

I am reclining on the davenport in the sitting room when Paní Kohler hands me a sizable stack of letters and telegrams from Franz. The postage date tells me that most were sent before I managed to trot up to Bennogasse to mail him my first reply in days, but there is a telegram from this morning as well. Today I attempted to draft outlines and notes for my translations of *The Metamorphosis*, "The Judgement," and *The Meditation*, but instead I flopped down on the davenport, still in my negligee, and stared at the ceiling for an hour.

I rip open the newest telegram and begin to read.

> YOUR LETTER HAS FRIGHTENED ME OUT OF THE COMPARATIVE CALM WHICH STILL REMAINED FROM OUR BEING TOGETHER...

"What's that you've got there?" Ernst suddenly appears in the salon and sits in the armchair next to the liquor cabinet, shaking me out of Kafka's world.

"Oh, these—" I look down at the envelopes, as if they might contain the explanation I'm searching for, "are letters from Prague."

"The *Tribuna* again?"

"Yes." What an excellent lie. "My editor at the *Tribuna*, responding to my story ideas and proffering some notes. You know how it is."

"Well, don't let me keep you," he says, but sits there, nonetheless.

Unsure whether this is a trick, I slowly pull my eyes away from him and back down to Kafka.

FORGIVE THE NONSENSE OF THE ELEVEN LETTERS, THROW THEM ASIDE ...

"Paní Kohler!" Ernst bellows like a town crier.

She sticks her head out from the larder, wiping her hands on her apron. "Sir?"

"Was there any post addressed to me?"

"Aye, sir, remember I told you about it this morning?"

Ernst chuckles. "I must have still been sleeping!" When he laughs, the back of his throat slaps against itself as though he's trying to swallow a rubber ball in one gulp. It's grotesque and mesmerizing in equal measure. "Tell me, dear, what was my reply?"

"You asked me to put them on the credenza near the entryway, sir."

"Right you are!" He leaps up and disappears around the lip of the wall.

I look down again:

THE ONLY THING TO FEAR AT THE MOMENT IS, I THINK, THE LOVE FOR YOUR HUSBAND...

"Voilà!" Ernst reappears holding his correspondence. He harumphs back into the armchair and the seat cushion makes a sizable *whoooooosh* as his rear end suffocates the trapped air. He flips through the envelopes, eyeing the postage dates and the return addresses.

YOU HAVE NOT BETRAYED HIM, FOR YOU LOVE HIM, AND IF WE SHOULD UNITE (I THANK YOU, SHOULDERS!), IT WOULD BE ON ANOTHER LEVEL, NOT WITHIN HIS DOMAIN...

"Paní Kohlerrrrr!"

Her head pokes out again like a gopher from a dark hole. "Sir?"

"My letter opener, if you please!"

She trots across the sitting room and opens the drawer to the hall side table. She rifles around, clanging keys and coins with Ernst's automatic lighter, before slamming the drawer shut empty-handed.

"Try my rolltop desk!" he yips over his shoulder.

Stomp-stomp-stomp-stomp.

Screeeeeeeeeeeeee.

Shuffle, rifle, shuffle, rifle.

"Maybe my bedside table drawer?" he yips again, his voice bouncing off the floor like a rabid dog.

Ka-chunk! Thack!

Stomp-stomp-stomp-stomp.

Screeeeeeeeeeee.

"Found it!"

Stomp-stomp-stomp-stomp.

She hands it to him, red-faced.

"What would I do without you, Paní Kohler?"

She disappears back into the pantry, and Ernst wields the letter opener in one hand.

Fwwwirrrrrrrrrrrrrp.

"Milena, darling, why is there murder in your eyes?"

I give myself a shake. "You're just . . . quite distracting."

He guffaws. "Just ignore me, darling."

"I've been endeavouring to for two years," I mumble under my breath.

He mocks me with laughter. "This is why I love you, Milena! You're the nicest, sweetest, most rage-filled person I know."

He finally turns his attention to his correspondence. I roll my eyes and do the same.

DON'T UNDERESTIMATE THE ENERGIES YOUR CLOSENESS GIVES ME ...

I look up, expecting Ernst to interrupt me in the most infuriating manner, but he's embroiled in his letter. I exhale and turn to the stack of older letters from Franz, ripping open the oldest one, sent last week.

> Today nothing at all. You said that you would write again immediately, and you haven't written. I told myself, "She doesn't want you, she has worries and doubts." How dark Vienna has become, and it had been so bright for four days...

Ernst sniffles, and then inhales sharply, but he doesn't say anything as he reads.

> Some malignant devil must be holding your letters. I sent a telegram to Paní Kohler. No answer either. You don't have to be afraid that I'll write to your husband; I don't actually have any great desire to do so. The only desire I have is to come back to Vienna...

I blink and reread that line again.

> I sent a telegram to Paní Kohler...

I hear Paní Kohler's name called, but rather than shrieking from my lips, it's from Ernst again. She emerges from the pantry, a slick of grease on her chin. "Sir?"

"You're here rather late, aren't you? Shouldn't you be getting back to your family?"

"Yes, sir, if you no longer need me, sir."

"So diligent and dedicated, that's why you're so indispensable to us."

"Thank you, sir."

"Give my regards to your husband."

Paní Kohler wipes her hands on her apron, disappears back into the pantry, and then reemerges without her dishrag and apron. She walks to the hall wardrobe, grabs her umbrella and hat, and makes her way to the front door.

I leap up from the davenport. "Let me see her out," I toss off meekly to Ernst, who is hardly paying attention.

Paní Kohler is reaching for the doorknob when I put my hand atop hers and hold her forcefully. "Did you receive a telegram?" I whisper.

"I beg your pardon?"

I look over her shoulder to see if Ernst has heard us, and of course he hasn't. I whisper again a little louder. "From Doktor Kafka. Did you receive a telegram from Doktor Kafka in Prague?"

Paní Kohler looks at me with a blank expression on her face, and then her brow drops. She clenches her jaw and wiggles her hand out from underneath mine. "Your correspondence is your business, meine Dame," she says as she yanks open the door, "and my correspondence is mine."

The door slams behind her, and I can hear her footfalls descending the spiral staircase until they blend with the indistinct echoes of the street and the city. As I stand facing the closed door, the rejection stings until it's all I can feel.

ERNST LIGHTS THE CIGARETTE between my lips; the glow of the tip reflects in his irises. I take a few puffs and then pick a small piece of tobacco off my tongue. Ernst rises from bed, a line of sweat descending from the nape of his neck to the curve of his lower spine and grabs his robe. Wrapping it but not tying it, he walks to the lavatory and, with the door wide open, relieves himself.

Saliva still on my nipples, I get a blast of cold air from the open window and throw the bedsheets over my body. The cigarette smoke rises to the ceiling in slow swirls. I reach up with my finger and draw shapes in the stream.

"One of the letters I received today is from the managing director of the bank," Ernst calls from the lavatory, his voice echoing off the tiles.

"Oh?" I call back.

"The inflation will continue unabated if foreign powers don't intervene and save Austria," he calls back. "The manager on duty wrote to tell me that, should push come to shove, my position at the bank might not be sustainable for more than five years."

I sit up. "What does that mean?"

I hear the gush of the toilet and running water. Ernst's silhouette appears in the doorway before he does. "It means the bank cannot print money fast enough to keep up with the rising inflation. Soon, even a twenty-crown note will be worthless. Austria is in a tailspin. And I don't want to be here when it all goes tits up."

He climbs into bed next to me, flopping his face on my chest, one leg encircling both of mine. I cradle his shoulders with one arm and keep myself and the cigarette upright with the other. "So, you want to quit your job?"

"I might. I haven't decided yet."

"But you love your job."

"Milena, we both know that isn't true. It just affords me a certain standard of living that I've grown accustomed to. What I'm really considering is moving us out of Austria."

I tilt my head to him. "Could we go back to Prague?!"

The excitement in my voice causes him to look up at me.

"Well, actually my dear, I was thinking of a fresh start for us elsewhere. Maybe Heidelberg."

"Heidelberg? That's a university town! I don't want to live near a bunch of drunken barristers in training and junior professors with delusions of grandeur."

"It doesn't have to be Heidelberg. Maybe we could go to Paris, or even Canada."

"Canada?! Where they strap blades to their feet and call it an Olympic sport? It's barely even a country. What do they have in Canada other than ice holes and moose sightings?"

"Milena, right now, you're being a bit of an ice hole."

"I just don't see why we can't go back to Prague."

"Look, we don't need to make a decision right now. It's just something to consider. I always knew this job in Vienna wouldn't be forever. Now we have time to really think about things."

Grabbing the ashtray from the bedside table, I blot out the cigarette and turn off the night light, but I am unable to sleep. Maybe it is the thought of moving so far away from everything I know and love and having to learn yet another foreign language. Maybe it is because this move might mean the death of Franz and me, and I'm not ready to give up all that he has to offer. Maybe it's because I'm just starting to realize my potential for love; I have so much more love to give than I ever thought I could, and there is a deep-seated need in me to spread it around, be it with a lover or with the readers of my column.

Or maybe it's because Ernst is snoring like a BFW fighter plane.

* * *

Dear Franz

There are three plans in motion, it would seem, and none of them involve me returning to Prague. Ernst wants to leave his position at the bank and move us to Heidelberg, Paris, or Canada. Can you imagine me in any of those places? It would be like the Kaiser riding the Stadtbahn to Kettenbrückengasse and then walking up and down the stalls of the Naschmarkt looking to buy dinner plates that bear his face! Completely out of place.

I don't really have many details, other than his wishes to leave Austria altogether. I wish I could plan for something more certain. I don't know the whens or the hows or the wheres of it all. So maybe you should come back to Vienna soon before it all bubbles over. I want to see you so much. I have been thinking of you daily.

I now think I might return to Prague to see you. I had no plans to come to that dark kingdom, but it will break my heart to miss you. What to do? Let me mull this for a bit. I am full of wonder at how you must view Prague at this juncture. It must be strange for you after so long in Italy, and then our four Viennese days. I cannot imagine it. I suppose your mother is over the moon. And all the Arconauts. Have you been to the new-old Café Arco? It's not as it was. But it is as it is.

Prague is definitely the heart of Bohemia. God, what a magical place. I think of it as your spiritual birthplace, rather than your physical one.

I wish you could come back to Lerchenfelderstraße for a visit. I would love to sit with you by the coal stove and hear the rush of your stories and your incredible mind. It has been a month since you left, and I miss that particular high you give. It has been absent for so long in my life.

I hope you are well and feel the love of family and friends. It is exciting to think of you walking the grey streets of the Vyšehrad district or the Hradčany area. You must be in the towering streets of Malá Strana somewhere.

In the meantime, soon you should receive notice from Stanislav Neumann. I wrote to him and proposed translations of *The Meditation*, "The Judgement," and *Metamorphosis*, to which he agreed! They should appear in the forthcoming Červan edition series, by *Borový* Press. It is Communist normally, but this edition will be non-partisan. I have already begun the deep dive into translation, which takes me inside your cluttered, beautiful head again. It's like visiting an art gallery. I can almost hear your voice echoing down the corridor. I miss your voice and startling eyes, your liveliness and wonderful way of seeing what everybody misses.

Milena

As I return from the Bennogasse post office, the summer of 1920 swirls all around me. The burning sun moves over the sidewalk like the moon over tidal waves—the families heading north to the theatres, the degenerates heading east to the cabaret music halls, the affluent heading west to the French restaurants where you're not allowed to bring your own wine, the tramps and vagrants staggering south to the wayward houses and shelters. The Alt Lerchenfelder church is ringing her bells incessantly; a wedding is on the steps. A young bride and bridegroom are surrounded by their family, and they even have a photographer! I smile as I enter our building and run up the stairs; that young couple has no idea how miserable they are about to make each other.

I open the door to the flat, drop my coin purse on the side table, and flop down on the davenport, kicking off my espadrilles. Exhale. It is only when I sit upright that I notice Paní Kohler has been standing in the entryway in silence.

"How long have you been there?" I ask.

She doesn't say anything, but she does take a few steps into the room.

"Is ... everything quite all right, Paní Kohler?" She isn't wearing her apron, and she has a peculiar look on her face. "Are you feeling all right?"

"Meine Dame, I'm afraid I must leave you," she finally says.

"But you just got here."

"No, Frau Pollak," she sits next to me on the davenport, "I mean, I must vacate this position."

"You ... want to resign?"

"My husband and I have talked about it, and we are going to leave Vienna."

I sit in stunned silence.

She continues, "My husband has a friend in Brno, a butcher. He wants to retire. There's a grand house attached to the butchery. It is a decent-sized property for a family of our caste. We'd have a yard, lots of open space, and most exciting of all, our own well system. No more faulty city pumps or contaminated brown water. So we—"

"You want to leave me?" I blurt out.

Paní Kohler places her hand atop mine. "I don't want to leave you, but I have to think of my family, Frau Pollak."

"Yes, but... but..."

"I know I've been with you for a long time, and I'm so grateful to have been taken in and treated like so much more than a servant. But now it's time for me to move on, though it breaks my heart to do it."

"No, but..."

"My family cannot survive in Vienna any longer. The lack of coal and wood, the rate of inflation... our living is not enough to sustain even the rent or the taxes. Leaving for Brno is the best thing for my family and—"

"But you're my family! This place will go to ruin without you." My chin collapses and my nose stings as I meekly add, "And so will I."

I fling my arms around her and sob into her blouse. She holds me close and rocks me back and forth very gently. "Oh, there, there, Frau Pollak. You'll be fine, I promise you."

I cry out of pure jealousy of her husband and children. Jealous that they get to leave this wretched city and go back to Czechoslovakia. Jealous that they get to move on to new beginnings and greater prospects, while I stay here in a perilous situation and miserable company. Jealous that they get to have her in their lives, forever. They get to benefit from her caring nature, and her incredible baking, which has kept me plump during the lean days as the war ended. Do they even know how lucky they are?

I sit up straight and wipe my nose with the back of my hand, taking a few deep breaths. "I guess the butchery is an important step for your family, and in that case, I wish you all the luck in the world."

She smiles. "Thank you. Our own life, with no masters. It's a dream, really."

I sigh. "It's everyone's dream." We nod in agreement for a moment as I calm my nerves. "I don't know if I'll be able to keep such a clean and warm home as you have for us, though."

She laughs. "Oh, take care, my love. I'm sure you'll have no problem."

"Please, I don't even know how to grind the coffee!"

"I'll teach you before I go ... how about that?"

"You'll have to teach me more than that! What about Herr Pollak?"

"Men are simple. If you want him to be happy, feed the brute. 'Course, the same could be said for sheepdogs, mind you ..."

I chortle a bit and sniffle. "I don't know how I'm ever going to survive without you, Paní Kohler."

She laces her fingers with mine once more and gives me a firm squeeze. "Don't underestimate yourself, Frau Pollak. You have a grace greater than many. When you fly, you fly."

She is the only one to whom I have ever shown all of myself: my vulnerabilities, my vices, and my faults. Nevertheless, she's only ever seen the beauty therein.

* * *

POŠTA ČESKASLOVENSKÁ

FRAU JESENSKÁ, POSTE RESTANTE, POSTAMT 65,

BENNOGASSE, WIEN VIII

TWO NEW FACTS I HAVE RECENTLY LEARNED FROM YOUR LETTER: FIRST, THE HEIDELBERG PLAN, SECOND, THE PLAN FOR PARIS OR CANADA AND THE BANK-FLIGHT. WHATEVER THE OTHERS SURROUNDING YOU IN THE WIDE CIRCLE AT THE HERRENHOF MAY SAY ABOUT YOU, IN SUPERIOR WISDOM, IN BESTIAL DENSENESS, IN DIABOLICAL KINDNESS, IN HOMICIDAL LOVE—I, I, MILENA, KNOW TO THE LAST FIBRE THAT WHATEVER YOU DO, YOU WILL BE DOING RIGHT, WHETHER YOU STAY IN VIENNA OR COME HERE, OR REMAIN HOVERING BETWEEN PRAGUE AND VIENNA.

~YOURS

FIRST AUSTRIAN REPUBLIC NATIONAL TELEGRAPH

DOKTOR KAFKA, OPPELTŮV DŮM, STAROMĚSTSKÉ

NÁM 5/934, PRAHA

PLEASE COME BACK. MY HEART IS ON FIRE. I FEEL A POWERFUL THING HAS HAPPENED TO ME. I AM ENERGIZED AS I TRANSLATE YOUR WORK BUT ALSO SHORT OF BREATH. A LIGHTNING BOLT TO THE HEART. WHY DID YOU WIRE PANÍ KOHLER BEHIND MY BACK? IN ANY CASE, SHE HAS LEFT US FOR BRNO. WHAT A GOD-FORSAKEN PLACE. IN PRAGUE I ONCE MET SOME BRNOVIANS AND THEY WENT ON AND ON ABOUT HOW PRAGUE IS FULL OF LAZY AND SELF-CENTRED PEOPLE. THEN, WHEN THEY ASKED WHAT PRAGUE MUST THINK OF BRNO, I REPLIED, “WE DON’T THINK OF YOU AT ALL.”

~M

POŠTA ČESKASLOVENSKÁ

FRAU JESENSKÁ, POSTE RESTANTE, POSTAMT 65, BENNOGASSE, WIEN VIII

NO, I WON'T COME TO VIENNA. LOOK, MILENA, IF IN VIENNA YOU HAD BEEN COMPLETELY CONVINCED BY ME, YOU WOULD NO LONGER BE IN VIENNA DESPITE EVERYTHING, OR RATHER THERE WOULD BE NO "DESPITE EVERYTHING." YOU WOULD SIMPLY BE IN PRAGUE. I ONLY WIRED PANÍ KOHLER BECAUSE, FOR DAYS, AND BAD DAYS, I WAS WITHOUT NEWS, WITHOUT AN ANSWER TO MY TELEGRAM, AND WAS ALMOST FORCED TO BELIEVE THAT YOU WERE GONE FROM THIS WORLD.

~YOURS

FIRST AUSTRIAN REPUBLIC NATIONAL TELEGRAPH

DOKTOR KAFKA, OPPELTŮV DŮM, STAROMĚSTSKÉ NÁM 5/934, PRAHA

MAYBE I AM GONE FROM THIS WORLD. YOU MUST UNDERSTAND, FRANZ, THAT I AM MARRIED. MARRIED TO A HUSBAND THAT I LOVE DESPITE ALL OF HIS BUFFOONERY AND ALL OF OUR MISGIVINGS. AND YOU. YOU ARE MARRIED AS WELL. TO YOUR FEAR. YOUR FEAR OF LIVING, OF TRULY LOVING, OF GIVING. NOT GIVING UP BUT GIVING OUT. GIVING YOURSELF AWAY. ALLOWING ME TO TAKE THOSE PIECES OF YOU WITH ME. YOU WORRY THAT I WILL LEAVE YOU HOLLOWED, THAT YOU'LL NEVER BE ABLE TO GROW THOSE PIECES INSIDE YOU AGAIN. BUT I AM TELLING YOU THAT YOUR HEART IS NOT WEAK OR FEEBLE. IT HAS A MEMORY. IT LEARNS AND GROWS STRONGER. GIVE UP THIS FEAR YOU HAVE, FRANZ.

YOU'RE THE ONLY REASON WHY I COULD EVER RETURN TO

PRAGUE. YOU'RE ALSO THE ONLY REASON WHY I WOULD HAVE TO LEAVE IT AGAIN. SO PLEASE, COME BACK TO VIENNA.

~M

POŠTA ČESKASLOVENSKÁ
FRAU JESENSKÁ, POSTE RESTANTE, POSTAMT 65, BENNOGASSE, WIEN VIII

YOU'RE RIGHT FOR REPROACHING ME IN THE NAME OF FEAR FOR MY BEHAVIOUR IN VIENNA, BUT YOU SHOULDN'T WRITE TO ME ABOUT VIENNA; I WON'T COME. YOU ARE THE MOST BEAUTIFUL CREATURE, BUT YOU DISTRACT MY TRAIN OF THOUGHT. I CANNOT DO ANY MORE TO THIS EFFECT; IT IS IN GOD'S HANDS NOW. LET HIM DECIDE WHERE WE SHALL MEET AGAIN.

~YOURS

FIRST AUSTRIAN REPUBLIC NATIONAL TELEGRAPH
DOKTOR KAFKA, OPPELTŮV DŮM, STAROMĚSTSKÉ NÁM 5/934, PRAHA

THESE TELEGRAMS ARE TIRESOME. YOU ARE STUBBORN AND YOU ARE ANGRY AT ME FOR THINGS I CANNOT CONTROL. YES, I AM MARRIED, I LIVE IN THIS WRETCHED COUNTRY, AND I AM QUICK TO ANGER. BUT WHO WOULDN'T WANT TO BE DISTRACTED FROM WHATEVER IT IS THEY'RE THINKING ABOUT? WHAT DO YOU THINK WE WERE PUT ON THIS EARTH FOR? WHEN WILL YOU BE TOUGH ENOUGH FOR TRUE AFFECTION AND LITERATURE?

~M

FIRST AUSTRIAN REPUBLIC NATIONAL TELEGRAPH
DOKTOR KAFKA, OPPELTŮV DŮM, STAROMĚSTSKÉ NÁM 5/934, PRAHA
I WAS TOO HARSH IN MY EARLIER TELEGRAM. LET'S STOP ALL OF THIS. TWO HOURS OF LIFE ARE BETTER THAN TWO PAGES OF WRITING. PLEASE MEET ME. IF NOT IN VIENNA, THEN WHERE?
~M

POŠTA ČESKASLOVENSKÁ
FRAU JESENSKÁ, POSTE RESTANTE, POSTAMT 65, BENNOGASSE, WIEN VIII
YOUR TWO TELEGRAMS LIE BEFORE ME. A PART OF YOUR TERRIBLE TORTURE CONSISTS IN YOUR WRITING TO ME EVERY DAY. WRITE LESS OFTEN. YOU WILL FIND PEACE THIS WAY.
~YOURS

POŠTA ČESKASLOVENSKÁ
FRAU JESENSKÁ, POSTE RESTANTE, POSTAMT 65, BENNOGASSE, WIEN VIII
YESTERDAY, I ADVISED YOU NOT TO WRITE TO ME EVERY DAY; THIS IS STILL MY OPINION TODAY AND IT WOULD BE VERY GOOD FOR US BOTH. ONLY PLEASE, MILENA, DON'T ACT UPON IT. WRITE ME DAILY ALL THE SAME. JUST TWO LINES. JUST ONE. JUST A WORD. BUT TO BE DEPRIVED OF THIS WORD WOULD MEAN TERRIBLE SUFFERING. IT SOMETIMES SEEMS TO ME THAT INSTEAD OF EVER LIVING TOGETHER, WE'LL JUST BE ABLE TO LIE DOWN CONTENTEDLY BESIDE ONE ANOTHER IN ORDER TO DIE. WHATEVER HAPPENS, AT LEAST I WILL BE CLOSE TO YOU. I WOULD

LIKE TO KISS YOUR HAND SO LONG THAT YOU WOULD NEVER BE ABLE TO USE IT FOR TRANSLATING AGAIN.

~YOURS

FIRST AUSTRIAN REPUBLIC NATIONAL TELEGRAPH
DOKTOR KAFKA, OPPELTŮV DŮM, STAROMĚSTSKÉ NÁM 5/934, PRAHA

NO STRING OF WORDS IN EITHER LANGUAGE, CZECH OR GERMAN, WOULD BE ABLE TO DESCRIBE THE PAIN YOUR TELEGRAM CAUSED ME. THIS ANXIETY YOU HAVE ABOUT A SECOND MEETING DOES NOT COME FROM A FEAR OF THE FUTURE, BUT YOUR DESIRE TO CONTROL IT. SO I ASK YOU AGAIN: IF NOT VIENNA, THEN WHERE? TOO MANY ARCONAUTS KNOW US IN PRAGUE, AND I CANNOT HAVE ANOTHER TELEGRAM SENT TO MY FATHER.

~M

POŠTA ČESKASLOVENSKÁ
FRAU JESENSKÁ, POSTE RESTANTE, POSTAMT 65, BENNOGASSE, WIEN VIII

WHY WOULD YOU NEED TO COME TO PRAGUE? YOU ARE PRAGUE, MILENA. AND PRAGUE DOESN'T LET GO OF EITHER OF US. THIS OLD CRONE HAS CLAWS; ONE MUST YIELD OR ELSE. WE WOULD HAVE TO SET FIRE TO HER ON BOTH SIDES; AT THE VYŠEHRAD AND THE HRADČANY. THEN IT WOULD BE POSSIBLE FOR US TO GET AWAY.

~YOURS

FIRST AUSTRIAN REPUBLIC NATIONAL TELEGRAPH

DOKTOR KAFKA, OPPELTŮV DŮM, STAROMĚSTSKÉ

NÁM 5/934, PRAHA

AS EURIPIDES ONCE WROTE:

"COME BACK. EVEN AS A SHADOW. EVEN AS A DREAM."

~M

* * *

TODAY IS THE 10TH of August. It is my twenty-fourth birthday.

Ernst and I are dining this evening at Zum Weisse Hahn, the public house and hotel on Josefstädterstraße—a treat to celebrate another year on this earth when the earth is still a weeping wound. We are seated in a booth near the front windows, where we watch war widows beg for handouts and urchins who lost their families to the Spanish flu rip the shoes off sleeping vagrants.

Our booth is outfitted with a gingham tablecloth and a basket of Swedish bread while we peruse the menu. I have never ordered from the dinner menu before; every time I've come here, I've asked for their tea menu, which consists of cold meats, cheese, pickles, bread and butter, steamed figs, and bergamot tea. That's all I've ever been able to afford, yet the portions have always been generous. But Ernst is treating me this evening, and I am spoiled for choice.

Tonight, the chef is offering Yarmouth bloaters, galantine of chicken parmentier, corned ox tongue, sauté of chicken Lyonnaise, stuffed vegetable marrow, lamb collops in mint sauce, pureed turnips, chateau potatoes in mousseline, and creamed carrots. I order the stuffed vegetable marrow, pureed turnips, and chateau potatoes. Ernst orders the corned ox tongue, creamed carrots, cream of barley, and a bottle of champagne. The server pours a sample of the champagne into a small tulip copita. When Ernst nods in approval, we are poured two coupe glasses of the bubbly stuff.

"To Milena," he raises his glass, and I raise mine, "whom I admire, appreciate, adore ... and ..."

And love? I think as he prevaricates.

"And ... whom I would so often like to smack the daylights out of, whether she deserves it or not."

"Ernst!"

"Happy birthday, darling. Prost!"

We clink glasses and I down mine in one. As far as toasts go, that one didn't go down smoothly. He is a man of few words and they're all the wrong ones.

Ernst's cream of barley with cucumbers arrives and he bibs himself with a serviette before leaning close to the bowl to slurp his first spoonful. "So tell me, my dear," he says between sloppy mouthfuls, "what is in store for you this week?

"Well," I say as I tear off a piece of sweet Swedish bread and nibble at it, "as you know, I'm obliged to translate more works of Doktor Kafka for Neumann in Prague."

"Yes. How is that coming along?"

"It's nothing I can't handle, but," I say, eyeing him, "I was thinking of returning briefly to Prague this week."

"Again?" He dunks a cucumber rondelle into the creamy soup before shoving it past his lips. "You were just there last autumn."

"Yes, that's true." I thumb the crusty bread as it crumbles on the tablecloth. "But I have some questions about the logistics of it all, and well, you know what a headache telegrams can be. I'd prefer to have a meeting with Neumann in person."

"Hmmm," he chomps away at a cucumber rondelle, expectorating as he talks, "if that's what you feel you need to get your work done, I have no objection. But the cost of passage these days is quite steep."

"Yes." I look down at the empty space before me as my stomach gurgles. "That is a concern."

"Why don't you call Neumann on the telephone?" he asks.

"The telephone?"

"Yes, I'm sure his offices would have one. Prague these days is catching up with all the modern comforts."

"I... never even considered that."

"You could use the telephone at the post office," he goes on, sucking on his spoon, "and their prices haven't increased by much. It's only five hellers a minute to Czechoslovakia, last time I enquired."

I tug at the pussy-bow collaring my blouse and smooth out the wrinkles in my pencil skirt. I've seen many people at the post office use the telephone box, though I've never had occasion to do so myself. Perhaps Ernst is right, and I should take advantage of the wonders of this new world.

This thought is interrupted when the head waiter approaches our table. "Forgive me, meine Dame," he leans in to speak to me, "but there is a telephone call for you at the server's station."

"Speak of the devil!" Ernst slaps his thigh in laughter.

"For me?" The server simply nods. I shimmy out of the booth. "I'll be right back."

"Take your time, my love!" Ernst calls after me as he returns to his steaming bowl.

I follow the waiter to the server's station near the front entrance, where the maitre d' turns away those without a reservation and keeps an immaculate logbook. I am handed a telephone shaped like an upturned black bell. The rotary dial juts from the bell, and the ear and voice receiver comes in one handy piece. This must be one of those new telephones from Siemens in Germany that the bourgeoisie keep in their homes. I cannot see these things becoming popular—who would want to have telephone conversations at home when you could have in-person conversations with tea and plum cakes at the café?

I hold the receiver to my mouth and ear. "Hello?"

"Überraschung!" The connection crackles, but I know that deep German voice at the end of the line. I would know it anywhere.

"Franz!" I exclaim a little too loudly. I cover my mouth and the mouthpiece with my palm. "Is that you?"

"I couldn't miss your birthday, could I?" he says. "And I don't trust a telegram to do it justice."

"How did you know I would be here?"

"Wild guess."

"It was not!"

"No, it wasn't. I called the Herrenhof, the Sperl, and the Central first before asking the operator to connect me to the Weisse Hahn. Luckily, you've mentioned it once or twice."

"How are you?"

"I'm feeling quite well. The lung hasn't been giving me too much trouble, but I've been sleeping poorly. How about you?"

I look toward the dining room, where Ernst has his back to me, but I still cower over the telephone and whisper. "I haven't slept either."

"Is that so?"

"Have you given more thought to coming to Vienna?"

"I have—" there is a pause on the line, and I wonder if I've lost him to a crossed wire, "and I wanted to ask you a question."

"Yes?"

"Do you have enough money for travel fare?"

"You mean, to come see you?"

"Precisely."

My heart begins to thump in my chest so loud I wonder if Franz will think there are cannons in the city of Vienna. "I'll think of something."

"Nonsense, Milenka." I cannot help but beam with delight as he says my sobriquet. "I will wire you some money tonight."

"So I can come see you in Prague? What about the gossip?"

"What if we met in Gmünd?" he says.

"The border town?" I ask.

His voice grows giddy and rapid. "Yes, hear me out. There is a station hotel next to the railway and customs control. At 4:38 in the afternoon there's a passenger train leaving for Prague, which would give us twenty-one hours together. Even if I have to leave on Sunday by the morning express, it won't be before 10:46 in the morning."

"Someone has been studying the train timetables!" I exclaim.

"I may have stopped inside the main train station on my way to and from work every day for the past few weeks. Then again, I may not. It's a mystery."

"Knock it off, you."

"Do you think you could get away this weekend?"

"Will I require my passport?"

"Well, the Gmünd station is Czech, but the town is Austrian. It is possible that the passport nonsense is carried so far that a Viennese requires a passport to cross the Czech station."

"Oh dear, I'm a Czech national with Viennese papers. I'm not even sure I have the proper documents or visas anymore."

"I'm not certain either, but it is bad enough that I may have to wait an hour at Customs before being allowed to leave the station, and thus the twenty-one hours would be shortened."

"I do really want to see you." I sigh. "And I have mentioned to Ernst that I might need to travel for a meeting with Neumann."

"I'll wire the money this evening so you can buy your passage tomorrow."

The head waiter mills about, casually eavesdropping in between showing guests to their tables. He inches closer to the station, as if to suggest that I am taking liberties.

"What a wonderful birthday surprise," I whisper into the receiver. "I'm so glad you found me."

"You found me, remember?" he says.

A short snicker escapes me. "Yes. I did."

"Do you know, by the way, that you were given to me as a present for my bar mitzvah?"

My snicker turns into a churlish giggle. "Was I!"

"I was born in 1883, so I was thirteen when you were born. The thirteenth birthday is a special occasion. I received many presents, but I was not entirely satisfied, because one particular present I missed. So I demanded it from heaven... which hesitated until the 10th of August."

When I return to the table, my hot plate of food is waiting for me, along with an inquisitive husband. "Look at that smile on your face!" he exclaims before I can wipe my expression clean. "Who called for you?"

I take my fork and knife in hand, slicing into the vegetable marrow with no urgency. "It was... Paní Kohler. She wanted to wish me a happy birthday."

Ernst is already a quarter through his corned ox tongue and little bits stick to his whiskers and top lip. "How is she doing?"

"She and her family made it to Brno," I say, after swallowing my first morsel. "The journey was long, and she was worried it wouldn't work out. She took a great chance leaving, you know. But she made it after all. And she is the most pleased she's ever been."

He nods, barely registering what I'm saying. "Good for her."

"Yes," I breathe, thinking of my own plans. "It looks like her happy ending is finally here."

17

Gmünd

1920

Today, as the express train hurtles me northwest and away from Vienna, another of my feuilletons has been published in the *Tribuna*. The words flowed from my fingers like a tide. The voice that commanded the next words in the sentence appeared as though it was an echo from someone else: a guru, a sage, a phantom, a lover. It came out in one seamless delirium. The same early morning that I bought my passage, I ran over to Bettina on Bennogasse and had her send the piece via courier to Lustig, my *Tribuna* editor. His reply via telegram informed me it would run in the Saturday edition.

My pieces have always been about the manners and fashions of modern people—and their absurdities—but this time, I wrote about the fashions of travellers that I have witnessed hundreds of times over as a porter at the

Westbahnhof, but more so, how too heavy a reliance on *things* is the mark of someone unwilling to embrace the freedom of the open road.

As I sit in my berth, staring out the window at the tower of Stephansdom that has become a dot on the distant horizon, the five men occupying the seats around me are all reading the issue. I read over the shoulder of the man next to me in a Styrian suit. He smells of toasted tobacco and Leone Violetta pastilles. Sensing my eyes, he shifts in his seat. So I turn my attention to the decorated officer on my other side. He has an expansive forehead and he's so tall that his knees keep knocking into the short man across from him. But his eyes are thoughtful as he reads my words.

He snorts a chuckle over my descriptions of how an Englishman packs his valise and keeps reading. As I peer over his shoulder, mouthing my own words back to myself, he suddenly catches wise and tilts his copy away. I look up at his face: he's not annoyed, more amused by my social indiscretion. I snap my neck back into place and keep my eyes forward.

It is still many hours until we reach Gmünd, and my thoughts bounce around my head like the sparks off a knife as it's sharpened. I pull out a book just to keep my mind occupied, though I have to reread every sentence two or three times before it actually sinks in. As the train begins to slow, the cabin attendant walks heavily through the carriage, bellowing the upcoming stop: "Tulln an der Donau! Alight here for Tulln an der Donau!"

The decorated officer looks up from the paper, sighs, and gathers his satchel and hat. I keep my eyes buried in my book.

"What's that you're reading?"

He's talking to me.

"Oh, it's... um..." I look at the title embossed on the front cover and realize that as a woman in a berth full of men, I probably don't have the social licence to say this out loud, so I just hold it up for him to see.

"*Beyond the Pleasure Principle*," he blurts loudly, "by Sigmund Freud."

There is a dip of newspapers, as the four other men in suits with bowler hats and black umbrellas eye me with sclerotic looks on their faces.

I jerk my chin to catch all their excited eyes, and they immediately hide behind my newspaper article again.

"Yes, that is indeed what I'm reading."

"Enjoying it?"

"No, not really." I fold the book in my lap and take a comprehensive look at this man. He isn't so much interrogating me as he is sizing me up.

Outside the window, the platform suddenly assembly-lines past. Families with young children, men in suits, single ladies, and other random characters populate the station.

"Tulln an der Donau!" the attendant shouts again before jumping on the platform to help passengers descend.

"Page sixty-four. First sentence."

I look back up at the officer.

"Pardon?"

He squeezes past all our feet, opens the sliding door to the berth, steps out, and takes one final look at me. "Page sixty-four. First sentence. Okay?"

Before I can answer, he slides the door shut and disappears. My curiosity is insatiable. So too is what can only be described as attraction.

I flip immediately to page sixty-four. I read the first sentence. I read it again. I don't understand what I have just read, but perhaps that man knows something I don't. Perhaps he knows I'm about to find out.

I drop the book, still open, to my lap.

> Thus the Libido of our sexual instincts would coincide with the Eros of poets of philosophers, which holds together all things living.

HALF PAST SEVEN IN the evening.

As I walk through the old town of Gmünd, voices grow louder. Life seems larger at night, swollen with dark shadows and strange creaks that terrify me, yet I cannot help exploring, wondering if there is anyone else like me, awake and glimpsing the unknown. People stroll the streets; some ride bicycles, pumping their legs to exhaustion in the August heat. Sapphire and amber dresses flap like flags. All the lights in the windows are lit. Voices break apart the town like war cannons once did. Old men hold up pints of beer, children devour ice cream, women cut melon slices. Singing musicians play tubas and accordions in the corner of the Old Town Square.

This small town nestled in the valley of the mountains is locked in an embrace. Lovers kiss under a dark sky. Young adolescents strip off their trousers and run into the fountains. They splash and dance in the water like toddlers on sugar. Cafés serve fresh cherries and peaches. Lemon tarts and plum puddings fly out of the bakeries, and cups of soft yogourt stain the children's teeth. I am in awe of this small border town. The villagers feel joy without mutilating themselves. How is that possible?

Over the hills, where the Czechoslovakian countryside begins, the sky is very quiet.

I made it here without a hiccup. But I couldn't go straight to the station hotel at the end of the railway tracks. How could I? When my eyes are glowing like warm candles, wishing to both savour and destroy the bodies of this world.

He is behind me. The crowd swallows us both, but the distance between us cannot be much. He is following me. He has always followed me. Since I stepped foot inside Café Arco last year, I have felt him behind me. I keep walking to prevent myself from dissolving into the ground, from splashing about in my own skin—skin that separates and joins the bricks and stones of my body.

Hair blows in my face.

Village voices like prayer chants infect my ears.

The night is an apple falling to the dirt.

The sloping shadows and hibiscus blooms all around me have quailed and folded.

Please catch up to me. Don't let me go. Don't let me. You have to catch me.

I think of Orpheus and Eurydice. If I look back, he'll disappear into death. Just let him follow.

Don't turn around, Milena.

His hand is on my shoulder.

Don't look now.

* * *

NINE O'CLOCK AT NIGHT.

The station hotel room is the colour of red clay. The kind of clay you can smooth, polish, stroke, and manipulate into what you want it to be. The light from the bedside lamp is hued like sandstone. His skin is an alabaster swath against a charcoal sky, like marks left by a lover on thigh and belly.

I take the pins out of my hair; curls whisk along my bare shoulders, folding and unfolding between my breasts. We both sit on our haunches atop the mattress, but our bodies are at opposite ends. Warm waves, like butter, travel across my skin. I bunch a goose-down pillow in my hands as he reaches for his satchel. I think he might pull out a prophylactic sheath, but instead he pulls out apples the pigment of wine, plums like blood.

I reach over and cup a plum in my hand. Cold skin. Perfect circle. He is about to bite down into his apple when he notices me holding the plum to my lips.

Freeze. Eyes lock. Move closer to each other, crawling like beetles across the bedsheets. Fruit to both our lips. My lips move. A pucker. A kiss. Kiss the cold skin of the blood plum. Eyes on him.

Protruding tongue. Licks the wine apple from stem to end. Eyes locked. Teeth bared.

Plum sucked down. Take it whole into my mouth. Puff my cheeks around the round lump. Suck until I open wide and let it slide back out slick, glistening, into my palm.

Teeth skin the apple. Indent of incisors. Bites. He bites down.

I bite down.

Juice drools down; mouths curled into smiles, lips cannot contain liquids. Tongues too slow to lick the juice away. My finger lifts to his chin; wetness makes its way through his dark stubble like a labyrinth. Finger his wetness until it's all I feel.

His fingers move across my lips and chin. He catches all the juice. Pushes his finger past my teeth, down the border of my throat.

There are talons emerging from my body. I want him to suffocate. I will carry him away like a field mouse in my grip. Squealing. The thought of swallowing him. And my talons will gouge him out. Because we both know he'll beg to be devoured.

MIDNIGHT.

The pearl-bleached curtains dance over the open window. Franz lies belly-down atop the linen, one arm slung over my ribs, imprisoning me. My eyes are closed, but I'm not sleeping; I refuse to say anything to break this moment. Franz's head is turned to me and I can feel his gaze lingering on my body. I can feel him languishing in my bone marrow. I am all over his face.

"How is Ernst?" he mumbles.

I place both hands below the small of his back, where there's a slight hint of soft mounds, and then let my head droop against his shoulder. Inhale deeply while running my fingers through the dark, coarse hair of his thighs. He smells like talcum powder, chocolate sweeties, and a musty, too-familiar scent. Breathe quickly now.

"Fine," I finally say. "But I don't think that's the question you really wanted to ask me."

"Have you told him about us?" He sounds as if he's in a trance: his tone even, then uneven.

Heart in my throat. "No."

"No?" His voice has an eerie, distant quality. He's beside me, but he's also somewhere else.

"Not yet."

"You know what I'm going to say to that, Milenka."

"Yes, but a lot must be considered before a conversation like that. I will. I promise."

He lifts his head from the pillow and props it up on his bent elbow and wrist. I open my eyes and look at him. Barbed wire is tightening around my throat. I swallow hard, tasting copper.

"I gave up the Girl for you. I left her because of the promise of us. Did I do it for nothing?"

"You can't compare—"

"Yes, I can."

"You weren't happy with her. You would have left her anyway."

"I'm not about to take my cues on happy marriages from you."

I sit straight up and yank his arm off me. His body lolls to one side as he watches me rise from the sheets still wet with our oils and scents. I grab his dressing gown and wrap it around my body. "Who do you think you're talking to like that?"

He bolts upright, his eyes burning fire and brimstone to match mine. "You don't plan on leaving him, do you?"

I am silent.

"You were never going to leave him. You made your

mind up a long time ago, didn't you?" Each word is like a pistol blast.

"I don't know."

"Your marriage is a lie."

Acid bile like a sulphur cocktail burns up my esophagus. My gullet contracts and dilates; I've been run through with a sword. Legs weakening, resolve and balance fading. I cannot blink away the stain of his words.

"Should you leave him, he will go live with another woman, or he'll go live in a bordello, but I guarantee you, in either event, that his boots will be cleaned better than they are now."

"How dare you!" I scream. The music in my head was previously soft, featuring an oboe and cello. Now it is the harsh crash of cymbals and trumpets.

"How dare I?"

"How dare you speak—"

"—You still love him!"

"Yes, I do love him, but I love him like an automatic lighter that only alights on the fifth or sixth try. Franz, I—"

"You don't even use *du* when you speak to each other. You say the informal, cold *sie*."

"It's complicated. I can't tell him this very second! I can't leave him this very second, can I! Perhaps I won't be able to ever. But you have to believe me, you are the most—"

"Please spare me *The Importance of Being* Ernst."

"Don't try to be clever, Kafka," I say through gritted teeth, "you'll be up way past your bedtime."

"You don't care about me, Milena."

"How would you know?"

He falls silent. There is a sharp edge to the night air now; it kicks up the corners of the curtains so I can see the lights of the locomotives as they round into the station.

"That night. That first night in Vienna. I told you what I thought of love, Franz. I told you how it burns hot, and then cold, for me. But you couldn't tell me what love is for you."

He says nothing.

"Franz Kafka, you've been engaged three times, twice to the same girl, and now you're here with me in this hotel room, and you pretend like you don't have an opinion on love? How brave of you to accuse me of that which you yourself are guilty! The view must be pretty spectacular from your seat on the fence! I'm telling you my heart is all yours and you dare to remain quiet. Tell me, why won't you look at me?"

He says nothing. My lungs are searing from yelling. Cheeks burning. A nail bores into my guts. A stitch runs from muscle to muscle, acid blazing inside my veins. An hour ago, I liked it when he traced my limbs with his lips: tender. But now, with those words on his lips, I want them to rot and break off in a fire.

"This is why, despite everything that Ernst has done to me, I won't leave him. At least he has a backbone. He takes a stance on things. He's uncomplicated. I can set my watch by him. I know Ernst isn't meek, or sickly, or poorly. He's robust in body and mind. He doesn't make a huge event out of little things, like how much change to give a beggar woman or which queue to join at the post office. He doesn't overthink a dance or a walk in the woods. He just lives! The same cannot be said for you."

"So the truth comes out," he finally spits back, narrowing his eyes and scrunching his nose. "This is what I suspected all along. You are revolted by my nervousness, my illness, my thinness ... my Jewishness."

"What revolts me is your lack of understanding. Matrimony is about companionship and tolerance, not scorched hearts!"

"You're so wrong, Frau Pollak."

"And how would you know?"

He doesn't reply, and I have never felt such a debilitating pain in my gut, as if a man is hammering on fresh stitches while the blood-clotting arteries are dying off and slowly shutting down.

"Tell me! I'm asking! How would you know what love is?"

"Because!" he yells back. He finally gets up from the bed, rising on his two long legs, his damned thighs, and closes the space between us. Gripping my forearms, he pulls me to him. "Because," he whispers up against my face, "you are the knife I turn inside myself. That is love. That, my dear, is love."

His lips sear mine. After all of this, I finally hear it. I suddenly have an urge I've never had before. I want to smash some bones. A clavicle or a rib. I want to draw blood. Have it spurt across my lips. I want to cast a spell. Drag him into a cauldron. I want to set fire to this place until we are both smouldering cinders fuming under the rubble.

* * *

I PERCH NAKED ON the windowsill, my knees to my chest. Beyond the open window, I can hear children playing ball games against a brick wall in an alley. Their voices ricochet. The rumble of express trains that do not stop here shakes the floorboards. The faintest hum of a klezmer street band reaches me, and I hum along to a song I've never heard before.

Franz is sitting up in the bed, atop the sheets, looking at me quietly. I trace a finger over my thigh: the spot where, as he was undressing me earlier, he snapped my garter belt against my skin. It has left a red welt. I think he did it on purpose, like he was trying to brand me as he might burn his name into a rose bed.

"Does it hurt?" he asks.

"Of course it does, you weasel-headed toad."

"My word, can you ever scold."

"I save my best insults for you."

"Truly? I'd like to hear them all."

"I don't think you would."

"Milenka," he gets up and stands next to me, "I would easily become your pupil and purposefully make mistakes at every interval, just to have the pleasure of being scolded by you."

I search his eyes. "Is that what you like?"

He nods slowly.

We hold each other's gaze. The night breeze blows the curtain between our faces, and now I can only see him through sheer gauze.

"Where does this come from?"

He drags a chair over from the wall and plants it beneath me. He sits and heaves his long legs upon the columns of the cast-iron radiator. I hold his dark, hooded eyes in mine as he tells me of his first sexual experience, which is at the heart of everything that has passed between us—

HE IS TWENTY AND a law student in Prague. On a hot summer day, as he is trying to learn a chapter on Roman law by heart, he looks out the window and sees the salesgirl from the confectionery across the street getting a breath of air on the sidewalk. She sees him and doesn't look away. He cannot look away either. They smile at each other. She raises her hand to wave. He does the same. She gives him a thumbs-up. He does the same. She points to both her eyes and then points to him. He does the same. He has the urge to lean out his window and holler a hello, but these hand signals hold on to him. He hasn't even heard her voice and already they have their own secret language. He's certain he has never seen her before, but she is familiar. How often do we really pay attention to the people who sell us postcards or licorice sticks or inkwells or shoelaces? He cannot believe all the time he's wasted not looking up as he walked along Celetná street when he could have been using his hands to speak to this girl. To touch this girl.

After a variety of hand signals, and misunderstandings, they agree to meet. At eight o'clock in the evening, when he arrives outside her confectionery shop, which has closed for the evening, she is there, but she's talking to a man in a straw hat and suspenders. Franz stands in a doorway across the way, watching, uncertain whether he should interrupt or wait until they're done. But then, she sees Franz standing there and laces her arm with the man. They walk off together, but she looks over her shoulder and signals Franz to follow. Why? He cannot say. He also cannot say why his instincts propel him forward with each step.

The pair walks to Café Slavia by the river promenade and orders beer. Franz takes a nearby table and does the same. He sits there for what feels like an eternity, never once sipping the brew, just eyeing the girl and the man, wondering if she's using him as some kind of chaperone without his consent.

The couple sets off again, and Franz is in close pursuit, ducking in and out of doorways to keep to the shadows. It is irritating, exciting, and horrible. All three of these emotions are blending; they all seem to react upon his body the same way. Following them has given him a pleasure he hasn't felt before. On Pařížská Street, she sends the man away. Franz watches as he runs to catch the tram and disappears around the corner.

The salesgirl still doesn't invite Franz to walk beside her. Instead, she walks to a hotel at the edge of the road. And Franz follows her.

Over the next twelve hours, he and the salesgirl exact upon each other a level of obscenity and disgust that only two lovers can. And during the game of their bodies, she scolds him. She uses words he has never heard a young Bohemian girl say before. As he moves inside her, there are profanities, and they include all the gross, beastly fantasies she wishes for him to fulfill. Had he been clothed, he would have been outraged. But her words, her scolds, gasped between thrusts, between skinfolds, between throbs, excite him frantically. His body, which has been in agonies for months, is finally satisfied. They emerge at dawn.

Afterward, his body is overtaken at irregular intervals by a keen desire for this dirty, repulsive indulgence. He wants it over and over.

He never walks past the confectionery again.

THE MEMORY OF THAT bit of filth stayed with him ever since, like a bad smell, a whiff of sulphur, a bit of hell lingering in the heart of pleasure. He tells me that sordidness and horror seem to be an integral part of how his body reacts to women. "It is a little thing that determined my sexual life," he explains, "just as in the great battles of history, the fate of big things has been decided by little things."

This is why he loves brothels, he admits. On his daily walks through Prague, he consistently chooses the streets with whores. "I walk by a brothel as though it is the house of a beloved," he says.

"Do you ever engage the whores?" I ask.

He inhales slowly. "Last year, in June, when Julie and I were affianced, there were six."

This is said without remorse or shame.

"Franz…"

"Yes?"

"Were you faithful to me in Prague?"

He tilts his head. "That's a strange question coming from a married woman."

"Were you?" I press.

He blinks. Somewhere in the distance, a bicycle bell

clangs and a woman's laughter bounces off the cobbles.

"Of course I was. I carry your locket with me everywhere I go. If any other woman were to undress me, the locket would scald her fingers like holy water would a demon."

I narrow my eyes. "Do I repulse you?"

His finger traces a line along my toes, from baby to big, as if he were lassoing a rope around them. "No. But you scold me so exquisitely."

He stands; his forehead is perilously close to mine. He doesn't touch me, but I can see his carotid artery pulsating in his neck as he clenches his jaw.

"You clueless, trumpeting nimrod," I hiss. It's almost a lullaby.

We hold each other's eyes, huffing. His body begins to react. This is what he wanted from Gmünd: trauma and hurt. Hate and rubble. Art and forgetting.

My eyes sting. They bleed salty tears and I want Franz to just claim victory already.

"Why are you crying?" he asks in a tone of voice he's never used before.

"Just ignore me."

"I could never." He cups my face. "You're perfect."

I want to take his clumsy, calloused hands in mine and run. As an adolescent I was this way: always plunging headfirst into the next vortex of human experience. Into the spectrum between loving and despising. I tend to view everyone emphatically—either I hate them or I love them.

But Franz, I have quickly learned, keeps changing. From hate to love. From love to hate.

The twilight passes through me like a wind that knocks down electricity poles. My love and his fear are fused together in a melding heat, but I can't feel anything except the welt left behind from its fire. I should be angry, but the red flames turn mauve and flicker out.

DAWN.

The sky is a dull amethyst. We sit on the floor with our backs against the door to the corridor. The satchel of apples and plums lies between us. We are quietly nibbling, tossing cores and pits out the window. Sometimes a pit hits the radiator and then tumbles down to our feet again.

"I was thinking," he says, "maybe I should return on the quarter-to-eleven train back to Prague, instead of waiting for the afternoon."

I don't look up from the apple in my hand. "I see."

"What do you think?"

"I think," I look the room over, "that you should do what you want."

The night crickets have gone to sleep, and the sparrows and swallows have taken up the charge. Shadows of leaves bouncing up and down fall upon the curtains.

He sucks on a plum pit, moving it about his molars, from one side of his mouth to the other. I lacerate the apple's red skin with my fingernails. He spits out the pit, after removing all the chewy meat, and launches it past the window.

"Shall we say what we're really thinking?" he asks.

I shoot him a look. "You first."

"I think I can't go on like this."

"Like this?"

"I want all of you, Milena. Not just four days between work, or a weekend away. I want all of you, all the time. I thought that's what you wanted as well."

"I do!"

"But you won't leave him."

"It's not a one-sided marriage, you know. I don't think he could live without me either, inwardly or outwardly. Knowing that makes it far harder to act upon my own wishes without considering his."

"What is his pain when compared to my eternal bondage?"

Exasperated, I get up off the floor and slam my apple into the wastepaper basket. "Why does everything always have to boil down to Ernst?"

"Because it does for me. I thought I knew where I stood with you."

"Even now, you doubt me?"

"What did you think this weekend was about, Milena?"

I fold my arms over my chest, holding his last question close. I narrow my eyes. "What did *you* think this weekend was about?"

He gets to his feet, wraps his dressing gown around his long torso, and crosses his arms. I stand there, naked and refusing to cover up.

"I thought you knew."

I close the space between us. "Was this entire thing an ultimatum?"

"Don't you want to run away? To leave all that hurts you in Vienna behind?"

"And live like Alma Mahler? No, thank you."

"She and Werfel are rapturously happy."

"She's been on more laps than a serviette, Franz. With her plunging necklines, I'm sure she's killed off more old men than a winter cold snap."

He sighs and reaches down to his satchel, pulling out another plum. "Well, if you won't come with me, I'm not sure why you even agreed to meet me in the first place." He bites into the plum, but it's mealy, past its prime. He spits out the chunk and hurls it and the plum out the window.

"I'm asking myself the same question."

Before he can reply, I notice something on his face that looks like a blossom.

"Franz?"

Diamonds of blood pepper his nose.

He wipes his nose and exhales. Then he coughs. Again and again. He coughs and covers his mouth, but when I tug at his arm, he shows me his palm. Wet. Blood.

"Franz, tell me what to do. Tell me what to do!"

The flow is river rapid; I can't capture it all. Blood seeps into my palm, so I grab his shoulders and manoeuvre him to the wash basin. Ventricles throbbing, blood pumps from his mouth with every hacking, wheezing cough. His breath is truncated. The cough is deep; I can hear it slicing into his throat, banging against his chest cavity in staccato bullets. No voice. Blood is on the floorboards. On our bodies, trailing down my toes. I pour icy water onto a washcloth and hold it to his face, and then I soak his handkerchief and hold it sopping on the back of his neck. His eyes are raw and bulging; there's blood on his chin and neck. I'm on my knees, holding his retching, convulsing body.

There is no chance to cry or curse God. Survival mode kicks in, and all I can do is hold him steady while his lung hemorrhages and pray that it ends swiftly. I've never seen such a violent attack, he was fine last—

"Milena!" he gasps through wet, scattered gargles. Bent over the basin, he reaches for me and I grip him tighter.

He struggles to inhale, but finally some air seems to be getting past his lips. The bloodletting slows. His shaking body seems to smooth out, nerves calming. His grip unclenches.

Before he can slump to the floor, I haul him with all my strength to the bed. I try to rub his temples as I did before, but my touch seems to have little effect now.

"Do you feel like you're suffering less?" I ask.

"Milena," he whispers at the very edge of his lung capacity, "I feel like my suffering has only just begun."

We lie there, him in a fetal ball and I wrapped around him, until his breathing evens. When he passes out, I sob into his shoulder.

MORNING.

The station hotel isn't far from the tracks, but we have to go at a snail's pace. The walk isn't paved, just pebbles and stones, and as Franz drags his feet, he kicks a dust pile forward. The jackdaws in the tree boughs above our head are silent for once, but they watch us like Pinkertons.

There is a stationery shop on the walk back to the railway, and Franz insists we make a stop. Once inside, he thumbs his way through a sliding stack of postcards, while I test different fountain pen nibs, dipping them slowly into the octopus ink, and then scrawling my name on the courtesy paper. *Milena. Milena.* I'm trying to remember who I was before Franz. And who I will be after.

He settles on a postcard featuring the dirt road leading into the centre of Gmünd: in the distance, the city hall tower looms above a canopy of trees and thatch rooftops.

"I think I'll send a postcard to Ottla," he says.

I peer at the postcard over his shoulder. "What's the point? It will get there long after you arrive home."

"Maybe," he turns to meet my eyes, "I want some lasting proof that this night happened."

The shopkeeper is paying us no mind, but I grab Franz by the arm and lead him behind the newspaper racks and shelves of typewriter ribbons. "I'm a married woman, Franz."

"Ottla will never tell." He smiles, grabs a courtesy fountain pen attached to a chain, and begins to draft his note to his sister. He writes in his obtuse penmanship that looks like musical notes written while driving along a bumpy road, but after a few lines he puts the pen down and begins to rub his wrists.

"What is it?" I ask.

"Median nerve compression, my physician says, though he cannot say why." He rotates his wrists in concentric circles, trying to stretch out the ligaments, but it doesn't seem to help. "I know it's from hours of writing." He nods down to his half-hearted postcard. "Could you?"

"Could I what?"

"I can't finish it."

"You want me to?"

"Just a line for the valediction."

"Franz, I can't duplicate your script. She'll know it wasn't written by you."

"Then don't pretend to be anyone other than yourself."

I purse my lips. "Franz ..."

"Oh, come off it, Milena, you look like you're mourning your dignity."

"Darling, my dignity committed suicide a long time ago." I yank the chained pen out of his twitching, claw-like hand and write two lines at the very bottom.

> He was unable to finish.
>
> Yours, cordially.

But I do not sign it.

QUARTER PAST TEN.

I stand on the platform while Franz finally makes his way out of the customs office, his passport bearing yet another Austrian exit visa stamp.

He walks toward me rather slowly, so I skip over to his side to hold him by the arm. I have his satchel in my other hand, but I don't give it to him just yet. Instead, I move us to a bench against a brick wall, and we sit, watching the porters load leather valises and hat carriers onto a dolly and an engineer heaving coal by the shovelful into the fire of a locomotive bound for Italy.

"Can I see your passport?" I ask.

He slides it to me, and I flip it open to the photograph page. His full, voluminous hair is parted in the middle, and his empty gaze trails somewhere beyond the photographer's shoulder.

"It's a good picture," I say, handing it back.

"Please," he shoves it into his breast pocket, "you can put that lie back in the garbage where you found it."

The clock in the arrivals hall ticks loudly before each strike. It mirrors the *tick-tick-tick* in my heart. I measure these seconds as if the clock hand were moving backward. There's a story behind our silence: all the truths that we were just before, and just after, are taken someplace new. Inside, my gut begins to pump bile up my esophagus. It's as though my liver's as fat as a partridge. I want to say something, but I'm hoping he'll speak first. Our silence grows heavy and dense. You could eat it with wooden salad tongs.

"My lungs feel black, as if they're submerged in a miner's shaft," he finally says.

"Are you sure you want to go now? Couldn't you wait until the afternoon train?" I say so quickly the words burn my tongue.

"Milenka, we've been over this."

"Don't call me that!" I snap, inhaling sharply, before continuing in a calmer tone. "Don't call me that unless you want me. Unless I'm yours and you're mine."

"You are not my possession, and I am not your property. That's not how this works."

"You will never, ever, find someone who loves you as much as I do."

"I know."

"And you'll give that up? Just because of—" I search for the right word "—details. For technicalities and footnotes."

"It's not just that."

"Then what?"

The custodian pushes a broom past us, and a little boy in lederhosen holds the hand of his governess as though she might float away on the breeze.

"It's being around you!" He is suddenly full of vigour, lungs be damned. "You suck up all my energy like one of Einstein's black holes, and I'm just a light particle floating through outer space, unable to resist your pull."

"You talk about me as if I'm some disease come to infect you!"

"Aren't you?"

"You really don't care how your words cut me, do you?"

"Not one moment of calm is granted me!" He throws his hands up in the air. "Nothing is granted me. Everything has to be earned. Always Milena, or not Milena. But never in between."

"Fine words of a coward."

He snorts and shakes his head, looking away toward the expanse of tracks that curve beyond the border into the wooded hills. "I may be many things, but a coward is not one of them." He gets up on shaky legs, grabs his satchel from my hand, and marches down the platform.

I come clomping up next to him. "Don't end it this way."

"Milena, nothing ever ends in the desired way. An ending is an ending."

I stop walking and turn my eyes upward to the sky. Stinging nose. Collapsing chin. I don't know how much longer I can withhold crying out.

He takes a few more steps down the platform, but then he turns back toward me. We stand a body length apart: a dead body. The distance could be a cavern, or an ocean. Untraversable.

Tears fall from my eyes in diamonds. They collect at my chin, a slow trickle. The ground beneath our feet starts to rumble. A steam whistle blows in the distance.

"I still have your blood on me," I call out to him. "It's on my hands, my legs. I won't rub it off."

"Don't turn my blood into a thing of beauty." He grips his satchel; his fists turn white. "It's not. It never was. It's only red."

He walks up to me finally. We are a breath apart, his nose close enough to kiss. He drops his satchel and puts his arms around me. The train thunders into the station like an infantry on the western front storming a beach head. He holds me like he did in the Schönbrunn gardens: so tight I think he might squeeze the life out of me. I want him to.

We rock back and forth in an embrace as the carriage doors slam open and travellers alight. Hats are removed and used to wave goodbye. Handshakes, kisses, and shouts from the train windows to the platforms. There are only seconds left, and I wish the clock hand truly did move backward.

Franz pulls away, lifts his satchel. He looks down upon me, as though he were on the top rung of a ladder, and I'm a fresco he longs to paint. Searching my face for something he won't reveal.

And suddenly he's moving away from me, swinging open a carriage door, and climbing up.

"Franz!" I call after him.

One foot in, one foot out, he stops and looks at me.

"Turning your back on the sun will not make it any less beautiful."

A smile tugs at his lips. The conductor blows his whistle and a sunbeam breaks through the railway's awning, haloing Franz's head.

Before I know it, he's disappeared into the berth and the train is moving away. The taillights are cruel and merciless. The cold gales whipping through the station chill my wet cheeks. I wipe them with the back of my hand, but it only sets my tears streaming.

18

Death and the Maiden

VIENNA

1920

Every day for the first week after my return to Vienna, I walk to the post office and poke my head inside. And every time, Bettina shakes her head. I'm beginning to question my addiction to the post. Was it the addiction to Franz's words that treated me to such passion and sweetness, or was it just that he was a willing audience to whom I could pour out my heart? It's all a blur and none of it seems real. Except for the withdrawal. Those symptoms are real.

Then, on the seventh day, there is a letter. I grab it from Bettina's hand without even a thank you and race to the parkette to sit in solitude and read. I notice immediately that he has returned to using the formal *sie*.

Frau Milena
So we seem to have drifted apart completely, and the only thing we should have in common is the intense desire that you should be here and your face somewhere near mine. But of course the death wish we also have in common; this wish for a comfortable death. But you want me to stand here on the Prague shore while you drown before my eyes in the Vienna sea, on purpose?

When you say you love your husband so much, that you can't leave him, I believe it and agree with you. When you say that although you could leave him, he nevertheless needs you inwardly and can't live without you, and that therefore you can't leave him, then I believe it too and also agree with you. But when you say that outwardly he can't cope with life without you and that you therefore can't leave him, then this is said either to cover up the above-mentioned reasons, or else it's one of those pranks of the brain under which the body (and not only the body) wriggles.

I've always known you would say those things to me before we met in Gmünd; it has been in the background of almost all your letters. It was in your eyes.

I can bear everything with you in my heart, and if I once wrote that the days without your letters were terrible, then it was not correct, they were only terribly heavy, the ship was heavy, its draught was terribly deep, nevertheless it sailed on your tide. Only one thing I can't bear: the "Fear." For this I'm much too weak, I can't even see the end of this vast Fear, it washes me away.

This brings us again and again to the conclusion that you're united by an all but sacramental indissoluble marriage (how nervous I am, my ship must somehow have lost its rudder during these last days) to your husband, and I by a similar marriage to Fear. This terrible wife often lies on me, I feel it. The indissolubility of the one marriage forms the indissolubility of the other, or at least strengthens it and vice versa. But what remains is nothing. It will never be. Let us never speak again of a future together. Let us not speak at all.

K

My body shatters like crystals caught between mortar and pestle. My face is a stone. Cold metal to the touch. No tears. I can't move. There are always two players in love: the wolves and the sheep. And I know which one I am.

I walk down to Lerchenfelderstraße, but I do not go home. I take the number 46 tram to the last stop next to the Volktheater. I walk across the Ringstraße to the Volksgarten, making sure I avoid all contact with the Grillparzer monument as I pass, and then cut behind the Burgtheater, weaving in and out of tiny thoroughfares, until I'm at the Herrenhof.

Anton-Moritz seats me at my regular table, but the gang isn't here. It's the odd hour between the early afternoon lunch rush and the evening service, when the café crowds disappear and the servers can be seen in the back booth near the kitchen, smoking and playing cards.

I order a sherry, but I do not drink it. My heart dangles from a fishhook so small that it slowly tears away at me with an extremely thin, horrible, sharp pain. I would be less hurt by the letter were I certain he still craved and desired my body next to his. But of this, I am no longer certain. The cold, hard *sie*. Addressing me as Frau, not even a mention of Milenka. And then, the signature. K. For months now, he lost his name. It was simply, "Yours." Because he was all mine. Now he shall no longer be known as mine, or even Franz. He is simply, K. That is how he might be addressed by his colleagues in insurance, or perhaps by an estate broker. I am no more important to him now than a distant acquaintance. Am I to address him as K? Really and truly? What kind of ludicrous name is that?

No more absurd than I have been made to be. I'm a fool. It's as though he was a sculptor with his potter's wheel, and I was a lump of clay, spinning around, dizzy and breathing heavy. He controlled the speed and I didn't know how to get off. I was moulded. Hardened. On display. Then shattered by a mallet to make room for a new masterpiece.

A figure stands over my table. "Is this seat taken?"

"Why don't you just—" I sneer as I tilt my head up but stop short. I know this tall drink of water, with his glossy hair slicked back with brilliantine and a neatly folded handkerchief in his jacket pocket. The only thing missing is his row of war decorations and medals. "It's … you," I say to the man from the Gmünd train.

"Count Franz Xaver Schaffgotsch, at your service." He tilts at the waist in a quick bow.

"Please—" I gesture to the seat opposite me.

He sits and unbuttons his suit jacket, relaxing his shoulders.

"What are you doing in Vienna?" I ask.

"I was an officer stationed in Russia when the

revolution happened, so I had to return to Vienna. I've been here for a year now, helping out with the communist cause."

"You're ... a Bolshevik?" I say in shock.

The Count smirks and says as nonchalantly as though he's hailing a taxi, "Communism will usher in a new world to the Republic, and the Social Democrats should be doing more to that end. Rosa Luxembourg defended democracy in her revolutionary writings, but her idea of the Communist Party's revolt against the German government resulted in her assassination in Berlin last year."

Anton-Moritz walks over, and the Count orders a tonic water and a lemon strudel, the meal of a juvenile.

"Forgive me, but how old did you say you were?" I ask.

"I didn't." He takes a bite of the strudel and a smear of lemon curd sits in the corner of his mouth. "I am twenty years old."

"A bit young to be spouting the merits of Communism, don't you think?"

"I was old enough to be sent into battle," he says through one corner of his mouth, chewing through the other. "Old enough to watch my brothers die around me. The youth of this country will be the ones to propel it forward into the twentieth century. Do not discount us."

"And old enough to know the works of Doktor Freud by heart, I suppose?"

The memory of our train exchange flashes across his face. "Freud is good for one's mind and soul."

"I can't seem to make heads or tails of him," I say, as though running my tongue over a broken tooth. "Besides,

I think Dostoevsky is a better psychoanalyst. He has already written about the same pleasures as Freud, and in less garbled language."

"Perhaps you just need a learned tutor?" He raises an eyebrow.

"Hmmm." I swill my sherry around before downing the small dose in one go. I slam the glass back down and meet his eyes. I do not look away. My hand flutters over the tablecloth.

"Forgive me," he says, leaning back to get a better look at me, "but I still don't know your name."

"Frau—" I begin to say but catch myself. I realize that I might be a scout of men. I find beguiling, attractive men in unlikely places. Or maybe they're not so unlikely. Perhaps they are the likeliest of spots. But I feel the need to defy the one man in my life who has hurt me so exquisitely. He is a king and I've been his pauper. So maybe it's time for a little regicide.

"Fraulein Milena Jesenská. Enchanté."

* * *

Doktor "K"

I received your letter. You forget that I am still working on the new translations for Neumann. Seeing as how you no longer wish to speak of the future, shall I simply do as I wish with these texts and run nothing by you? It would be a shame to see your words in Czech do your German words no justice, don't you think?

If we were still talking, I know you would be proud to hear that artistically I have developed colossally; I battled to make a business out of writing and am happy that I have attained a degree of toughness. Someone in a café wanted to chat with me about how to break into journalism; I replied that an audience with me would cost 300 crowns; he was horrified by my intelligence, my pride in myself, and my assertiveness. He was so horrified that he invited me out to dinner. And then for an evening drink. Oh, the horror. I may not be rich in money, but I'm rich in character. So rich that I give myself away for free every time I sit at my typewriter. This is because, as you well know, it is indeed possible to take my dignity. But as you shall never learn, you can never take my independence. You'll never take my career.

Back to your letter. If we were talking, I would assure you that I know you fear death, but complete death is not possible, so long as you are published. You will never be close to degeneration so long as you crave putting pen to page. I think one day you will reach the point where people will be shocked by the magnitude of your works. A single living piece of literature suffices to ensure the immortality of the writer. Like a petroglyph. You will live many lives. Your novels will be placed in temples and worshipped daily.

But as you have so delicately stated, we should no longer speak. We clearly are nothing to each other. So if you'll excuse me, I have to go work on your translations, and then entertain the man with the horrors again and again. He's not afraid of a little horror. In fact, he has no Fear whatsoever.

Isn't that refreshing?

Frau Pollak

POŠTA ČESKASLOVENSKÁ

FRAU POLLAK, POSTE RESTANTE, POSTAMT 65, BENNOGASSE, WIEN VIII

I CAN'T GO ON WRITING THESE LETTERS. PLEASE, LET'S NOT WRITE AGAIN. MAKE IT IMPOSSIBLE FOR US TO MEET. PLEASE FULFILL MY ONE REQUEST IN SILENCE. IT IS THE ONLY THING THAT CAN ENABLE ME TO GO ON LIVING. EVERYTHING ELSE CAUSES FURTHER DESTRUCTION. DO NOT WRITE.

~K

I sit at my typewriter, my fingers hovering over the keys. Outside my window, the world is still spinning as if nothing has happened. Caterwauls echo inside the Alt Lerchenfelder parish gardens. Bicycle bells mingle with automobile horns. Rainwater runs down the sewer grates in a heavy stream. It seems the world wants to take scissors to my flesh, to cut away all the pieces of me it does not like and does not understand, until only glass and mud is left.

But it wants to cut away the core as well, until my very nature capsizes.

I rip the typewriter off the table and throw it across the room. It smashes my sanity.

For a moment I am frozen by what I've just done. Clarity in the lunacy. But the moment passes, and I scream. The wail tolls. I am dissolving, tearing at my flesh as if I were stripping wallpaper. Sparks crawl up my skin. I am smashing everything that I cannot handle.

Ernst rushes in. "Milena!" His stocky, olive body crashes into me, grabs me by the waist, and slams me on the floor. His weight keeps me down. "What in God's name?" he yells. I fight against him. "Okay! Okay, calm down! It's okay, just calm down!"

He tries to lift my head, but I turn away so I don't have to see my face reflected in his eyes. I bellow into the floor. Ernst rubs my back until my sobs slow.

Later, in the quiet of the evening, I hear Ernst's bedchamber door click and a small voice is ushered in. He closes the door quickly again. It must be Mitzi. I do not mind in the slightest. An hour passes, and I open my bedchamber door to let in Count Schaffgotsch, his smile, and the way his eyes fall upon the bell of my hips. He closes my bedchamber door behind him, and the night thickens.

* * *

Dear Herr Doktor Max Brod,

Forgive me for bothering you; I simply don't know what to do. I can't take it anymore, I don't know anything, I don't feel anything, and I don't understand anything. I don't even know what I want to ask of you! But to Franz, I don't dare write a word. I won't write to him. How could I! I understand his fear down to my deepest nerve. I knew his fear before I knew him. In the four days he was with me in Vienna, he lost it. We laughed about it. But he will never be healthy, Max, as long as he has this fear.

I am bordering on insanity. Please understand what I want: I want to know whether I have caused Franz to suffer as he has with other women, so that he had to flee from me too into his fear. Whether I am to blame, or whether it is a consequence of his nature. You are the only one who may know something. I beg you. Answer me.

I won't write to him, not a line, and I don't know what will happen further. But I'm coming to Prague soon.

I thank you once again.

M.P.

P.S. One more request, a silly one: My translations of "The Judgement," *The Metamorphosis*, and *The Meditation* are appearing with Neumann in the *Červen* edition, but Neumann wants me to write a foreword or an introduction about Franz for the Czech reading public. Franz doesn't want me to write TO him, but Jesus Christ, now I have to write ABOUT him? I just can't. Translating these pieces has already eaten away at my heart and soul. Would you like to write the introduction? Please, if you don't have any reservations, do this for me. You are frank and clairvoyant and you write so beautifully. Please I beg you.

And don't tell F. anything. We'll surprise him, agreed? Perhaps—perhaps it will bring him a little joy.

Bettina stamps the letter, and I stroll out of the post office to jump on the next tram heading to the Meidling district. Alighting at Pohlgasse, I find the black-market men I once knew so well. Showing them what the Affable Thief has procured, I am paid a few thousand crowns. "We haven't seen you around for some time," the man with the gapped yellow teeth and muttonchops says from under his tweed cap.

I shove the notes inside the cup of my camisole. "I haven't been myself," I say. Then I head back toward the Westbahnhof in my dingy porter shirt and blouse.

19

Prague Doesn't Let Go

1920

In October there is an election, and the Christian Socialists take more seats than the Social Democrats, but Vienna remains in the hands of the SDP. Schaffgotsch dubs it "Red Vienna," because even though Austria is still negotiating a settlement with the War Reparations Commission, taxes on the wealthy are introduced in the thirtieth and fortieth percentile. At first, Vienna thinks this will alleviate the tension from inflation, but instead it pushes food and coal prices up. The clash between rich and poor begins to fester and rot in the streets. Nineteen thousand crowns is only worth one American dollar, and half the Republic is unemployed. Hungary has blockaded the export of food. Property is easily requisitioned and repossessed. Interest accrues on unpaid debts. Loans are recalled. Avarice is the only language. Despair guts me. Ernst now does not see a pressing need to leave his employment and move us elsewhere, as hard times always bring prosperity to the banks. I don't want to stay here among the jagged shards of a once-virtuous, bright, and limitless Vienna. I want to go home!

I bought my passage home with the extra funds provided by the dexterity of the Affable Thief and sent a telegram to my father that I will be visiting for a few days. He doesn't reply. He never does. At this point, I think he would swim through an ocean of beer with his mouth closed just to exchange me for a son. Maybe I should steal one for him.

The work on the translations all these months since I last saw Franz has been a torment. A part of me wishes I could buy back my introduction to him, but another part of me—a very vocal part—just wants to go back to the spring, when we were both so besotted. When every trip to the post office felt like being cocooned in a warm sheath. Like growing wings every day. How fitting that I've been translating *The Metamorphosis* then, isn't it? Max agreed to pen the foreword, bless his heart, but he was a bit annoyed by my words that attempted to diagnose Franz. I asked him not to tell Franz, but deep down, I hope he does. I hope Franz knows all about my collaboration with Max. I hope he swims in jealousy. I hope it eats away at his flesh like a pestilence.

Stepping foot outside Prague's main train station, I hop on tram 26 and take the short ride to Wenceslas Square, where I hop off and run north through the narrow, cobbled streets, the streets that I could walk blindfolded. Every time I return to Prague, I am undone. The smell of the oil lamps, the thick Czech accent that looks good on men with full mouths, the light that bounces off the astronomical clock, the feeling that I belong. The progressive Masaryk government makes fools of the Austrian Republic.

I cross the massive Old Town Square and pass the vendors selling wrought iron tools, stained leather hides, rabbit's feet, and pickled turnips until I am standing face to face with the Oppelt house on the north side. The entrance is flanked by a portico colonnade, adorned with decorative plinths where two Roman gods sit in judgement on each other. The latticework grille gate guards the front entrance, and directly above the lunette is a balcony with a grille parapet and balustrade. Two oak doors with glazed windows and an iron handle keep intrusions at bay.

As I ring the doorbell for the apartment marked *Kafka*, a herd of harlots passes giddily behind me and turns up the corner to Pařížská street. I wonder how many of them Franz has bedded.

A woman in black, both skirt and blouse, fabric woven from domestic silks, opens the door. She has a swagger that denotes her queendom; I am a serf. Her hair curls to the sky. The hefty queen puts her hands on her hips and inhales. Oh dear.

"Ahoj," I offer in Czech.

"Guten tag," she replies in German.

I try to smile, but my gullet contracts. So I continue in my best German.

"I'm Frau Pollak from Vienna. I am a friend of Franz Kafka." My heart skips.

"You know my son?" So this is the famous mother I've

heard so much about. Her voice rises. "That most definitely is a Viennese accent you're working with."

I blink. "Please tell me which accent you would most like to hear. I would be happy to oblige your discerning tastes."

She grimaces, turns on her heel, and walks back into the building. I take this as my cue to follow. Closing the heavy oak door behind me, I enter the tiled rez-de-chaussée that bounces my footfalls up the stairwell long before I climb it. Frau Kafka leads me up to the third floor, where they are the only tenants. Entering the mahogany stained door, I immediately feel like I've made a mistake. Like I'm intruding in a private world where I have no business to be.

"Please do be seated," his mother says, but I remain cemented in place. "Hermann!" she bellows.

A short, burly man, with thin-rimmed spectacles and a newspaper in his hands appears in the sitting room. He nods to me but says nothing.

"Go fetch your son. He has a visitor," she barks at her husband, and he dutifully scuttles away. I feel an immediate respect and admiration for her, having trained her husband so diligently.

I hear footfalls coming down the corridor. I don't dare look.

"Someone here to see you, Franz."

I stand in the middle of the sitting room, staring at the sheer curtains over the windows, wondering if I should jump.

Franz and his long strides reach me in seconds. He stands in front of me, his eyes wide. His collared shirt is unbuttoned to his sternum, his black slacks held up by suspenders, but one strap is slipping off his shoulder. He is barefoot and his breath smells like verbena tea. I decide not to let him see my burgeoning regret and straighten my back defiantly, meeting his stare, holding it until one of us breaks.

"This is Frau Pollak," he tells his mother standing beyond my shoulder. "She has been translating my stories into Czech for Neumann's editions."

"Ah, so this is the one who has been filling our letter box every day," she responds, and both Franz and I let out a snicker before covering our mouths.

Franz clears his throat and sits across from me in an armchair as I slowly ease myself onto the settee. We sit uncomfortably, even though the cushions are plush and shapely. His father reappears with a silver tray. A pot of hot ginger mint tea, a creamer, cups, a sugar dish full of rock candy, saucers, and spoons are placed on the coffee table between us. Hermann pours a cup for me, and then one for his son before helping himself. His wife holds a hand up to refuse. He turns to me, this quiet stalk of a man, and whispers in Czech, "She is angry because we are low on provisions. The aid relief we received wasn't enough."

"Wasn't enough, Hermann?" she yips, switching to Czech. "Barely enough to live. No grain, no olive oil, one tin of milk powder, and a small sack of polenta. How am I supposed to feed a family on that? You tell me."

I hold my hot cup in my hands, unsure if this is the right moment to sip. "I didn't know Czechoslovakia was suffering as much as we are in Austria."

I look to Franz for salvation, and he finally replaces his

cup in his saucer. "Our aid relief was supposed to come from Austria's share, but it was delayed at Customs," he explains.

She collapses into her palms and grunts out a loaded wail. Sonorous, her echo ricochets between our ears. Dead music. Franz doesn't rush to her side; instead, he stares angrily at me. Her sobs end as she searches hastily for composure, wiping her cheeks with rigid fingers, her face a seething red bloom. All her wiping simply encourages further tears, but silent ones. "I'm sure there's plenty of grain in Austria," her voice palpitates. I bite at the dead skin on my lip.

"Julie ..." her husband cautions, and I raise my head to gape. That is his mother's name?

She lights a cigarette and passes it to Hermann before lighting another for herself. I can picture her drawing baths for him and drying him off before plunging into the leftover soapy water herself. Franz coughs and swipes at the air.

I finish my tea, replacing the cup on the saucer, my throat warm and moist now. His mother reaches for my cup, peers down into the china, swivels the cup, letting the light hit it in spheres and cones.

"She reads tea leaves," Franz informs me. I want to snatch my cup back. What could my soggy leaves tell her? I want all things about me hidden.

Julie looks up at me. "You'll live a long time," is all she says and hands the cup back.

Silence. The shotgun hidden in my chest is cocked. Then Franz smiles, the corners of his mouth curved. That handsome devil.

Outside the open window, down in the Old Town Square, a young man in a grey suit is arguing with a buggy driver over the size of the basket that he wants to bring into the carriage. He screams and gesticulates the way I wish I could right now.

Everyone sits in awkward silence.

Hermann finally says, "Franz, perhaps..."

"Yes." Franz gets up and closes the distance between us. "Come, Frau Pollak, perhaps you would like to see the view from our terrace?"

Setting down my cup and saucer, I smooth out the wrinkles of my dress and take his offered hand. He leads me out onto the balcony with a balustrade that adorns the front entrance. He closes the French doors behind us, and the October wind whips through our clothes with ease. He folds his arms over his chest, and I try to keep my hairpins in place. It is futile and soon wisps of hair are dancing in the air and slapping against my lips.

"Your mother's name is Julie?" I ask, with exaggerated incredulity.

Franz holds my stare but says nothing.

"What kind of man can be engaged to a woman with the same name as his mother? Unless of course that was seen as an incentive rather than a hindrance."

"I don't know what you're implying." He says each word with distaste.

"Well, even Oedipus didn't see his own mother coming."

"Why did you come here, Milena?" he snaps.

"I tried writing..."

"I told you not to."

"I know but ..." I search for an acceptable answer. Below our feet, in the square, pigeons nibble at cigarette butts and empty walnut shells. "The translations ..."

"Ah, yes, Max told me all about how you strong-armed him into your little scheme," he sneers in a manner that I've never seen before. It cuts deep, to the bone.

"It was supposed to be a surprise for you! A gift, even!" I say. "I told him not to tell you."

"Yes, but you knew he would, didn't you?" He brings his face so close to mine that I have to jerk my neck back to see him clearly. "You were trying to provoke contact with me."

I throw my hands up in the air. "So I wanted to speak to you! Call in the troops! I wanted to talk to the man that I love! Shoot me in my goddamned head!"

"Milena!" He grabs my arms and yanks me forward. "Lower your voice and watch your language."

Across the square, the astronomical clock tolls the hour. Marionettes pop out of cubby holes and do a little dance before retreating inside the clock-face, to the delight and applause of an easily entertained crowd.

"Look, I was in Prague anyway to visit my father and to liaise with Neumann over the translations. I didn't see the harm in saying hello. In fact, I thought it would be rude if I didn't. And frankly ..."

"Yes?" He places both hands on the balustrade and glares down at the people rushing about below, trying to keep their hats from blowing off their heads.

"Frankly, I thought you would have calmed down after a few months and reconsidered your position."

"Well, as you can see, that isn't the case. So I ask you

once again," he looks at me with eyes of brimstone, "what are you doing here?"

I place my hand atop his on the balustrade. "Because Prague doesn't let go. Of either of us. This old crone has claws. One has to yield or else ... remember?"

He snatches his hand from underneath mine like he's been burned. "The crone is you, Milena."

"Oh, for chrissakes!" I say. "Then set me on fire and be done with it."

"I think you're holding on to something that is not meant for you."

"You told me you loved me."

"I did."

"Well, you don't get to take it back when things get rough. You can't be a fully formed adult in any meaningful sense if you renege on your obligations just because things aren't going your way."

"My obligations?"

"When I say that I love someone, it's not some fleeting feeling that will pass with time!" I shout over the wind. "It's because I feel it all the way down to my bones, and I will always feel it."

"You're married!" he shouts back.

"And you said I could leave him and live with you. You said you made enough for us to live comfortably and—"

"Milena, we shall never live together," he says to gut me. "We shall never lie body to body, sit at the same table. We won't even live in the same town."

"Can you predict our future?"

"Why do you talk about a common future? It doesn't exist."

"It existed for us in Vienna."

"No, Milena, it didn't even exist then."

"And do you know why, Franz? Because you do not have the capacity for living. The rest of us, at some time or other, have taken refuge in enthusiasm, in optimism, in some conviction or other, even in pessimism. But you have never escaped to any such sheltering refuge. You are incapable of living! You will never get well. And you will die." Tears well up and tumble down. My forehead burns like scarlet fever.

He nods. The full weight of my words lands on my feet like a planet falling out of the sky.

"I'm sorry," I breathe. "I shouldn't have said that."

"No, you're right," he says. "All these things in life that you mention are glorious. Only not for me. And rightly so," he moves closer to me. "From now on, when you talk about me, speak as if I were dead."

Hot tears speckle my cheeks. My heart is a bushfire, atomizing every branch and leaf into cinders. This charred love of mine would be better suited to kissing all the parts of his body. That is how death will besot me. Teeth and blood, once used in wild acts, will be all that's left to identify my remains. I'll leave behind a scorched landscape. Much like what I've scorched here between us.

"I'm sorry for the pain I have caused you," Franz says, as I turn my face away, hoping the wind will dry my cheeks. "I know this has been a Boschian nightmare."

"Don't worry, I'm sure one day they'll name nightmares after you."

"What?"

My words were eaten by the wind.

"I said," I clear my throat, "that it seems to me that you cannot see the sun unless you first read a novel about how to feel its warm rays. My wish for you is that you might one day see beauty in everything in the world."

"Youth is happy because it has the capacity to see beauty," he says. "Anyone who holds on to the ability to see beauty never grows old."

I turn back to him and place my hand on his cheek. "That's why you're dying, Franz."

He shrugs. "I cannot help it if I love all kinds of people—including the dead."

His words hang briefly in the air before the breeze takes them over the canopy of thatched roofs and church steeples. He reaches into his pocket and pulls out the locket. My scorched heart grips me, like blood is seeping into my lungs. He places it in my hands, then turns, and disappears back inside his apartment. My tears teethe, chewing out my eyes like a golem until all I can see is a black Prague.

STANDING BEFORE MY MOTHER'S grave, I realize I can't remember the last time I paid her a visit. She lies next to my infant brother, Jan. Together for eternity in a way they couldn't be in life. Her stone is overgrown with vines of ivy; I tear at the branches and then wipe down her name. Which is my name.

Here lies Milena.

The sky is changing colours; the cerulean blue has creamed into a salmon haze. The veins behind my eyes pulse and the flesh of my throat singes like dying embers. I clench my fists as acid blazes up my esophagus. Tooth enamel melting. Nostrils exploding. A sucker punch to my gut. Blast to the head. I'm disintegrating into nothing. My mother's death suffocates my veins.

I steady myself on her stone, but I still fall to my knees. I'm praying to her, but the prayers aren't benedictions or wishes of much weight. I tell her hello. I tell her I miss her.

Gophers and chipmunks dart into holes. Wind skips the stones off the dusty path. Jackdaws sing.

Then, for a moment, before it is buried again, I hear her voice, *There are two possibilities in life, Milena: to accept one's fate, or to seek one's fate.*

ON THE TRAIN BACK to Vienna, I have a berth all to myself, so I sink into the cushions and close my eyes. When I stand up again, the cushions keep my shape briefly before they retake their form and my body is lost, craving the pressure and heat of another—laps, thighs, bones.

I get off the train early at the Meidling Hauptbahnhof instead of the main train station. Winding past the crowds of people navigating market day, I walk across Pohlgasse and find the black marketeers loitering like spider monkeys in a doorway. My man, the one with the cap and teeth like a chess board, greets me and I show him the locket. He looks it over, opens it, and finds my portraits and my words. He stuffs 100 crowns into my hand, but not before asking, "Why wouldn't you want to keep this?"

I do not say, "Because I had a great love and I lost it." Instead, I just shake his hand and walk away.

Back at Lerchenfelderstraße, I sit on the lavatory floor,

naked and cold. Guilt follows me like a dopplegänger. What is there to do? What can free me from the mad inner voices? They are like hungry coyotes: you can't kill them and you can't feed them and they never shut up.

So I drink an entire tincture bottle of laudanum while thumbing the old scars on my wrists. But I do not die. I just sleep it off.

In the morning I receive a telegram, sent directly to my home:

YOUR LETTERS WERE THE MOST BEAUTIFUL THING THAT EVER HAPPENED TO ME IN MY LIFE.

~K

20

The Drawings of Lamentable Artists

VIENNA

NOVEMBER 1923

Last night I had a dream. War broke out across the globe, and we had to flee in a great hurry, but to where? Endless trains, one after another, departed from the main railway station, going out into the world, but all of them were overcrowded. Panic gripped us. People were fighting for seats. "Please let me sit," they cried, "I have a child!" Or "I am sick!" Or "I have to see my family again!" Neverending throngs of people blocked my way to the platform, and I couldn't even summon the hope that I would ever push through them. Despair coursed through me. Somehow, I was given a ticket from someone; I didn't really see his face, but he was an old acquaintance. Someone I once loved, I was sure of it. He told me the ticket would take me over the border. Eight carriages to a train, and everyone sat shoulder to shoulder, heads motionless in their laps, faces carved from melancholy stone. We all sat in anguish for five hours. Then six. Until the train finally moved. The departure of the train heralded a catastrophe. As we moved away at high speed, the earth behind us collapsed into a great void, and the world was transformed into merely a series of railroads over which the displaced people travel. At the border, officials shouted, "All out for control!" But when I unfolded my ticket, I discovered that it contained only one message: *Condemned to death*.

The images of this dream—I cannot shake them. The dream keeps me gripped like a fox in a trap. I must write about this. I have continued writing my fashion columns for the *Tribuna*, but over the past few years, I have contributed personal and political essays and op-eds to the *Národní listy* and even the *Lidové Noviny*, all from my home on Lerchenfelderstraße. And curiously, this has put me in the new position of receiving what my editor calls "fan mail"; apparently, my musings and diatribes are considered required reading in the cafés, literary salons, and social circles of Prague. A cause célèbre, they say. A strange experience it is indeed to be recognized on the street whenever I visit Jarmila or Staša, or even my father. He is mellowing a bit in his advanced years. Perhaps his shame of me is tempered by the fact that I am his only child. His only family. Even my aunt Růžena keeps him at arm's length. And although he will never approve of Ernst, I can't blame him, since I hardly approve of him either. Ernst keeps himself busy with Mitzi; I occupy myself with Schaffgotsch, and neither of us asks questions. It is a marriage sailing perilously on still waters; should anyone dare stick in an oar and try to push the boat one way or the other, we will all capsize.

And as for Franz...

We still write to each other, though it is sporadic. I don't like the new clerk at the post office with the horseshoe-ring hair and the face that looks like a haunted doorknocker. Franz is now living in Berlin with a woman named Dora, whom I suspect he might marry soon. Surprise, surprise. He is now miraculously able to have a healthy relationship with a woman. I do all the renovations, but someone else gets the house.

I'm at Café Sperl, writing to him about his good fortune.

> It seems you are not lacking in female interest. But the lung keeps gasping. I suppose that's the way you're built. You have real blood pumping through that heart of yours. All arteries are working. Bless you, K, may a day come when it hurts no more. Although, I think some of us, and maybe you as well, live in a kind of sea of unacknowledged grief. Women and wives come and go, but the river of sadness flows through it all.

I do not use *du*. We have been corresponding in the formal, distant *sie* for years now. Perhaps it is better this way.

I add a few more pleasantries and platitudes before signing and folding the letter. Placing it in my satchel, I get up and head for the magazine rack. I select the

Frankfurter Zeitung, the *Prager Tagblatt*, the *Kronenzeitung*, and a few penny dreadfuls just for the laughs.

Taking my seat, I stir my cappuccino with extra mounds of foam and spread out the papers. All of them have screaming black headlines. Something has happened in Munich. I scan each histrionic article. It appears a group of outcasts, a fascist branch of the German National Socialists, have tried to overthrow the Bavarian government. No, wait. As I read, I discover it wasn't just some disgruntled political miscreants; it was a massive march of thousands. It resulted in a pogrom, and four police officers were massacred. The papers cannot tell if the goal of the attempted coup was pure agitation or real political gain, but the men were shouting for revolution. They want what they are calling "lebensraum." What an odd little concept; sounds like white noise to me. There has been a manhunt, as the Weimar Republic will not accept any such threats or attacks, but the riots on the streets continue. They have arrested the ringleader of this incident, which the press is now calling the Beer Hall Putsch.

I read this instigator's name and something in me flashes and clicks. I know this name. How do I know this name? It tugs at me like a tick tapping into my veins. Rising from my seat, I look up at the walls of Café Sperl. The first day that Franz visited me in Vienna all those years ago, he pointed out the watercolours. What was it that our server said? Something about ... Oh, it's on the tip of my tongue.

I lean right up against the booths lining the walls so I can inspect the paintings with greater precision.

"Meine Dame, your knee!" an old man with a bottle of Apfelschorle exclaims as I nearly mount him, but I am oblivious. I devour the watercolours like the answer lies inside their pithy pictures. Something is pulling me into them like an ebbing tide. They are the lighthouse, revealing what I cannot see on my own.

Then I come across one picture—of a town square with a stone fountain and wood beam façades framing the buildings. It isn't very skilled; the hand that drew it must have shaken a bit, but I wouldn't call it horrible either. Probably worth a cup of coffee.

That's it! Our server told us the café would give struggling artists a free brew in exchange for a watercolour, as it was so close to the Art Academy.

I dash back to my table, grab the *Frankfurter Zeitung*, and rush back to the watercolour. I hold up the paper with the headline screaming the criminal's name. The name of the man now awaiting trial. I shift my glance back to the artist's name on the bottom right of the watercolour. I squint at the scrawl.

A. Hitler. 1908

21

Lebensraum

PRAGUE

1939

The Obergruppenführer pushed back his chair and clasped his hands behind his back as he paced the length of the room. Milena's swollen lip throbbed like it needed to be drained. She took shallow, drawn-out breaths. There wasn't enough air in the basement cellars. From down the corridor, she heard the sounds of a door crashing open and a woman screaming as she was dragged from one cell to another. Men shouted and grunted. Her shrieks were a death knell.

"Who is Joachim von Zedtwitz, Frau Jesenská?" the Obergruppenführer asked. He did not raise his voice. It was almost as though he didn't care for the answer.

She glanced up at him, but when he turned to her, she quickly looked away. "Now, let me think..."

"You might know him as Jochi," he clarified.

When she didn't answer, he shoved his face mere millimetres from her nose. His breath inflated her shirt and made her lashes dance. She didn't retreat. "Why do you ask me questions you already know the answer to?" She clenched her jaw.

He smiled like he'd just been handed a newborn. "I've never seen a woman delight so in defying me. It's stupendous, it really is."

He stood upright and appeared to move away, but before Milena could breathe a sigh of relief, his body wound back and he swung a kick at the legs of her chair. She hit the concrete floor with a thud. Face scraped, tooth chipped, she gasped for air, but only hotness filled her lungs. He stood over her and said again in his flatlining voice, "Who is Jochi, Frau Jesenská?"

She wheezed, "He's a German Count!"

He read from his folded report. "With a nice two-seater Aero coupé sports car, isn't that right?"

"He's a member of the Nazi Party, for chrissakes!"

He reached down and grabbed Milena by the cheeks; she winced as his fingers dug into the exposed nerve of her tooth. "He's a Jew sympathizer, as are you." He held her eyes with his, and she couldn't help but notice the beautiful aquamarine colour of his irises. Over the past few years, it had come to her attention that the most beautiful of creatures, both wild and tame, were capable of the most gruesome acts. A lioness will rip the beating heart right out of an antelope without so much as a nod of apology. A snow-white polar bear will eat an otter while it's still alive, without a care or a second thought. And these majestic Aryans, with their peaches-and-cream complexions and crystal eyes, will garrotte and disembowel a raven-haired Slav for attempting to cross the border with an extra ten Reichsmarks sewn into the lining of her dress.

"We have intelligence," the Obergruppenführer continued, "suggesting that he smuggled Jews into Poland in that car—Jews who hid in your house on Kouřimskà street."

"Why do you care so much about where the Jews sleep at night?" she hissed.

"It's for their own protection," he responded, his boilerplate reply.

"Look," she pushed down on the cold floor and up on her forearms, drenched in sweat, and raised her upper torso just enough to regain a modicum of dignity, "you don't want any Jews to remain in Czechoslovakia, so I did you a favour by helping them leave. What does it matter to you if you don't have to deal with them?" She scolded herself quietly for allowing her voice to land on the wrong side of pleading.

"Poland is ours now." He smirked. "We'll find them nevertheless."

She thought of Ernst, who had sent her a telegram the week prior from his exile in London, thanking her for facilitating his escape through Poland during the summer. Their marriage may have been a failure, but family is family. And Milena was never one to forsake blood in favour of settling old scores.

The Obergruppenführer shook his head as though he were shaking off a jab to the chin. His brows dropped, his nostrils flared. "They should die," he breathed. "They should all die. And you along with them."

For the briefest of moments, Milena heard Czech folk songs ringing through Wenceslas Square as her neighbours and friends bought roasted chestnuts and bunches of pasqueflowers. The bells of Jakob's Church echoed up and down the meat market where kitchen wenches haggled for the best price for fat geese and plucky hens. The spicy paprika scent wafted around her in a swirl. The number 15 tram dinged its bell as it rumbled by the Café Arco. Inside, writers and philosophers debated the merits of Dostoevsky. She heard their voices now with a resounding clarity.

"Perhaps it is beautiful to die in vain," she snarled. "Perhaps it is beautiful to shed blood in a heroic gesture for your country. But we won't be doing that. We will live, Herr Obergruppenführer. My only interest is the culture of Czechoslovakia's past, and the future of the Czech people."

"We have all sorts of people here, Frau Jesenská, not just your blessed Czechs. Some are good racial quality—they are quite simple to handle; in fact, they have welcomed us. We can Germanize them with ease. But on the other hand, there are—" he chose his words like he was choosing which pastry to order from the patisserie "—racially inferior *elements*. These we must get rid of. There's plenty of space eastward."

Milena stared at the row of medals and emblems over his heart: the Iron Cross First Class, the winged eagle, and the swastika. Eastward, he'd said; she knew what that meant. There were stories of the Makotřasy village. Men executed in the garden of a farm. Women and children put in a schoolhouse in Kladno that was locked and set ablaze. She couldn't decide if that fate was preferable to the stories of the camps in the east. The forced labour. The disease and squalid conditions. The electrified fences and the dead rotting all around. The bodies in piles. The firing squads and the mass graves. The stories had been swirling since 1933, when reports from Munich circulated of a camp deep in the forest from which there was no escape.

"Finally," he continued, "there is a group of people who are acceptable in racial terms, but hostile to us in their thinking. Sound familiar, Frau Jesenská? They are most dangerous, because they—"

"Think for themselves?" she interjected.

"Precisely." He took a turn about the cold room as though he were going for a stroll on the promenade. "Naturally, we can try to relocate some of them to the Reich, put them in a purely German environment, and then Germanize and re-educate them. But should that prove to be impossible, we must..."

"Must what?"

He stood over her like he was inspecting a rose bed, keeping his mouth closed just long enough to crack a smile. "Put them against the wall."

Milena recoiled and her guts flipped. She thought of her beautiful daughter, Honza, and the grandchildren she would never see: their tiny voices, their sun-scented hair, hard candies in their hands. Would they be able to count to forty? Would they eat their Brussels sprouts? What would they dream about? Would they be girls? Would they suffer the same injustices, or would they break free?

"The Reichsprotektor will never allow you to do that," she squeaked out.

"Von Neurath? Ha!" He smirked. "He may not hold that position much longer. I am a personal friend of the Führer and of the SS-Reichsführer Himmler. I expect big things." He tugged at his suit. "And I look great with an army under my command."

"We will strike back!" she barked, like the last gasps of a rabid dog.

"All resistance will be butchered," he whispered. "The Czech people will cease to exist. You will all be Deutsches Reich."

"We are not your untermenschen. We won't give you lebensraum."

When he kicked her in the stomach, she vomited bile and blood. When she began to choke on it, he let her. She writhed on her back, unable to clear her airway, her eyes bulging like balloons, her capillaries bursting in the skin under her eyes.

Finally, he grabbed her shoulder and rolled her onto her side and she expectorated the last bits of acid and flesh. Darkness fell across her eyes, and she hoped for its long and sublime friendship. The solitude, the quiet, the lack of echoes, where the distance was buried behind a cornucopia of grey, for that's where she felt warm. It was freeing—the dark bringing on liberty.

22

Metamorphosis

JUNE 1924

The times have changed so quickly. Dresses and hairdos are shorter, lips are redder, music is faster, nights are hotter. The drinks are less salubrious, the affairs more scandalous, and inflation is but a bad dream. Czechoslovakia, Italy, France, and the British Empire collectively loaned Austria more than one billion crowns and the League of Nations now controls our economy. Things stabilized rather quickly, and now they tell us that by the end of the year, they will replace the crown with a new currency: the shilling. Will Franz live to see the dawn of a new age?

When I received a letter from Franz addressed directly to my home, I noticed straight away that it was not sent from Prague. Or Italy. Or Berlin. Or any of the other myriad locations from which he has written to me over the years. It was sent from Austria, a village on the outskirts of Vienna, in fact. The letterhead was from the Kierling sanatorium. He was asking to see me.

With some perspective from Schaffgotsch, I spoke to Ernst about visiting Franz in the sanatorium. Last year, I finally told him about the affair back in the summer of 1920. To my surprise, he took the news rather well. His main complaint was that I had kept it a secret, rather than trusting him. He said Kafka was always someone he respected and admired. With some small, strange degree of pride, it gave him pleasure to know that his wife was regarded highest among all by such a man and mind as Kafka. And to my utter astonishment, he admitted that it would have been rather hypocritical of him to punish me for my affairs while Mitzi was now practically living with us at Lerchenfelderstraße.

An agreement was hatched: for as long as it was working for us, we would remain married and continue to build our lives together but still be free to have our dalliances as we wished. The one rule was honesty. Ernst didn't mind that I sometimes spent three or four consecutive nights away with Schaffgotsch, so long as I gave him a ring on our new residential telephone. And conversely, I would humbly share our living space with Mitzi, so long as her presence didn't interfere with my work and deadlines. She and I have become civil, so much so that sometimes I even do her the favour of drawing her bath. For all I care, she can drown in the damn thing.

So, Ernst gave me his blessing to travel to Kierling. These were the acts of kindness and compassion that made me fall for Ernst all those years ago as we ran wild through the streets of Prague like no scandal could ever touch us. Now there is respect and admiration between us, but if I'm being honest, there is no love left. We are partners. Ernst knows me better than anyone. He never cared that I was a radical, a thief, or even a mouthy charlatan who terminated a pregnancy and escaped from an asylum just to be with him. And for that, I stay with him.

Today, the train ride to Kierling is short and uneventful, though I can't stop fidgeting with my silk turban over my slicked and pinned bob. My hair has always been an unruly beast.

Inside the sanatorium, a deaconess nurse in a white tunic and cap leads me to the intensive care salon in the east wing. Beyond the doors of the private care rooms, I can hear nothing but coughing and wailing. There is a strong smell of septic waste and industrial solvent cleaners. Most windows remain closed because of a fear of spores. I am given a cloth mask that ties behind my ears to wear over my mouth and nose. It looks like a garment for a ridiculous clown.

The deaconess leads me into the salon, and I see a row of backs huddled over a cast-iron hospital cot. They turn to me, all of them wearing masks.

"Milena," a voice says. The man pulls down his mask.

"Max." I step forward and shake his hand.

The others eye me curiously. I smile weakly but then remember my mask.

"Milena, you remember Franz's parents, Hermann and Julie."

Hermann's eyes are blotched red and glassy. Julie

wobbles as if the inside of her head has been scraped clean. "Yes, of course." I shake their hands, but they say nothing.

"And this is his sister Ottla."

The famous younger sister. I am impressed by her femininity and graceful features despite bearing a striking resemblance to her brother—the aquiline nose, the hooded brows. But when she pulls down her mask to greet me, I am met with a pair of plush lips, a tiny round chin, and a soft voice.

"I wish we had met under better circumstances," I say, and she lowers her eyes in a sombre nod.

"And this," Max brings me to the final sentry by the bed, "is Dora Diamant."

Her thick shock of midnight hair, so heavy and wavy, turns first before I even see her face.

"Hello." I extend my hand. Her gaze holds mine longer than normal, before she grips my hand in hers and gives it a firm shake. She says nothing.

"God in heaven," Max suddenly exclaims, "don't you two look alike!"

Ottla, Dora, and I stand there, staring at him. If our eyes were pistols, he'd have more holes in him than Swiss cheese.

He clears his throat and pushes his glasses back up the bridge of his nose. "Mother always said I was bad at reading social cues."

There is a groan from behind the row of people and a withered arm rises above the canopy of heads and hats. "Might I have a word with Frau Pollak?"

"Franz," I gasp, and bring my hands up to my chest.

Under the ivory-white sheets lies a body thin as an ice

pick. Veins bulge purple at the skin's surface, which has the texture of sandpaper. His throat and jugular are a mottled yellow-jade colour with deep purple bruises. The skin around his eye sockets has sunk beneath his brow bone, and the hair on his head has been shaved down to the nub. His lips are chapped and chafed, his fingernails black. He has never looked so small.

"He can't sit up," Ottla whispers to me.

"Come sit with me," he says, and pats the mattress by his hip.

"My darling," Dora pipes up and moves toward him, "don't you think you should rest your voice? The doctor said—"

"Dora, my love," he interjects, "would you be a dear and fetch me some ice chips?"

She pauses, her face loaded with unspoken protests. But after she looks from him to the rest of us, she quietly nods. She leans down to give him a kiss on the forehead and then gives me a look that could cut glass before heading toward the door. Hermann, Julie, Ottla, and Max follow, closing the door behind them.

The air around us is still and quiet like twilight on the quiet side streets of Prague. I take a seat at his bedside. "So," I say anxiously, taking in the gruesome state of his body, "what a sloth you've become."

He narrows his eyes. "What's that?"

"Just what do you think you're doing lying here all day, lazy bones? Don't you have novels to write?"

"I—"

"Wasting everyone's time and energy too, I bet. I'd expect this kind of behaviour from a truant child, or a criminal scoundrel, but not from you, you trumpetting shit-gibbon."

His sunken, bloodshot eyes glisten suddenly with life and a smile curls his raw lips. "I love it when you scold me."

Gazing upon him, I reach over and place his skeletal hand in mine. "I came as soon as I received your letter, my dear." I yank off my face mask and toss it aside.

"Thank you for coming." His cheek disappears into the down pillow as he turns his head gingerly to look at me. He breathes aftertastes onto my lips. "I have tried to keep up my correspondence while here. In fact, I'm almost done a new novel."

I exhale. "Well, chop, chop, mister, there's no time to lose."

He smiles. "Yes, Teacher Milenka."

I haven't heard my sobriquet pass his lips in so long. It's bittersweet. A window into a past life that no longer exists. "What's the novel?"

"It's not finished yet," he says hoarsely. "But you'll like it. I promise."

"What's it called?"

"I was thinking of going with *The Castle*."

"*The Castle*," I roll the title around my mouth like a peach pit. "Sounds mysterious and regal."

His fingers grip mine weakly. "It's been so long since I've seen you."

"I know."

"I'm sorry you have to see me like this."

"Don't be daft!" I squeeze his fingers delicately for fear they might break. "Besides, you look fine to me. You're clearly getting better. This won't last long, Franz. Not at all. Mark my words. You're getting stronger every day, I can tell. Soon you'll be up and about and we'll laugh about this..."

I ramble on like a parrot in a cage, but then he gives me a look that chastises me without a single utterance. "You don't have to, you know."

"You're going to live, Franz." My nose stings. "Soon we'll celebrate your forty-first birthday!"

"No, Milenka." A single tear spills out the corner of his eye and slowly marches to the pillow, where it disappears.

"Don't give up the fight," I whisper.

"Trust me, I will stay here until death comes and finds me, but..."

"What?"

"Don't dream dreams."

"I thought that's what you liked about me," I quip.

He furrows his heavy brow. "You know, when it comes to us, sometimes I feel as though we have a room with two doors on opposite sides, and each of us is holding a doorknob. At the bat of an eyelash, if one of us utters a single word, the other is sure to close the door behind them, so they can no longer be seen."

My chin collapses and I bite my lip. "I see it differently, Franz."

"Oh?"

"I picture myself standing behind your door, with my face pressed to the keyhole. And I am waiting to see what will happen inside. Yet this whole time, I could have just climbed through your window. Don't you see? It is the window, not the door, that is the gateway to freedom.

Beyond the window lies the whole world, the big expanse of blue sky. It's where longing and desire lies. To see the countryside through a window means to see it twice: through the eyes, and through longing. At the door lies only real life."

He begins to cough, so I reach for the pitcher of water, quickly pour a glass, and then I bring it to his lips, raising his head slightly with the palm of my other hand. He takes small gulps before he gurgles, and I put the glass down. Blood appears, and I soak a washcloth to clean up his chin. When the attack subsides, I place the cold washcloth on his forehead.

"That feels nice," he sighs and swallows hard. "Speaking of real life, how is Herr Pollak?"

I slump back in my chair and look about the salon. Cold, white tiles crawl up the walls. A wood-handled mop soaks inside a metal pail; a single fly buzzes about it but never lands. A linen chest of towels, sheets, face cloths, rubber tubes, metal instruments, and trays fills the corner by the closed window. The drapes are open, however, so the jackdaws and magpies resting on the branch of the apricot tree beyond the glass can say hello and dance about.

"Oh dear, that bad, eh?" he says, and I catch myself.

"Well," I start, "I guess I thought we'd have children by now. I so long to be a mother."

"You have a lot of love to give," he whispers.

"But no one to give it to me." I shrug. "I do have bright spots in every day, and I don't take them for granted. That much is true. But I want so much more than what's on offer. I want a daughter. I want to go back to Prague. I want a love that could fill a Russian novel."

He closes his eyes to soak in the chill of the washcloth, and when he opens them again, the rich brown abyss that once made me peel off my dress in the Wittgensteins' front entrance has returned in full force. "Milenka," he breathes, "you have always remained staunchly yourself. The lesson it has taught me is that no matter what, following your own path is infinitely better than doing what is expected. It is awfully easy to fall victim to the voices of jealous naysayers and abandon your goals. But you, Milena Jesenská, you continue to ignore them. And not subtly either, but outrageously loudly and defiantly. That is a trait worth celebrating in a world where many diminish their own voices. Milena, you are the bravest woman I've ever known."

Hot tears fall, and I clasp his hand in mine once again. "Do you really believe that?"

His fingers caress the scars on my wrist. "I believe," he whispers, "that there are two possibilities in life: to accept one's fate, or to seek one's fate."

BY NIGHTFALL, THE LESIONS on Franz's gullet make swallowing unbearable, and he is coughing up bits of flesh from the back of his throat. He cannot even swallow water. He cannot even swallow his own saliva. Sputum fills a small gathering pan placed under his chin. Dora sends us all home, but I return in the morning, and he has lost the ability to speak.

Franz hasn't eaten for three days, I learn from the deaconess, as Dora and Ottla go to the nearby synagogue to pray. A team of doctors tried a procedure called intubation—it is explained to me as tubes that are passed down the esophagus so that liquid food can reach the stomach—but the tubes were too big for Franz's swollen throat. I enter the east wing salon as the doctors throw about ideas: *A tracheotomy perhaps so that he can breathe more easily? Perhaps the intubation can be inserted via the tracheotomy?* Franz lies before them as they surround his bed like merchants of death, deciding his fate.

I push through them—he is awake, his eyelids fluttering. Creases and furrows ripple across his face; the pain must be acute. His cheeks have collapsed into hollows, and the cartilage in his nose and ears appears to have melted away, as these appendages are now pointy protrusions like those found on a vampire bat.

"Well?" I spit at the men in white coats. "Do something! He's starving to death!"

"Who is this?" a doctor with whiskers yells over his shoulder to the deaconess.

"I'm with him!" I snap.

The doctor grabs me by the forearm. "I will have no histrionics in front of the patient," he hisses. "Out in the corridor now."

"Don't you dare touch me, you spineless oaf." I wrench his hand off me. "He can still hear us, and he is smarter than all of you stuffed shirts put together, so tell him what's going on."

"There's no need to send him into a panic," the whiskered doctor sneers.

"Doctor," I straighten my back, "do you know who you're dealing with?"

"I beg your pardon?"

"Franz isn't afraid of death. So, if he is about to die, let him know so he can make his peace and say his goodbyes."

The doctor sighs and shoves his hands in his long coat's pockets. "It's too late," he says in a monotone, before motioning for the deaconess to step forward. "Call the rabbi and bring back his wife."

"She's not his wife!" I shriek, but the men in coats and the deaconess have already made a move for the door.

Two nurses remain behind, wheeling a metal table to his bedside. "Sit yourself down, meine Dame," one of them says in a pleasant voice, pointing to a bedside chair. "We can make him more comfortable."

Sitting and grasping Franz's hand, I see that his eyes are now open and alert. "Franz?" I say, keeping control of my voice. "Can you hear me?"

A tear crumples from the corner of his eye and rolls quickly into his ear. Below fluttering lids, he shifts his gaze and looks right at me.

"My darling," I cup his cheek. It is scaly and clammy.

His lips move as the nurse files off the tip of a morphine capsule, breaks off the glass, and plunges a syringe into the clear, drippy kiss of relief.

"What's that, darling?"

I place my ear right up against his lips, careful not to smother him. His breath is hot and stale, and his cracked lips scratch at my skin.

The nurse retracts the plunger, and the needle fills in the vacuum slowly.

I pull away and look him in the eyes. For the briefest moment, this room, the nurses, the sanatorium, everything disappears, and we are sitting face to face in the bright Café Arco, swimming in each other's gaze, a wealth of possibilities laid before us. We are cycling along the Danube, the wind in our hair and the sun bronzing our skin. We are dancing the Charleston in the speak-easy, laughing as we step over each other's toes. We are standing in the Hotel Riva lobby, counting the bed bug bites on each other's shoulders. We are sitting in the parkette, stealing kisses when the coast is clear. We are holding each other close among a sea of night revellers in Gmünd town square, my arms slung around his neck, his strong hands along my back. We are lying naked beside one another, our skin mingling to become one body. We are standing on his balcony, overlooking all of Prague, the wind stealing all the things we wish we could say to each other.

He once told me I was a gift to him from God, and I want so badly to offer him one more miracle. But as the nurses leave the room, I see their exchange of glances. This is it.

So, I lie down on the bed next to Franz's emaciated body. We are so close that he cannot look at me, but his temple rests against mine. His eyes traverse the expanse of the ceiling, until they fall upon the window. A solitary jackdaw sits on a branch, observing us.

"My darling," I whisper, my voice trembling. "Just think, you'll never have to meet another living soul ever again. What a relief. From now on, you can lie in the grass and look at the clouds in peace. And when you feel sad, you'll remember just how pleasant it is to be alone. You will finally have the only kind of solitude that revives."

He blinks his glossy eyes, and for a time, I think he might smile. I admire his finely wrought cheekbones. If

I begin to weep, I promise myself, I will look away. The thought of finally being wrapped in a kittel must surely be giving him solace.

I pull out from my brassiere a telegram he wrote to me before we were lost to each other. There are voices calling down the corridor. There are footfalls and echoing shoe squeaks and door slams. I bargain with God to give us just a few minutes more. Unfolding the telegram, I clear my throat and begin to read. My words are softer than egg yolks, my tongue as clear as wine.

"'It sometimes seems to me that instead of ever living together, we'll just be able to contentedly lie down beside one another in order to die. But whatever happens, it will be close to you.'"

I lace my fingers with his. His eyes roll back in his head.

I gasp. Hands shake. Spine bolts. Stomach flips. Lungs thud. I place my cheek against his chest and listen for a heartbeat. My fingernails dig into his cotton hospital gown. But all I do—all I can do—is close my eyes.

The jackdaw outside the window flaps its wings and lifts off into the sky.

23

Decree Nisi

VIENNA

1925

The Herrenhof is at capacity. Servers rush about in their ridiculous waistcoats and money belts, serving Linzertorte slices, small cups of espresso, and mineral water sourced from the Alps. Women with feathered turbans and boas cross their legs to flash the buckles of their brogue Mary Janes. Men with hair parted in the centre and slicked from root to ear with brilliantine talk with cigarettes hanging on their lips and drink imported plum brandy from Poland.

Ernst and I sit at a small marble-topped table in the corner, against the vermillion damask wallpaper. The clatter of cutlery, low-pitched voices, and high-pitched cackles fills our ears. Beyond the window, horse-drawn carriages trot around Michaelerplatz. When the glass doors swing open, a gust of cool autumn air rushes through the café, chilling our feet. The summer is coming to a close.

I open the silver caddy that Ernst gave me for our fifth wedding anniversary, take out a slim cigarette, and pop it between my ruby lips. I never would have dared to wear such a garish colour of lipstick when I was younger, but this is the 1920s, darling, and the times have come for all of us with great urgency. Retrieving his lighter from his breast pocket, Ernst thumbs the ignition four or five times, shaking the fluid, until finally an orange flame with a blue centre bursts forth. I lean into it, sucking on the tip of the cigarette until the kiss of smoke fills my mouth and throat, and I breathe deeply. My head lolls back to exhale. I leave a ruby kiss on the rim of the filter.

"So do you have any plans, or..." Ernst trails off.

"Not as such," I say, as I shake my head. "I think I'll just see how it goes, really."

His fingers nervously tap out time on the table. "Well, I... I can't say I'm surprised."

"I know." I lower my eyes.

"I guess," he looks up from his percussive fingers as a waiter rushes by with a bill of service, "I thought perhaps after all these years, you might learn to be happy with me and the way things are."

I ponder this as I flick my cigarette into the glass ashtray. "At this age, I know myself well enough to know that I am only happy with the way things should be."

He nods. "You know, in my way, I have loved you. Very much."

"Darling, this is no one's fault." I reach out and cover his hand. "I'm not asking you to take any blame. All I'm asking is for both of us, you and me, to take responsibility. We have to at least demand that of ourselves."

His fingers lattice with mine, his thumb slowly caressing my palm. "Was there something more I could have given you?"

I look at our hands entwined, much like the way they were the day we got married. "Ernst, remember when you first met me in Prague? What was I, sixteen? All I wanted to be then was beautiful, because I thought that's all I had to offer the world. But now that I'm grown, I want to threaten people with my wit. I want to charm people with my charisma. I want to be otherworldly. I want to scorch every heart and engulf every spirit I encounter. I want to be loved and helplessly adored for the power of my thoughts. And nothing else, Ernst. Not one damn thing more."

"Well," he lifts his copita of port in a toast, "here's to being otherworldly and vaguely threatening."

Clinking my hot glass of glühwein, I smile and sip. "You know, that's probably the nicest toast with which you've ever saluted me."

"I have my moments." He grins. "Besides, I wanted to do it right just once."

I've already signed and filed my documents requesting a decree nisi; he simply needs to sign his, and our request should be granted within twelve weeks. The year 1925 will begin with a new outlook: no longer "we," but simply "I."

He doesn't prevaricate over the fine print or the obfuscating legal jargon. He just looks for the X and signs his name.

"Thank you," I say, and gather the documents in a manila envelope before sliding them into my satchel.

"You're welcome," he says. "Now we can at least enjoy our drinks."

As we sip, a young couple two tables over is having a disagreement. She pulls his folded handkerchief right from his breast pocket and dabs at her eyes; he leans in and fights his case. Some words carry across the café.

I snort as I sip my glühwein. *I love you* and *I'm telling the truth* are the two most popular phrases in the world. And neither offers any guarantee.

SCHAFFGOTSCH BEGAN AN AFFAIR with Gina Kaus, much to the chagrin of her husband, Otto, so I took the opportunity to make a clean break from Vienna and return to the windswept shores of the Vltava. Prague is just as I left her, under a canopy of blue. The street sweepers use wire-bristled brooms on the sixteenth-century cobblestones, cleaning the day's debris off the face of the city. The gauze of night sets in and lamps illuminate the long streets that stretch from the riverbanks to the rail tracks to the cemeteries and then disappear. The tall, lean houses, the dip and curve of the terraces that climb up the façades, the red and brown leaves falling upon wooden benches—I wish Franz were here with me to see it all. He'd love this more than I could. He'd infuse it with something extra. He'd go out on the water and cast his net.

The air is wet and likes my nose. There's a band setting up on the promenade, tourists lining up for boat rides along the river; I even hear some bagpipes playing. Brash women with full mouths and platinum bleached hair like film siren Anita Page sell me milk cakes from Café Slavia. When I speak, they tell me I must be foreign because of my accented Czech. What a kick in the teeth.

I move back in with my father, and he is unapologetically pleased to hear of the end of my marriage. He never liked that charlatan, he says, but I don't want to get into another lengthy and exhausting clash with my father. Not having a husband or household to care for feels strange, and there are now so many hours to do the devil's bidding. I listen to live broadcasts on the wireless, direct from the Folies Bergères in Paris, and hum along to songs sung in French by Josephine Baker, of which I understand only a little.

Staša and Jarmila are ecstatic that I'm back and insist on reintroducing me to society to stave off idleness. The latter even chats me up to the editor of *Cesta*, the cultural newspaper, who commissions a series of columns. My regular work as a columnist for all these many publications will keep me in shoes and brews for the foreseeable future, but I hope one day to be a staff journalist. What a dream: to chase the scoops with all the men in hats.

After seeing him at a few dinner parties hosted by Jarmila and Willy Haas, I begin a dalliance with Jaromír Krejcar, a Bauhaus architect who favours function over form. He has boxcutter eyes and a very strict ethos for furnishings: simple and understated. The florid decorativeness and extravagant details that made up the Art Nouveau movement should be banished and abolished as far as he's concerned. The man cannot stand the look of a dust ruffle or a nail head trim. I can see my unborn children in his eyes.

I hadn't seen Max since Franz's funeral in the New Jewish Cemetery, where I laid a fountain pen on his grave and said a quiet prayer by his side. When I opened my eyes again, Max had walked away. The entire family had left me there on my own. No one wanted to indulge my piety or my grief. They could not stomach the sight of me. But today, Max sent me a telegram and asked to meet at the Arco.

When I push through the wood-framed glass doors, headwaiter Mr. Počta leads me to Max's quiet corner in the rear salon. None of the Arconauts I once knew are here. It's as if the café has fallen from grace. The once-loud German voices of Prague's intellectuals have been traded for Czech. But no one speaks of Rainer Maria Rilke or Karel Čapek. Instead, the topic of the day is the communist worker.

Max doesn't greet me with a warm embrace, or with an awkward joke like he once did at Café Prückel. He simply stands, pulls out my chair, and orders me a cup of the strong black stuff without even giving me the pleasure of small talk or chit-chat. Several times he removes and replaces his new round wire-framed glasses that hook behind his ears.

"I'm glad you came," he says, after I take a sip of my coffee.

"It's been, what? Six months?" I ask.

"Just about." He crinkles the bridge of his nose. "Who would have thought we'd start 1925 without him?"

I nod my head and purse my lips. "It's gutting, isn't it?"

He nods and we swim in silence for what feels like the length of a Buster Keaton feature.

"Have you checked in on his family?" I ask.

"I did," he says, folding his hands. "That's part of the reason I asked to see you."

"Oh?" I'm worried he might regale me with all their horrid insults.

"They asked me to go through his things." He lifts his briefcase from the floor, unhooks the latch, and pulls out a stack of papers. "When they let me into his room, everything was the way he left it, even though he had moved to Berlin with Dora almost a year before his death. They said they didn't see why his right to privacy should end just because his life did. In any case, among his work documentation and employment contracts at the insurance company, there were diaries and manuscripts. So many stories and novels that he never finished."

"He told me in the sanatorium that he was working on a novel," I say.

"I also found a trove of letters," he adds.

I gulp. "Oh. I see. From ... whom?"

"From many people. His first fiancée. His second, as well. From me, of course. And, yes, from you."

I grip my coffee cup so tightly it burns my hands.

"Don't worry, Milena, I didn't read them."

I exhale.

"But I also found, curiously, handwritten instructions from him."

"I don't understand."

"I think he knew his family would seek me out to organize his affairs, so before going to the sanatorium, he must have written this letter and kept it in his room for me."

He slides me a small, delicate note. It is definitely from Franz; the penmanship is too garish to be mistaken. But it is clearly written with a weak hand. The ink barely bleeds through the page.

> Dearest Max,
> my last wish: Everything that I leave behind in the way of diaries, manuscripts, letters of my own and from others, drawings, etc. (whether in my bookcase, clothes cupboard, writing desk at home or at the office, or in any other place anything may have gotten and you find it) should be burned, completely and unread, as should everything written or drawn in your possession or in the possession of others whom you should ask, in my name, to do likewise. People who do not want to hand over letters to you should at least be made to promise that they themselves will burn them.
> Yours,
> Franz Kafka

"God in heaven," I gasp. "He wants it all burned?"

"Yes."

"Why?"

"Probably to free his soul from his ghosts."

"Will you?" I ask incredulously.

"Here," Max extracts from the stack of papers a large manila envelope that is thicker than chocolate ganache on a vanilla-lemon cake. "He asked me to burn yours too."

All my letters to him. The telegrams. The postcards. The little missives. The briefest notes and the longest tomes. They're all there, carefully preserved in chronological order and without a tear or tea stain.

"But... you want *me* to burn them?"

"And the letters he sent you."

"Max!"

"Milena, I'm not the right person for this job."

"Well, thank you for giving these to me," I say.

"You're welcome. They're back where they belong."

"What about his other things?"

"There's a lot to sort through." He shrugs, feeling the full weight of the task. "He had many unpublished and unfinished stories. Maybe … one day …"

"I'm sure you'll do what's best." I place a hand over his and give it an encouraging squeeze.

For a solemn, sombre moment, both our minds are occupied by a memory, a cipher that hangs in the café with us for one second and then dissipates like fog.

"Before you go," Max reaches into his briefcase, "I wanted to show you something."

I lift my brows. "I don't know how much more I can handle."

He pulls out a folded letter from an envelope. It is in poor shape: jagged tears, dog-eared folds, bleeding ink, and yellowing foolscap. "A few years ago, after you and he had broken off your affair, he wrote to me about you. He had read your feuilleton in the *Narodní Listy* called 'Devil at the Hearth' about unhappy marriages."

"Ha," I smile, remembering. "It was a thinly veiled critique of male companionship, but perhaps it was also about all the places I wish I could have been—anywhere but with Ernst."

"Franz thought so too." He places the letter on the table between our two coffee cups. "He said men are pathetic communicators with limited abilities to describe the mystery of women, and he longed to send his list of your qualities to your husband, who was too simple and myopic to notice them."

I pick up the letter and narrow my eyes. "You've never really been good at keeping his secrets, have you, Max?"

"Now, now," he folds his arms, "I have a reputation to maintain."

Delicately unfolding the paper so as not to worsen the tears, I quickly locate the passage that begins with my name:

> Milena Jesenská is a woman of many surprises; an iridescent woman who walks and feels much unlike others do. She is someone who jazzes herself up in fantastic outfits and does the boulevard as well as it can be done. She does not hate men or women. She is open to ideas and impulses that would not occur to many. She is gifted in so many ways that it is almost an offence to speak of her gifts. She has a face that is difficult not to look at. When she is in the room everyone becomes aware of where she is in that room. Her hair demands a conscious look. Her sculpted physical form is of a shape that invites a master's painting. Her eyes look through things and dance with humour and understandings. She has a kind of Medean strength. She walks in a manner that calls out to bystanders; everyone wants a chance to comment on her. She has the kind of bosom a majority of men are drawn to. Her lips could start wars and probably have. But she needs to be loved like everyone else. She suffers from insecurity, self-loathing, heightened dreads, but mostly she suffers from an active mind that races ahead of others. She has already imagined mostly everything that can occur. I think she likes surprises.

My chin collapses as the final line sinks in. I fold the letter along its demarcations and slide it back to Max. "The first day he spent with me in Vienna, he asked me right away if I liked surprises."

"It's always puzzled me that he surprised you that day," Max nods as the letter disappears back into his briefcase, "because he loathed them with a passion."

"What?"

"He hated being surprised. It was his biggest and most grandiose annoyance. No one could tempt him with an unexpected arrival, a gift for no occasion, or even a party."

My eyes widen. "I didn't know this about him."

"Probably because you surprised him more than anyone else ever did. People are predictable, he used to say. You can map out their routines by the lines in their hands. But with you, he said, he never knew in which direction of the road to look before crossing, because no matter what, a truck would run him over. And he'd lie in the road, bleeding from the head, marvelling at how he never saw it coming."

The words clutch at my heart. Sometimes, I suppose, even in brittle human relationships, the enduring beauty of our natural selves will shine through, binding us forever.

UPON MY RETURN TO my father's apartment, I realize I only have an hour to get ready until my rendezvous with Jaromír. My father is in the next room, jiggling the temperamental handle to the china hutch and calling for the housekeeper to help him with the damn thing. The small spinet piano stands at the end of the sitting room, untouched in the sunlight. Dust particles dance around it before resting on the ivory keys. My letters to Franz should mingle with his. When I moved back here, I hid all of Franz's letters, postcards, and telegrams in the hollow of the piano for fear my father might find them. Quickly opening the lid of the piano's back, I locate the stack wrapped in brown paper and tied with twine. But now, as I hold the stack of my own handwriting, my own desires, urges, wishes, affections, and all the disasters therein, something in me hesitates.

I gingerly close the lid and turn to look out the window that faces Na Příkopě. Men emerge from haberdashery shops. Women drag little boys by the hand and take them to church. A cobbler places a new pair of leather brogue Oxfords in his window. Shimmering brown mares are led from the blacksmiths to the saddle-maker. Somewhere in the quarters, a caterwaul rises.

My nose stings and my cheeks are wet, but I do not make a sound. I hold my letters to Kafka in my hands, but they are stained with his face.

24

The Castle

PRAGUE

1939

When Milena came to, the acrid tang of vomit infected her nostrils. Her body was cold on the cell floor and the pain in her gut felt like her intestines were trying to eat their way out of her torso. The side of her face that hit the concrete was scraped and full of grit, her chipped tooth throbbed, and one eye was swollen shut. Lifting her head, she saw the chair she had been sitting on was smashed. Jagged splinters mingled with her vomit on the floor.

The Obergruppenführer was sitting in his chair opposite her, reading a hardcover book. One leg was crossed over the other, as though he were relaxing in the sunlit window of Café Union with a cup of rosehip tea, rather than in the dank basement cellar of Pankrác Prison.

What time is it? she wondered. There were no windows, and she had no idea how long she had been down here. Hours? Days? The Obergruppenführer was still wearing the same suit, but he looked like he'd had a shower and shave. She wondered what Honza was doing right at that very moment. Probably taking a bath at her father Jaromír's house with his new wife. Maybe she was reading a book on the davenport at Milena's father's apartment. Occasionally, when money was tight, Milena had even sent Honza over to Ernst's apartment. Honza always came back with glowing reviews.

"Mama, he gave me candied nuts and fizzy drinks."

"Mama, his housekeeper gave me a pot pie to take home, and it's still hot!"

"Mama, he walked with me to the bank and put one thousand korunas in my savings account. Here, Mama, this cheque is for you."

Now that Ernst had escaped, Milena wondered if Honza had enough sense to use her key to his place and hide. Of course she did. Honza was too clever for her age. She could sell spoiled ham to pigs and curdled cheese to cows.

Milena sat up and wiped the vomit from her cheek and prison smock.

"You know, he's really quite good," said the Obergruppenführer, without looking up from his book.

Milena froze. She looked at him with wide eyes but said nothing.

"He is quite the novelist," he said, eyes still down in the book. "Remarkable, affecting, utterly convincing, though he is a bit long-winded."

Milena squinted, trying to read the fine print on the spine of the book in his large hands.

He looked up at Milena with rifle fire in his stare. "I remember reading it many years ago when it was published, but after hearing your story, Frau Jesenská, I was moved to revisit it."

Suddenly he was up on his feet, grabbing the extra chair from against the wall, dragging it by its hind feet across the floor, and screeching it to a halt at Milena's side. He kicked the pieces of the splintered chair behind her. "Here, have a seat." He picked up the book and flipped through the pages. He walked the length of the room, which seemed to be getting smaller and smaller now that Milena only had one good eye. She heaved herself onto her haunches, steadied herself on the chair back, and sat down.

"Have you read it?" he asked from the shadows of the back wall. She wished he would walk toward her and the single bare bulb hanging above her head.

"Have I read it?" She repeated his question as if the answer lay within.

"*The Castle.*"

"Yes, I've read it."

He marched back—one, two, three—sat in his chair and crossed his long legs—four, five, six—and flipped open to the back of the book, clearing his throat—seven, eight, nine.

"The last lines I find to be remarkably thought-provoking. Listen," he augmented his voice, "'She held out her trembling hand to K. and had him sit down beside her. She spoke with great difficulty, it is hard to understand her, but what she said...'"

He looked at Milena and she stared blankly back at him. "And poof!" He slammed the book closed in one hand. "The novel is over. Unfinished. Although I suspect you know how that sentence ends."

"How would I?"

The Obergruppenführer smiled. "In the book, there is a love triangle between our protagonist K., Frieda, and Klamm. Since you've read the novel, surely you remember this triangle."

"Yes ... Are you suggesting—"

"See this?" He picked up a long white envelope from underneath his chair that she hadn't noticed before and pulled out a huge stack of crumpled paper bound with metal fasteners. Penmanship assaulted every corner of the pages, front to back, up the sides, and red marker broke it up. "It's his first draft."

"How on earth did you get that?"

He scanned the pages, licking his fingers as he flipped each crumpled sheet. "Yours wasn't the only house we raided, Frau Jesenská."

"Please tell me you didn't ..."

"Kafka's parents died a few years ago, so we took the three sisters into custody. Two we've sent to Chelmno, the other is still in custody, but she's scheduled for hard labour at Thereisenstadt. We also have arrested his former fiancée Julie Wohryzek. She is on a transport to Auschwitz."

"But why?! You cannot mean—"

"And furthermore," he retrieved the book from the lap of the chair and flipped through it, approaching her under the hot bare bulb. "When K. first seduces Frieda away from Klamm, he takes her to a quintessentially named castle inn. I don't need to tell you what it is. You know it already, don't you, Frau Jesenská?"

Somehow, her hand covered her mouth, though she didn't remember raising it. Then it was on her forehead, as if her mind might ooze out. She couldn't believe this was happening.

"Let me hear it." He grinned like the curve of Lucifer's bifurcated tail.

She closed her eyes. "The Herrenhof."

The book dropped from his hands and made a thud on the floor.

"Music to my ears," he said, and retook his seat across from her.

Her eyes welled with tears. When Max had published the novel back in 1926 after refusing to burn the manuscripts, she had felt an engulfing gratitude. Even in his final days, Franz had held her in the highest regard. That had never faded with time or distance. But now, she couldn't think of a worse fate for his words. Because his words would determine her fate.

"All the dissidents we've arrested say, 'Oh, this woman is the voice and heartbeat of Prague! The moral leader of the Czech people!' But they need to see you as the Jew-fucker we know you to be."

There was a knock at the big heavy iron door, and the Obergruppenführer sighed and slipped out to the corridor.

Milena heard muffled voices. She couldn't make out what was being said, but she knew this was her moment. She knew he would regret all the times he had leaned in too closely to her face, trying to intimidate her, his jacket pocket swaying low from his body, ever-so-lightly brushing against her fingers. She knew he was so consumed with his performance, with attempting to extinguish a woman who was made of fire, that he wouldn't notice her sleight of hand. And it would be too late for him and this wretched prison. She would turn bricks to brimstone. By the time he burst back into the interrogation room, the cell was ablaze like Hades. The book, the documents, the wooden chairs, the wiring along the wall and ceiling, the lightbulb exploding in blue sparks of electricity, and Milena—standing in the middle of the room, naked. Her clothes were in a fiery heap at her feet, forcing him back against the wall. She raised the broken leg of her chair—it morphed into a torch—and waved the liquid hot end in his face.

The Obergruppenführer rushed the room, but Milena hit him with her blazing cudgel. He grunted. She screamed something in Czech that he didn't understand. The room was a powder keg, heat like flowing magma. He lunged for her, making contact with her torso and forcing himself on top of her. She screamed and screamed as she bludgeoned him, but he wrenched the flaming club out of her hands. He wrestled with her tiny body, her wellspring of strength limitless. She was like a hydra: every time he cut off one of her heads, another grew back.

Guards rushed in. They sprayed water at the walls, sand on the floor. It took five men to wrench Milena's nails from under the Obergruppenführer's skin and drag her out of the room. His blood, flesh, and hair were gripped in her fists.

"There will be no more peace now!" she screamed, as the men dragged her kicking and writhing down the corridor. "Not for a day! Not even for an hour! Do you hear me!"

Sounds of her being beaten echoed throughout the building as the fire was extinguished. As the Obergruppenführer rose to his feet among the smouldering cinders and the choking smoke of the cellar room, he remembered her words at the beginning of the interrogation.

I wouldn't even blink if my hair was on fire.

25

Ravensbrück

1940

Milena was sent to trial in Dresden, but all the charges against her were dropped. News of her acquittal reached Prague. Honza, who had been staying with her grandfather Doktor Jesenský, rejoiced at the news, and together they made sweet cakes and plum pudding for Milena's imminent return. Her colleagues and compatriots who remained in Czechoslovakia raised money for her care and well-being once she returned. News even reached Ernst in Britain. He sent Doktor Jesenský fifty pounds.

But the Reichsprotektor, at the urging of Berlin, stopped her return. Berlin sent a cable expressing their concern over repatriating someone so incendiary back to Prague to inspire further tumult and upset among the people they meant to rule. At the suggestion of the

Obergruppenführer, it was decided that she would be sent to Ravensbrück, the women's camp outside Berlin. It was for her own protection, their official documents asserted. But when her father tried to pay for her release, the money was taken, and then no further information was provided.

Upon arrival at Ravensbrück, the women's heads were shaved and their clothes were removed. They were given black-and-white striped work smocks and a handkerchief to cover their shorn scalps. If they tied it under their chin instead of behind their head, they would be shot. If they were caught hoarding slices of bread, they would be shot. If they didn't pass the delousing checks, they would be shot. The matron held out her walking stick and all the women had to run, naked in the dead of winter, and leap over the stick without tripping. If they were infected with typhus, if they became too gaunt and sickly, if they stole clothes from the administration office, if they looked the matrons in the eye, if they were pregnant or had a venereal disease, if they darned the Wehrmacht's socks shut in an act of sabotage, if they caught the eye of a male SS guard and a matron became enraged with jealousy, if they were caught in a lesbian relationship, if they were just unlucky—they would be shot. Or hanged. Or sent on a march for five days into Poland, which was certain death. No one could outsmart the camp. If you were smart and tried to stick to a stratagem, you were the first to be hanged. If you were strong and thought your strength would serve you in the labour, you were the first to be hanged. The only way to survive was to be lucky. There weren't enough rags to go around, so the matrons put sodium in the soup to prevent menstruation. Some women whispered the sodium would make them barren, but most women did not think of a future. Survival was minute to minute, hour to hour.

The Nazis realized women had smaller, more dexterous fingers so they forced them to hammer down old batteries and then extract the still usable filaments of wire for Siemens, which supplied electrical parts for the German war effort. The Siemens factory was just beyond the south wall of Ravensbrück. One inmate found a long scrap of brown paper that had blown over the wall to the ground at her feet. She picked it up and hid it on her body. She then stole a small pencil and small fabric scissors and sat on the floor of the barracks and cut the paper into pieces. Women gathered around her, wondering what she was doing. The women were from every corner of Europe: Hungary, Greece, Poland, France, Vienna, Russia. They were communists, criminals, dissidents, asocials, political opponents, Gypsies, the mentally insane, the infirm, the prostitutes, the women who had carnal relations with Jews, the Jews, the Muhammadans—and there was Milena.

The inmate wrote a recipe for potato dumplings, from memory, on the scraps. The recipe was confiscated, naturally. The inmate was hanged in the yard and the women had to watch.

When Milena arrived at Ravensbrück, she had to hammer the batteries for the filaments of wire just like the criminals and prostitutes. Her inmate serial number sewn onto her sleeve was 4714, but because she carried herself as if she were at a hot spring retreat rather than a forced labour camp, the other women called her 4711 after the celebrated eau de cologne. When a matron or a kapo had her back turned, she would eat a raw tadpole or any kind of green weed to heal the scabies that had infested the barracks.

The winter of 1940 came quickly, and a cold snap swept through the barracks. Every morning, frozen bodies were lifted out of the bunks.

As she carried a box of metal tools, instruments, and lubricating oil from the work yard to the office, Milena walked along the south territory wall of the camp. The boots she was issued were taken off a dead woman. They were too big and sliced into her ankles and the backs of her feet. She was too dirty to prevent infection. If a kapo or matron saw her hobbling, she would face selection. So, she allowed her boots to cut into her, deforming her toes. After all this time, she didn't even feel the pain anymore.

As she walked, something above her head caught her attention. Another brown piece of paper blew over the Siemens factory wall. It danced in the air like the Blue Danube was leading it in a waltz. She willed it to approach her. It floated on an invisible wave, and she chased it along the perimeter wall, tools jangling in her box as she trotted breathlessly along. The paper in flight seemingly had no rest. It had wings. As she chased it, the jackdaws in the spruce trees cawed and crowed among themselves. She remembered how their bright eyes had watched over every interaction between her and Franz. After all, the name Kafka is an old spelling of the Czech word *kavka*. Which means jackdaw.

Suddenly, ash blew in the air and stuck to her face like flakes of snow or potato shavings. She stopped in her tracks and stood there, staring over the wall beyond the linden trees. The ash and the paper were suspended in the air. If she could just reach up and grab the paper, she could write down everything that she had witnessed here. She could smuggle a letter out to her daughter. She could hide scraps of evidence all over the camp until the war was over. She could record every single rape, every single execution, or at the very least, the dwindling remnants of her burning character. But she didn't do this. Because she couldn't. The brown paper danced away in the gale.

She would never write again.

With great exaltation, the jackdaws took off in flight, but one remained behind on a tree limb. It watched her as she walked away from the perimeter wall, deeper into the shadows of the camp, until she disappeared behind a row of barracks. He hopped on one leg, then on the other. A strange little dance. When the raining ash stuck to his wings, he groomed himself and then let out a harmonious call of solitude.

26

A Living Fire

PRAGUE

1925

I walk along the Náplavka promenade in the Malá Strana district that stretches along the banks of the Vltava River until I arrive at the cobblestoned slip. During the day, a bevy of swans, long necked and white as snow, occupies the slip. They hiss at poodles and chase tourists for breadcrumbs. But now, in the cocoon of twilight, they float quietly under the Charles Bridge, two by two, asleep. From this vantage point, Prague has never looked lovelier. Oil lamps cast almond hues across the bridge. The moon, clear as glass, stares at its reflection in the river. Lovers duck into nooks and stairwells, arms wrapped around each other, crushing lips against lips, and then breaking into giggles. The river laps lazily against the cobbles, smoothing the stones and breaking them in two. Beneath the moonlight, empty dinghies tied to shore clack softly against one another when a small ripple disturbs them. Steeples, domes, and towers jut out across the cityscape. Lime trees and aspens tremble in the chilly breeze. The river carries voices to me from the other shore. Someone underneath the Bridge Tower has just said, "The party's over. Let's go home."

It is a cold winter, but I have never felt warmer. I have been set steaming. Grabbing some of the broken cobbles, stray rocks, and driftwood that litter the slip, I slowly build a pit, arranging dried leaves and twigs artfully for kindling. Soft music emanates from somewhere behind me, like an operetta. Joyous and victorious, it reaches me in fragmented notes. Someone must have left their window open.

I strike a match against the heel of my boot and toss it. The fire pit smokes a bit on account of the waterlogged timber, but I've always had faith in fire. There's nothing a little arson won't fix. It doesn't take long for the flames to find their footing. Double-winged samara seeds flutter down from the Norwegian maples like whirlybirds. I throw handfuls of them into the fire just to hear them pop.

With blackened fingertips, I pull the bundle from my satchel. I could read my letters to Kafka one last time, laugh over my verbosity, my moody hypocrisy, my engulfing need to be loved, my silly manners and morals. But he once wrote to me that we should set ourselves ablaze on both sides. *Then it would be possible for us to get away...*

A rich perfume wafts along the promenade and the soft music is abruptly truncated. So I throw the letters into the inferno one by one, without so much as a blink, hurling everything that I am into this sacrifice.

The bonfire grows and grows, and embers fly through the night sky. I watch as they drift over the water, gusting in all directions, until the little glowing cinders disappear over the horizon. A mournful howl dopplers through the air like the echo of a distant storm. Kafka's description of me has never been truer.

In this quiet moment, perceptible to no one, I am a living fire.

Postscript

Obergruppenführer Reinhard Heydrich, known as the Butcher of Prague, was one of the orchestrators of the Final Solution at the Wannsee Conference, the genocide of Europe's Jews. He was assassinated on the streets of Prague by Czech and Slovak patriots in 1942.

After his divorce from Milena, Ernst Pollak stayed in Vienna until he was forced to flee back to Prague during the 1938 Anschluss. After the Nazis occupied Czechoslovakia, Milena helped Pollak escape Prague, and he eventually settled in London, England, where he died in 1947.

Jana Černá, known lovingly as "Honza," was the only daughter of Milena Jesenská and her second husband, Czech architect Jaromír Krejcar. Following in her mother's footsteps, Honza became a celebrated poet and writer in communist Czechoslovakia, even authoring a biography on her late mother. She died in a car crash in 1981.

After his death from tuberculosis in 1924, Franz Kafka's manuscripts and diaries were kept by his friend and editor Max Brod, who had them published, launching Kafka into posthumous fame. Kafka's letters to Milena

Jesenská, which were preserved by editor Willy Haas, were published in the epistolary book *Letters to Milena* in 1953.

Milena Jesenská died in Ravensbrück concentration camp on May 17, 1944, a few months before it was liberated by the Soviet Red Army.

Her letters to Kafka were never found.

Permissions Acknowledgements

Excerpt from *Kafka's Last Trial: The Case of a Literary Legacy*, (c) 2017, used by permission of W.W. Norton.

Excerpts from LETTERS TO MILENA by Franz Kafka, translated by Tania Stern and James Stern, edited by Willi Haas, translation copyright 1953 and © renewed 1981 by Penguin Random House LLC. Used by permission of Schocken Books, an imprint of the Knopf Doubleday Publishing Group, a division of Penguin Random House LLC. All rights reserved.

Excerpts from LETTERS TO FRIENDS, FAMILY, AND EDITORS by Franz Kafka, translated by Richard and Clara Winston, translation copyright © 1977 by Penguin Random House LLC. Used by permission of Schocken Books, an imprint of the Knopf Doubleday Publishing Group, a division of Penguin Random House LLC. All rights reserved.

Bibliography

Buber-Neumann, Margarete. *Milena: The Tragic Story of Kafka's Great Love*. Arcade Publishing, 1997.

Černá, Jana. *Kafka's Milena*. Translated by A.G. Brain. Souvenir Press, 1988.

Hockaday, Mary. *Kafka, Love and Courage: The Life of Milena Jesenská*. Overlook Press, 1997.

Jesenská, Milena. *The Journalism of Milena Jesenská: A Critical Voice in Interwar Central Europe*. Edited and translated by Kathleen Hayes. Berghahn Books, 2003.

Kafka, Franz. *Letters to Milena*. Edited by Willi Haas, translated by Tania Stern and James Stern. Schocken Books, 1953.

O'Connor, Anne Marie. *The Lady in Gold: The Extraordinary Tale of Gustav Klimt's Masterpiece,* Portrait of Adele Bloch-Bauer. Knopf, 2012.

Acknowledgements

Toni Morrison once said, "If there is a book that you want to read, but it hasn't been written yet, then you must write it."

That was the impetus behind bringing Milena's story to light since I first came across her name twelve years ago, and I'm so glad this all-consuming obsession has finally come to fruition. This would not have been possible without the support and encouragement of several people and organizations.

I owe a debt of gratitude to my long-suffering agent, Chris Bucci, for believing in, and championing, this novel in the face of so many obstacles and years in development. You're a mensch.

Major high-fives must go to my editor, Shirarose Wilensky, who elevated the heart of this story up to the heavens and fully supported the ethos behind this book. Thank you for believing in me.

Major fist-bumps go to the House of Anansi team, including publisher Karen Brochu, for your continued support of, and dedication to, my bonkers scribblings.

I gratefully acknowledge funding from the Canada Council for the Arts, the Toronto Arts Council, and the Access Copyright Foundation for supporting the creation of this work.

Thank you to the organizers behind the 2023 Lee Smith Novel Prize who selected this manuscript as a Top 3 finalist out of more than five hundred submissions. That honour restored my belief in this manuscript; had that not happened, this book might still be buried somewhere on my hard drive.

Thank you to *Kafka, Love and Courage: The Life of Milena Jesenská* author Mary Hockaday for speaking with me that day in London. I can't believe you covered the bill. I got the next one.

Major inspiration for this book came from the ethereal and ephemeral streets of Vienna and Prague, which have remained mostly untouched since Milena and Kafka ran breathless along them. To these cities, I am forever obliged.

During the creation of this novel, I went through something that I never thought I would. In the midst of it, I discovered a huge community rallying around me. Thank you to all those who held my hand, gave me endless hugs, stayed up all night listening to me, drove hours to be by my side, and checked in on me regularly. Miruna, Jodie, Elamin, Chris, Leroy, Teresa Wing Yee, April, Victoria, Kyle, Katie, Robin, Sue, Ada, Derrick, Craig, Allegra, Erin, K.J., Alix, Sarahjane, and many more. You are my people.

The largest thanks and debt of gratitude must go to the inspirational woman of the hour—Milena Jesenská. Wherever you are, just know: ya did good.

© Panther Sohi

CHRISTINE ESTIMA is an Arab woman of mixed ethnicity (Lebanese, Syrian, and Portuguese) and the author of the short story collection *The Syrian Ladies Benevolent Society*, which the CBC called one of the Best Fiction Books of 2023. She has written for *The New York Times*, *The Walrus*, *VICE*, *The Globe and Mail*, *Chatelaine*, *Maisonneuve*, the *Toronto Star*, and the CBC. Her story "Your Hands Are Blessed" was included in *Best Canadian Stories 2023*. She was a finalist for the 2023 Lee Smith Novel Prize and was shortlisted for the 2018 Allan Slaight Prize for Journalism. Christine has a master's degree in interdisciplinary studies from York University and lives in Toronto.